THE
HOLLY KING

Mark Stay got a part-time Christmas job at Waterstone's in the nineties (back when it still had an apostrophe) and somehow ended up working in publishing for over 25 years. He would write in his spare time and (he can admit this now) on company time, and sometimes those writings would get turned into books and films. Mark is also co-presenter of the Bestseller Experiment podcast, which has inspired writers all over the world to finish and publish their books. Born in London, he lives in Kent with YouTube gardener Claire Burgess and a declining assortment of retired chickens.

@markstay
markstaywrites.com
witchesofwoodville.com

Also by Mark Stay

Robot Overlords
Back to Reality (with Mark Oliver)
The End of Magic

The Witches of Woodville series

The Crow Folk
Babes in the Wood
The Ghost of Ivy Barn

THE
HOLLY KING

The Witches of Woodville IV

Mark Stay

**SIMON &
SCHUSTER**

London · New York · Sydney · Toronto · New Delhi

First published in Great Britain by Simon & Schuster UK Ltd, 2023

Copyright © Unusually Tall Stories, Ltd 2023

The right of Mark Stay to be identified as author
of this work has been asserted in accordance with the
Copyright, Designs and Patents Act, 1988.

1 3 5 7 9 10 8 6 4 2

Simon & Schuster UK Ltd
1st Floor
222 Gray's Inn Road
London WC1X 8HB

Simon & Schuster Australia, Sydney
Simon & Schuster India, New Delhi

www.simonandschuster.co.uk
www.simonandschuster.com.au
www.simonandschuster.co.in

A CIP catalogue record for this book
is available from the British Library

Paperback ISBN: 978-1-3985-2079-0
eBook ISBN: 978-1-3985-2080-6
Audio ISBN: 978-1-3985-2081-3

Typeset in Sabon by M Rules
Printed and Bound in the UK using 100% Renewable Electricity
at CPI Group (UK) Ltd

For Emily & George.
Hardly ever on the naughty list.

December, 1940

The war has reached its second winter, bringing deadly bombing campaigns to Britain's cities, and a terrible loss of life. Morale is low among the beleaguered Allied forces, and on the Home Front there is increased rationing, shortages of essentials and inclement weather to contend with. Meanwhile, a small village in Kent prepares for the Christmas festivities as best it can in the bleak midwinter, unaware of the coming magical chaos that will make this a Yuletide like no other ...

Dream a Little Dream

Faye knew she was dreaming because she was in the woods. Despite the foggy night, she was wearing nothing but her blue-and-white-striped jim-jams and the fluffy pink slippers she got last Christmas.

Faye knew she was dreaming because somewhere unseen in the depths of the wood a gramophone was playing 'I'll See You in My Dreams', the singer's heartbroken voice drifting between the trees.

Faye Bright knew she was dreaming because she was floating just a few inches above the ground.

At least, she hoped it was a dream, otherwise she'd clearly gone completely doolally.

Faye had learned to fly quite recently – and she was a dab hand at it, thank you very much – but floating this close to the ground was just showing off, and she wasn't the sort to go drifting about when she was in possession of two perfectly good legs. This was definitely, most assuredly, a dream.

The singer continued to pine about tender eyes

shining and lighting the way. This was the third night in a row that she'd had this same dream, though it always stopped too soon.

The fog was starting to clear, and Faye found herself on the path to the hollow oak at the centre of the wood. The bitter-cold air nipped at the skin between her slippers and pyjama legs. The tip of her nose was numb and her eyes were streaming. Faye wondered if she should be able to feel the cold so vividly in a dream.

Snowflakes began to tumble silently through the empty trees. As the fog melted away, it revealed a blanket of snow a foot deep covering the whole wood, though this December had been damp and grey, with not so much as a drop of sleet, let alone snow.

The snow made everything bright. The light of the moon reflected off every flake, and Faye could find her way easily.

A heavy rustling and scraping filtered through the trees. The sound of something being dragged across the ground, accompanied by a constant groan. Someone in pain.

Faye leaned forward, heart racing as she floated faster through the wood, picking up the pace to find the source of the noise. Every night for the last three nights she had done the same. She couldn't help herself. She had to know.

Somewhere in the wood the gramophone got stuck, and the words *I'll see you ... I'll see you ... I'll see you ...* repeated over and over.

A new sound of exhausted huffing and puffing dared

Faye to come closer. She took the dare, weaving through the trees. Up ahead, a figure was dragging what looked like a stretcher along the path, silhouetted against the bright snow. There was a body on the stretcher, held in place by leather straps. The figure pulling it wore a winter coat with a fur-lined hood.

I'll see you ... I'll see you ...

The groans came from the person on the stretcher. A young woman with light brown skin and long black hair that tumbled away in shiny waves, she grimaced in agony with every bump on the path.

'I'm hurtin' real bad,' the girl on the stretcher hissed through gritted teeth. She spoke with an American accent, and Faye was reminded of a gangster's moll from the movies. 'Give a girl a break, honey. Please. I can't take the pain no more.'

The figure pulling the stretcher glanced back, though the fur of the hood obscured her face.

'Pearl, don't you dare die, you silly girl. Not yet. We're so close.' The voice was female, and oddly familiar to Faye. A villager, maybe. About her age.

I'll see you ... I'll see you ...

This was where the dream had ended the last three nights. Faye would wake up, desperate to know more. Tonight, she willed herself to remain in the dream.

Faye flew faster, though she began to feel a creeping sensation of dread. Maybe she woke at the same time each night for a good reason. Did she really need to know who the girl in the fur hood was? Mysteries are much more enjoyable before the truth is revealed. Faye recalled a night before the war when a travelling conjuror had to be turfed out of the pub for having one too many, but not before he insisted on showing her how to pluck a coin from behind someone's ear. The disappointment had lingered for days. Yes, Faye determined she was better off not knowing. She would wake herself up and this would all be forgotten by breakfast.

But try as she might, she could not wake.

As Faye turned a bend, she could suddenly see the girl more clearly. She was wearing an old-fashioned red velvet dress under the winter coat. She pulled back her hood, revealing nut-brown hair, a pale face and red lips. It was like looking in a carnival mirror.

'M-Mum?'

⚲

Faye woke in the darkness of her room, the tip of her nose still cold. She pressed the palm of her hand against it to warm it up.

The only noise was the gentle *tock* of the longcase clock downstairs. Faye's heart gradually slowed to a steady beat, her head still light as a feather.

'Blimmin' 'eck,' she whispered.

Summer and autumn had given Faye plenty of time to get used to the idea that, like her late mother Kathryn, she was a witch. During those turbulent months she'd had more than a few opportunities to learn how to harness her powers, and after a few close shaves with the occult in which she'd saved the village – and, arguably, the country – she'd finally felt like she'd earned the right to call herself one. Then along came one dream to make her realise just how little she knew.

She'd had dreams about her mother before, of course, but they were little more than snatches of childhood memories jumbled through a filter of grief and love. This one had arrived like a gatecrasher at a party, and Faye wasn't sure if she liked it. Each night it had teased her with a little more, and she had feared what tonight might bring. She didn't much enjoy the idea that her own mind was winding her up and made a note to discuss it with her mentors in witchcraft, Mrs Teach and Miss Charlotte. Perhaps they knew how to control dreams? After all, it played in her head like a big Hollywood Technicolor movie, so who's to say she couldn't whizz forward to the final reel and see the ending?

The only person she'd told about the dream so far was Mr Paine. They'd been on ARP duty the night before and it had been fairly quiet, so she'd decided to describe the whole thing to him in detail, all while sucking on a succession of his sherbet lemons. He'd shuffled about as she spoke, avoiding eye contact, and Faye had realised with a start that perhaps the dreams of an eighteen-year-old girl weren't as interesting to a respectable middle-aged man as she'd first thought they might be. They hadn't spoken much after that, and it had all been a bit awkward. She also got the feeling he was annoyed that she was so quick to take his sherbet lemons. Faye recalled she had a bag of Liquorice Allsorts from Bertie. She didn't have the heart to tell him that they gave her wind, so she would offer them to Mr Paine as a peace offering on their next ARP shift.

Faye shook her head clear. Her thoughts turned to tea. There was no way she was getting back to sleep after that, so why not enjoy a cuppa and clear her mind?

There was a new noise from outside. Boots splashing through puddles.

Faye popped her glasses on, wriggled her feet into the pink fluffy slippers waiting for her on the rug, then shuffled over to the window, hands tucked into her armpits for warmth. The glass was wet with condensation, so she used a finger to wipe a clear patch on one of the panes. She peered through the criss-cross of the window's anti-blast tape to the Wode Road beyond. As she suspected, it was the village postie, Eric Birdwhistle, out on his rounds in the dark morning's mizzle. Faye smiled to herself, happy to see that some things remained the same in all this madness.

She still had an hour or so before Dad got up, but that didn't mean she couldn't put the kettle on. Faye wrapped herself in her dressing gown and made her way downstairs. Which was a shame. If she had just waited at the window a few moments longer, she might have noticed that Eric's postbag was much lighter than usual. She might even have seen a telltale flicker of dread on Eric's face and realised something was terribly wrong, and perhaps Faye could have saved Eric and the village from the series of Yuletide disasters to come.

Special Delivery

Save the mail, Eric thought over and over as his boots splashed through deep puddles at the top of Gibbet Lane. *Save the mail*.

Save the mail had become a clarion call for Royal Mail workers since the war started. Not only did they have rain, fog and sleet to deal with this winter, but now also bombs falling from the sky, pillar boxes smashed by debris, and parcels and letters charred and mangled. But it didn't matter how much damage had been inflicted, it was a matter of pride for any postie – not least Eric Birdwhistle – to save the mail. Delivering the Royal Mail was his calling, and one he could not resist, even at four o'clock in the morning.

At this time of day, the village was all his, like a stage before the curtain went up. All the scenery was in place, the players in the wings anticipating their cues, the orchestra waiting for the baton to move.

In the distance came the urgent whistle of a train and the growl of Merlin engines as Spitfires and Hurricanes patrolled overhead. The wind toyed with telephone wires, and somewhere a cat screeched, disturbed by Eric's footfalls.

The others would come later. Doris on her milk round, the whistling newspaper boys, the shovellers of coal into rattling buckets, dogs let out to bark at shadows.

A Birdwhistle had delivered the letters and parcels in the village of Woodville for three generations, and Eric wasn't about to let a little something like bombing raids stop him. Not that anyone in the village gave a tinker's cuss. They all took him for granted. Four deliveries a day when it was busy, up before the sun and never late. Eric considered himself to be the hardest-working man in the village, but did he ever get any gratitude? Not a sausage. All right, there was the odd cup of tea and some cakes on special occasions, but just the other day Mr Paine, who owned the newsagent's in which the letters were sorted and collected, had referred to Eric as 'part of the furniture' of Woodville. It was a compliment, apparently, but Eric wondered how Freddie Paine would like to be compared to a footstool or an armchair.

A chill wind danced around Eric, biting at his nose and ears. Last year had been bitterly cold. Ice had been the real enemy then. Far more threatening than that loon Adolf Hitler and his goose-stepping Nazis. It had burst pipes and left little rinks for Eric to slip on. He hated ice, but he didn't mind the cold and grey winter they were having now. No snow, no ice, just a bit dull and damp. He could put on a few layers and stay snug and dry.

As he left the road by Gibbet Lane, the silent shadow of a barn owl slid over the path and into the wood. Eric's destination.

This morning's delivery was a peculiar one. Truth be told, he wasn't strictly on Royal Mail business. He had risen earlier than usual, careful not to wake his wife Shirley, then gone about his usual ablutions. There had been no need to go to the Post Office in the newsagent's as the package had been waiting for him by the front door.

Eric had stood and stared at it, unblinking, arms limp, wondering how it had arrived there. For some time, a tiny hollow of dread gnawed at his belly and there was a peculiar ringing in his ears. But a sweet voice whispered to him, and any fear was soon washed away by a welcome sense of serenity. Eric had popped the package into his sack and headed for the woods.

Of course, he was curious to know whose package this was. There was no name on the box. Simply a destination. The hollow oak.

Eric knew precisely where that was. Everyone in the village did. It was one of the few fixed points in the wood, at its very centre. No one ever talked about this openly, but the wood had a habit of shifting around as you passed through it. Trees would shuffle in the corner of your eye. The sun would mysteriously set in the east. You could walk in a straight line for an hour and end up exactly where you started.

There was none of that this morning. Other than the *splish-splosh* of Eric's boots in the occasional puddle, the wood was silent, still and dark.

Of course, the wood did have one permanent resident. But Miss Charlotte Southill collected her letters and parcels directly from the Post Office, and those occasions were very rare. She corresponded infrequently with someone in Folkestone, and she would sometimes take deliveries of exotic pipe tobaccos from around the world, but other than that she barely got a postcard.

Eric was certain this parcel wasn't for her.

As he moved deeper into the wood the canopy above offered a little more cover from the bone-chilling wind, but the waning moon was still bright enough to show him the way, and Eric recognised the path. He was close. It wouldn't be long now.

A little part of his brain was wondering just what the blazes he was doing here, treading through the leaf litter of the wood. He should have been warm in bed with Shirley. But that sweet voice had whispered in his ear while he slept. This was one delivery that could not be late.

The house was so much colder now their son Sidney was away serving with the army. The last thing Eric had heard was that Sidney was back in England, training in Salisbury. And he'd been promoted. A lance corporal, no less. Perhaps Sidney would be allowed home for Christmas. Shirley kept talking like it was a certainty, but Eric knew the odds were slim. The best they could hope for was a card. One that Eric would take delivery of personally.

All that would come in its own time. Eric still had his regular morning round to do after this. No rest for the wicked.

He spotted the hollow oak's clearing up ahead and stopped.

The lonely silence was such that he could hear the blood rushing in his ears. He gripped the strap of his sack a little tighter and cleared his throat.

'Hello?' The sound of his voice was muffled by a sudden rumbling wind. He stepped into the clearing and announced, 'Special delivery.'

No one answered.

The roots of the hollow oak wound across the clearing. Eric tried to recall if they had stretched that far before. The tree's hollow was at its base, and he instinctively knew that was where he should leave the parcel. Yes, get that done and then head back home to Shirley as soon as possible. Eric needed his porridge and a cuddle from his beloved.

He took a deep breath and marched to the hollow, crouching down and feeling a twinge in his right knee and a slight spasm in his back. Too old to serve in the forces, Eric had stayed in the village as an essential worker. He would do his bit the way he always had. By getting the post through, come rain, snow or bombs. *Save the mail*, indeed.

He placed the parcel in the hollow. The box looked about the right size for a hat. One with a wide brim. He nudged it a little further in to protect it from the damp. Normally that would be it for any delivery, but Eric had one more task. The voice had told him to bring a mirror. Any mirror would do. It whispered to him now as he took his little round shaving mirror from inside his coat and angled it at the moon. Its light reflected off the glass and fell onto the box, giving it the same chilly glow. Done. Eric felt complete. He tucked the mirror away, dusted off his hands and stood carefully, so as not to set off another back spasm. That was the last thing he needed with such a busy week ahead—

The ground trembled, tickling the arches of his feet.

Eric wondered if he'd imagined it, but then it happened again. The whole wood groaned. No. It was more like an old man's yawn.

Something was awakening beneath the roots of the hollow oak.

A cracking noise came from deep in the earth. Eric spun to find dirt and dust tossed into the air as the oak's roots stretched and extended, breaking free from the earth, flexing like muscles.

As a low growl erupted from below, Eric had a brief and panicked debate with himself about whether to run like the clappers or stand firm and see what was making that ungodly racket. Fear gripped his spine, making the decision for him. He simply couldn't move. He watched, paralysed, as the tree's roots rolled back and a fissure cracked open in the ground.

Something burst from the jagged fracture, knocking him onto his backside. A wooden box, twice as long as a coffin, was hoisted into place by creaking, writhing roots.

Made from oak streaked with reds and pinks and carved with the most ornate decorations of oak leaves, acorns and mighty trees, it was possibly the most beautiful thing Eric had ever seen (and he had been to the sorting office at Mount Pleasant one halcyon summer). He spied intricately chiselled fauns and pixies peering out from behind the lattice of leaves and entwined branches. It told a story – a kind of fairy-tale Bayeux Tapestry whittled in wood – but its twists and turns were beyond his understanding. It looked brand new, though there was something about its design that felt ancient and unknowable. A sarcophagus from another time.

For a moment, there was silence.

Then the lid juddered.

'Ow, nuts.' The voice came from inside the sarcophagus. Eric chuckled despite himself. He was completely terrified, but the voice made him think of a gangster's moll he'd seen in a movie. There followed some huffing as the voice's owner struggled to heft the lid open. Never let it be said that Eric was anything less than a gentleman and a public servant – if there was a lady in need of assistance, it was his duty to help her. On legs of jelly, he staggered over to the sarcophagus and heaved. The lid hardly budged.

Gritting his teeth, Eric got a better grip on the lip of the lid and was able to shove it off in one go.

In that moment he started to lose his mind.

What lay beyond was an iridescent infinity. A swirling mass of light and dark matter, leftovers from the birth of the universe idling on another plane. Eric's thoughts and senses abandoned him. His eyes vibrated as they struggled to cope with new colours, his ears throbbed numbly at frequencies from other dimensions, and his brain snapped and flipped like a cheap brolly in a storm.

It was all so beyond his understanding that when a pretty girl with light brown skin and silver shimmering wings fluttered out of the sarcophagus, he wasn't remotely surprised.

'Thanks, sugar,' she said, whizzing around the clearing. She glowed like the rising sun, and her translucent wings left a trail of glitter as they flapped. She wore a long dress of gossamer lace, white stockings and black Balmoral lace-up boots. Her ears were pointed. Eric felt like she belonged at the top of a Christmas tree, albeit one that had been abandoned in a dark cellar and left to rot. There was something distinctly un-Christmassy about this fairy. Not least that she was a good six inches taller than he was. She darted about, looking into the darkness of the wood, before hollering, 'All clear!' back into the morass of interstellar dust.

There was a drawn-out pause, then a gnarled hand gripped the edge of the sarcophagus with a thud. Eric's heart hammered. A figure ten feet tall with limbs of hoary wood eased itself out of the ancient coffin. Creaking legs strode over him as the thing moved to the centre of the clearing. As it stepped into the moonlight, he was able to get a better look at the creature. It was a tree that looked like a man. Or a man that looked like a tree. He couldn't be entirely sure. It arched its back, bellowing at the distant moon. Its branch-like fingers bunched into formidable fists.

This was an unfortunate moment for Eric to make an involuntary noise from his bottom.

The creature's head – a tangle of branches and bark twisted into a ball – snapped around towards him. Its inhuman eyes were infused with amber.

'Oh blimey,' Eric said.

The oak man stalked across the clearing in a few strides, arm extended, twiggy fingers splayed out. Eric found to his horror that he had quite lost the use of his limbs. His legs in particular were impotent, seeming to weigh several tonnes each. He stood among the roots, utterly helpless, as the creature advanced. He wished he could see his son at Christmas, yearned to hold Shirley one more time.

Eric cried out as one of the oak man's legs slammed down on his chest, breaking his little shaving mirror, pinning him to the ground, crushing every rib and snapping his spine.

ENTER THE HOLLY KING

Eric couldn't feel anything below his neck. He'd had a few near misses in the Great War, but he was done for now, that was for sure. He thought he ought to be panicking, but a strange acceptance seemed to have come over him. He thought again about Shirley and his son Sidney, and wondered if they would ever know what had really happened to him.

The creature's hand reached past Eric, grasping the parcel and lifting it from the oak tree's hollow.

The clearing fell silent once more as the oak man stepped off Eric and contemplated the cardboard parcel, much like Hamlet looking at the skull of that Yorick chap. Eric had been dragged to see the play once, but after a week of early starts found himself nodding off throughout, much to Shirley's annoyance.

With a delicate touch that belied its bulk, the creature peeled back the lid of the box. It reached in and removed a wooden crown laced with oak and holly leaves.

Eric recognised it immediately. He flinched, confused. His wife Shirley had spent the last month making it. He had told her it looked a bit like a crown, but she insisted it was a fancy Christmas wreath for the front door. It had taken up every spare minute of her time, and whenever she worked on it her eyes had glazed over as if in a trance. Every now and then, she would nod and mutter as if she was listening to instructions. Eric had put her behaviour down to the peculiar changes that a woman went through in middle age. For years his mother had been prone to staring into space for long periods of time, before becoming her old self again. Eric had simply assumed it was something that happened to all women in their fifties.

Shirley must have left the package by the door. Had the sweet voice been talking to her, too?

The oak man's mouth creaked into a smile as it raised the crown high. Like a child on Christmas morning, it admired its new toy from every angle, savouring its beauty, brushing its hands over its surface.

'It's here!' The hush was broken as the fairy called back into the coffin, and suddenly Eric recognised her sugary-sweet voice. She had been the one whispering to him in his sleep. 'The crown is here. He has it!'

There was no immediate reply, though the oak man swiped a mighty hand at the fairy, who spiralled up out of range.

A chill wind rushed through the clearing, rattling the sparse branches. Lightning flashed high above.

'Ow!' Eric felt something scratch against his ear.

Holly leaves whipped through the air from all directions as if summoned by some clarion call. Countless little pointy darts of dark green swirled around the oak creature. It roared, swatting at them with one hand, gripping the crown with the other. Eric was now reminded of that *King Kong* film. He'd definitely stayed awake through that one. He instinctively wanted to cover his face, but his limbs were still useless. He could only look on as something incredible began to happen.

One by one, the holly leaves started to stick to the oak man. Some stabbed into his mouth and eyes. Others slipped between his joints, shivering as they formed clusters, working to prise him open.

The oak man dropped the crown, using both hands to paw at the leaves that now covered him from head to toe, infesting him completely. Each handful that he tossed away was replaced by twice as many. The holly leaves knitted together, forming their own limbs. An arm reached around the oak man's neck, throttling him. His legs snapped as ropes of holly tightened around them, first at the thighs, then at the shins. He collapsed in a heap, his now-feeble fingers clawing at the air.

The wood trembled as lightning struck. A direct hit on the hollow oak issuing a deafening crack. The tree spat glowing slivers of bark across the clearing. The fairy squealed and dived behind a bush.

Eric snapped his eyes shut, streaks of white light darting over his retinas.

The ground trembled as a new sound emanated from

within the oak sarcophagus. A deep, bellowing laugh that rattled Eric's skull. It was all he could do to force his eyes open as a new creature clambered out of the box and stood in the clearing.

This one looked more obviously like a man, apart from standing nearly twice as tall. Impressive antlers erupted from his head. His face was as wrinkled as bark and his eyes as red as berries. His hooded cloak was Lincoln green, and his beard was the biggest that Eric had ever seen – a bib as white as snow, peppered with vivid green leaves and scarlet berries. His antlers were decorated with holly and ivy, twisted around like tinsel.

Eric held his breath as the holly man stooped and picked at the remains of the oak creature. What only moments ago had been arms and legs were tossed aside like firewood. The holly man paused when he found the oak creature's head, still attached to neck and shoulders. Crouching, he gripped it and, with a sharp twist, snapped it free. He pressed his gloved hands against his foe's temples, gritting his teeth.

Eric watched in horror as the oak man's eyes opened and his jaw moved about. He was still alive! The oak man emitted a wordless wail of agony before his skull caved in, crushed between the holly man's hands. What remained was carried away on the bitter breeze.

Satisfied, the holly man stood and strode back to the sarcophagus, reaching with a massive, black-gloved hand into its depths. With a heave, he pulled out a giant sack, half his size and tied shut with thick rope.

He tossed it onto the ground where it wriggled and kicked. There was something – some *things* – inside it.

The fairy bobbed out from her hiding place and flew to the holly man, covering her mouth and whispering in his ear. Every now and then their eyes darted to Eric. The postman had a well-developed sense of paranoia. He knew that many of the villagers made disparaging comments about him, especially when something arrived late or damaged, and he had a sixth sense for when someone was gossiping about him. However, he suspected this was the first time any of the gossips had wings or antlers.

'Eric Birdwhistle.' The holly man's voice made every branch on every tree tremble as he raised himself to his full height. 'Come hither.'

He beckoned to Eric, who wanted to shrug, but could only bobble his head from side to side.

The fairy whispered in the holly man's ears again. He nodded.

'I see my clumsy brother has broken you, Eric Birdwhistle. That will not do.'

He strode over to Eric, tugging at the fingers of a black glove before resting a surprisingly warm giant hand over Eric's face.

What happened next would baffle Eric for the rest of his life. He would never speak of it to anyone, not even Shirley. A pleasant tingle spread through him, rising like hot water, healing cuts and bruises, knitting broken bones together. His fingers twitched, his toes wiggled, and that twinge in his shoulder blade that had been annoying him for weeks was suddenly gone. Eric was whole again. Even his little shaving mirror. He felt better than ever before. He hopped to his feet and the holly man stood back, chuckling as he held his belly.

'Thank you,' Eric said, tears springing from his eyes. 'A thousand thank yous!'

'Think nothing of it, Eric Birdwhistle. You delivered the crown. Where is it?' the creature asked. 'I must have it now.'

Eric shuffled in a circle. He recalled the crown being dropped by the oak man and—

'Here ... here it is,' Eric stammered as he scuttled to where the crown rested by the hollow oak. The tree had a fresh lightning scar, embers glistening inside. It remained standing, though it looked like it had been stripped by bark enthusiasts on a bender.

Eric carefully picked up the crown, surprised by how heavy it was. His Shirley had done an incredible job. A solid ring of holly and oak wood intertwined and decorated with the leaves, berries and acorns of both trees. He never knew she had it in her to make something so beautiful.

'Bring it to me, Eric Birdwhistle,' the holly man said, with a trace of excited impatience. 'Bear witness to my coronation.'

The fairy hovered over his shoulder, motioning for Eric to come closer. Behind her, the giant sack continued to undulate and make muffled, angry noises.

Eric's fingers tightened around the crown. Its immense power slowed his heart to a sluggish pace, and he feared that it would become so heavy it might fall through him. Eric was not a particularly pious man. Oh, he went to church, of course, and heard others talk about feeling the presence of God ... but surely they didn't mean this? An exhausting sense of inevitability washed over him. A bleak dizziness accompanied a growing darkness at the edge of his vision. All compelled him to complete one simple task. *Deliver the crown.*

Eric moved as close as he dared, offering the crown in a way that he hoped was sufficiently ceremonial.

The holly man knelt, bowing his head and very nearly poking Eric's eyes out with his antlers. Eric didn't need to be told what to do next. There was a space between the antlers that was perfect for the crown. With all care and deference, he put it in place.

Thunder rumbled and lightning once again split the clearing with dazzling white light. The excited fairy clapped her hands and beamed.

Eric found himself weeping tears of joy, a bright and shining happiness abruptly coursing through him. He knew now what his purpose in life was. To worship this bringer of light.

The holly man's white hair writhed, entangling itself in the branches of the crown and holding it firmly in place. With a deep growl of satisfaction, he stood. It might have been Eric's imagination, but the creature looked even taller than before.

'Behold!' it bellowed. 'The Holly King!'

The waning moon glowed intensely, like a light bulb about to burst, and the whole world shook.

The Holly King looked down at Eric, who had by now quite lost his mind.

'You have done well, Eric Birdwhistle. *God Jól.*'

Eric twitched with blissful incomprehension.

As they stood together, snow began to tumble gently into the clearing. Fat flakes, heavy and ready to settle, silvery white in the rays of the moon.

The Holly King leaned forward, voice growling, 'Merry Christmas.'

CHRISTMAS CANOODLING

Faye Bright and Bertie Butterworth could not keep their hands off one another. Since their first kiss in August – a hurried smacker grabbed just before Faye flew off to save her fellow witches – they had taken every opportunity to indulge in heavy petting.

Growing up, Faye had never had much interest in boys, nor the accompanying hanky-panky that might ensue, but over the summer something inside her had changed. It wasn't just the blossoming of her magical powers. She found she wanted to get all up close with Bertie. She couldn't help herself. Every time she saw his big smile, freckled cheeks and ever-curious eyes she wanted to grab him by the ears and plant one on him. Perhaps it *was* the magic? Had it stoked some passionate fire in her belly? She didn't care. All Faye knew was that whenever she was with Bertie she lost track of time, didn't have a care in the world, felt warm and safe. She liked it. And now, with Christmas around the corner, they'd managed to find even more opportunities

27

for smooching by liberally hanging mistletoe from every available ceiling.

'Oh dear, Bertie. Would you look at that?' Faye and Bertie stood on the threshold between the Green Man pub's lounge and saloon bars, where a sprig of mistletoe was pinned to a beam. 'Who put that there?' Faye asked, all innocence.

Bertie's freckles reddened. 'Can't imagine,' he said with a shrug.

Faye glanced around. It was early. Long before opening time. Dad was in the cellar sorting the barrels for the day. She and Bertie were supposed to be sweeping and dusting, but they had a bit of time to spare.

'It would be rude not to.' Faye's eyes rose suggestively to the mistletoe.

'It's tradition,' Bertie agreed. 'And traditions should be— *mmf*!'

His last words were lost as Faye pressed her lips against his. She wrapped her arms around him, and he did the same to her. It was clumsy and a little uncomfortable, but this was why they needed to practise. How were they supposed to do this sort of thing properly if they didn't put the hours in?

Faye's heart quickened as Bertie pulled away to take a breath. She gave him all of half a second before pulling him back.

'Ooh, Bertie,' she said between kisses. Her eyes were closed but the heat from his blushes radiated on her face. 'Whatever shall we do with you?' They kissed again. The glass of Faye's specs began to mist at the edges, and she felt a welcome and familiar excitement building within her as she yearned for—

'Will you two pack it in?' Terrence's voice was like a bucket of cold water. 'This is a pub, not a knocking shop!'

With a swiftness that somehow managed to contradict many of Professor Einstein's theories about the speed of light, Bertie was on the other side of the bar, pushing a broom, concentrating on gathering dust into a neat pile, and avoiding eye contact as if his life depended on it.

It was Faye's turn to blush. She hurriedly cleaned the mist off her specs on a bit of blouse that was poking out of her dungarees for just this purpose. 'If you meet your beloved under the mistletoe, you *have* to kiss them, Dad. It's tradition.'

'Is it really?' Terrence's voice was heavy with unseasonal cynicism. 'All I know is your dear departed mother was always suspicious of mistletoe. Wouldn't have it in the house.'

'Really?' Faye looked up again at the sprig of green leaves and white berries. 'Why's that?'

'It's poisonous for a start,' Terrence said as he wandered over, eyeing the cutting like he would an intruder. 'And it's a parasite. When other trees shed their leaves and look as good as dead during the winter, mistletoe moves in and lords it over them. That always used to irk her. That, and it also gave licence to any Tom, Dick and Harry to try and kiss her.'

Faye shuddered a little. She'd dodged a few attempts

at unwanted pecks from a couple of worse-for-wear punters last Christmas, and the threat of a bunch of fives if they did it again had soon put an end to that.

'Your mother was always curious about why we did things. Especially if it was some old tradition. Most people don't know or can't be bothered to know, but Kathryn would always dig a little deeper.' Terrence trailed off for a moment as if remembering something. 'She was a wise one, your mother. A wise angel.'

'She married you, so how wise was she really, eh?' Faye chuckled and kissed her dad on the cheek. 'Last one. Promise,' she said with a bold smile, getting back to dusting the pub. The task had become much more difficult ever since the Christmas decorations had gone up. Every dado rail was draped with colourful paper chains or strings of Christmas cards. Terrence had discovered a knack for sketching jolly snowmen with top hats and cob pipes, which he drew in chalk on the blackout boards placed over the windows. Bertie had made a two-foot-high Christmas tree from a broken beer crate, which he'd painted green and decked out with little glass baubles. The pub was as festive as it had ever been. Christmas in Woodville was always jolly, but after the shenanigans of the past year the villagers felt they had earned the right to a bit of knees-up. Or as much of a knees-up as they could afford, what with shortages of almost everything – the sugar allowance down to eight ounces, tea down to two ounces, margarine now on the ration books, and a penny on a pint.

Terrence wiped away the wet patch Faye had left on

his cheek, then made his way to the bar. Faye noticed that he was limping.

'Your war wound playing up again, Dad?'

Bertie jerked upright, eyes wide in admiration. He all but saluted at Terrence. 'I didn't know you fought in the Great War, Mr Bright.'

'I didn't.' Terrence patted his left leg by the knee. 'Tore a ligament in a football match before the war, and it flares up whenever it's damp or cold. I failed the medical and spent most of the war in the catering corps in Dover, serving slop to Tommies before they went to France.'

'I call it his war wound because it kept him out of the war,' Faye told Bertie. 'And thank gawd it did, otherwise I might not be here.'

'We should start a double act,' Bertie said with a grin. He got puzzled stares in return. 'You've got a limp, and I've got a limp. We should do something for the Christmas cabaret. We could call it "Two Left Feet"!'

Terrence's eyes rolled around their sockets. 'Back to work, Bertie.'

The lad flashed a nervous smile. 'Yes, Mr Bright.'

Faye couldn't help but notice that Bertie had begun using more formalities around her dad ever since they started stepping out.

Her dad had clearly noticed, too. 'Mr Bright,' Terrence repeated softly to himself with a chuckle. He nudged Faye. 'Watch this. *Bertie!*' Terrence had developed a strong sergeant major voice since joining the Home Guard, even if he was still only a private. 'When are you going to make an honest woman of my daughter?'

'Dad!' Faye slapped her father on the arm.

Bertie stiffened, his cheeks crimson and knuckles white as he gripped his broom so hard it was close to breaking.

'She's ... quite honest enough,' he managed, sounding as if he was constipated.

'You don't have to answer him, Bertie,' Faye told him. 'Dad, stop winding him up.'

Terrence gave a throaty cackle and moved to return to the cellar, but as he glanced at the pub's doors something occurred to him. 'We had any post yet?'

Faye shook her head.

'Not like Eric to be so late,' Terrence mused. Mr Paine's newsagent's shop with the village Post Office inside was just up the road, and the Green Man was usually one of Eric's first stops.

'He'll have loads of Christmas cards,' Faye reasoned. She was about to suggest that their mail might turn up in the second post when a scream pierced the air. It echoed from the direction of the Wode Road, followed swiftly by another, then a crash and the clatter of running footsteps.

Faye was quick to unlock the doors and rush outside. Terrence, with his dodgy knee, and Bertie, born with one leg shorter than the other, shuffled after her.

The morning sun reflected off puddles in the street, and the brightness made Faye's eyes throb. A few folk were already braving the chill to queue outside the butcher's and baker's for their ration. It was Mrs Marshall, clutching a wicker basket, who was screaming. She pointed down the road.

Faye followed her finger and stopped short at a peculiar sight.

Eric Birdwhistle, village postman, was staggering up past the war memorial. He was naked as the day he was born, apart from a cloak of what looked like holly leaves.

'He is coming!' Eric cried in a voice that wasn't entirely his own. It was deep, rumbling like a bass drum. 'Shed no tears, good people. Rejoice, for it is time. The Holly King cometh!'

THORNY CLOAK

Faye heard the clatter of a bicycle. Reverend Jacobs rattled to a stop outside the baker's and hurried towards Eric.

Eric continued bellowing, regardless. 'Celebrate, good people, for He has defeated the Oak King and taken his crown.'

'Now, now, Eric old chap,' the young Reverend said, breath puffing in the cold as he wriggled out of his long winter coat. 'I don't know what all this non-sense is about, but let's see if we can cover you up, hmmm?' The Reverend held out the coat like a matador facing a bull.

'Don't touch him!' a familiar and commanding voice cried.

All heads winched around to find Mrs Teach stepping out of her terraced house, arms raised. She was immaculately turned out in her green Women's Voluntary Service woollen coat and hat with its distinct red band. As she strode towards Eric and the Reverend, the onlookers in her path took an instinctive step back to clear her way. She might not dress like a witch from a fairy tale, but she didn't need to. The residents of Woodville knew who was in charge here.

All except one, perhaps.

'Ah, Mrs Teach, yes, thank you for your contribution,' the Reverend said with a nervous smile. 'But I rather think we should first—' Reverend Jacobs laid a hand on Eric's forearm. Faye felt the tremor right through her boots as a shock wave sent the poor Reverend flying through the air. He landed in a heap by his bicycle outside Mrs Yorke's bakery. The sound made Faye's ears ring, and rainwater fell from gutters all around. Eric looked at his forearm with a puzzled expression.

'Don't say I didn't warn him,' Mrs Teach shrugged as folk splashed through the puddles to help the Reverend to his feet. 'Next time, good Reverend, you would do well to heed my advice.' She turned to the watching villagers. 'Blankets!' she cried, and a dozen women snapped to attention and dashed away to their homes, leaving the men gawping in their wake.

Faye instinctively hurried to Mrs Teach's side. 'Morning, Mrs Teach. Any clue why Eric the postie is wandering about in nary but a cloak of holly?'

Suddenly Eric cried out in pain. He began to writhe as the holly leaves dug themselves into his cold, bare skin.

Faye noticed little clumps of snow on Eric's head and feet. Had it snowed last night? She glanced around, but the village looked as grey and damp as before. It had been a miserable winter so far, and a little Christmas snow would do wonders to put a smile on the villagers' faces.

'The Holly King will tolerate no defiance,' Eric said between gasps. 'All who transgress will be punished come Yuletide. The wood belongs to my master now. All who trespass shall face His wrath.' Blood began to seep from tiny wounds between the leaves.

Faye started to rush forward to help him, but Mrs Teach took a firm grip on her arm. 'Don't,' she warned.

'The poor fella's in pain.' Faye tried to shake her off, but the older woman's grip only tightened.

'Don't touch him until we know what we're dealing with.' Mrs Teach spoke low enough that only Faye could hear. 'If I'm right, and I sincerely hope I'm not, it appears that our Eric has become the emissary of a demigod, which makes no sense whatsoever.'

'A demigod? Is that this Holly King he keeps harping on about?'

'The Holly King is a myth. He's not real, at least . . .' Mrs Teach pursed her lips as she thought. 'Whatever this is, Eric is protected with some very old magic. Reverend Jacobs got off lightly, and I suspect the next to interfere won't be as lucky, so keep your distance. Ah, here we are.'

The first of the women returned with blankets and bedsheets.

'Ladies, form a circle, please,' Mrs Teach directed them, and they obeyed.

More came with sheets, an eiderdown and bath

towels. They stood shoulder to shoulder, creating a barrier around Eric, Faye and Mrs Teach, averting their eyes from Eric's nakedness.

'Do not fear, good women,' Eric said, his voice trembling as he shivered. 'The Holly King will reward the just and the good. He healed me, and now I worship Him, rightly. He can heal us all. Only those who have committed an egregious sin should fear Him.'

'That would be most of us, then,' Mrs Teach muttered as she stood before Eric, Faye right behind her. The poor man looked like the last turkey in a butcher's window. All goosebumps and fatty folds. His belly covered his nethers and his knees were pink. His fingers trembled, blue at the tips, but his eyes burned like a zealot's. Unblinking and wide.

'Eric, look at me.' Mrs Teach's voice softened.

Eric's gaze drifted to her. 'Philomena Teach,' he said, an eerie smile creeping across his face. 'You are named in the Holly King's scroll of sinners, I am sad to report.'

'Am I indeed? Why am I not surprised.'

'Come the reckoning you will be punished.'

'Yes, we'll discuss that later, Eric. For now, I need you to look at me here.' Mrs Teach raised a red-painted fingernail to her right eye. The effect was immediate. Eric's grin dropped and his eyelids became heavy. The cloak of holly leaves began to shake, as if in a strong wind, and fall away.

'Whatever you're doing, it's working,' Faye whispered.

'Stand by, girl.' Mrs Teach tensed her shoulders. 'We need to—'

'Eric!' a voice cried from outside the circle. 'Where's my Eric?'

It was enough to break Mrs Teach's spell. Eric glanced up and his eyes darkened once more as the cloak of holly tightened around him, the points digging deeper into his flesh. He grimaced, as if in pain, but let out a gasp of ecstasy.

'Eric! Let me through!'

'It's Eric's Shirley,' Faye told Mrs Teach, who regained eye contact with Eric. His face contorted in confusion and pain.

'Go to her, Faye. Keep her out. Do not let her in.'

'Righto.' Faye ducked under the wall of blankets to find Shirley Birdwhistle being held back by her dad, Bertie and Captain Marshall of the Home Guard. The three men were struggling to keep a grip on the woman as she reached out for her husband.

'Eric! What's going on?'

'Yes, indeed,' Captain Marshall snapped at Faye. 'What is the meaning of this hullaballoo, young lady?'

'Captain, whatever happens, don't let anyone in there.' Faye jabbed a thumb back beyond the circle of blankets. 'Mrs Teach's strict orders.'

'Mrs Teach?' Captain Marshall grimaced. 'Who's she to be giving orders?'

'Oh, she's Mrs Teach,' Bertie said, as Mrs Birdwhistle once again made to lunge forward.

'I find life's far less complicated if you do as she says,' Terrence added.

Captain Marshall grunted in reluctant agreement.

'Let me through!' Shirley cried.

'Shirley, it's me, Faye Bright.' Faye gently took the woman's hand. Mrs Birdwhistle rarely came into the pub. She much preferred to be helping others, being one of the first in the village to sign up to the Women's Voluntary Service, and always ready to run a raffle, knit a cuddly toy or bake a cake. She made an incredible Victoria sponge. She also worked in the Post Office with Eric and was always very proper and neat, so it was odd to see her hair so unkempt this morning, her floral housecoat and heavy winter coat clearly thrown on in a hurry.

'Faye, he wasn't there when I woke this morning.' Mrs Birdwhistle gripped Faye's shoulders. 'Where's he been? What's going on?'

Faye decided that the whole *possessed-by-a-demigod* explanation would only make things worse. 'He's ... he's had a funny turn, that's all.'

'Funny turn? What do you mean? Eric doesn't have funny turns.'

'Mrs Teach is helping him,' Faye began. 'So there's no need to—'

An agonised cry came from behind the wall of blankets, straight from the depths of Eric's soul. The air above him and Mrs Teach shimmered like heat haze on a summer's day.

'Eric!' Shirley Birdwhistle broke free from Terrence, Bertie and Captain Marshall, shoved Faye aside, and ploughed through the wall of quilting.

What she found had her sobbing in heavy gulps.

Eric was on his knees on the wet cobbles, surrounded by holly leaves and with countless scratches and pin-pricks of blood all over his back. Mrs Teach crouched beside him, covering him with a blanket, but still the blood seeped through.

'Shirley?' Eric looked up at his wife. His eyes and voice were his own again, but his mind seemed addled, as if he had woken from a bad dream. 'Oh, Shirley,' he said, before collapsing into Mrs Teach's arms.

Interlude: The Trees Awaken

Across the wood, the trees stir. The hollow oak is singing. A low note, pulsing through their roots. A song of warning. He has returned. And it will only be a matter of time before He calls on them. They must prepare.

MISS CHARLOTTE
ATTEMPTS A LIE-IN

Miss Charlotte Southill slept alone.

Not that this was unusual. For decades, centuries even, she had been used to sleeping solo. The life she had chosen meant moving from place to place and grabbing a bit of shut-eye wherever she could – in ditches, trees, carts, barns and, on one memorable occasion, a palace in Lucknow.

She had always been a light sleeper, even as a child. Memories of her early life were stretched thin these days, but she could recall her mother Ursula staying up all night creating explosive concoctions. The young Charlotte had learned it was wise to sleep fully clothed, boots on, and within dashing distance of the nearest exit. As she grew older, she preferred to sleep in the nude, but in the winter she wore a bright red men's all-in-one union suit. Snug and practical, it kept her warm from neck to ankles, and was all she needed. She still wore her boots to bed, though. Some habits die hard.

Of course, she had shared her bed on many nights in the past. Mostly for one night only, and on the understanding that afterwards they would never see one another again. Though there had been exceptions. Lizzie in Pudding Lane. That was a very long time ago, but the memory was a pink, glistening scar.

Most recently, Charlotte had shared her bed with Martine de la Barre. The rambunctious events of the summer had culminated in her unexpectedly finding herself completely infatuated with the tempestuous French scryer. Their autumn affair was as fiery and passionate as one might expect, but each night had ended with them gently holding one another in bed, and Charlotte had become rather used to having Martine around. It was the little things she enjoyed. The scent of Martine's Gauloises mingling with her own pipe smoke. The way she cursed in French. The hours of consensual, happy silence. The warmth of Martine's hand in hers. Waking each morning to find her still there.

Last week that had all changed. Martine had received a coded communiqué from the Conseil Français de la Magie, summoning her to join the magical resistance effort in occupied France. Martine felt compelled to fight for her country's freedom and Charlotte knew there was nothing she could say or do to stop her.

Neither wept on her departure – they both agreed that tears were a waste of time and energy – but nor could they find the words to say a proper goodbye. Charlotte saw Martine off at the train station, returned to her cottage in the middle of the wood and slept alone once more.

Which was a bugger because this morning was bloody freezing and the fire had died hours ago.

Charlotte was in dire need of some shared bodily warmth. Even the goat would do.

It had been a long night. Charlotte had been hearing whispers on the aether from a voice she did not recognise. It was a woman, American. A New Yorker, if she wasn't mistaken. Not anyone she knew, but still oddly familiar. Not wanting a repeat of Mrs Teach's disastrous summoning of the demon Kefapepo earlier that summer, Charlotte had put aside her yearning for Martine and thrown herself into finding out who this mysterious voice belonged to. For the last week she had stayed up till dawn, dabbling in divination, haruspicy, augury, mirror magic, and even Tarot, to discover the owner of the voice, but whoever it was remained elusive.

It was almost as if she was teasing Charlotte. Toying with her to draw her in. Charlotte had first suspected the involvement of the Bavarian Druid Otto Kopp, but he had gone quiet after evading capture in Dover once his plan to kill them all had failed, and this wasn't his style, anyway. That egotistical buffoon liked everyone to know he was involved. This felt more snide. This felt like a witch.

Charlotte had then wondered if it was that minx Jennifer Gentle putting on a silly voice. After her arrest on the Dover cliffs in August she had every reason to want revenge on her fellow witches. Faye had spoken for her at the trial, which was held in private to avoid any scandal and revealing the role of witchcraft in the war effort, but there was no getting around the fact that Jennifer had murdered three witches in cold blood, possibly more, and had colluded with the enemy. She had been sentenced to death by hanging, though she was now appealing the verdict on some dull technicality. Charlotte had asked Vera Fivetrees to check if Jennifer had access to any kind of scrying material, but the High Witch had confirmed that she was kept under constant surveillance in her cell and was, so far, behaving herself.

Last night, Charlotte had attempted scrying herself – not her forte – to summon the voice, but it had stayed stubbornly silent. Not for the first time since Martine had left did Charlotte wish that she was there. After hours of fruitless fumbling in the aether, she had finally flopped onto her bed at around 4 a.m.

Her sleep never went as deep as she would like. She could hear the creak of branches under the weight of fresh snow outside. The padding of a fox hunting around the ferns. The squeal of a field mouse as it was caught in the talons of a barn owl. That goat munching straw at first light. Every little sound waged war on her efforts to sleep, and together they were winning. She was on the verge of getting up to mix a sleeping draught when—

Charlotte Southill ...

The voice again. Clearer than ever. Tickling her ears.

Charlotte Southill. Have you been a good girl this year?

It was a young woman's voice. Definitely New York in origin. Possibly Harlem.

He knows, y'know, so don't tell no lies.

She spoke in a way that suggested a mischievous grin.

Hold onto your hat, Charlie girl. He's a-comin'!

The wood fell silent. Not a creature was stirring.

Then the goat started bleating in fear. It scampered away, the sound of its cloven hooves fading into the distance.

Charlotte opened her eyes and sat upright at the end of her bed, boots on the floor, fists bunched. She listened intently. Her cobwood cottage was protected. There was iron over the doors and windows. She regularly refreshed the black salt around the perimeter of the clearing, though if there had been snow last night it might be less effective. Not that it mattered. Nothing would get in or out without her permission.

The thud on the roof made her heart jerk in her chest. Something was up there and moving about, so heavy it made the beams creak. Her roof was made of turf and wood. She kept intending to build something sturdier, with slate tiles and proper insulation, but it never quite reached the top of her to-do list. She made up her mind to remedy that as soon as she scared off this invader.

She moved carefully from her bedroom to the main room, following the thing as it paced from the west gable end of the cottage to the chimney. Dust fell from the eaves and the teacups hanging from pegs rattled with each of its footsteps.

Charlotte stayed silent. Whatever it was might assume that, because she wasn't screaming like a ninny, she was either asleep or the cottage was empty. She tiptoed to the fireplace, avoiding the creaky floorboards – she took great pains to ensure they creaked loudly in case anyone was stupid enough to try and burgle her in her sleep – and reached for the katana sword hanging in its scabbard over the fireplace, where she kept it for special occasions, such as duels and home invasions. If this thing wasn't stopped by the iron over the doors and windows, it would be stopped by a swift slice of tamahagane steel.

The footsteps paused at the chimney.

'Whoever you are, you have exactly three seconds to leave,' Charlotte cried, silently drawing the sword and surprising herself with the loudness of her voice.

'*God Jól*, Charlotte Southill,' a man's voice boomed from above. 'You have been *such* a naughty girl.'

Charlotte's blood chilled. If this wasn't some transatlantic witch, then who the bloody hell was it?

'You are a trespasser on my land, Charlotte Southill, and you shall pay the price.'

The thing gave a grunt, not dissimilar to the sound Mrs Teach made when putting her boots on, as if squeezing into something too small for it. More strained noises came, followed by the grinding and shifting of bricks and mortar as the plaster above the fireplace cracked from ceiling to mantle.

He was coming down the chimney.

Soot billowed over the ashes of last night's fire, filling the room.

Blood rushing in her ears, Charlotte snatched up a scarf from where it hung on the door and wrapped it around her mouth and nose.

As the black dust began to clear, she saw a pair of shiny black boots suspended over the coals. He was stuck. Good. That gave her time to think.

God Jól. Trespassing on his land. A hefty man who comes down a chimney. Knows if you're lying.

Charlotte's heart almost stopped. No. It couldn't be him. He wasn't real, was he?

And if he was, then her magic wouldn't work. Nothing would. He was a demigod. As powerful as they got. If the stories were true, then nothing short of a bolt of lightning would stop him, and even that would only be a temporary measure that would do little more than make him very cross.

But Charlotte Southill was not one for running, and she wasn't about to let some reprobate half-deity invade her home. She would let this uninvited guest know just how unwelcome he was.

If he ever got out of her chimney.

Just then a ghastly noise came from the flue, an almighty roar like the howl of a storm. The crack in the plaster spread like a spiderweb, and the cobwood cottage's beams twisted and snapped as it was prised apart as easily as a Brazil nut. Plates and cups smashed to the ground, window frames buckled, the glass broke into shards. The cold winter air swept in, stirring up papers and books. Before Charlotte could react, roof beams slammed down fast and hard, knocking the katana from her hand. She was buried in the rubble as her cottage came tumbling down around her.

THE IRON CONTRAPTION

The Holly King stood triumphant in the wreckage of the witch's abode, his chest heaving. It had been a while since his last physical manifestation, but his strength was returning. All thanks to the crown.

He kicked aside the cottage door frame with its iron decorations. As if a few shards of old metal could stop him. He chuckled to himself at the very idea, startling a nearby vixen with a bright orange coat. She stiffened, watching him from between the leaning alder trees. Eyes unblinking, ears pricked, limbs tense. The Holly King gave her a bow of his head. With a flick of her tail, she turned and skipped away. He followed her darting run, past where he had left his sarcophagus and sack, happy to see they were both undamaged. The sack's impatient inhabitants continued to kick and curse. Their time would come soon enough.

If the wood was to be his, then he needed to clear it of any unwanted intruders. This witch was a trespasser, and he knew she would not leave without a fight.

'Is she dead?' The fairy fluttered to his side, an eager grin on her face. She was a necessity – after all, it was she who had arranged for the creation of his crown. But she was starting to grate on the Holly King's nerves. He would tolerate her for the moment, but he looked forward to the day when he would pluck her wings off. 'Well, is she?'

The Holly King motioned for her to be quiet. This witch was no ordinary foe. Now to see if she had perished or, like a wounded bird, needed finishing off.

The Holly King bent down and gripped the edge of a fallen wall in his fist. With a mighty growl, he hurled it to one side, sending it crashing to the far end of the clearing. He waved the swirling dust away. Curled up as if asleep, the witch looked remarkably undamaged. He reached out to prod her. Suddenly her eyes bulged open and she gulped in air, limbs flailing. A mercy killing it would be, then.

The Holly King raised a foot to stomp on her, but she rolled aside, grabbing a poker and swinging it into his knee. He roared in pain as she scrabbled clear of his boot.

The fairy squealed and flew away, hiding in the trees, just as the Holly King received another whack from the witch and her poker, this time on his back. The blow jarred his crown of oak and holly, but it did not fall. How dare she? How *dare* this jumped-up practitioner of childish tricks desecrate his sacred crown? He would punish her for this. A quick death was too merciful. She moved to strike him again, but he caught the bar in his hand, bending it like rubber. Wide-eyed, she fell back, crabbing away from him, but she did not run. Defiant to the last. He liked that. He would break her legs first, then her arms, then pick off her limbs like petals from a daisy.

As he stooped down to snap the first leg, the witch reached into her pocket and threw a fine black powder into his eyes.

The Holly King felt the world tilting around him. Magic. So tedious. But it wouldn't last long. A few moments to clear his head, then he would simply rip hers from her body. He had no time for this nonsense.

'Miss Charlotte!'

A new voice. Strangely, it seemed to be coming from above.

The Holly King blinked his eyes clear. A leather-clad girl on some kind of iron contraption floated down into the clearing. She wore a helm, like Freyja of old, but her eyes were shielded by glass.

'Miss Charlotte, jump on!' she cried.

The witch staggered over to the iron frame, swung a leg over the thing's saddle and wrapped her arms around the girl. In a heartbeat, they were soaring into the night sky.

The fairy leapt into the air in pursuit, but the Holly King was quick to pinch her by the ankle. Her wings fluttered in frustration, then folded neatly along her spine. She craned her head, watching them go.

'Let the little pests flee,' the Holly King told her. 'They will spread the word of my coming. For now, let me enjoy my prize. The wood is mine.'

My Hero, the Goat

Faye had seen some peculiar stuff in the wood, but the oversized fella with the antlers and the great big bushy beard really took the biscuit. She was more than happy to put some distance between them as she rose above the tree line astride the Griffin, her Pashley Model-A bicycle, recently customised for flight.

'Hold tight!' Faye called to Miss Charlotte as she leaned forward, and they tore across the chilly morning sky.

Using the tower of Saint Irene's Church as a guide, Faye pointed them away from the village. The wind rushed by as they skimmed the treetops, heading towards Larry Dell's farm. It wasn't long before their destination came into view. Larry had offered Faye the use of Ivy Barn as a workshop for the Griffin after she had helped him sort that business with the poltergeist earlier in the autumn. Since then, it had become something of a second home as Faye, Bertie and her father tinkered with the flying bicycle. The Griffin now had a compass, a clock, two saddles and two new wheels so that it could still function as a regular bike when needed. It sported a new paint job, too. Bertie had given it the same camouflage colours as a Spitfire, using the paints from his model kits.

Faye circled the snow-covered barn before bringing the Griffin down by the doors. Mrs Teach was waiting for them, along with Miss Charlotte's goat.

Miss Charlotte gave Faye a slight squeeze on the shoulder as she got off the bicycle. 'Thank you, Faye.'

Faye heard something new in Miss Charlotte's voice. A hint of fear, and vulnerability. She wasn't sure she liked that in her Miss Charlotte. She leaned the bicycle against the barn doors.

'Just in the nick of time.' Charlotte straightened her back, becoming her old self once more. 'How did you know?'

'Your goat told us.' Faye gestured to where Mrs Teach stroked the creature's back. It stood idly munching on some hay.

'He's not my goat.'

'Whoever he is, he came haring up the Wode Road and Mrs Teach somehow knew what he was going on about.'

Charlotte strode over to the goat. She crouched before it, as if she was going to propose, then gently placed her hands on either side of its head.

'Well, old friend, I think your debt is paid,' she said.

The goat bleated.

'In full,' Charlotte agreed, then tipped her head

forward to meet the goat's. They briefly closed their eyes.

Faye looked to Mrs Teach with a *what-the-flip-is-going-on?* expression on her face. Mrs Teach remained respectfully silent.

The goat bleated again, and Miss Charlotte stood and took a step back, allowing it to trot away down the snow-edged path to its new life.

Charlotte caught Faye's puzzled expression. 'It's none of your business.' She stood with her hands on her hips. Even in her bright red long johns and boots she was an imposing figure. 'Did I just encounter the bloody Holly King? And what is he doing in my wood?'

'*Our* wood,' Mrs Teach corrected her sweetly. 'Tea, anyone?' She didn't wait for a reply as she hurried into the relative warmth of the barn, because the answer was always yes. 'And just what was he doing in *our* wood?'

'Demolishing my cottage.'

'It's true.' Faye took off her helmet and shook her hair free. She placed the helmet on the workbench and started cleaning her specs. 'And he was about to demolish Miss Charlotte, too.'

'Let's not get carried away.' Charlotte slumped into an armchair, one of the many home comforts installed in the barn by Faye, Bertie and Terrence. Mrs Teach lit a small gas stove for the tea. 'I had everything under control.'

'If you say so.' Faye pushed her specs up her nose.

'I do.' Charlotte crossed her legs. 'Anyway, there's more. Before he arrived, I heard a voice on the aether.'

'Anyone we know?' Mrs Teach asked, popping open the tea caddy.

'Not the foggiest. But she was there, too, in the clearing. She sounded American.'

Faye found herself thinking of the girl on the stretcher in her dream with the American accent. *I'm hurtin' real bad*. What was her name? Pearl?

'I've been dreaming about an American girl,' she said, taking a step back as the other witches' eyes turned on her. She shrugged. 'I thought it might mean something.'

'Does she look like a fairy?' Miss Charlotte asked. 'With wings?'

Faye gave her a puzzled look.

'Like one you'd stick on a Christmas tree, but as tall as you with sensible boots?' Miss Charlotte added.

Faye folded her arms. 'You two told me fairies don't exist.'

'They don't,' Miss Charlotte said. 'I think she's something else that *looks* like a fairy.'

'A demon?' Faye grimaced at the thought of another demonic encounter. They never ended well.

'Perhaps. She knew me and warned me that someone was coming. Or she might be a witch.' Miss Charlotte narrowed her eyes at the others. 'I must say, you're all taking this rather well.'

Mrs Teach perched herself on the arm of a divan as she waited for the kettle to boil. 'You're not the first to encounter the Holly King today. Eric Birdwhistle bumped into him on his rounds this morning. Poor chap has gone quite doolally.'

'Hold on, you two.' Faye hopped up and sat on the workbench. 'Who's the Holly King? That grumpy Father Christmas-type with the antlers?'

'That's actually a fairly decent description.' Miss Charlotte got to her feet and started opening drawers in an old sideboard. 'Ah!' She took out a clay pipe, tobacco pouch and matches. 'Legend has it that a very long time ago the wood was ruled by the Holly King in winter and the Oak King in summer.' Miss Charlotte busied herself lighting her pipe and Mrs Teach took over the story.

'Twice a year, at the turning of the seasons . . .' Mrs Teach left an expectant pause and Faye realised she had to fill in the gap like a schoolgirl.

'Oh, er, Lammas and Yule?'

'Very good.' Mrs Teach smiled. 'At Lammas and Yule, they would have a right royal punch-up to decide who wore the crown and ruled the wood. In summer the Oak King was strongest, in winter it was the Holly King.'

'Couldn't they just share it?'

Charlotte snorted. 'Demigods have a streak of inadequacy a mile wide, Faye. The story goes that they were both promised the wood by their mother the Goddess, and when they discovered the lie, their perverse reaction was to blame the other. Besides, no one likes a good scrap more than a pair of competitive brothers.'

'That can't have been much fun for the locals,' Faye mused. 'Having a couple of bloody great tree men knocking seven bells out of each other.'

'Demigods.' Miss Charlotte puffed on her pipe as she corrected Faye. 'Not tree men. They're nigh-on invincible, especially when they're wearing the crown. And you're right, it wasn't fun. They vented their anger on any poor soul who dared wander into their wood.'

'Yule starts tomorrow, doesn't it?' Faye half closed one eye as she recalled her feasts and festivals, and Mrs Teach insisting that she burn an oak log for twelve days. 'Twenty-first of December, right? So maybe that's why he's here?'

'He's a relic of the past. He's not been worshipped for centuries.' Mrs Teach looked to Miss Charlotte for an explanation. 'Why return now?'

Miss Charlotte exhaled a cloud of blue pipe smoke. 'He wouldn't be able to on his own. Someone had to make a crown and use it to summon him.'

'The voice you heard?' Faye suggested.

'Very likely. This is no accident.'

'Why did they go away in the first place?' Faye hopped off the workbench as the kettle started to whistle. 'Someone must've got rid of them. How do we do it, too?'

Mrs Teach poured the tea. 'No one knows.'

'Lost to time,' Miss Charlotte added.

Faye shook her head. 'If only someone had written it down, eh? But oh no. The Council of Witches can't be having books with helpful information like that lying about, can they? Oh deary me, heaven forbid.'

'Stop being so impudent,' Mrs Teach snapped. 'We'll

find a way to rid the wood of this interloper. We're witches, after all.'

'How long will that take?' Faye asked. 'Half the village walks their dogs in that wood. What if someone else gets flattened?'

'Already dealt with,' Mrs Teach said, handing out teacups. 'I've spread the word there's a rabid dog on the loose. That should keep everyone away.'

'Let's talk to Eric.' Faye took her cuppa, enjoying the warmth on her hands. 'He was the first one to meet His Majesty the Holly King. Maybe he can tell us something?'

'And I'll keep trying to find out whose voice I've been hearing.' Miss Charlotte tugged at the sleeves of her union suit. 'But first, I need to get some new clothes.'

'Very good.' Mrs Teach stirred her tea. 'I shall report to Vera Fivetrees.'

The skin on Faye's back tingled at the mention of the High Witch of the British Empire. Vera Fivetrees had been urging Faye to volunteer for special missions for the war effort after Faye's actions in Dover had, in Vera's words, 'Saved the nation.'

Faye had reminded Vera that she hadn't done it single-handedly, but what she'd kept to herself was just how terrified she had been, and how close she had come to failing. She didn't much fancy going through that again, and so politely declined every mission that Vera offered her. And anyway, she was needed here. After all, who better to fix a problem like a deluded demigod? The witches of Woodville, that's who.

Homeward Bound

As the bus passed under the railway bridge, its tyres splashing through bright puddles, Sidney Birdwhistle felt like he had suddenly gulped a pint of ice-cold water. The sensation spread from his chest to his trembling fingers and toes. His heart tripped over itself, and his body tensed with pain.

It was ridiculous. Sid had fought at Ardennes, Escaut and Dunkirk, but it was coming home that scared him the most.

He peered through the anti-blast netting on the bus window, scanning the rooftops, windows and hedges for any sudden movements, flashes of light or unusual gatherings. The village looked much as he had left it, though Dougie Allen's garage on the Unthank Road was gone and a pair of Daimler armoured cars were parked on its blackened forecourt. There were sandbags piled on every corner, but the villagers were going about their business as usual. Folk queued up outside the butcher's and baker's, ration books in hand, exchanging gossip for smiles. They didn't have a clue. Not the foggiest that there were people just like them over the water who had been blown to bits on streets just like this one. Sid had watched as men, women and children fled from Stukas and Panzers. Had seen bullets execute their deadly dance, spitting brick dust from the walls, punching into the bodies of civilians and soldiers whose only mistake had been to take a wrong turn. Sid kept his eyes open. He knew that if he closed them he would see it all again, clear as day. See poor old Alfie. Or what was left of him. One minute he'd been chatting and laughing away, the next—

A hand landed on Sid's shoulder.

Instinctively, Sid grabbed it, squeezing hard. He looked up to see someone he half recognised. A female bus conductor. He knew her face but couldn't place her, especially in that uniform. She spoke to him, smiling, but her voice was silent as blood pounded in his ears. Wrenched out of his trance, he struggled to clear his head. Nothing could hurt him here.

'Sorry if I startled you, duck.' The bus conductor fanned her hand, shaking life back into it. Her voice became clearer as she spoke, like water draining from Sid's ear after a swim. 'That's a strong old grip you've got there, I'll say. You're Eric and Shirley's lad, aren't you?'

Sid still struggled to recognise the woman, but she clearly knew him. He gave a numb nod.

'Thought so. You've missed your stop! Staring out the window, was yer? What's so interesting out there, eh?' She chuckled as she spoke. Her voice was beginning to grate on him. 'You'll have to hop off now and walk back into the village. Come on, off you pop.'

Sid did as he was told, barging past roughly and ignoring her protestations and the disapproving stares of the other passengers. He staggered off the bus. His boots splashed in a grey puddle by the side of the road and cold air brushed against his face. He found himself standing by a lollipop bus stop. Edge Road. A bit of a walk from the village. He could see the bell tower of Saint Irene's.

It was happening more and more. Sid knew that sometimes whole hours of the day passed without him knowing. What would Alfie say? 'Get your act together, Sid. You can't let them see you like this.'

He hefted his kitbag over his shoulder and readied himself for the long hike to the village.

Then he saw it.

A man. Or something that looked like a man. As tall as a bear on its hind legs, standing silently in the middle of the road with a club made of oak in its hand.

Its hunched shoulders slowly rose and fell with each breath. Moisture evaporated from the coarse brown bristles that covered its body. It was too far away for Sid to make out the expression on its face, but the light caught its black eyes. Even from this distance, there was something ancient and pitiless about them. Sid wanted to run, but he somehow knew that the thing would be on him in seconds.

This wasn't the first time Sid had seen the creature. The hairy man had been there on the beach at

Dunkirk, watching him from the lapping waves as the bombs fell. He was there when the train had pulled into Waterloo, waiting at the back of the crowd. Sid had seen him out of the window at the barracks in Salisbury, standing in the fields, the club resting on his shoulder. And here he was now. Each time, as inevitable as the grave, he got a little closer, and each time Sid felt a weight in his chest get heavier.

The creature had a name.

Woodwose.

It came to Sid from childhood stories. Yes. The wild man of the wood.

The woodwose drew its hunched shoulders back and raised its right arm. It held out its club to Sid.

Sid swallowed, looking from the club to the woodwose. He shook his head, but the woodwose only offered the club again.

Sid took a breath and closed his eyes. When he opened them again, the thing was gone. Of course it was. The woodwose was nothing but a figment, a hangover from his nightmares.

Sid needed a rest. He needed to go home.

He started marching down towards the village, staying in the centre of the road. He kept his eyes front, certain that if he looked into the trees on either side, he would see the thing again.

The voice of his old drill instructor came to him as he marched.

BY THE CENTRE, DEFT-IGHT, DEFT-IGHT, DEFT-IGHT!

The old goat never said 'Left, right'. He had changed the words so he could be heard over the wind and rain. Sid had enjoyed training on Salisbury Plain. He'd especially loved the long cross-country runs. Alfie had thought he was barmy, but all Sid had to do was put one foot in front of the other and lose himself until it was done. His mind was always clear after a run. Finally, something he was good at.

He'd been eighteen when he got his call-up papers. He'd passed the medical A-1, gone straight to a camp in Salisbury, and every day from six in the morning till ten at night it had been all drills and training.

Teachers at school had scolded Sid for daydreaming, but at the training camp the NCOs praised him for his concentration, endurance and determination. He was going to be a fine soldier, they told him.

Day after day he would run in the rain and the cold, his only reward some reconstituted spuds and what Alfie reckoned to be horse meat. This would be followed by a night under thin blankets, his head on a pillow filled with straw. The others tossed and turned. Sid slept like a log.

Then they went to France.

Sid hadn't slept properly since.

'Sid! That you?'

Sid blinked to discover he was by the lychgate at Saint Irene's. How had he got here so quickly? Someone slapped him on the arm. Sid spun on his heels, fists clenched and ready to thump his attacker, but found only a man wearing shorts, smiling at him.

'What were you chatting to yourself about, eh?'

Who would be mad enough to wear shorts in this weather? The man had bright pink knees and long white socks. A name came to Sid. Mr Hodgson. The local busybody. He tried to recall what the man had just asked him. It was important to appear normal. To act like there was nothing wrong.

'Hello, Mr Hodgson. Sorry. Miles away. What was that?'

'You looked like you were talking to yourself, lad. Army sent you half barmy, has it?'

Sid flashed a smile, though he was kicking himself. He had to stop talking to himself. Especially when there were others around. 'No, Mr Hodgson, just, ah, singing a song. Got to keep warm somehow, I s'pose.'

Mr Hodgson's smile faded slightly. He wasn't convinced, but was too polite to take it any further. 'Good to see you home, Sid. And just in time for Christmas, you lucky thing.'

Was it really Christmas? Already? He'd lost all track of time.

'Send my best to your parents, won't you?' Mr Hodgson folded his face into a sincere frown. 'Especially your dear old dad. Bless him. What a palaver this morning. Poor chap. I'm sure he'll be right as rain in no time. I saw Doctor Hamm knocking on the door, so—'

'Palaver?' Sid stiffened. 'What happened? What's wrong with Dad?'

Mr Hodgson started to explain, but Sid was already

running. He ducked down Perry Lane, the shortcut that took him behind the houses and shops. The world around him was a blur, only a few familiar landmarks standing out. The back alley, his garden gate, the kitchen door. He tumbled through the hall and the living room. No one. There was a creak on the floorboards from upstairs. Sid dropped his kitbag and dashed up to the landing.

'Mum? Dad?'

'Sidney? Don't come in here!' His mother rushed from their bedroom and across the landing, arms outstretched.

Through the open bedroom door Sid could see movement. He dodged past his mother and barged in. He scanned the room in seconds – the curtains, under the bed, behind the door – looking for threats, traps.

Doctor Hamm stood over his dad, who lay in bed with ceramic hot water bottles under his armpits and between his legs.

The doctor raised a finger to his lips, but Sid needed answers.

'What's happened to Dad?'

Eric's eyes snapped open. They were yellowing and bloodshot. Dribble oozed from his mouth.

'Don't go into the woods. It is His domain now. Stay away from the woods!'

'What's he on about?' Sid had never seen his father like this before. His dear old pa was a solid fellow, never missed a day's work in his life.

'He called to me! He knows,' Eric raved. 'He knows everything. There's no pretending.'

71

Sid's mother put herself between her son and the bed. 'No, Sidney, you shouldn't see him like this.'

'Mum, what's going on?' Sid looked from her to Doctor Hamm, who was leaning over his dad. 'Tell me!' A familiar rage began to build inside Sid as his mother tried to shoo him out of the room. Her eyes were pink from weeping, and she gripped his hand in an effort to pull him away.

'Mrs Birdwhistle, please calm down.' Doctor Hamm's voice was soft with a Lancastrian lilt, even though he had worked in the village for as long as Sid could remember. The doctor had treated him when he had a fever as a child. If anyone in this room could talk sense, it was him. 'It's only fair that your son know what's happened to his father.'

'A reckoning!' Sid's dad cried out, pointing at the ceiling. 'A reckoning is coming!'

Sid's mother fell into a chair by the bed and buried her head in her hands.

Sid flinched as Doctor Hamm rested a hand on his shoulder. Why did everyone keep touching him?

'Your father is suffering from exposure to the cold,' the doctor said, calmly but loudly enough to be heard over his mother's tears and his father's ramblings. 'For reasons we have yet to understand, he wandered alone into the wood first thing this morning and got lost.'

'Beware the Holly King's wrath!' Eric cried, and Shirley wailed in despair.

Doctor Hamm gestured to the landing. He and Sid stepped out of the room. The doctor closed the door behind them and spoke in a low voice. 'Sidney, I'm sorry you had to come home to this.'

'What's wrong with him, Doctor? Why's my dad lost his marbles?'

Doctor Hamm shook his head. 'I expect him to make a full recovery. Thanks to Mrs Teach, your father got the right kind of help. This could have been much worse. But . . .' He hesitated, glancing back to the bedroom where the ranting and wailing was beginning to fade. 'Sidney, you're going to hear some strange stories about your father.'

'Like what?'

'There's no easy way of saying this, so I shall be straight with you. Your father was found naked on the Wode Road. He was behaving like a wild man.'

Sid heard the words that came from the doctor's mouth, but he had to take a moment to put them in some order that made sense.

'No, that's not true,' Sid said. 'It can't be.'

'If I hadn't seen it with my own eyes, I would have struggled to believe it myself. But that's what prolonged exposure to extreme cold does to people. It scrambles the mind like eggs. My father was a doctor in the Navy. He told me about a chap who fell overboard off the coast of Norway. After he was rescued, he complained he was burning up and took all his clothes off. The fellow had a kind of delirium brought on by the cold. I believe that's what happened here.'

Sid shook his head in confusion. 'Dad didn't fall overboard. What are you—'

'Sidney, listen to me. The good news is your father will recover with the right care. You've come home at the best possible time.'

'What am I supposed to do?'

'Keep him warm, top up the hot water bottles and keep him hydrated. Warm cordial will be best.' Doctor Hamm made to leave, but Sid gripped his arm.

'That's it? You're leaving?'

'I've done all I can.' Doctor Hamm glanced down at his arm. 'Could you let go, Sidney?'

Sid nodded and released his hand. A wave of exhaustion washed over him. He just wanted to curl up and sleep.

'I'll be back in the morning. Don't worry, your father will soon be himself again.' For the first time, the doctor's voice faltered, and Sid wondered if he was lying. 'I'll see myself out.'

As the doctor made his way down the stairs, Sid's mother called from the bedroom. 'Sidney? Are you there?'

Sid hurried back in. His dad was now lying on his front, eyes closed, breathing slowly.

Sid embraced his mother. Her thin arms held him tight and he felt like a little boy again. Home at last. 'What was he doing in the woods, Mum?'

'I don't know, Sidney, I don't know. I woke up and he was gone. I can't fathom what's come over him.'

Sid helped his mother back into the chair, then knelt down to pick up one of the hot water bottles by the bed.

'I knew you were coming home.' Sid's mother pressed

her hands together, as if offering a prayer. 'Your father told me not to get my hopes up, but I had a feeling in my bones. I just knew it, and now here you are. Here we are. A family again. Your father needs a rest. That's all. He'll get better and put all this strangeness behind him, and it'll be like it always was.'

Sid sat on the edge of the bed and watched his father sleeping. This made no sense at all. His dad was the most normal man he had ever known. As straight as a die. Logical. A thinker who planned everything. A man who—

A hand gripped Sid around the back of his neck. His father jerked him closer until they were nose to nose. Eric's eyes were wide, his cheeks trembling. 'He knows, Sidney!' Eric bellowed in his son's face. 'He knows what you did. The Holly King knows what happened to Alfie, and He's going to make you pay!'

CRYPTIC CLUE

The good news for Miss Charlotte was that the twice-weekly Women's Voluntary Service Clothing Exchange was in full swing at Saint Irene's.

The bad news for Miss Charlotte was that Mrs Teach insisted on accompanying her there.

'You can't be seen walking around like that. It's indecent.'

'I care little for decency.'

'That much is evident. How's Martine, by the way?'

Charlotte's shoulders tensed as they came to the church doors. 'No idea.'

'Aren't you concerned?'

'As if worrying about her will help. There's no time to waste, and it's chilly, and I need something warmer so that I can get back to what remains of my home. I'm hoping there's a sword in the rubble there that might help us.'

They stepped into the church, a formidable pair. Mrs Teach had changed into her best fur coat and hat.

Miss Charlotte was still in her bright red union suit long johns and boots, though now with Mrs Teach's Women's Voluntary Service woollen coat draped on top to fend off the cold.

The church was packed, and barely recognisable as a place of worship. Only last week, the precious stained-glass windows had been removed – in case of bomb damage – and replaced with plain glass, criss-crossed with anti-blast tape. The pews had been swept aside to make room for dozens of rickety trestle tables and clothes racks, all heaving under the weight of donated garments. Volunteers scurried about finding the right sizes for those doing the rummaging. Most were desperate mothers, accompanied by boys wearing trousers that barely reached their ankles, or girls in dresses so tight it made their faces red.

Miss Charlotte looked on in fear. 'What have you dragged me to, woman?'

'It's just a clothing exchange. You won't catch anything.' Mrs Teach stamped her shoes on the church's welcome mat. 'It's cheaper than buying new, and there's always something good.'

'And you shop here, do you?'

Mrs Teach brushed a hand over the collar of her fur coat. 'Where do you think I got this?'

'And there I was thinking you had personally skinned fifty minks to make it yourself.'

'If you don't want my help, just say so.'

'I don't want your help.'

'Good morning, ladies.' Reverend Jacobs appeared in

their path, wringing his hands together. The Reverend was young and relatively new to the parish. Mrs Teach generally found him to be pleasant and enthusiastic. He took much of the village's strangeness in his stride and didn't ask too many impertinent questions. Miss Charlotte generally found him to be harmless, if intermittently annoying. Much like one of Mrs Pritchett's Yorkshire Terriers.

The Reverend was usually polite and knew to keep it brief, but this morning he seemed somewhat twitchy. His smile quivered as he studiously avoided looking at Miss Charlotte's long johns.

'Good day to you, Reverend.' Mrs Teach greeted him with a smile. 'Have you recovered from this morning's fall?'

A moment passed between them. They all knew that something very strange had occurred this morning, but in the longstanding Woodvillian tradition, they would do all they could to avoid talking about it directly.

'I have indeed, Mrs Teach, thank you. And I have attempted to offer solace to the Birdwhistles this morning, but they are not taking visitors at this time, it seems.'

The Reverend hoisted a brief smile back into place. Miss Charlotte almost felt sorry for the man, who so often found his role as village pastor supplanted by the wisdom of the witches. Almost.

He continued. 'Th-that's actually something I was hoping to discuss with you both at some point. I appreciate that the village has a fascinating and colourful history, peppered with some remarkable events, many of which have a hint of the … well …' He made the mistake of catching Miss Charlotte's eyes and faltered.

'Do go on, Reverend,' she said, arching a brow. 'A hint of … ?'

Reverend Jacobs smacked his lips together nervously. 'A hint of the, ah, pagan.' His nostrils quivered in an involuntary display of disapproval. 'To be frank, Miss Charlotte, all this talk of Holly Kings and Yuletide and such. It's … well, it's not exactly the done thing, is it?'

'Reverend Jacobs.' Mrs Teach's voice was all brandy sauce oozing over a Christmas pudding. 'Leave all that to us. We're in the process of nipping it in the bud.'

'Are you? How splendid. I suppose the real question is how to stop this becoming a regular thing? Especially after the summer we've had. It's been very peculiar, indeed.'

Miss Charlotte did not like this one little bit. The Reverend's predecessor, a man called Skipwith, had understood the old ways enough to not interfere. If anyone needed nipping in the bud, it was this little man.

'Perhaps we could discuss it further another time?' The Reverend turned his attention to Mrs Teach. 'On an unrelated matter, I should like to extend an invitation to you, Mrs Teach, to stop by the vicarage over the Christmas festivities.'

Mrs Teach glanced over at Miss Charlotte.

'That's very kind of you, Reverend Jacobs, though I don't see why I should receive such special treatment.'

'It's a service I offer to all those in my parish who face Christmas without a loved one. A warm hearth, tea, Christmas pudding and, one hopes, good company and a sympathetic ear.'

'And that will compensate for the loss of my Ernie, will it?'

The sudden chill in Mrs Teach's voice drew an involuntary gasp from the Reverend, and a tightening in Miss Charlotte's belly as she tried not to chuckle. The iciness was fleeting, and in moments Mrs Teach's charm was back in full force.

'Forgive me, Reverend, I must decline your kind offer. I have made plans for the festivities already. Good day.'

She levelled her fingers as if to press against a door, and the Reverend instinctively stood aside. The two witches strode past him into the bustle of the clothing exchange.

Miss Charlotte pursed her lips in admiration. 'Mrs Teach, I am both shocked and bursting with pride.'

Mrs Teach lifted her chin slightly. 'Miss Charlotte, when have you ever known me to be patronised or pitied?'

'Never, to be fair.'

'Indeed. Anyway, I'm surprised he's got time for entertaining. Last I heard he was up in Edith Palmer's drawers.'

'Scandalous,' Miss Charlotte smirked, having heard similar rumours from Mrs Yorke in the bakery.

'"Sympathetic ear". I sometimes wonder if these

people know who I am,' Mrs Teach muttered, before smiling sweetly and gesturing to the clothes. 'Shall we?'

'We shall.'

They moved from stall to stall where each of Mrs Teach's exhortations – 'Isn't this divine?', 'What a charming frock!', 'You would look spectacular in these' – was received with stony silence or a baleful glare.

'Ah, now this looks practical.' Miss Charlotte picked up a white cricket jumper with red and blue trim around the V-neck collar.

'You're not a cricketer.' Mrs Teach snatched it away from her. 'Don't be so ridiculous. What about this? Marshall and Snelgrove, if I'm not mistaken.'

'You are not, Mrs Teach.' Mrs Pritchett, Woodville's second-oldest resident after Miss Charlotte, wandered over to the stall with a box marked 'Odds & Sods'. She let it drop onto the trestle table, which creaked under the added weight, then took a drag on the roll-up cigarette that seemed permanently stuck to her lip. 'That came in just this morning.'

'Try it on.' Mrs Teach thrust the frock at Miss Charlotte.

'I'd rather die,' came the reply.

Mrs Pritchett looked Miss Charlotte up and down in her red union suit. 'Rough night?'

'Something like that.'

'I've got just the thing for you.' Mrs Pritchett plunged a bony arm into the box and retrieved something long, trousered and green. 'Try that for size.'

She handed it to Miss Charlotte who let it unravel. 'Oh, I love it.'

It was a siren suit. One piece with little buttons up the front, useful pockets and slightly flared trousers.

'You'll look like a man,' Mrs Teach said in disapproval.

'Mrs Teach, I've known men who wear skirts, tights and frilly powdered wigs. Kindly refrain from lecturing me on how to dress for my sex.' She pivoted to Mrs Pritchett. 'How much?'

'It's an exchange. You're supposed to bring some-thing to, y'know, exchange.'

'I don't have anything to exchange. As I said, it's been a rough night.'

'We could accept a cash donation, I suppose.' Mrs Pritchett sucked on her ciggie, assessing the siren suit. 'This is good as new. Buy one of these in the shops and it would set you back thirty bob, but I can do it for twenty.'

'Twenty bob?' Mrs Teach pressed a hand to her chest. 'That's outrageous.'

'Times are hard, Mrs Teach, as I'm sure you've noticed.' Mrs Pritchett flicked the tip of her cigarette into a tin ashtray. 'And besides, it all goes towards the war effort.'

'Does it indeed?' Mrs Teach leaned over the trestle table until she was eye to eye with Mrs Pritchett. 'And might I ask where you found such a pristine item? This has a whiff of the black market about it.'

There were few women in the village who could hold

their own against Mrs Teach, but Evangelina Pritchett was one of them. She folded her arms and lowered her eyelids to half-mast.

'It disappoints me, Mrs Teach, that you would impugn my good name so readily. It belonged to a young lady of my acquaintance who bought this for a factory job, then found herself in the family way only a few days ago.'

'Oh.' Mrs Teach shrank a little. 'I see.'

Mrs Pritchett paused, then lowered her voice. 'Though quite how she got herself pregnant when her husband's been in a POW camp in Germany since Dunkirk remains a mystery.' She waggled her eyebrows suggestively at Miss Charlotte, who smirked.

Mrs Teach gave a small bow. 'My apologies for the slander, Mrs Pritchett.'

'Accepted.' Mrs Pritchett rummaged in the box again, extracting a selection of slightly worse-for-wear thermal undergarments. 'I'll chuck these in for another ten bob.'

'Throw that in, too, and you've got a deal.' Miss Charlotte pointed to the cricket jumper.

'Done.' Mrs Pritchett nodded.

'Excellent. Mrs Teach, pay the woman.'

'What?'

'I'm good for it,' Charlotte reassured her. 'However, due to this morning's *incident* I find myself lacking in cash funds. Where can I change?' she asked Mrs Pritchett as Mrs Teach grumbled into her purse.

A corner of the church had been cordoned off for women and children to try on clothes, but it was agreed that Miss Charlotte frightened enough people already without subjecting them to her snowy-white flesh. Which is how the pair found themselves descending into the crypt.

Mrs Teach tugged on a cord and a handful of electric light bulbs dangling from cables arrayed around the room sprang into life. The crypt was built of Kentish ragstone – a hard, grey limestone – and hosted just one sarcophagus, that of some poor soul lost to history. Any names, dates and eulogies had crumbled away long ago. It sat in the centre like a forgotten altar and was draped in a red gingham tablecloth on which lay tin mugs, a tea caddy, a biscuit tin and a sugar bowl with spoons. The crypt was used regularly as an air raid shelter, and armchairs were scattered about for the benefit of those sheltering from Luftwaffe bombs. Half-read magazines lay open on their arms.

Miss Charlotte began to undress. 'Cosy.'

'Hardly.' Mrs Teach peered into some of the darker recesses beyond the arches. 'What this place needs is a good spring clean. Look at this.' She brushed away a veil of cobwebs on the north wall, revealing a network of ominous fissures running up the ragstone. 'That's not terribly reassuring,' Mrs Teach noted.

'After all the bombs we've had dropped on us over

the summer,' Miss Charlotte said as she eased herself into the siren suit, 'I think we can allow for a few cracks here and there.'

'That's subsidence.' Mrs Teach stood back and angled her head as she inspected the wall. 'The old yew tree in the graveyard. Reverend Jacobs should see to that before plying ladies with tea, Christmas pudding and misplaced sympathy. I say, this is new.' A section of the wall had been plastered, though this, too, had a crack that ran from floor to ceiling. Mrs Teach scratched at the crack, picking off a small shard.

'Since when are you an expert on plaster?'

'My Ernie worked on the renovations of the church nave years ago. He warned them about the yew even then. Every night he would come home covered in lime stucco – old Norman plaster. It smelled all musky and damp. But this –' she sniffed it '– this is modern plaster. It can't have been done all that long ago.'

'How simply fascinating,' Miss Charlotte said, with the absolute minimum of enthusiasm.

'I don't understand.' Mrs Teach stepped back. 'Why plaster this wall and none of the others?'

Miss Charlotte smoothed down the cricket jumper over the siren suit. 'I think that's rather fetching, don't you?'

Mrs Teach glanced over her shoulder. 'You look like you've just been bowled for a duck. You're entirely sure you're happy with this get-up?'

'I am.'

'Then you owe me thirty shillings.'

'You shall have it by the end of next week. Now leave that plaster alone and let's find Faye.'

Mrs Teach pressed the little shard back into its divot in the wall. As she did, the crack in the plaster spread like a spiderweb.

'I am not paying for *that*,' Miss Charlotte declared.

'In for a penny . . .' Mrs Teach pounded on the plaster like a debt collector. More cracks appeared and great chunks of the plaster fell away, revealing twentieth-century red bricks blocking an archway made from Norman stone.

'Well, well, Mrs Teach.' Miss Charlotte stood beside her fellow witch. Something was painted in white on the bricks.

An old rune. An arrow bisected with a cross.

'You finally have my interest. What the bloody hell is this?'

ALFIE ISN'T ALL THERE

'You should listen to your old man, Sid. I know you think he's off his chump, but he's right, y'know.'

'Don't talk about my dad like that.' Sid made sure to keep his voice low. His dad was still asleep upstairs. He stood by the sink in the kitchen and looked out to the backyard where icicles dripped from the guttering on the outside lavvy, and the rainwater on the Anderson shelter was slowly evaporating off its roof. Sid and his father had built the shelter together that fateful September in 1939, days after Mr Chamberlain made his speech on the radio, and just before Sid went off for his first bout of training. His dad had been bursting with pride that his only child was the first in the village to volunteer after war was declared. He shook his boy's hand. 'Never been more proud of you, son.' That was the dad Sidney knew. He didn't have a clue who that fella upstairs was, raving about kings and reckonings. Maybe the doc was right? Exposure to the cold did things to the brain.

'Yeah, yeah, keep your hair on,' Alfie said. 'Your pa got lost in the woods and it froze his noggin', but why was he out there in the first place, eh? Ask yourself that.'

'Keep your voice down,' Sid told Alfie. He had a gob on him, that one. He sat at the kitchen table, rolling a ciggie as always. Sid couldn't bear to look at him, because if he did, he might not be there.

Alfie came and went, you see.

Sometimes he was just a voice in Sid's head. Other times, he was a shadow on the edge of his vision. Sid would catch sight of a boot, or a fidgety knee, or fingers sorting tobacco into neat piles. He found it easier to just let Alfie have his say and then he'd go. Though he seemed to be hanging around for longer and longer since Sid left the barracks.

'What the bloody hell is a Holly King, anyway?' Sid sneered. 'Stupid sodding name, for a start.'

'I reckon you'll know soon enough,' Alfie said, a hint of menace in his voice.

Sid said nothing. If the Holly King knew what had happened to Alfie, did that mean that Alfie knew the Holly King? How? Sid was thinking about the best way to ask him without arousing suspicion when there was a knock at the door.

'Aye-aye,' Alfie said. 'Fate comes a-knockin'. Don't answer. Let your mum get it.'

'She's gone to work,' Sid reminded him. Even with his dad poorly upstairs, she'd insisted on doing her bit in the Post Office sorting room in the back of

90

the newsagent's. She'd told Sid that the vicar's lodger Edith Palmer had offered to step in and cover Dad's round and needed to be shown the ropes. Sid's mum had a busy day. Sid envied her. Better than stewing in this place.

Another knock.

Sid moved silently from the kitchen to the hall, staying close to the walls. Through the criss-crossed blast tape on the front door's frosted glass panel, he could see a silhouette moving about.

'Mrs Birdwhistle? You there? It's Faye Bright.'

'A bit of skirt?' Alfie's voice became excited. 'Who's she?'

'Landlord's daughter,' Sid whispered.

'A bit of skirt with her own pub? That's a dream come true, that is. Get in there.'

'She's a child.'

Faye pressed her nose against the frosted glass. 'Mrs Birdwhistle? I just came to ask after Mr Birdwhistle and see if you need anything.'

'She's persistent, I'll give her that. Get rid of her,' Alfie said, and he was gone. Sid didn't need to look to know it. He could feel the emptiness where Alfie had been. Instead, he looked at the wall where his mother had hung a painting of Jesus carrying the cross. She always straightened it whenever she walked past. Sid saw something odd in his reflection in the glass. Two shadows. He blinked to clear his eyes.

There came a creak as Faye raised the flap of the brass letterbox. 'Sid? That you?'

'Hold your horses, I'm coming.' Sid yanked the door open, ready to give this little brat an earful.

'Sidney Birdwhistle, as I live and breathe.' Faye Bright stood on the doorstep, dressed in what looked like an RAF fighter pilot's jacket. Her hair was tucked into a green bobble hat, but she wasn't the childish imp that Sid remembered from before. 'You're looking good in your uniform, Sid. Suits ya.'

Sid found himself smiling. Faye had always been lippy for a girl, but she had a swagger about her now that was all new.

'Look at you, Faye Bright. All grown up.'

'We've all had to do a lot of growin' up, I s'pose. Been a funny old year. You on leave?'

Sid bristled. Why were people so nosy? He nodded, giving away as few details as possible. 'For Christmas.'

'Lucky thing. How's your dad?'

And there it was. She knew. Everyone in the village must know that Sid's father was a raving loon.

'He's asleep. He's been exposed to the cold.' Sid closed the door a little. 'And it's probably not wise to keep the door open too long and let all this winter air in, eh?'

Faye shuffled her feet. 'Sid, I know this might be a bit of an imposition and all that, but any chance I can pop in and see him?'

'No.' Sid stared at her. Usually, a dead-eyed glare from him sent folk scurrying, but Faye didn't budge. She was looking at the empty space next to him. The place where Alfie had been just a moment ago.

'What're you looking at?' he snapped.

She crinkled her lips. 'Not sure.'

'I never had you down as a nosy parker, Faye. Why don't you mind your own business and leave us—'

'It's not like that, Sid. I was there, when he came into the village. I just want to help if I can. Make sure he's all tickety-boo.'

'I bet you do.' Sid spoke to release the tension in his jaw. He bunched his hands into fists as he felt the old rage growing. 'He's fine. Now do me a favour and let us be.'

'Is your mum there?'

'And that includes my mother!' Sid thumped the wall. The picture of Jesus juddered and tipped at an angle. 'If I find out you've upset her, then you'll have me to answer to.' He made to close the door.

'Sid, I'm sorry. But ... has he said anything?' Faye craned her neck to keep eye contact with Sid. 'Did he mention something called the Holly King?'

Sid slammed the door shut. 'No. Go away.'

He could see Faye through the frosted glass in the front door. She stood silent for a moment before turning away. He heard the squeak and clatter of the gate and she was gone.

There was a movement in the corner of his eye. A blurry reflection in the hall mirror.

'She knows.' Alfie stood behind him. 'The Holly King will come for you sooner or later, Sid. You'd better watch out.'

∞

The wood was not as the Holly King remembered.

The air was tinged with lead and oil and cordite. Great swathes of his domain had been chopped down and replaced with farmland. Paths made by the boots of men cut through the undergrowth like scars. In the sky, giant birds growled. Their wings were eerily still. Now and then he heard distant booms, but they were not thunder. He could sense the heartbeats of the creatures of the wood, but so many were missing. No bears. No wolves.

The trees murmured in their roots, trembling at his return. One of them sang. They thought he couldn't hear them, and he would let them continue to think that.

There was one other like him. A naiad in a pond. But when he called on her, she dived so deep that not even he could reach her.

He was alone. King of nothing. Was it any better than when he and the fairy had first concocted this plan? Two souls lost in the aether, both victims of their own folly and too weak to succeed alone, they had put aside their rage to conspire their return. She had promised him a kingdom worthy of his might, but all he had found was a shrunken wood surrounded by the stench of mankind. He was beginning to think she wasn't quite all she made herself out to be. She wouldn't even tell him her name, and it grated that even he – the keeper of secrets – couldn't identify her. She knew the value of names. She was no fool, despite her foolishness.

'You okay with that, Your Majesty?' The fairy's abrasive voice shattered the moment. 'Startin' to get heavy?'

She was referring to the ancient sarcophagus that he insisted on carrying with him wherever they went. It was bulky and weighty, but he didn't want it leaving his sight. It was his way out if things didn't go to plan.

There was another, of course. He wondered where that might be.

'Need a rest, O Holly King?' she persisted.

He winced, almost lashing out at her, but then he remembered that she could still be useful. The time would come, however, when he would shut her up for good. 'Where are the Druids with their worship and sacrifice?' He turned to survey his diminished domain. The fairy had to take evasive action to avoid being swiped by the coffin. 'Where are the gifts and offerings? Man has become lazy and ungrateful in my absence.'

'It's the twentieth century, Your Majesty,' the fairy shrugged, making her insect-like wings buzz. 'People don't got no respect.'

The Holly King made a grim face. It was true, she had tried to explain to him how things had changed. But it was worse than he had thought. Humans had the arrogance to think they could lord it over this plane. They had built countless homes of brick and plaster that belched smoke, places of worship for false gods. They came and went without so much as a curtsey to their betters.

'I know all their lies. Every one of them.' The Holly

King shifted the sarcophagus on his shoulder. 'And they will all be judged and found guilty. I will toy with them, test them. A Feast of Fools to expose their secrets. Then I will summon the trees to rise and wipe away any trace of their pestilent village. The woodland's return will renew my kingdom and my rule, and they shall all cower in the shadows between trees as order is restored!' The Holly King finished his speech by clenching a gloved fist.

'That's very exciting.' The fairy flashed a smile and scrunched her nose before hovering closer to him. 'But I'm concerned, Your Holly King-ness.' She pouted and tipped her head. 'It's been so long ... Are you still the demigod you used to be? What I mean is – and don't get all huffy – but tearing down one itsy-bitsy witch's cottage got you all outta breath. Are you up to destroying a whole village?'

He hated to admit it, but she had a point. It might take a day or so for him to regain his full strength.

'Especially with them witches so close by.' She looked around as if they might jump out at her. 'We need some kinda leverage.'

'What do you mean?'

The fairy curled her lips and arched an eyebrow. He had to concede, she was a cunning minx. 'I got a few ideas. There's someone I've been—'

'Heartbeats!' The Holly King raised a hand to silence the fairy. 'Fresh and fearful. I can sense them closing in.' He sniffed the air, then turned to her. 'Man has entered the wood.'

Interlude: The Trees' Warning

The hollow oak's song moves to its second note. Creatures scurry to hedgerows and ditches. Birds flap to the sky, seeking safer nests. The only ones who do not hear are the humans. They chose to stop listening to the songs of the trees long ago. They are going to have to learn the hard way.

WE'RE GOING ON A
DEMIGOD HUNT

The Woodville Village Home Guard volunteers moved deeper into the shimmering, snowy wood.

Captain Marshall led from the front. 'Stay in close formation, men. Eyes and ears alert.'

Bertie admired that in his captain. He would never ask his platoon to do anything that he wouldn't do himself. Bertie had his own doubts about their mission, though, and he wasn't the only one.

'Have I mentioned that this is an utter waste of everyone's time?' Mr Gilbert raised his majestic Roman nose, while at the same time keeping his voice carefully low.

'Only every five minutes,' Mr Brewer replied. He was the shorter of the pair, resplendent in his big round specs with thick lenses. The two gents lived together above their antiques shop on the corner of the Wode Road and Rood Lane and had a very special, if private, relationship. Bertie somehow felt safer when he was on patrol with these two. They had all fought side by side earlier in the summer, seeing off a bunch of hardened Kriegsmarine sailors, although since they had signed the Official Secrets Act they weren't allowed to talk about that. It was their secret victory, and together they all walked a little taller.

That said, they were all hunched over at the moment in an effort to be stealthy. Bertie – having been born with one leg shorter than the other – found that a little trickier than most, especially with all the snow and ice about. Quite how it had snowed in the wood and nowhere else was just one more mystery thrown up by the day's strange events.

Faye's dad had chosen not to join the patrol because of his dodgy knee, though Bertie had offered to keep him company at the back, as his own limp often slowed him down. Mr Bright had said he appreciated the gesture, but in truth he didn't much fancy traipsing about in the cold playing silly buggers. He'd told Bertie that he was welcome to stay and help stack a few crates in the pub's backyard, but given a choice between chores and adventure, Bertie always chose the latter.

Captain Marshall said that at the very least this patrol would be good guerrilla warfare practice. There had been a short period during the briefing when Bertie had wondered if the Nazis were now secretly sending giant apes into battle, but Mr Brewer had kindly explained the difference to him.

'Who saw this rabid dog in the first place?' Mr Gilbert asked.

'Captain Marshall said his daughter Betty heard it

from Dotty Baxter.' Mr Brewer tipped his tin helmet back a little as he thought. 'She claims she heard it from Miss Gordon, who heard it from Mr Loaf.'

'And where did he hear it?'

'Ask him yourself. He's up front with the captain.'

Mr Gilbert shook his head. 'I swear this is a bloody wild good chase.'

'Rabid goose chase.' Bertie snorted at his own joke.

'Quiet back there!' Captain Marshall barked.

Bertie buttoned up. From what he'd seen of poor Mr Birdwhistle, and from the snatches of conversation he'd heard between Faye and the other witches, he was sure there was something stranger than a rabid dog in the wood. But how could Bertie explain that to someone as ramrod rigid as Captain Marshall?

They continued to trudge through the snow. Birdsong trickled down from the trees, and Bertie spotted a badger trail. Fresh prints in the snow, ambling off into the shadows where ice and fungus lingered patiently. The path dwindled to nothing, and they snaked between barbed-wire brambles behind their captain, who Bertie sincerely hoped had some idea of where they were going. The wood, as always, was playing games. Moving trees around like chess pieces but making up its own rules as it went along. The line of Home Guard volunteers became a single file, and Bertie decided he was sufficiently far away from Captain Marshall to rekindle the conversation. However, Mr Gilbert and Mr Brewer were already embroiled in their own intense chat regarding preparations for Christmas.

'Did you pick any Brussels sprouts from the allotment?' Mr Gilbert asked.

Mr Brewer gave a guilty sigh. 'I was hoping to pick some this afternoon, but then our esteemed captain decided to surprise us with this enchanting excursion. I'll do it as soon as I get back.'

'See that you do. I don't want another Christmas ruined.'

'You must really like your Brussels, Mr Gilbert,' Bertie said.

Mr Gilbert stiffened. 'Can't stand the things, Bertie, but it wouldn't be Christmas without them.'

Mr Brewer brightened. 'I *did* collect the Christmas cake from Mrs Yorke.'

'How much?'

'Five shillings.'

'Good god, that woman's a mercenary.'

'It is a jolly good cake, though. Any luck with the ballcock?'

Mr Gilbert noted Bertie's puzzled expression and felt obliged to explain. 'We've had some issues with our lavatory. You wouldn't believe how difficult it is to find replacement parts these days. Combine that with the sudden increase in the cost of lavatory paper – *eleven* pence, if you please – and my daily ablutions have transformed from the one moment of peace in the day to a tiresome and challenging experience.'

'I'm sure we've got a spare,' Bertie offered. 'I'll have a rummage in me dad's shed.'

'Would you, Bertie?' Mr Gilbert crinkled his brow in gratitude. 'You're a brick, young man.'

Bertie smiled, before clearing his throat and steering the conversation back to his own agenda.

'Mr Gilbert? Mr Brewer?' he whispered. 'You've lived in this village a long time and you've seen some queer stuff ...'

The two men shared a silent look.

'The crow folk, and all that palaver at the Summer Fair, and that pilot in Larry Dell's barn ...' Bertie trailed off as he struggled to formulate his question.

'What are you trying to say, Bertie?' Mr Gilbert asked.

'I s'pose I'm sayin' that all this strange stuff happens, but we never stop to think about it.'

'There's a war on, Bertie.' Mr Brewer held up his rifle in evidence. He was indeed the last man you would expect to go to war, even as a Home Guard volunteer. In his antiques shop he was the most soft-spoken and polite chap you could ever hope to meet, with an astonishing level of expertise on Victorian teapots. 'We find ourselves somewhat preoccupied with the dread reality of the Nazi jackboot.'

'And these strange occurrences are nothing new.' Mr Gilbert nodded his head back the way they'd come. 'We had a house clearance a few years ago and some old chap left us hundreds of years of old newspapers. Do you recall?'

'How could I forget?' Mr Brewer raised an eyebrow. 'You insisted on reading them all. We didn't speak for weeks.'

'I couldn't help myself. It was absolutely fascinating. This village has a strange and bloody history of the unexplained, Bertie. There was one story about three highwaymen in 1752 who would rob any poor soul fool enough to pass through the wood at night. Then one April morning they were found torn to pieces at the Gibbet Lane crossroads. Throats ripped out and their guts eviscerated.'

'Blimey.' Bertie wasn't entirely sure what 'eviscerated' meant and made a mental note to look it up in his dictionary when he got home.

Mr Gilbert smiled to see the lad so enthralled and continued. 'And before that, Bertie, in 1651 we have a very detailed eyewitness account of a woman wearing a powdered wig and not much else who came screaming into the village claiming that a wild and crazed man, tall as a bear and covered from head to foot in bristles, had attacked her and her betrothed in the wood. Her paramour fought the creature while she escaped. Although the account offers no explanation for why she was in her bloomers, I'm sure you can draw your own conclusions.'

Mr Brewer tutted. 'You're incorrigible, Mr Gilbert.'

'Takes one to know one, Mr Brewer.'

'What happened to her fella?' Bertie asked.

Mr Gilbert raised his impressive nose. 'That's the real mystery, Bertie. He was found with his leg slashed open, which caused him to bleed to death, and something had bitten his hand off. It was never found.'

'P'raps it *was* a bear?' Bertie mused, before adding

hurriedly, 'I know we've not had wild bears here for centuries, but people used to keep them in chains for bear baiting and such. That'd make me want to bite some hands off.'

'Perhaps. A hunting party went looking for the beast, but nothing – hairy man or bear – was ever found. To return to your original point, Bertie, this village and this wood are soaked in the blood of those who have fallen victim to the strange and the peculiar. It's why the soil has a reddish tinge.'

'Really?' Bertie curled his lip.

'Don't tell him that,' Mr Brewer snapped. 'Honestly, Bertie, take anything he says with a pinch of salt.' Mr Gilbert prodded his partner with the butt of his rifle.

'Will you lot be quiet?' Captain Marshall snapped, at what Bertie thought was a much louder volume than their whispering, though he decided against pointing this out.

Mr Brewer, ever the peacemaker, raised a palm in acknowledgement of his captain's order and their march continued.

Mr Gilbert, ever the rebel, walked by Bertie's side and spoke to him out of the corner of his mouth. 'The village is indeed an odd place, Bertie, and yes, those carnival folk were strange, and the kerfuffle at the Summer Fair gave us awful headaches for days afterwards.'

Mr Brewer pressed a palm to his forehead in agreement. 'Didn't it just.'

Mr Gilbert rested a hand on Bertie's shoulder. 'But

I've found that if one starts picking at old threads, then we might all start to unravel. And if we are to endure this war, then we need to put such considerations aside and focus on what's in front of us.'

'Like . . . like that?' Bertie pointed ahead to a shadow in the wood.

Captain Marshall had seen it, too. He raised a hand, and the platoon came to a halt.

No birds sang, no creatures scurried. The wood's soundscape was paralysed by snow, though even the flakes had taken a break from tumbling.

Their way was blocked by what Bertie thought was the stump of a fallen tree. At least, he hoped it was a stump and not a giant bear or a hairy man. He craned his head to see around the others. He caught a glimpse what seemed like a large bird hovering about some odd-shaped branches, but it darted off before Bertie got a proper look at it. He couldn't be certain, but this bird looked like it had human legs, and it chuckled like Betty Boop from the cartoons at the cinema.

The odd-shaped branches began to rise, and Bertie realised they were antlers, though bigger than any he had seen before. As they rose, they brushed against the surrounding trees, spilling snow in a whispered flurry as the creature's shape became clearer, resolving itself into a giant bearded man in a cloak. He strode towards them, antlers sprouting around the wooden crown on his head. Apart from the beard, he wasn't particularly hairy, which reassured Bertie a little, though he was carrying what looked like an enormous coffin over one shoulder, and a giant sack over the other.

'Who goes there?' Captain Marshall hollered, but the giant kept coming. 'Defensive positions!' he ordered, and immediately the Home Guard volunteers fanned out, taking cover behind trees and in ditches.

'Bertie, come on!' Mr Gilbert beckoned Bertie to join him and Mr Brewer behind an ash tree, but Bertie found that his feet were too heavy to move.

'Halt!' Captain Marshall demanded, but the cloaked man let out a deep, booming chuckle that didn't sound terribly friendly. 'Advance and be recognised!'

Perhaps misunderstanding the request, the man began to run straight towards them, the coffin rattling and the big sack slapping against his back with every stride.

Man Down

'Open fire!' Captain Marshall commanded, drawing his revolver and shooting at the fast-approaching giant. The volunteers of the Woodville Village Home Guard let rip with their assorted weapons. All except Bertie, who remained stock-still, feet rooted to the ground.

The bullets veered round the antlered man, ricocheting off trees and spitting splinters into the air. A handful began to whizz around him, like planets around a star, faster and faster before suddenly breaking free of his gravity and pinging back towards the amateur soldiers.

'Oh, bugger!' Mr Gilbert cried out, clutching his arm and collapsing onto the snow.

'Ralphie!' Mr Brewer tossed aside his rifle and crouched by his fallen partner.

'Well, that's Christmas definitely ruined,' Mr Gilbert managed between gasps of pain.

'How bad is it? Let me see.'

'Stop fussing. It's barely a scratch.' Mr Gilbert moved

his hand from where he had been hit, revealing a large gash across his biceps. Blood glistened and dripped down upon the snow. 'Oh no, actually, that looks quite horrid.'

As Mr Brewer attended to Mr Gilbert, there came a scream from the front as Mr Loaf from the funeral parlour was hurled through the air, landing in an ungainly fashion in a ditch. Having dispatched him in this manner, the giant carefully placed the coffin and the sack upon the ground, raising his fists like a boxer.

Enough was enough. Bertie raised both hands. 'O Holly King!' he cried at the top of his voice. And just in the nick of time. The demigod paused as he loomed over Captain Marshall, gripping him in a clenched glove. 'O, er, great and wise and merciful Holly King.' Bertie limped slowly towards the giant, adopting a tone that he hoped was suitably humble.

'Bertie, what are you doing?' Mr Brewer hissed at him. 'Get down.'

Bertie kept walking, his mind racing to recall the things he had heard Eric Birdwhistle say this morning. This wasn't a bear, or a wild hairy man, but something magical. 'O slayer of the Oak King and wearer of his crown.'

The Holly King released Captain Marshall, leaving him to slump into a bush.

'You know me, boy?' The Holly King's voice reverberated off every tree trunk.

Bertie found his mouth was suddenly dry. 'I've ... I've heard your name.'

'Private Butterworth, stand down,' Captain Marshall ordered from his bush. 'That's a direct order!'

Bertie ignored his captain, focused on what was in front of him, and took a deep breath. 'I've heard others talk about how powerful you are. I'm sorry we've been shooting at you, but the thing is, we were told there was a rabid dog in the wood, and that's what we've been looking for, and when we spotted you ... Not that you look like a dog, but everyone's a bit twitchy, what with there being a war on and all that. So, what I'm hoping is that we can all put this little misunderstanding behind us and have a good laugh about it down the pub.' Bertie paused for breath. 'What ... what do you say?'

The Holly King crouched to meet his eyes, scrutinising the lad like a curio in Mr Gilbert and Mr Brewer's antiques shop.

'Herbert Butterworth,' he said after a while. 'I know your secrets, boy. All of them.'

Bertie quickly tried to bury any lustful thoughts about Faye. Then something else pricked at the edge of his mind. Something buried deep, hidden in its darkest corners. He shook it away. No one could know about that.

A gasp of pain distracted him. He glanced around to see Mr Brewer bravely staying exposed as he gave Mr Gilbert a drink from his canteen. The rest of the platoon had taken cover behind trees and in ditches, other than Mr Loaf, who groaned as he crawled through the slush to Captain Marshall's side, clutching his head.

The Holly King surveyed the men. 'So many

111

shameful secrets among you. But you have very few, Herbert Butterworth. You're quite unusual.' The Holly King's beard rustled. 'I might let you live.'

Bertie's heart all but stopped, and the world suddenly felt excruciatingly real, as if his mind was trying to take everything in before it all ended.

'I'd like that.' Bertie extended a shaky hand to his Home Guard comrades. 'What I'd like even more is for you to let my friends go.'

'They are trespassers in my wood, Herbert Butterworth. Why would I set them free, unpunished?'

'W-we didn't rightly know this was your wood now.'

'I sent forth my herald, Eric Birdwhistle. Did he not proclaim my message loud and clear in the village?'

'Yes, but not everyone heard him and, like I said, there was a lot of confusion about a rabid dog and ...' Bertie was beginning to falter. He looked into the Holly King's pitiless eyes, the enormous white beard laced with berries and holly, and began to realise just who he was dealing with. 'And ... and they have rehearsals for the village Christmas show this afternoon. They're helping to keep the Yuletide traditions alive.'

'Are they indeed?'

'They're good people, Holly King.'

'I beg to differ.' In a sudden movement, the Holly King snatched up Captain Marshall by the throat and began to squeeze.

'Me!' Bertie blurted, resting a hand on the demi-god's enormous forearm. 'Take me instead. As a ... Yuletide gift.'

The Holly King considered the offer, Captain Marshall gasping wide-eyed in his grip.

'You *are* a good boy, aren't you, Herbert Butterworth?' He dropped the captain again. 'You amuse me. I think I shall take you up on your offer. I shall test your goodness. I shall test it, and see how long before you break.'

The Holly King swirled his arms in an almost balletic fashion and flurries of snow took to the air, whirling into a maelstrom and roaring in Bertie's ears. Everything went white.

AGGRESSIVE ARCHAEOLOGY

Faye found her father out in the backyard of the pub, stacking beer crates into a maze of teetering piles. Many of the towers were already taller than Terrence, and creaked as they gently swayed. Still limping, he pushed one of the piles against the back wall to join the others.

Faye stood, hands on hips, squinting at him. 'Bonfire night was last month, Father.'

He started at her voice. 'Don't sneak up on me like that, Faye. Blimey.' He patted the crates to ensure they were firmly in place. 'And I'm not going to burn them. The brewery wants these back so they can reuse the wood to build bomb shelters. Thought I'd tidy them up, but they won't all fit unless I stack them high, and they'll all come tumbling down unless I pack them in tight. It's going to be quite a stack. I think I'll call it "The Great Pyramid of Boozer".'

'Very grand. You should charge a penny a time for people to see it.'

'I just might do that. Oh, I have a message for you.'

Terrence turned his eyes skyward as he tried to recall. 'Mrs Teach and Miss Charlotte say you need to go and meet them at the crypt at Saint Irene's.'

'What are they doing there?'

'I'm merely the messenger, and that's all I was told. You all right? You're doing that frowny thing where your nose crinkles.'

'Did you know Sid Birdwhistle is back on leave for Christmas?'

'Perfect timing.' Terrence resumed stacking crates. A smaller pile of six this time. 'Just in time to see his poor dad lose his marbles.'

'I had a little chat with him.'

'How was he?'

'Rather snippy, if I'm honest.'

'Sid's always had a bit of a temper on him. He used to play for the village footie team and he wasn't above a bit of two-footed argy-bargy when it suited him. Mind you, after what he's been through recently, I can't say I blame him if he's got the 'ump.'

'He was at Dunkirk, wasn't he?'

'One of the last to get out. By the skin of his teeth, I heard. Then they promoted him to lance corporal and sent him back into training.'

Faye remembered that day. Eric had been proud as punch and told everyone he met. It had taken him all day to do one round of post.

There was a knock at the back gate.

'Get that will you, Faye?' Terrence asked as he slid his latest pile of crates into place.

Faye opened the gate with a flourish, startling the young Reverend Jacobs. The contorted expression of fear on his face made her realise why Miss Charlotte enjoyed winding him up so much. Behind him stood Edith Palmer, the cheery ambulance driver, looking smart in her uniform as she sorted through a Royal Mail sack. Faye had heard rumours that the pair might be stepping out since he took Edith in as a lodger. She gave them a smile.

'Wotcha, Edith, Rev. Howdo?'

'All right, duck?' Edith greeted Faye with a grin. 'Got your post here somewhere. This job is harder than it looks.'

The Reverend must have detected something in the air between Faye and Terrence, as he abruptly blurted out, 'Edith has volunteered to cover Eric's round while he recuperates. I had some free time and thought I would offer my assistance.'

There followed a silence that mingled disbelief, politeness and unspoken judgement in equal measure.

'Here you go, ducks.' Edith handed over a clutch of envelopes.

'Ooh, ta very much.' Faye took the ones that looked like Christmas cards, then handed her father the bills.

The Reverend hurriedly continued, more flustered than usual, 'I also have a message from Miss Charlotte and Mrs Teach.' He handed her a folded piece of notepaper. 'And I should be eternally grateful, Faye, if you could kindly persuade them to cease demolishing my church.'

'Demolishing the church?' Faye unfolded the note in a hurry.

'What does it say?' Terrence asked.

'"*Stop gossiping with your father and move your arse to the crypt as requested. P.S. Bring a torch, mallet and crowbar.*"' Faye scrunched the note in her fist. 'I'll see what I can do, Reverend.'

⌘

Minutes later, Faye was descending the steps of Saint Irene's crypt, tools in a bag slung over her shoulder and a lit oil lamp in her grip. She found Mrs Teach standing by as Miss Charlotte used a claw hammer to chip away at the mortar in a brick wall. She hadn't got very far. The red bricks looked oddly modern amid all the ancient stone, and someone had painted a white arrow with a line through it on the wall.

Miss Charlotte glanced up when she heard Faye's footsteps, her brow glistening with sweat. 'I said bring a torch.'

'Batteries have run out. What are you doing?'

'Supervising,' Mrs Teach replied.

'Not you. Her.' Faye nodded to Miss Charlotte as she placed the oil lamp on the sarcophagus with the red gingham tablecloth. 'What's going on?'

'Tools?' Miss Charlotte nodded at the bag.

'Yes.' Faye slipped the bag from her shoulder and slid it towards her. 'Reverend Jacobs asked that you stop demolishing his church.'

'It's not his church.' Miss Charlotte took off her

cricket sweater and tossed it onto an armchair. 'He just works here.' She crouched down to take the mallet and crowbar from the bag.

'Well, I tried.' Faye stood back and surveyed the bricked-up arch. 'That's not a supporting wall, is it? And look at those cracks. That's subsidence, that is. Should we be banging around down here?'

Miss Charlotte twirled the crowbar like a baton. 'Why ever not?'

'We don't want the whole church crashing down on us.'

'This church has stood for centuries, Faye. We're perfectly safe.' Mrs Teach gestured at the painted arrow on the wall. 'What do you make of this?'

Faye peered closer at the rune. 'X marks the spot? I don't know. What I *do* know is we have a big beardy demigod on the loose in our wood and I'm wondering why we're banging away at a crypt wall.'

'We think the two are connected.' Mrs Teach had to raise her voice as Miss Charlotte resumed hammering with the mallet and crowbar.

'Connected how?'

Mrs Teach adopted her teacher voice. 'Tell me what you see.'

Faye bristled a little. These two were still testing her. Even after the summer they'd endured and everything Faye had done, she was still the junior partner in this trio.

'Come along,' Mrs Teach chivvied Faye.

'Some sort of rune?' Faye scrunched her nose again

as she examined the bisected arrow. 'Oh, wait, it's a zodiac sign.' She snapped her fingers. 'Sagittarius.'

'Very good, though this symbol is also associated with the festival of Yule. That's when the Holly King is said to be at his most powerful. We are standing in one of the oldest parts of the church, and if there's something behind that wall that might help us, we should investigate.'

One of Miss Charlotte's strokes sent a brick sliding into the dark beyond, giving the wall a gap-tooth.

'You're desecrating a church because someone painted a sign of the zodiac on a wall?'

Mrs Teach grimaced. 'When you put it like that, you make it sound so unseemly. Besides, these bricks are hardly ancient.'

'This isn't desecration.' Miss Charlotte's voice strained as she swung the mallet. 'It's archaeology.' Her words were almost lost in the avalanche of red bricks that went tumbling into the shadows beyond the arch. 'Light. Quickly.' Miss Charlotte beckoned Faye, who dashed to grab the oil lamp. She raised it high, revealing a secret chamber beyond the arch.

Faye edged closer, waving away the eddies of brick dust in the air. 'Hello? Anyone home? We've come about the plumbing.'

Mrs Teach gently took the oil lamp from her and stepped over the fallen bricks. 'I know you're trying to be amusing, young lady, but one should not tempt the darkness.'

Faye thought that was rich coming from a woman

who just a few months ago had managed to accidentally summon a demon, but she reckoned now was probably not a good time to bring that up. Besides, something had caught her eye in the gloom. 'Ooh, that's pretty.'

Inside the chamber was a sarcophagus made from ancient wood. Resting on its back, it was bigger and more elaborate than its counterpart in the main room of the crypt, and it was decorated with intricate carvings of trees, their branches laced together, and bizarre creatures leaping between them.

Mrs Teach squinted in the lamplight as she inspected the carvings.

'Anyone we know?' Miss Charlotte gripped the mallet as if half expecting something to leap out.

Mrs Teach traced a finger along the branches. 'Holly leaves,' she said. 'This might belong to You-Know-Who.'

'The Holly King?' Faye hopped over the bricks and into the tomb, followed by Miss Charlotte. The air was chill, with a musty odour of damp and death. 'He has his own coffin?'

'Look at this.' Mrs Teach pointed to a carving on the lid, where a figure was depicted leaping from a box that looked much like the sarcophagus. 'This is more than a coffin. I think our mischievous brothers used this as a gateway.'

'To where?'

'Some very unpleasant places.' Miss Charlotte gently touched a part of the carving featuring tormented souls on spikes surrounded by flames.

Faye grimaced. 'Hell?'

'Hell is an invention of men, and not nearly as terrible as the alternatives.' Miss Charlotte took the oil lamp from Mrs Teach and began to look around. 'Oh now, that's interesting.'

She gently clasped Faye's elbow and turned her until she was facing the north wall.

The lamp's light revealed a fresco painted from floor to ceiling on lime plaster. The backdrop was blue and bright as a summer's day. In the centre was an intricately designed circle depicting the seasons and phases of the moon. Flowers, crops, berries, trees, deer, lambs and bears were depicted in painstaking detail. At the northern cardinal point, Faye recognised the Holly King, resplendent in his beard, antlers and cloak. At the southern point was a figure who must have been his brother, the Oak King, a formidable tree man with fists like anvils. At the east and west points, there were wooden coffins much like the one in the chamber.

Faye broke the awed silence. 'It looks like it was painted yesterday.' She oh-so-gently touched the fresco with the tips of her fingers.

Miss Charlotte joined her. 'There are parts of this church that date back to the Romans. And there was sacred ground here before them. I don't know who painted this, but I doubt it was done yesterday.'

'There's your new lodger.' Mrs Teach singled out the Holly King. 'And his brother. Oh, who's this?' She stood on her tiptoes to get a closer look.

'Who's who?' Faye asked.

'There, look, behind the Holly King. Something's creeping up on him.' Mrs Teach pointed to a sketchy rendering of a tall, hairy man wielding a club as if about to clobber the Holly King.

'Well, well.' Miss Charlotte tilted her head to one side. 'A woodwose.'

Faye did the same, as if it might make the thing more distinct. It didn't. 'A woo-what?'

'A woodwose is a wild man of the woods.' Miss Charlotte's eyebrows twitched. 'And this is the infamous Wild Man of Woodville, if I'm not mistaken.'

'That's a fairy tale,' Mrs Teach said dismissively.

'After today's events, let's not be so quick to dismiss fairy tales.' Miss Charlotte scrutinised the hairy man's image. 'He was a knight returning from the Crusades—'

'Or a Viking fresh from pillaging, or a lost Roman centurion on the run from the Celts.' Mrs Teach shook her head. 'The story changes every time I hear it. Either way, he's a soldier returning from a terrible war who finds his lands have been stolen, and so he becomes a violent hermit in the woods, robbing anyone foolish enough to trespass in his—'

'No, no, no.' Miss Charlotte shook her head. 'That's the version told by the victors. The true story is, yes, he was a soldier, but he was so appalled by what he saw on the battlefield that he could no longer face civilisation, and so became a hermit in the wood. But the wood was also the home of a witch, and she didn't take kindly to this intruder. They fought, but then she made him an offer. She would give him the wood if he would agree to become its guardian. He did, and so she turned him into a woodwose, bestowing gifts of great strength and speed upon him. He kept the wood safe for centuries until some fool of a nobleman ran him through at the hollow oak in the eighteenth century. It's said the blood of the woodwose is what gives the hollow oak its long life.'

Mrs Teach flicked the air with her fingers. 'Like I said, a fairy tale.'

'And does he have anything to do with our mate in the woods with the antlers?' Faye nodded at the Holly King. 'Does any of this?'

Miss Charlotte narrowed her eyes and was about to answer when a cry came from the crypt behind them. 'Oh my goodness!'

They all spun around to find Reverend Jacobs frozen at the bottom of the crypt stairs, looking aghast.

'What have you done? What blasphemy is this?' His hand reached for the cross around his neck.

Miss Charlotte exhaled wearily. 'Get a grip, man.'

Mrs Teach, feeling that she had tortured the poor man enough for one day, was far more conciliatory. 'Reverend, you're just in time. We're simply dabbling in a little light archaeology. We've made quite the discovery.'

'A little ... light ... what?' The poor Reverend was starting to lose what little grasp he had on reality.

'It's all tickety-boo, Rev.' Faye negotiated the fallen bricks and took his elbow, steering him to the nearest armchair. His eyes widened as he registered who she was.

'Faye, oh Faye.' There was sorrow in the Reverend's eyes as he squeezed her hand. 'It's Bertie.'

Granny Joan

Bertie found himself in a place that was neither here nor there. There was no up and no down, and everything was white. A ringing started in his ears, getting louder and rising in pitch. It was accompanied by the cries of strange beasts circling unseen. Bertie wasn't one to be afraid of animals. Oh, there were some dogs he would keep a respectful distance from – Mrs Pritchett's Yorkshire Terriers, for a start – but he found that, on the whole, if you respected animals, they let you be. Though from the sounds of these growls, Bertie knew there would be no placating whatever beasts were making them with a biccie and a pat on the head. They wanted to rip him to pieces and would have great fun doing so. Which is why he was so relieved when the real world slammed into him like that time the scenery fell on Mr Hodgson in the village panto last year.

Bertie lay still as he felt the weight of the world return. He was by the hollow oak in the middle of the wood. With a groan, he got to his knees and brushed snow and ice from his uniform. Fresh flakes fell lazily into the clearing and something else fluttered above. Too big for a bird, it giggled as it darted between the trees. It sounded like a girl, but the only girl Bertie knew who could fly was Faye. More giggles. There was a cruelty in that laughter. It definitely wasn't Faye.

Bertie could sense the Holly King behind him. The ground trembled at the demigod's every step. 'Welcome, Herbert Butterworth.'

'Where're my friends?' Bertie got to his feet, still lightheaded.

'They have fled the wood. At the first sign of danger, they abandoned you. That must make you very angry.'

'Mr Gilbert was wounded.' Bertie gave a reasonable shrug. 'And I asked you to spare them, so I got what I wanted. I ain't angry one little bit. If anyone should be narked, it should be you.'

Another chuckle from above. It echoed through the branches.

The Holly King's beard shifted as he smirked. 'Should I, indeed?'

Bertie squared his shoulders, trying to look braver than he actually felt. 'You just set free some of the finest men in the village in exchange for little old me. Not sure you got the best deal there, chum.'

'If that's the village's finest men, then I have nothing to fear.'

You wait till you meet the women, Bertie thought to himself. 'Now we're here, what do we do?'

'You are to be tested, Herbert Butterworth. You—'

128

'Call me Bertie.'

The Holly King glared at the interruption.

'Everyone does. Except my gran on my dad's side. She insists on calling me Herbert. Not sure why, but every time I see her, every birthday card, every Christmas card, I'm 'er Herbert. So, if you think that calling me by my full name is scary, then you should know that all you're doing is making me think of my dear old Granny Joan.' Bertie scratched under his cap. He wasn't sure where this bravado was coming from, but he was enjoying it.

However, all that bravado bade him a fond farewell as something descended from the trees. It was a girl about Faye's age, dressed as a Christmas tree fairy, complete with wings that hummed like a dragonfly's. She hovered close to the Holly King and whispered in his ear. All the while her eyes stayed fixed on Bertie.

The Holly King brushed her off. 'Not now.'

The fairy buzzed away from the Holly King. 'As you wish, Your Majesty.' She shrugged, gave Bertie a sly wink, then spiralled back up into the trees.

The Holly King sneered in irritation, then returned his full attention to Bertie. Still reeling after getting a wink from what looked like a fairy, the lad felt his skin start to tingle under the intense gaze of the demigod. Fighting an overwhelming compulsion to splay his body on the ground before him, Bertie began to understand why poor Eric Birdwhistle had ended up in the nuddy that morning.

Bertie cleared his throat and decided to try to get the

conversation back onto something he was comfortable with. 'W-Where were we? Oh, yes. My Granny Joan. She calls me Herbert, so—'

'What about your mother, Bertie? What does she call you?' The Holly King leaned forward, hands on his knees. Bertie half expected the demigod to pat him on the head.

His mother. He felt his chest tighten and his palms begin to itch. He could tell by the Holly King's grim smile that he knew all about Bertie's mother, and Bertie's shameful secret.

'Ah, yes, there it is.' The Holly King closed his eyes and inhaled deeply. 'So much guilt for one so young. How delicious.' His eyes opened, pinning Bertie to the spot. 'Will you summon the courage to confess, Bertie? Or shall I do it for you?'

THREE SHILLINGS

Sid's mum had come home from work early and wouldn't stop sobbing. Sid couldn't bear it, so he made his excuses and went to the pub. He wore his uniform. You never knew when some kindly soul would offer to buy you a pint for serving your country. Though the uniform also made him a target – in the pubs around Salisbury there was always some chancer who'd take a pop at a lone soldier in uniform to impress his bird. Sid was confident that sort of thing wouldn't happen in a quiet little village like Woodville. Then again, in Salisbury, he'd had his lads to back him up in a scrap. Tonight, he was alone. Almost.

'Looks cosy.' Alfie's voice came from just behind Sid as they approached the Green Man. Its windows were boarded up inside because of the blackout and to protect it from bomb blasts, but a warm glow could be seen around the edges of the door, and the hubbub of pub life was unmistakable.

'It is.' Sid stamped his boots on the brewery mat

before pushing the saloon door open. 'Don't start any trouble.'

'Who, me?' Alfie chuckled.

The warmth of the fireplace and the melange of bitters, ales and tobaccos wafted over Sid. Out of habit, he quickly checked the doors and windows for escape routes, and the punters for possible threats, but the atmosphere was cheerful. The place was festooned with colourful Christmas decorations, and heaving with a mixture of villagers, pilots in RAF blues, engineers in overalls, and girls in Women's Auxiliary Air Force uniforms. They were all chatting and laughing away without a care in the world. If only they'd seen what he'd seen. And the bloody racket they made. The noise set his ears ringing. Sudden barks of laughter, the sharp clink of glasses, the unexpected hack of a cough. He flinched.

A woman struck a match and the tang of phosphorous had him reaching instinctively for a rifle that wasn't there.

He wiped a hand across his face. No threats here. Just a jolly pub. Calm down. He thought about turning around and going home, but the only things waiting for him there were a wailing mother and a raving father. No, the pub had pints, and that's what he needed more than anything.

He headed for the bar, moving between clumps of people, and noticed a chalkboard over one of the windows as he passed. The names of several pilots were scribbled on it, and above it someone had written 'The Few'. Bloody hell. So what? They'd won one battle, and now everyone thought their farts didn't stink. What did pilots know about real combat? Swanning about up there in their crates, then coming back to Blighty to snatch up all the local skirt. They had it bloody good and didn't even know it. Sid and his fellow soldiers at Dunkirk had expected the RAF to give them cover as the Nazis closed in, but only a handful of Spitfires had bothered to make the trip and even they didn't stay long. *The Few*. Too bloody few by far.

Sid bumped up against a man standing between him and the bar. The man didn't budge, so Sid roughly barged past him.

'Steady on, old chap!' A toff's voice. Strained and indignant, it reminded Sid of his commanding officers. Full to the brim with entitlement, but they couldn't find their own arses with both hands and a map. Sid turned on the voice to find a pilot with a ginger moustache. That's probably what they all called him. Ginger. Like he was one of Biggles' chums. This was all a lark to them.

Ginger held a pint glass, though his hand was covered in suds from where Sid had knocked into him. He wasn't alone. Three other pilots flanked him, looking just as appalled.

'What's that?' Sid angled his head towards Ginger. 'You say something?' He could feel a familiar temper building inside of him, but this time he welcomed it.

'Watch yourself, Sid.' Alfie's voice was so close to Sid's ear that it tickled his earlobe, making him twitch involuntarily. He noticed the pilots flinch in response.

'You're outnumbered, sunshine. Get a pint or two inside you first.'

Ginger raised his own pint and pointed towards the mess of spilled beer and suds. 'I said, steady on.'

Sid angled his back to the bar, once again checking the exits. His hands trembled, and he clenched them into fists. He kept them by his sides, at least for now.

'Not now, Sidney, old son,' Alfie told him. 'His time will come.'

'Sorry, chum.' A sickly smile crossed Sid's face as he turned back to Ginger and his mates. 'Didn't see you there. But then I never saw you at Dunkirk either. I expect you were busy here, having a pint or two.'

Ginger's moustache quivered. 'What's that supposed to mean?'

'Whatever you want it to. Merry Christmas, Smiler.' Giving the pilot a wink, Sid patted him on the cheek and eased his way along the bar. He was sure the pilots were making disparaging comments in his wake, but Alfie was right. He needed a drink.

'What can I get you, Sid?' Terrence Bright never missed a trick. He must have seen Sid's little altercation but would do whatever it took to keep the peace.

'Pint of mild, please, Terrence.'

The landlord got to work, expertly pulling a pint. 'How's your old man?'

Sid shrugged, not wanting to get into a conversation, and especially not on this topic. His dad had slept for most of the day, not a word spoken since his raving about the Holly King. That suited Sid fine.

'Send him and your mother our best regards, will you?' Terrence slid a pint towards Sid. 'That'll be a shilling.'

Sid blinked. 'A shilling?'

Terrence chuckled. 'They put a penny on a pint while you were away. There's a war on, y'know.'

'I'm aware of that, Terrence. I've been in the thick of it.' He slapped a shilling on the counter. 'What would you know about it, eh?'

Terrence's smile faded, though his pleasant tone remained. 'You're not going to give me any trouble, are you, Sid?'

Sid's reply was to down his pint in one, letting it dribble around his mouth and chin. He wiped his lips with the back of his hand, baring his teeth and slapping a second shilling on the counter. 'Another.'

'Easy, tiger.' Alfie again. He had somehow found a spot next to Sid in the crowded pub, just on the edge of his vision. 'You don't want to get chucked out, do you? Not yet, anyway. Get a few more down yer.'

A pilot started playing 'Hark! The Herald Angels Sing' on the upright piano. The rest of the pub joined in the singing. The noise made Sid's head pulse. He wanted the sound to fade away, but it never seemed to happen when he wanted it to. His breathing became shallow. The tips of his fingers were cold.

Sid rigidly sipped at his second pint until the song came to an end. He stared into the amber liquid. Why had he come here tonight? In Salisbury, he'd gone to the Rising Sun so that he and the lads could let off a bit of steam, which usually meant a punch-up and a dash through town when the MPs arrived. This place was like another planet. If it weren't for the uniforms, you'd never have a clue there was a war on. He knew it should provide him with some sort of solace, but it just made him sick.

'Did you see this, Terrence?' A familiar voice from the corner of the bar. Mr Hodgson, still wearing his bloody shorts, peeked over the top of a copy of the *Daily Mail*. He prodded a headline. '"Churchill urges Italians to oust Mussolini." Surely it won't be long before they're on our side again.'

Terrence cleaned a pint glass. 'Here's hoping, Mr Aitch.'

'Fat lot of good that'll do,' Sid said, loudly enough for Mr Hodgson to hear over the others now singing 'While Shepherds Watched Their Flocks'.

'You ... you don't think so, Sid?' Mr Hodgson was polite, but there was a tremor in his voice. Weakness. Sid was trained to spot any sign of weakness and stab it, shoot it, trample on it. After months of drills, it came so easily to him now. There was an empty sherry glass by Mr Hodgson's elbow. Sid could smash it and use it to cut the man's carotid artery in seconds.

Instead, he just downed the rest of his pint. 'I know so,' he replied, tossing a third shilling at Terrence, who caught it in the pint glass he was drying.

'You in a hurry, Sid?' Terrence stood the pint glass on its head on the bar. The shilling spun for a while before settling. 'Got somewhere to be?' Terrence was still smiling, but Sid knew he kept a knobkerry hidden behind the bar and was handy in a scrap.

Mr Hodgson, on the other hand, never knew when to shut up. 'I must object to your grim outlook on the situation, Sid. After all, our lads here won the Battle of Britain decisively. We have troops in Egypt ready to give the Hun a bloody nose. And we snatched victory from the jaws of defeat at Dunkirk. We can—'

'Victory?' The word erupted from Sid's belly, laced with anger and cynicism, and loud enough to be heard over the singing. The piano player stumbled and came to a stop. The bar fell silent. All eyes were on Sid. 'Dunkirk was a victory, was it?' The people around him stepped back, like he was a lit firework. 'Read that in the papers, did yer?' He could hear himself snarling. He snatched the *Daily Mail* from Mr Hodgson's grip, scrunching it up in his fist. 'Ever occur to you that they might not be telling you the whole story? How we ran like children from the tanks and bombers? How our commanding officers didn't have the first clue what to do? How some of them were shot by their own men? How we got lost? How we pissed ourselves as the tanks closed in? How we . . .' He trailed off, aware of Alfie by his side. 'You wanna know what else they're not telling you?' Sid raised his chin and addressed the whole pub. 'I was a lance corporal till yesterday, but I got busted down to private. Yeah, don't tell my old man. It'll break his heart. You know why I got bust? Couldn't control my section. All of them deserted overnight. Hopped the fence at the barracks in Salisbury, never to be seen again. But it's not just them. Oh no. Two hundred and fifty deserters from Salisbury alone in the last month. Y'see, soldiers like me, we've seen what we're up against. We don't want to go back, so we leg it. And the new recruits come from borstals. They're either thick as two short planks or thugs. We're training them to go to Egypt, Mr Hodgson. You're right, that's where we're off to next. That's where they want to send me. But we won't be giving the Hun a bloody nose. We're being lined up as cannon fodder to die in the desert. That's what this war is. It's not victories, it's not speeches. It's all about which side is gonna run out of lads like me first.'

'Sid, I think you need to go home, son,' Terrence said, a new firmness in his voice.

'This upsetting you, Terrence? Is this not what you want to hear? You.' Sid pointed at Ginger. 'You lads in the RAF know. How many mates did you lose this summer?' He gestured at the blackboard with the names. 'How many this week?'

Ginger lowered his eyes.

Sid stepped up to him, the old bloodlust coursing through his veins. 'How many of you will even make it to the New Year?'

The pilot looked up again with red-rimmed eyes. 'Watch your mouth, *Private.*'

'Now, Sid!' Alfie's voice was gleeful in anticipation of the coming fight. 'Smack him in the schnozz. Do it now!'

Sid didn't need telling twice. His fist was a blur as

it connected with the bridge of the pilot's nose. Before anyone could react, he'd landed a second punch on the flight lieutenant next to him. Fists began to fly in an ugly, clumsy scrap. Hopelessly outnumbered, Sid was pummelled from all sides by men in RAF blues. He saw stars as he struggled to stay upright, kicking and biting. The pain made him feel alive in a way he hadn't in months. Sid heard Alfie cackling hysterically as a fist cracked into one of his ribs. He looked around for his mate, but he was obscured by the rabble. Instead, Sid found the woodwose at the back of the room, leaning on its club, stooping as its head brushed the ceiling, face obscured by shadows as it watched the fray. No one else saw it, and it didn't speak. It didn't need to. It raised the club, offering it to Sid, encouraging Sid to fight back. Sid grinned, shook his head and roared as he went down fighting.

MEETING AT THE CROSSROADS

Faye flew low above the trees as fast as she could, leaning over the handlebars of the Griffin. She wore her second-hand RAF flight jacket, boots, helmet and goggles, with a white silk scarf over her nose and mouth. It was bitterly cold, and what looked like gently drifting snowflakes from the ground were streaks of dizzying white up here.

Reverend Jacobs had informed Faye that the Home Guard patrol sent to find the 'rabid dog' had returned without Bertie. Overwhelmed by the sudden tingling in her chest and the tips of her fingers, the warning voices around her had become distant and hollow. All that mattered was Bertie.

She had dashed straight to Captain Marshall, who was helping a wounded Mr Gilbert into an army ambu-lance outside the church. The captain had remained tight-lipped about what had happened, stating over and over that he had everything under control. Faye was about to give him an earful when Mr Brewer gently took her to one side.

'Bertie saved us, Faye. We were on the path to the hollow oak. He might be there.'

That was all she needed. She ran to the Green Man, donned her flying kit and, ignoring the protestations of Miss Charlotte and Mrs Teach, took to the skies.

Faye slowed as she approached the middle of the wood, concentrating hard to create a glamour of stars around her. She circled above the hollow oak's clearing, but it was empty. Spiralling lower, she spotted footprints in the snow. One huge-booted pair and one regular-sized pair, with a leg that dragged slightly, suggesting a limp. Both headed north. Faye followed them until she came to the crossroads at the northern end of Gibbet Lane and found what she was looking for.

'Oh, Bertie.'

You didn't have to be much of a historian to deduce how Gibbet Lane had got its name. Previously the main coast road to the village, over time it had been reduced to little more than a meandering path just wide enough for carts and motor cars. But back in its heyday, it had been the perfect place to remind any travellers with illicit intent what would happen to those who broke the law, by displaying the previous unfortunate lawbreaker in a gibbet. In ancient times, there had been a wooden gallows, but in the seventeenth century the village had held a whip-round to pay for one of those fancy new iron gibbets. Tight-fitting and profoundly uncomfortable, the iron cage could hold a malingerer in full public view until they eventually starved to death and rotted to their bones,

becoming a less lively – but no less effective – disin-
centive to other criminals.

The gibbet itself had been abandoned sometime in
the 1800s, but it had somehow returned to the crossroads tonight. And crammed inside its iron framework
was one Bertie Butterworth.

Faye's heart tightened, and she took the Griffin into
a dive, her ears popping as she landed with a skid and
shed her glamour.

'Faye!' Bertie's voice cracked. His hands were pinned
to his sides, but he flexed his fingers, trying to wave her
away. 'Faye, no, it's a trap!'

'I'm sure it is, Bertie.' Faye looked up and down the
darkened roads as she pushed her bike towards the
tall gallows holding the gibbet, leaning it against the
wooden pole. 'But what sort of person would I be if I
left you up there, eh?'

'What sorta person, indeed?' A woman's voice
came echoing from the darkness. It had an American
accent, and Faye's shoulders tensed as she recognised
it immediately.

'I guess all the Wynter girls are loyal to the bitter
end, huh?' A fairy flew out of the mist on the eastern
path. Her diaphanous wings glowed bright and golden
as they flapped, and her long black hair fell in waves
to her waist. Her clinging gossamer lace dress shone
iridescent in the moonlight, by turns blossom pink,
duck-egg blue, sapphire white. Even with the dress and
the wings, there was no mistaking her.

'Pearl.' Faye's voice was a shocked whisper.

'She remembers me!' Pearl clasped her hands to her chest. 'Ain't that sweet?'

Bertie looked back and forth between them in his cage. 'You ... you know each other?'

'I guess you could say that.' Pearl circled over the boy in the gibbet, all the while keeping her bright hazel eyes on Faye. 'How does the song go? *I'll See You in My Dreams.*' Pearl twirled above the two of them, making it look effortless. She settled into a swaying hover over Bertie, arms folded. Faye saw that around her waist she wore a belt and a dagger within easy reach. 'Oh, I've waited a long time for this. And now I'm here, I'm so excited I just don't know what to do.'

Faye stood her ground. 'Who are you, Pearl, and just what the bloody hell do you want?'

'Direct and to the point. I like that. Do you have any idea how long it's been since I had a proper conversation with another woman? Let's not rush things, sugar. Take your time.' Pearl flicked her hair back. 'You know what it's like out there? Between worlds?'

Faye shrugged. 'I've had a quick peek.'

The fairy snorted. 'A peek? Try a few decades, sweetheart. Years of nothin' but an endless void. Only lonely voices on the aether. Magical voices. Like yours ... Oh, and the radio.' She chuckled. 'If you know how, you can pick up New York radio. I know all the latest tunes, *cha-cha-cha*!' She giggled as she danced in the air, arms wide.

'Why were you in my dreams?' Faye asked.

'A good question, kiddo.' The spinning stopped, the

smile vanished, and any trace of warmth was gone. 'Why would I cross the aether and risk being snuffed out like a candle, all in order to get to you, Faye Wynter?' Pearl spat. 'Why would I make a deal with a demigod and have him transform me into a goddamn fairy to make your lousy acquaintance? Why would I crawl from the coldest depths of limbo to pay your scrawny ass a visit? What? She never told you the story? Well, I gotta say, I'm kinda hurt.'

Faye's spine tightened. She desperately wanted to run from this place and this woman. Never had Faye met anyone who radiated such instant hate.

'Call me Cousin Pearl,' the fairy said, her smile returning, but this time dripping with malice. 'Your mom did.'

SECRETS AT THE CROSSROADS

The cold clutched at Faye, icy barbs stabbing into her skin. 'I don't have a cousin called Pearl, and neither did me mum. And my name's Bright, not Wynter.' Her words had an uncertain shiver to them, and she tried her best to sound bold. 'And if my mum did know any Christmas fairies, I'm sure she would've mentioned it.'

The night air closed in around the crossroads, a silent dread broken only by the creak of the gibbet. Faye glanced up at the rusty old thing. Poor Bertie was squirming inside in a vain effort to get comfortable. She wanted to reassure him that it was all going to be tickety-boo and they'd be back in the pub enjoying a hot toddy before closing time. But he knew her well enough to know when she was fibbing, so she kept quiet and gave him the most confident smile she could muster.

'Don't that just break my heart.' Pearl pouted theatrically and pressed the back of her hand against her forehead. 'She didn't mention me even once?'

Faye was afraid to ask, but she took the bait. 'Why would she?'

'You look confused, Faye, and I don't blame ya. I wasn't always like this, y'know.' Pearl's wings and eyelashes fluttered in time as she struck a coquettish pose. 'No, this is your mother's fault. She's the reason I died.'

'My dream.' Faye's eyes widened. 'Mum was dragging you through the snow. "Pearl, don't you dare die," she said. She was trying to help you! What happened?'

Pearl gleefully patted her hands together. 'You really don't know? Good. I can't wait to see the look on your face when I tell ya. I thought the dreams would show you everything, but that's the trouble with dream projection. It filters out the heartache sometimes. And then you wake up right before the end—'

'Tell me what happened.' Faye stopped short of stamping her feet, but she was ready to wring the fairy's neck. She took a deep breath and tried a more peaceable approach. 'Who are you, Pearl? And how are we cousins?'

Pearl drifted up towards Bertie, who did his best to shrink inside the gibbet. 'I got roots here that go way back. Did you know that? 'Course you didn't.' Her voice turned colder. 'But how else would I know there was a gibbet left to rust in the deep river under the old Roman bridge, huh?' She reached through the bars towards Bertie and patted him on the cheek. 'Hey, Bertie boy, ask me how I know that.'

Bertie obliged. 'H-how do you know that?'

'Because, sweet Bertie, in the year of our Lord 1631,

the people of Woodville locked my great-great-great-grammy in it, paid a witchfinder to prick her skin, and drowned her in the river.' Pearl's smile remained in place, though her hazel eyes burned. 'Ain't history fun!' She shoved herself away from Bertie, leaving him to creak back and forth like a grisly pendulum.

'Most of the Wynter family decided it would be a good time to get the hell outta Dodge, so they packed their bags and boarded the first boat to the New World. Not that anyone in my immediate family told me this, mind. If there's one thing our kin's good at, Faye, it's keeping secrets. But you and me ...' Pearl swooped down to Faye's height, her feet dangling just above the road as her wings flapped, puffing the gentle snow around her in a hypnotic display. 'We're different. We know when something ain't right. Your mom was the same. *My* momma, one Rowena Wynter – an English Rose left to rot in New York – wouldn't speak a word about the past, and neither would my aunties. So I did a little digging to discover the truth. The only one who would tell me was my estranged poppa.' Pearl's voice softened, her eyes fixed on an empty spot in the air before her. 'Billy J. Pinkett was a God-fearin' black man from Georgia who came to New York to be a poet, which meant he was sweet, wise, romantic and dirt poor. He was seduced by a pretty girl with an English accent, my momma Rowena.' Pearl smiled and gently shook her head. 'He confessed to me like I was a priest. It all came pouring out. He cried as he told me how they lay together every day one hot summer.' Pearl looked at Faye, and both young women knew what Rowena had done. 'I was the consequence of their little summer tryst. But Billy J. didn't even know I existed. When I found him, I gave him the shock of his life. He begged forgiveness and promised to be a good daddy. Then he told me his secret.' Pearl edged closer to Faye. 'You see, he and Rowena were very much in love. This weren't no infatuation. They did what lovers do, which is they shared everything. Momma told him all there was to know about our family. Including the magic. You may recall I said Billy J. Pinkett was a God-fearin' man. Well, he went and did what God-fearin' men are supposed to do. He tried to change her ways, the poor sap. Rowena wasn't about to betray her heritage for one dirt-poor poet, so Billy J. hightailed it outta there, not knowin' that Momma was already carrying me. But you know what that wonderful man did next?' Pearl's bright hazel eyes glistened, and Faye couldn't help but lean forward. 'He wrote it all down, Faye. He showed it to me. A book that he was going to publish and make his fortune. *The Complete History of the Wynter Witches.*' Pearl spread her palms wide, like she was imagining the words in lights on a Broadway billboard. 'It took him years to write. It was like the story didn't want to be written down. Every pen and pencil he used broke. Notebook after notebook went missing. He wrote every day, skipping meals, losing work. Billy rarely left his apartment. He lost every friend he ever had, and he never took another lover. The book was his obsession. It turned his hair grey, his back bent over, and his eyes could barely see, but he did it!' Pearl fluttered away from Faye, jabbing a defiant finger in the air. 'God damn, he did it, Faye. And me, sweet l'il Pearl Wynter, got to read it first. It was his masterpiece. The man put his heart and soul into tellin' Momma's stories. How the family fled England in fear, how they struggled to be accepted in the New World, how they learned to hide in plain sight. That man mighta been spurned by Rowena Wynter, but he loved her on every page of that book, and he did the impossible. He made me love my momma, too. I suddenly understood her pain. After that, I returned to her. I told her about the book, how Billy J. still loved her, and now I loved her, too. She didn't say a word, except to tell me to stay away from Billy J. Pinkett if I knew what was good for me.' Pearl's body rocked with a sad chuckle. 'He died that same week. Fire burned down the whole tenement. My daddy and his book burned with it.' Pearl bit her lip, tears in her eyes.

Faye moved a step closer, wondering if she should try to take her hand. 'Pearl, I'm so sorry. Witches ... they don't like stuff being written down.'

'You're tellin' me.' Pearl flashed an angry grin. 'But it was too late, y'see. The whole book's up here.' Pearl tapped the side of her head. 'And guess what? I found out I had one remaining relative right here in jolly old England. A distant cousin called Kathryn who still lived in that crazy little village that murdered my great-great-great-grammy.'

'In 1631,' Faye reminded her. 'Talk about holding a grudge.'

'Oh no, you misunderstand me. I wasn't here for revenge. I wanted to learn about magic. Sincerely. My momma refused to tell me anything, so I went to where it all started. I wanted to discover more about my family. About the power that we share. Your momma, bless her heart, taught me everything she knew.'

Faye's belly tightened. What she wouldn't have given to have her mother teach her about magic. And somehow Pearl had beaten her to it. Faye desperately wanted to ask what it had been like, what her mother had been like, but Pearl was in full flow.

'We started with candle magic, mirrors, healing – all that good stuff. But I wanted more. I pushed her to tell me about dreams, the aether and the voices in the dark. And y'know what? She showed me everything, Faye. We became friends. Close friends. Like sisters.'

'Then why is it I'm only hearing about this now?'

'You remember what I said about this family and secrets?' Pearl teased a smile, which faded as she looked Faye up and down. 'You're not much like her, y'know. She was pretty. She wore pretty dresses. You look like a boy.'

Faye tugged at the wool collar of her flight jacket. 'This was given to me by a pilot, if you must know. It's warm and cosy and I like it, and I'll wear what I want if it's all the same to you.' She squared her shoulders. 'Why don't we let Bertie go on his merry way home and we can have this out over a cuppa?'

'Your mom knew the value of silence. You talk too

much, sugar. I'm wondering if I should tell you the rest
of the story, or just kill you now.'

'You blimmin' won't!' Bertie protested, rattling his cage.

Faye reeled a little at such a casual mention of her
imminent demise. At least when someone like Otto
Kopp threatened to kill her, he did it with a bit of
Bavarian Druidic melodrama. Cousin Pearl sounded
chillingly like she was deciding whether to put the bins
out or do the washing-up.

Faye took a deep breath, trying to buy some
thinking time.

'Why do you want to kill me, if you don't mind me
asking? I ain't done you no wrong.'

'Sins of the mother, Faye. Your mom may be long
gone, but if there's one thing I've learned, it's that
Wynter women don't forgive.' Pearl's eyes were dark
and pitiless. 'I'm gonna have my vengeance on the
blood of the one who killed me. That's what all this
is about. I'm going to watch you die the way she
watched me.'

Faye tried to suppress a shocked laugh, but it came
out as a snort. The idea that her mother – who was
kindness itself – would kill anyone was ridiculous.

'You think it's funny?' Pearl hissed.

Faye straightened her face. 'I feel sorry for you, Pearl,
but I also think you're off your rocker.'

'I get that plenty.' Pearl chuckled mirthlessly. 'That's
a real shame. I was gonna tell you what your momma
did that cold December day in 1903, but now I'm

thinking you don't deserve to know. I was hoping you'd be different, Faye, but you're just like the rest of our family with their secrets. At least Kathryn knew the value of the truth.' Pearl fluttered up to Bertie's gibbet and the lad cowered as she planted her feet on its top. She cupped a hand to her mouth, calling into the darkness. 'Your Majesty! It's time.'

'I'm already here.' The voice was deep, and each word was accompanied by a tremor beneath Faye's boots.

Faye spun to find a giant standing in the road, silhouetted by the moon.

The Holly King.

STAND-OFF AT THE
CROSSROADS

Faye was so discombobulated that it took her a moment to comprehend what she was looking at. The last time she had encountered the Holly King she had been some distance away and airborne. Having him tower over her now was a different experience altogether. Gigantic antlers branched from his head, which she now noticed was adorned by a crown of holly and oak, and his shining white beard was a bustling hedgerow of winter foliage. He carried a wooden box on one shoulder that looked remarkably like the one Faye had just left in the crypt of Saint Irene's, and over his other shoulder was a huge wriggling sack. He tossed the sack to one side, and it landed with muffled curses from within. He lowered the sarcophagus to the ground much more carefully, smoothing his hand over the lid and giving it a reassuring pat. Pearl buzzed over it, standing guard.

'Your Majesty, the Holly King, I presume?' Faye politely bowed her head and tried to keep her voice from wobbling. She wasn't usually much of a one for deference, but when in the presence of a king, not least one three times as tall as her, she reasoned it was probably wise to be polite. 'I reckon there's been some misunderstanding with my friend Bertie here.'

The Holly King tipped his head to one side, inspecting her the way a blackbird might look at a worm before plucking it from the soil.

A chill wind swept the crossroads, buffeting Faye. She shifted on a patch of grey ice and tried again. 'How can we sort this, Your Highness?'

'There is nothing to sort.' The Holly King turned his gloved hand to Bertie in the gibbet. 'Your friend was trespassing in my wood, and he surrendered of his own free will.'

Of course he did, Faye thought as she glanced up at Bertie. *One day, Bertie, that selflessness of yours is going to get you into real trouble.*

Faye bit her lip and raised a finger. 'I think I have the nub of it, Your Majesty. Y'see, you've been away for some time, and much has changed in your absence. Not least that folk can come and go as they please in these woods.'

'No longer.' The Holly King's words had the weight and certainty of an avalanche. 'The wood belongs to me.'

'That's news to me, and will be to everyone in the village, including Bertie. So, can't we let him off with a warning and—'

'I sent an emissary. Eric Birdwhistle. Did he not make my decree clear? All trespassers shall incur my wrath.'

'Eric said a lot of things, to be fair. It was quite a bit to take in. Have you considered popping something on the church noticeboard? Or—'

'Silence!' The Holly King loomed over Faye and Bertie. 'The wood will be mine. Your ghastly village will be consumed by its roots.'

Faye held her ground. 'Over my dead body.'

'Very likely, though it doesn't have to be that way. The villagers will be given a simple choice. Surrender and worship me, or face oblivion. Herbert Butterworth is merely the first of those who will be judged and found wanting.'

'Bertie?' Faye snorted. 'Found wanting?' She looked up at the lad in the man-shaped cage. His eyes were downcast. She wanted nothing more than to rip those bars away and give him a hug. 'He's the least wanting fella you'll find. He'd do anything for—'

'Faye, no, he's right,' Bertie began, his eyes glistening with tears. 'I did do something awful, I—'

The Holly King closed his fists around the gibbet. Its iron buckled, squeezing the boy tighter in its grip as Pearl chuckled and applauded.

'Stop! Please, don't hurt him.' Faye took a few steps closer to the sarcophagus, hoping against hope that this might distract the Holly King. His eyes snapped towards her, and he released his grip on the gibbet. 'What could Bertie possibly have done that could be so terrible, eh? Why don't you let him go and we'll have a proper chinwag?'

'I will do as I please, Faye Bright.' The Holly King

lunged forward, bending his knee to meet her eyes. 'He has brought shame upon his family, and he will be punished.'

This close to the Holly King, Faye could see the rage and madness in his darting eyes. A demigod out of place and time, angry and confused. Her body clenched in fear, and she wondered how he knew her name. All the same, she met his gaze and took a moment to allow her heart to find its rhythm again. When she spoke, her voice was steady.

'Then I reckon we have a problem, Your Majesty. Cos I can't allow my friend here to be punished on your say-so.'

'Foolish girl.' The Holly King leaned closer. 'Do you have any idea who you're dealing with?'

Faye set her jaw. 'Do you?'

The Holly King's beard rustled as he smiled. 'Faye Bright, daughter of Terrence Bright and Kathryn Wynter, you are a noviciate witch of some little renown. I could crush you before you could even blink.'

'Then what are you waitin' for?' Pearl cried.

The Holly King craned his head towards her with a growl.

Pearl flashed a smile through gritted teeth and curt-seyed, her eyes burning with fury. 'Your Majesty.'

The Holly King turned back to Faye, continuing in a conspiratorial voice. 'I confess, the fairy vexes me greatly. Though, on this occasion, I must admit that her judgement is flawless.'

His fist came swinging around in a blur.

Faye just had time to duck and roll. Fighting off blind panic, she closed her eyes, concentrating hard on rising quickly and silently into the falling snow.

'Faye! Go! Get out of it!' Bertie cried.

The Holly King, frustrated at missing his target, lashed out at the boy. He hit the gibbet so hard that it swung in a loop on the chain, snapping the gallows wood. The cage spun wildly before clattering to the ground.

'Bertie!' Faye cried.

The Holly King raised his arms, summoning swirling snowflakes and sending them into a whirling frenzy around her as she stood, paralysed. Blinded by icy shards and crying in pain, Faye stumbled into the branches of a tree before hitting the ground with a thud. Her lungs empty, she began to panic, thrashing about as she felt the thumping footsteps of the approaching Holly King.

'Geronimo!' Bertie cried, rolling in the gibbet and colliding with the giant's ankles. The Holly King barely broke his stride as he kicked the poor lad into the woods, where Bertie landed in a bush with an explosion of snow.

'Offside!' a familiar voice cried.

Faye, gasping for breath, managed to roll herself over. A pear-shaped woman and her tall, thin companion strode towards the crossroads.

'That's not offside.' Miss Charlotte rolled her eyes. She was wearing a fetching cricket jumper over her siren suit and had something strapped to her waist, though Faye couldn't make out what it was.

'I thought it was when the ball goes off the pitch?'

Mrs Teach was wearing her best fur coat and hat and gripping a red handbag. '"Off the side" – offside?'

'No, it's when you pass the ball forward to a— Look, we don't have time for this.'

Mrs Teach stopped to take in the bizarre tableau. 'Miss Charlotte, the sarcophagus. Looks familiar, doesn't it?'

'Indeed,' Miss Charlotte replied.

'I wondered when you two would show up,' Pearl said, with so much loathing in her voice that Faye thought she might retch.

'Oh look, a fairy for the tree.' Mrs Teach cocked an ear. 'I'm sorry. Have we met?'

'This is Pearl.' Faye sat upright, having got some of her breath back. 'She's a distant cousin who wants to kill me.'

'I've got a few of those,' Miss Charlotte muttered. 'Sorry we're late, Faye. I had to collect something from the remains of my cottage.'

'Pearl Wynter?' Mrs Teach's voice rose in pitch.

The fairy dipped her head in a mocking bow.

Faye looked from one woman to the other. 'You know her?'

'I met her once. Very briefly. That was enough.' Mrs Teach arched an eyebrow. 'Hello, Pearl. You're look-ing ... well, like an overstuffed moth, frankly.'

'You got old,' Pearl snapped back. 'And fat.'

Mrs Teach's reaction was to stand stock-still, though Faye knew from the look on her face that the remark was being filed away for eventual retribution.

'Now, now, let's not start with personal insults,' Miss Charlotte said. 'We could be here all night.'

'Indeed.' Mrs Teach cleared her throat and affected her most commanding voice. 'Pearl Wynter, you are to leave this plane immediately. Taking this one with you.' She gestured to the Holly King, who now stood with one foot raised above Bertie like a centre forward waiting for the ref's whistle to resume play (presumably after an offside decision).

Faye, realising that no one was taking much notice of her, started to slowly inch her way over to the gibbet.

'Seein' as I'm the one with the demigod on my side,' Pearl said, 'I think I'll stay right here.'

Charlotte nodded in appreciation. 'Always handy to have one of those. Especially when demolishing someone's home.'

'I was there, sweetheart. He was supposed to kill ya, too, but I guess better late than never. *Don't move!*' This last was screeched at Faye, who was just a few feet away from Bertie. She stopped in her tracks, giving Bertie a helpless shrug. 'And stay on the ground,' Pearl added. 'If I see your sweet little tush rise a single inch, the kid in the cage gets it.'

'We appear to be at something of an impasse,' Mrs Teach noted calmly. 'All of us are rather tense and twitchy. I suggest we sit down like adults and discuss the best way to settle whatever differences we may have.'

'I suggest you say your prayers and prepare to die.' Pearl drew the dagger from her belt.

Mrs Teach made an unimpressed noise. 'As opening negotiation gambits go, that's a bit extreme. Your Majesty, do you have anything to add that might pour oil on these troubled waters?'

The Holly King considered. 'Once again, I find myself in the remarkable position of agreeing with the fairy. Witches are such a petty little nuisance. Not a significant threat, of course, but having you all dead would make what I have planned infinitely simpler.'

Miss Charlotte slowly adjusted her stance, a hand moving to her waist and the object strapped there. 'And what exactly do you have planned?'

'I will take back what is rightfully mine. This wood once stretched across the land. I will begin by reclaiming that village of squatters up the road. After that, we shall see. If you intend to try and stop me, then yes, it will be a vote for death from me.' An idea occurred to the Holly King and he stroked his beard. 'If you were to worship me and offer your undying allegiance, then I think I could be convinced to spare your lives.' He chuckled to himself. 'I could even turn you into fairies.'

'Hmm.' Mrs Teach pursed her lips. 'I think I'd rather die. What do you say, Miss Charlotte?'

Moonlight flashed on metal as Miss Charlotte drew her katana sword.

From the bushes, Bertie gave an appreciative, 'Ooh!'

Miss Charlotte smiled, her lips blood-red. 'To the death it is.'

BLOODSHED AT
THE CROSSROADS

Faye admired Miss Charlotte's unusual sword. 'It's very nice,' Faye said. 'What is it?'

'Something I picked up when climbing Mount Haguro with the Yamabushi.' Miss Charlotte said this like it should mean something important, but Faye hadn't the first clue and made a mental note to ask more later. If there was a later. 'The blade has a name,' Miss Charlotte continued, eyes now fixed solely on the Holly King. ' "Kamigoroshi" – it means "God Slayer". In keeping with the Samurai tradition, the blade must taste blood once drawn, and it's very, very thirsty.'

Mrs Teach grimaced. 'You never told me it was Japanese.'

'What difference does that make?'

'They're the enemy. It's not very patriotic.'

Miss Charlotte rolled her eyes. 'They weren't the enemy at the time. And I have no doubt that they won't be the enemy in the future. You have to take a long-term view on these things, Mrs Teach.'

'That's as may be, but next time make sure you bring a proper British sword.'

'Good grief,' Miss Charlotte muttered.

The Holly King laughed. 'You think you can prick me with that little needle? It might have an impressive name, but for as long as I wear this crown, I am impervious to your flimsy blades and feeble magic.'

Miss Charlotte shrugged. 'True, but as a wise old crook once told me, "There's a time for magic, and there's a time for putting the boot in."' She gave a quick nod. 'Now, Mrs Teach.'

With a flick of her wrist, Mrs Teach sent her red handbag hurtling with the velocity of a cannonball and pinpoint accuracy. It landed slap bang on the Holly King's nose.

He cried and staggered back. Miss Charlotte leapt forward with the katana. She was quick, but the Holly King was no slouch, and he ducked her first slash, then the next. Spinning, he swung at her backhanded, hitting her in the chest and sending her flying over the crossroads and crashing into a tree.

Pearl hooted with laughter, rising high above them. Faye saw her chance and scurried over to Bertie in the gibbet, gripping its iron bars.

'Hold tight, Bertie,' she said, and they rose into the air, the chain of the gibbet clinking as it swung about. Faye gasped at the extra weight. Since first learning to fly at the end of the summer, it had become an instinctive thing. She merely had to concentrate a bit, and up she went. But now the extra weight of Bertie and the iron cage had her gasping for air.

She closed her eyes, reminding herself of the principles of magical flight. She was a tiny planet, hurtling through the vastness of space, in very, very close proximity to Earth. She simply had to detach herself from the world and ...

Faye, Bertie and the gibbet were one, rising together.

Without the Griffin, flight would be unbalanced and tricky, but getting away from here as quickly as possible was Faye's top priority. She brought them about, pointing the gibbet in the direction of the village, ready to go.

Just then Pearl slammed into Faye like a sledgehammer.

Faye felt the rusty bars slip through her fingers and heard Bertie's wail as he dropped towards the ground.

She tumbled head over heels but was quick to right herself. She dived after him, hands outstretched. As she grabbed the bars again, the added weight threatened to yank her arms from their sockets, but she held tight, teeth clenched, and they stopped inches from the road. Bertie's head dinged against the metal with the sudden deceleration, but he was able to blurt, 'Crikey, Faye, thanks!' She gave him a slightly shaky wink and heaved them aloft again.

'Philomena!' Miss Charlotte cried out.

Faye glanced over just in time to see Mrs Teach swiped aside by the Holly King. She arced through the air, landing heavily and flopping like a rag doll before rolling into a ditch. 'Mrs Teach!'

Miss Charlotte looked up at Faye, sweat on her face as she gripped her sword. 'Faye, what are you still doing here? Get—'

The Holly King grabbed Miss Charlotte's hair, yanking her backwards. Her sword clattered to the icy road. He shoved her to the ground, resting a boot on her chest, scooping up the katana as she gasped for air. The thing looked like a dagger in his enormous gloved hands.

The blade gleamed in the moonlight, slicing at Miss Charlotte's face. Her cry was hoarse and shocking. She clutched her eye, scrabbling about in agony. The Holly King kicked her aside like a flat football.

'No!' Faye roared. But before she could help Miss Charlotte, Pearl landed on her back, wrapping an arm around her throat in a clumsy choke hold and pressing a hand against the nape of her neck. Faye couldn't breathe. Blood rushed in her ears and her head lolled about heavily. Any second now, she and Bertie would drop like stones.

'This is more fun than I thought,' Pearl hissed in her ear.

The edge of Faye's vision darkened, though she could just about see Bertie wriggle one arm free through the bars of the gibbet. Gritting his teeth, he reached up to one of Pearl's fluttering wings, grabbed it by the humerus, and twisted hard. The fragile bone snapped like celery and Pearl screamed in pain. She loosened her grip on Faye, who gasped for air and elbowed the fairy in the face. Pearl spiralled like a sycamore seed, landing clumsily on her remaining good wing. It broke with a sharp crack.

The world slowed as Faye took in the chaos below. Cousin Pearl thrashing and kicking on the ground like a toddler. Mrs Teach semi-conscious in a ditch. Miss Charlotte blinded and defenceless. The Holly King raising his fist for the kill.

Faye looked beyond him to the sarcophagus left in the middle of the crossroads. She had a flash of inspiration.

'Bertie.' She grabbed the gibbet's chain. 'Geronimo?'

He looked from Faye to the Holly King and understood. 'Geronimo,' he said with a nod.

Faye began to fly in rapid circles, building up momentum. Just when she thought she couldn't hold on any longer, she released Bertie in the gibbet like she was throwing a hammer at the Olympics. The iron cage smashed into the giant's head, sending him toppling and knocking over the sarcophagus. Its lid spun away as Bertie crashed to the ground and rolled along the road. Faye swooped down, grabbing Mrs Teach by the wrists and lifting her effortlessly to where the wooden sarcophagus lay on its side. She came to, her eyes struggling to focus as Faye gently set her down.

'Get in!' Faye ordered.

Mrs Teach blinked for a second as she got her bearings, then recoiled. 'Are you mad?'

'Look at it.' Faye slapped a hand on the sarcophagus.

'It's almost the same as the one in the crypt at Saint Irene's. And what do you smell?'

Mrs Teach dared to flex her nostrils. A musky odour of damp and death. Her eyes flashed. 'The crypt!'

'In you go.' Faye helped the older woman clamber in. Mrs Teach vanished from sight.

'What do you see?' Faye called after her into the void.

'It's the crypt!' Mrs Teach hollered back. 'I'm in Saint Irene's crypt.'

'Good work.' Miss Charlotte's voice was a shocked whisper as she hobbled over to the sarcophagus, one hand gripping the katana, the other covering her bloody right eye. She leapt in without hesitation. 'Faye, hurry!' she called back.

A scream of anger from Cousin Pearl sent a new chill through Faye's bones. She looked around to find the wounded, broken-winged fairy rushing at her. Behind Pearl, the Holly King was back on his feet, his left antler broken and dangling. Never had two beings wanted to kill her so badly.

The Holly King reached up to a nearby oak and snapped off a thick branch. He held it between his hands and closed his eyes, letting out a savage roar as the air around him undulated. The branch was enveloped in an intense orange flame, taking on the festive air of a yule log. He hurled the missile at Faye, who soared up high. The fireball slammed into the sarcophagus, blowing it to splinters.

Pearl and the Holly King ducked from the explosion. Faye stretched her arms wide. She shut out the din and the chaos and focused on her breathing. The light of the waning moon washed over her, and she felt for its power, letting it course through her. The two objects she sought rose into the air. The gibbet and the Griffin. Faye called them to her, leaping onto the Griffin's saddle and grasping the gibbet's chain. Light-headed and gasping for breath from the effort, she leaned forward and flew into the night.

Chokey

Woodville Village Police Station was situated at the bottom of the Wode Road and looked much like any other house. The only clues as to its real purpose were the blue door and the lamp post with 'Police' stencilled on its glass, as it had been decided long ago that, in the interests of maintaining the village's peaceful aesthetic, the building should be somewhat anonymous. As far as the village burghers were concerned, the police were public servants to be called on in times of need rather than official overlords of law. And besides, if they ever needed to cope with anything more threatening than burglars or rowdy revellers, then a mob of locals with flaming torches could be rustled up at very short notice.

Beyond the bland exterior – the walls currently shored up with sandbags, and the windows criss-crossed with anti-blast tape – the house was anything but ordinary, with three cells, two interview rooms, and a secure basement of confiscated items rumoured to contain enough weapons to repel a Nazi invasion.

Tonight, the cells were full to the brim. Two were crammed with RAF pilots fresh from a scrap in the Green Man, awaiting MPs to take them back to base for a rollicking. Constable Muldoon had arrived at the altercation with nothing more than his truncheon and a whistle but soon had the rabble marching to the cells in a sorry line. These lads knew how to obey orders and were suitably chastened when the MPs eventually collected them just before midnight.

The troubled young man in the third cell was a different story. It had taken the combined might of Constable Muldoon, Terrence Bright and Mr Hodgson to pin the boy down. Even when cuffed, he had thrashed about like a wild thing, and had needed to be all but dragged over to the station. It had been a full hour before the lad had finally stopped screaming.

ß

Sid curled up on the bunk in his cell. To anyone peeking through the slot in the steel door he was alone. But Sid was never alone.

'That was all goin' our way till that rozzer bopped you on the 'ead with Constable Dunlop.' Out of the corner of Sid's eye, he saw Alfie's hand mime the swiping of a police truncheon. 'Weapons in a fist fight? That's just not the done thing, Sidney. Strictly against the unwritten rules of the noble Great British public house ruckus, that is.'

Sid wanted to sleep, but the bunk wasn't exactly designed for comfort and Alfie could yak for England.

'Still, you showed 'em, though, eh? They'll think twice before giving you any more lip. Well done, sunshine. I'm proud of yer.'

Pride wasn't quite what Sid was feeling. As a boy, he had been warned about the kind of men who spent a night in the cells, and the shame they brought upon their families. Sid's dad had told him time and again about the civic pride he felt at being a postman. That he was a public servant who was part of the glue that held society together. These sermons were usually delivered over dinner, and it was only when Mum served up that Dad put a sock in it, because speaking with your mouth full was another unforgivable sin, apparently.

Alfie's voice faded as Sid disappeared into himself.

He stared at a blank spot on the wall, eyes drifting over the flaky paint, the tiny imperfections, the remnants of brushstrokes, until it all became a blurred nothing. Despite the lingering smell of urine and tobacco, Sid quite liked it here. He didn't have to listen. He didn't have to care. He barely had to breathe.

The clang of the cell door yanked him from his reverie. He didn't know how long he'd been lost in his own mind, but his cheeks were wet and he was curled up underneath the bunk now, arms wrapped around his knees. The blanket formed a curtain of sorts, and Sid watched as a shadow stood before the bed and spoke.

'Most of our guests prefer to sleep on top.'

Sid shuffled out from under the bunk to find Constable Muldoon and his astonishing moustache staring down at him.

'It's hardly the Ritz, but I can say with all confidence that of the two options available – bed or floor – you have chosen by far the less luxurious.' He extended a hand to Sid, hefting him up onto the bunk. Sid scrubbed at his eyes.

'Do I have your full attention, Sidney?' The constable stood before him, hands clasped behind his back.

Sid glanced around the cell. Alfie was nowhere to be seen. He nodded and stood to attention.

'Good. What with last night's scrap being a first offence, and in recognition of your service in His Majesty's Armed Forces, and this being the season of goodwill to all men and all that, I am prepared to let you off with a warning.'

Sid tried to summon the energy to thank the constable, but all that came out was a vague grunt.

'This comes with two conditions.' Muldoon raised a pair of fingers, just to make it perfectly clear. 'One, you will be released into your mother's custody, where she can keep a close eye on you.' The constable waited for an acknowledgment that Sid understood. Sid gave a nod that made his skull ache. 'And two, I'll need to see your movement orders.'

Sid's belly did a flip. He had been dreading this. 'What do you need those for?'

Constable Muldoon leaned forward till he was almost nose to nose with Sid. 'I've spoken to a few of the chaps who witnessed your little display at the Green Man, and they all agreed that you were somewhat het up about deserters and such. You're not the only one, my lad. We, too, in the constabulary, have been tasked with keeping an eye out for those who decide to go Absent Without Official Leave. I've called your barracks in Salisbury on the telephone ...'

Here it comes, Sid thought, a wave of nausea shuddering through him.

'But there's a bit of snow in their neck of the woods, apparently, and the lines are down. So until that gets sorted, I'd like to see your movement orders.'

Sid did all he could to subdue the panic making his heart thump. Every soldier on leave was given movement orders to tell them where to report once their leave was over. He scrunched his nose and squinted his eyes as he pretended to think where he might have left his.

'Ooh, the jig is up, Sonny Jim.' Alfie's voice made him flinch.

'Anything wrong, laddie?' the constable asked.

'No, I ... I don't have my movement orders with me.'

'That's cos he don't have any,' Alfie said with a cackle. 'He's bunked off, in't he?'

'They're at Mum and Dad's. Not sure where,' Sid added hurriedly. 'It was such a rush, what with Dad's funny turn.'

Constable Muldoon nodded sympathetically, patting him on the shoulder. 'I understand. I'm on shift for the next two hours. If you can bring them here for me to inspect before then, we're all square. Is that clear?'

Sid nodded.

'Good. Your mother's waiting for you.' Constable Muldoon pointed an unwavering finger at Sid's nose. It came so close that he went cross-eyed. 'That poor woman's been through enough. Don't make it any worse.'

※

Sid and his mother trudged home in silence through the gentle rain. Closing the front door and drawing the blackout curtain, he stepped into a house that felt colder inside than out.

'Goodnight,' he muttered, taking a first step onto the stairs, but his mother's hand gripped his forearm.

'I've never known such shame.' Shirley Birdwhistle stood in the shadows. Sid could only make out his mother's silhouette, her head hanging heavily. She was no flake. She had worked in the village Post Office and newsagent's since before he was born. Always the first one in, she got straight to it each morning at the sorting frame out the back, sifting through the deliveries from the main sorting office. She knew everyone in Woodville, and they all knew her for her cheery, can-do attitude. There was little that could cause her to falter.

'Mum, I—'

'Be quiet. Let me speak. I don't know what's happened to your father, Sidney. I'm not sure we'll ever know, and we can only pray that he gets better. But you ...' She let go of his arm, her trembling hand fishing for a hankie tucked into her sleeve. She dabbed the corners of her eyes. 'What were you thinking? Starting a fight in a pub like a common thug. I couldn't believe it when they told me. Mrs Baxter, of all people, came to my front door. Went out of her way to be the first to let me know. God, she'll love this, won't she? The nosy bitch.'

Sid had never heard his mother use language like that before. He wasn't the only one who had changed, clearly.

'What's become of you, Sidney?' She raised her head to look at him, eyes glistening. She brushed her fingers gently against his cheek. 'When you were little, you'd skip along ahead of me in your sandals and shorts, chasing birds and butterflies. You were all pleases and thank yous.' A smile trembled briefly on her lips. 'Whatever happened to that little boy? Where's my Sidney?'

Sid thought back to those childhood summers. Ghostly memories that felt like they belonged to someone else. 'I think he's gone, Mum. He went away when I was training. I didn't think he'd ever come back, but then . . .'

His mother gripped her hankie as she listened. The hope in her eyes was heartbreaking, but he had to tell her the truth. Sid would never lie to his mother.

'It was the strangest thing. I found the old me on the beach at Dunkirk. I would lie there face down in the sand as the bombers came screaming overhead and my mates were blown to bits around me. I would lie there and cry just like that little boy.' Sid didn't dare close his eyes for fear of hearing those bombs fall again. He thought of the woodwose standing in the lapping waves, watching and waiting. 'I had to leave him there,

Mum. If I'd stayed with him, I'd have died, too. I survived because I'm a trained soldier. I killed people, Mum. Other boys just like me.'

His mother shook her head, lips clamped together to stop the sobs.

Sid gently rested a hand on her arm. 'That's who I am, Mum. I'm sorry, but your little boy is gone.'

Sid's mother took a sudden breath as if she'd been deep underwater and could only now come up for air. 'This is the drink talking.' Her eyes zigzagged around him, looking for some clue that he was making a twisted joke. 'Get to bed and sober up, and we'll forget all this nonsense.'

'You ain't told her everything, have you, Sid?' Alfie's shadow stood by the door. 'You ain't told her about me. What you did. I wonder why?'

There was a wailing from upstairs. Sid's dad calling for help. As his mother began to move past him, Sid recalled Constable Muldoon's words. 'You're right, Mum. I'm still hungover. Bad head. Sorry.' He glanced upstairs as his father's cries intensified. 'I'll look after Dad. You get some rest.'

He left her at the foot of the stairs, sure that she didn't believe him. He crossed the landing and hurried into the main bedroom to find his father in his pyjamas, peeking between the blackout curtains, transfixed by the clouds. Eric's mouth hung open slackly as he moaned in fear, a droning sound that rose and fell like an air raid siren. It made Sid sick to see his father like this. It couldn't just be the cold.

This once kind and cheery man had completely lost his marbles.

'Dad, come on. Back to bed.' Sid joined his father at the window. As he did so, a tall, silent silhouette loomed out of the darkness by the Andersen shelter. He knew with just a glance that it was the woodwose.

Sid snapped the blackout curtains shut and took his father by the elbow, but the old man spun, grabbing Sid's jaw and squeezing hard. His eyes revolved slowly, like a kaleidoscope, and the voice that came from his mouth was not his own.

'The Holly King has a task for you, boy.' Eric's spine arched and spittle formed on his lips. He jerked and fell backwards onto the bedside cabinet, sending a ceramic hot water bottle rolling across the floor. As he flailed about, he pointed straight at his son. 'Kill the witches! Kill them, or your father dies! Do it. Do it now!'

GOD JÓL

Clocks across the village chimed midnight as Faye ran breathlessly out of Mrs Teach's front door. It was the twenty-first of December. Yule. Not that you'd know it from Mrs Teach's house. Apart from a few Christmas cards on the mantle, there wasn't a single decoration in the place. Which, for the home of a woman devoted to doilies and chintz, struck Faye as a surprise. She wondered if it had to do with this being Mrs Teach's first Christmas without her Ernie. But that was a thought for another day. Faye had no time to waste right now.

She jumped onto the Griffin and flew the short distance to Saint Irene's Church through the cold drizzle. She was still a little woozy from drawing on the power of the moon, which made flight perilous, but every second counted.

Faye hopped off the bike while it was still airborne, leaving it to land, roll and clatter into a gravestone. She ducked into the little wooden devil's door on the north side of the church and dashed down into the crypt.

Descending the worn stone steps, she emerged into a scene from a nightmare.

Miss Charlotte lay writhing in pain on the old stone tomb, twisting the red gingham tablecloth beneath her. Mrs Teach, hands spattered with blood, held a cold compress made from a flannel to Miss Charlotte's eye.

Bertie was still locked in his gibbet, which he kept insisting was perfectly fine, though he was wide-eyed and trembling and sporting fresh cuts and bruises after their encounter with Pearl and the Holly King.

'Did you find them?' Mrs Teach beckoned Faye closer.

'Poppy juice and cabbage lotion.' Faye opened her palms, an apothecary bottle in each, not knowing which one Mrs Teach needed first. She had found them shelved alphabetically in the woman's extensive cellar, which was crammed from floor to ceiling with countless remedies in tiny bottles.

'Good work. Thank you, Faye.' Mrs Teach snatched up the brown bottle containing the poppy juice, unscrewing the lid to reveal a glass pipette. 'This will help with the pain,' she told Miss Charlotte.

Faye had been convinced that Miss Charlotte owed her long life to some kind of magical invincibility, but tonight it had been made horribly clear that she was as vulnerable to the edge of a blade as any of them. Faye winced to see Charlotte's hands trembling. She had said nothing since their return from the crossroads, only gritting her teeth and occasionally hissing in agony as she struggled to manage the pain.

Mrs Teach squeezed the bottle dropper and filled

the glass pipette with poppy juice. Miss Charlotte opened her mouth like a baby bird receiving worms from its mother.

Mrs Teach leaned back. 'No dear, not orally.'

Miss Charlotte's lips shook as she spoke. 'W-what?'

'For instant relief, this needs to take a more direct route.' Mrs Teach cleared her throat and lowered her voice to a tone better suited for such a delicate conversation. 'Via the *derrière*.'

'You're sticking it up her bum?' Bertie blurted.

'I'd rather die,' Miss Charlotte said, some strength returning to her voice.

'Fine, we'll just sit around and make idle chit-chat while we wait, shall we?' Mrs Teach inspected the little brown bottle. 'I thought you were rather desperate for pain relief a short while ago.'

'Not that desperate. You never mentioned anything about shoving it up my bottom.'

'I won't be *shoving* anything. I promise to be delicate.'

'Are you enjoying this?'

'Certainly not. I had very different plans for the Yule festivities, and none of them included your backside.'

'Come on, you two.' Faye raised her voice. 'Pack it in. This ain't the time for—'

Miss Charlotte's hand was a blur as she grabbed the bottle and gulped the juice down.

'Two drops!' Mrs Teach swiped it back. 'You were supposed to have two drops, not the whole bloody bottle. That would kill an ordinary person.'

183

Miss Charlotte let out a relieved sigh. Her hands slowly stopped shaking and her breathing gradually settled into a deep ebb and flow. 'I'm not ordinary,' she said, looking around as if becoming aware of where she was for the first time. 'My eye.' Her spindly fingers dabbed at the cold compress over her wounded right eye. 'Philomena, can you save it?'

Mrs Teach set her jaw, glancing briefly over to Faye. Her usual confident upright posture sagged as she gently lifted the compress. For a moment she said nothing, simply staring at a puzzle she knew she couldn't solve. 'Charlotte, dear, this is going to sting like buggery, but can you open the eye for me, please?'

Faye angled her head to get a better look, then wished she hadn't. Most of the blood had been cleaned up, revealing a cut that ran from Miss Charlotte's eyebrow to her cheek. Her eyelashes fluttered like a butterfly's wings as they opened, revealing a mess of raw pink and off-white jelly.

Miss Charlotte's chest heaved. Even with the poppy juice, this was excruciating.

'Can you close your good eye?' Mrs Teach asked, leaning closer to the wounded one. 'What can you see?'

'It's ... it's all milky white.' Panic rose in Miss Charlotte's voice. 'I ... I see nothing.'

'My darling, I can't save it.' Mrs Teach took her hand. 'The cut is too deep. There's a chunk missing. It ... it looks like someone's taken a nibble out of a grape.'

Astonishingly, a laugh erupted from Miss Charlotte,

followed promptly by a gasp of pain. 'Ow! Don't make me laugh.'

'Sorry. All I can do is heal the wound.' Mrs Teach turned to Faye. 'Cabbage lotion, please, Faye.'

Faye handed her the second bottle. Small and made from clear glass, it contained a thick white paste. The confused look on Faye's face prompted an explanation.

'It's a concoction of my own.' Mrs Teach unscrewed the lid and scooped out a pea-sized portion using a teaspoon left by the previous air raid shelter occupants. 'Hastens the healing of eyes and such. Look up, please.' This last was directed at Miss Charlotte who, for once, did as she was told. Mrs Teach applied the paste to the damaged eye. 'Now look down. Left. Right. That's it. And blink.' She placed the cold compress back over the eye. 'Rest for a while. It should stop hurting soon.'

'But . . .' Faye bit her lip. 'She won't be able to see out of that eye ever again?'

'No, but now I get to wear an eyepatch. It's long been an ambition of mine.' Miss Charlotte was already sounding like her old self again, and Faye wondered if she could ever be that strong.

Mrs Teach took a cushion from an armchair and gently slid it under Miss Charlotte's head. There was a shawl, too, and she moved to drape it over the wounded witch. As she did, her foot clanged against Bertie's gibbet. 'Sorry, Bertie.'

'Quite all right.' He was lying on his side, head propped up on a balled fist he'd somehow managed to wedge alongside his cheek.

Faye inspected the gibbet. It was secured with a rusty old padlock.

'I'm sorry, Miss Charlotte, but getting Bertie out of this thing is going to make one hell of a racket.'

'I'm fine,' Bertie insisted. 'I can wait. If anything, I prefer having a solid bit of iron between me and any angry Father Christmases that might be around.'

'If I don't get you out now, you might be in this all Christmas, Bertie.'

He smiled. 'I've had worse.'

'Bang away.' Miss Charlotte curled up on the stone tomb. 'I've slept through entire battles. I'm sure I can manage.'

'If you're sure.' Faye picked up the mallet they had used to smash down the hidden crypt's wall. 'What do you reckon, Bertie? Whack the lock or the hinges?'

'Before you start deafening us all,' Mrs Teach interjected, 'how did you know the Holly King's sarcophagus would bring us here?'

'I didn't, to start with.' Faye pursed her lips as she recalled what had come to her in a flash. 'There was something about the way he handled it when he arrived. All gentle and cautious, like. It was precious to him. Important. And it might look like a fancy wooden coffin from down here, but from above it looks like a door. I remembered his brother's box here, and you said they might have used it like a gateway. When I got close and could smell this place, I knew.'

'Nicely deduced,' Miss Charlotte muttered, sounding drowsy.

'And don't worry.' Faye pointed the mallet at the shadows of the crypt where the remaining wooden sarcophagus stood, its lid ajar where Mrs Teach and Miss Charlotte had clambered out after the fray. 'He blew up the other one, so he can't follow us here.'

'Good work.' Mrs Teach dried her hands on a towel. 'That was something of a disaster, but it could have been much, much worse.'

Faye gripped the mallet harder. 'Do you think she was telling the truth about my mum? I've seen them together in my dreams, but that could just be Pearl putting ideas in my head.' She was rattled more than she cared to admit. Not only did it seem that her mother was *not* the wise angel that everyone else made her out to be, but she might actually have blood on her hands. 'Could she have killed Pearl?'

Mrs Teach lit a gas lamp, moving to join Faye. 'I didn't know your mother then, Faye, but it seems jolly unlikely to me.'

'And I wash in Russsha,' Miss Charlotte drawled, getting sleepier as the potions took hold. 'Good vodka.'

'You said you met Pearl,' Faye said to Mrs Teach.

'Briefly. When she first arrived in England – the autumn of 1903, if I recall – she came to Lady Sage in London. I was on a special assignment there with Vera Fivetrees. There was something of a kerfuffle, and Pearl left with angry promises of vengeance and such. Never heard from her again. We assumed she had returned to New York, though it seems she came here and found your mother.'

'I wonder if Dad knows what happened?'

'Are you sure *you* want to know?' Mrs Teach asked.

'Don't be daft. Of course I do.'

'Faye, you remember your mother as a kind and wise woman, but who's to say she was always like that? In 1903 she would have been the same age you are now. And to say that you can be somewhat flighty and reckless is the understatement of the century.'

Faye would normally have rushed to her mother's defence, but Mrs Teach was only saying what she was already thinking. Her heart sank in her chest.

Mrs Teach must have registered her despair. She rested a hand on Faye's shoulder, and her voice softened. 'We've all done things in the heady rush of youth that, looking back, we might regret. Have we not, Miss Charlotte?'

The wounded witch grunted a reply in the affirmative.

'You believe her, don't you?' Faye felt her eyes burning. 'You think my mum killed her.'

Mrs Teach took Faye gently by the arms. 'I do not, but it doesn't matter what I believe, only what you do. You can't let this change anything, Faye. Your mother loved you and wanted the best for you. All the time I knew her, she was a good woman, dedicated to helping others.'

Faye sniffed and nodded, but she was far from convinced. 'Dad'll know.' She hefted the mallet and circled Bertie in the gibbet. 'Let's get you free, Bertie, and then we'll go and find him. Maybe he'll know what Pearl wants.'

'I care little for what Pearl wants.' Mrs Teach's voice hardened. 'There's more to this than your family squabbles, Faye. You heard what the Holly King said. He intends to destroy the village. We have to stop them.'

Faye looked at the helpless Miss Charlotte, Bertie in his cage, and Mrs Teach's bloodstained fingers. 'The pair of them just gave us a good hiding. How the bloody hell are we supposed to stop them?'

'Get Bertie out of the gibbet while I think about that.'

BROKEN ANTLER

The Holly King's left antler dangled by a thread. He toyed with one of the tines, twirling it between finger and thumb like a giant hangnail. It didn't hurt. He rarely felt pain of any kind. But the humiliation was searing. What good was a woodland demigod with only one antler? It completely ruined his otherwise immaculate symmetry. And that was important when he appeared to cowering mortals in a silhouette of light and shade. The desired effect was to induce fear and awe, not to have some fool raise their hand and ask, 'Where's the other one?'

The Holly King sat in the snow by the crossroads and came to a decision. He grasped his antlers – one broken, the other whole – in each hand. Gritting his teeth, he snapped them both off with a snarl and tossed them over to where the gibbet's wooden scaffold lay in pieces. Feeling a little better about himself, he reached up. His good antler had broken away cleanly, leaving a smooth stump. The previously broken antler had left a small shard jutting out like a tiny, off-centre rhinoceros horn.

The Holly King muttered an ancient curse.

The Oak King would have been the first to laugh at his predicament. His brother was always looking for ways to humiliate him. They had been in constant competition since birth. A tempestuous sibling rivalry that intensified when the Holly King was promised stewardship of the woodland realm by their mother.

Little did he know that she had made the same promise to his brother.

The Goddess took a perverse glee at seeing her children fight for what they both believed was their birthright. A cycle of violence and rebirth, in parallel with the turning of the year. By the time the brothers discovered the lie, their hatred had already set, just as lava turns to stone. The carnage continued, and for each of them, every victory was followed by a defeat.

Until now.

Finally, the Holly King had the upper hand. The whole wood was in his grasp. Though this was not the wood of old. Oh, there were some remnants of its former glory. His eyes fell upon a nearby row of silver birch. Snow queens awaiting coronation. A fox foraged around their roots for food as a goldcrest teased seeds from an alder's tightly packed cones. Rabbits had scratched at the tree itself, leaving little pink welts on its roots. From deep in the maze of foliage came the hand-clap echo of pigeons taking flight. A wood in winter was nature stripped back to its bare essentials, and the

Holly King revelled in its bleakness. But this wood was now little more than a copse compared to the majesty of what had been here before. Pearl had explained to him how the humans had cut down the trees, so many of them, to make warships, bows and arrows, homes, furniture, toys, even pencils.

Pencils.

Things had got out of hand in his absence. He thought back to when he had last been here. Back then, people huddled together in little clusters of mud huts. They lived, rightly, in fear of the darkness, and they were more than happy to worship a demigod who promised the return of the light after the darkest day.

Those who had dared to defy the way of the wood had been punished. They could only take dead or fallen wood, by hook or by crook. That was the way, and it was understood. Cutting holly without permission meant a fine. And if they were to do something truly dreadful – say, killing a tree by peeling its bark – then they would be cut open at the navel, nailed to that same tree, and have their entrails wound around them and the tree as a warning to others. It was a fair system, and everyone had known their place back then. They'd had the decency to understand that living meant sacrifice and pain. He would never have encountered the disgraceful resistance that he'd had to endure today. Appalling manners from a rabble of witches, if you can believe that.

He glanced over at the smouldering remains of his sarcophagus and a tiny thought niggled at him. Had he made a terrible mistake?

After all, out there, in the aether, he had known peace. Time was meaningless, and he was accountable to no one as he communed with the greater universe.

Until Pearl had found him and reminded him of his greatness. She had stoked the fires of his ambition. There was so much more to prove. Yes, mistakes had been made in the past. Yes, those who had once worshipped him had turned their backs. But he had given up too easily.

The light of the old gods had faded – even his mother was silent – and now they were all but forgotten. The Oak King was dead, for good this time, and that left only him – the Holly King. Finally, he could reign supreme and fulfil his purpose in this realm. If he couldn't achieve something as simple as that, then he had no business calling himself a demigod.

The Holly King tried to recall who had first told him that. He suspected it was his mother. It was so long ago that only the words – and the hurt – remained.

The confrontation with the witches had not exactly gone to plan. With them dead, everything would have been so simple. Instead, they had survived and now things were getting complicated. The Holly King did not enjoy complicated. He enjoyed ritual and tradition in all of its splendour. A sense of order that the people could adhere to. It was time to restore that order.

'That was something of a calamity.' The Holly King gestured at the scorched road where the remains of the sarcophagus were scattered about. 'I think you underestimated them.'

Pearl sat in the centre of the crossroads, eyes closed, wings broken. If they caused her any pain, she didn't show it. She was remarkably calm. Perhaps she was replaying the confrontation in her mind's eye and wondering where she had gone wrong. Of course, the Holly King couldn't trust the little witch as far as he could throw her – which was quite some distance, to be fair – but other than this most recent mistake, he had to admit that she had been a useful ally. His resurrection had all been down to her, and she had certainly followed through on her promises for the creation and delivery of his crown. That kind of magic had its uses. But he had more than indulged Pearl in her games and in satisfying her own lust for revenge. Now came the hour of the Holly King.

'It is the darkest moment of the longest night of the bleak midwinter.' The Holly King brushed his beard down. 'The veil has lifted, and we should strike now before they have time to lick their wounds.'

Pearl flapped an irritated hand at him. It came with rapid shushing.

The Holly King bristled. *How dare she?*

As if sensing his ire, Pearl opened one eye and pasted on a smile. 'Sorry, Your Majesty, but this requires a lotta concentration.'

The lack of respect was breathtaking. He was the Holly King. He had been there when this wood was naught but ash. He and his brother had sown the first seeds, nurtured the first shoots. This was *his* wood, and she would do well to remember that. He knew her ministrations were self-serving – he was no fool – but he demanded respect. Not a veil of fawning lies. Oh, how the Holly King loathed secrets and lies. He would expose them all until none were left.

'Forgive me, O Holly King,' she said at length, all contrition, as if she were reading his thoughts. 'I'm having two conversations at once and it's kinda tricky.'

The Holly King had seen her do this before. She could speak with others through the aether using only her mind. Witch magic. Petty stuff, but not an ability that he could summon. Not yet, at least.

'With whom do you commune?'

'I'm sending someone to take care of them for good,' she said, the strain in her voice making it crack. 'A killer. Though they think he's a friend. He'll do the job. My only regret is that I won't be there to see it.'

The Holly King self-consciously touched the stub of antler on his head. 'How can you be so sure of your assassin?'

'I'm not the only voice in his head. He's a broken soul. Burdened by grief and guilt, angry and violent, easy to manipulate. And he's motivated.' Pearl smiled, tongue licking her teeth. 'If he fails, I've made it clear that someone he loves will be punished. I think we have an understanding.'

The Holly King sneered. 'You *think*?'

'I *know*. I won't fail you.'

'Recent events suggest otherwise.'

'You're right, I underestimated the witches. Especially the Wynter girl.'

The Holly King couldn't deny he had enjoyed seeing the look on Pearl's face as she was sent tumbling to the ground by the girl. Beaten, and with both wings broken, it was the first time he had seen the fairy show any fear.

'Bright,' he said, standing to inspect his writhing sack. At least he still had his bag of surprises.

'What?'

'Her name is Faye Bright.' He hefted the sack over his shoulder, ignoring the complaints and kicks from within. 'Her father's name.'

'Nah, she's her mother's daughter.' Pearl opened her eyes. 'She's a Wynter. Like me.'

'Not quite,' the Holly King mused. 'She doesn't have your duplicitous cunning. There are few secrets of consequence in her past.'

'Maybe it's time we gave her one?'

'What do you mean?'

'Ahh, don't matter. She'll be dead soon, so who cares?' Pearl stood and smiled sweetly.

'I care, Pearl Wynter.' The Holly King exhaled, his chilly breath swirling before him. He enjoyed watching her smile vanish as he spoke her name. He continued in a calm, even voice, towering over her. 'I care very much that these witches present no further threat to my plans. Mark me, if your assassin fails, if I lay eyes on Faye Bright or any other witch from this moment forth, I shall hold you responsible. I shall pluck your pretty head from your shoulders and crush it to dust. Do *we* have an understanding?'

All flippancy and lightness drained from Pearl. Her chest heaved and her jaw set as fear took hold. She might try to hide it, but he knew she was terrified. He smiled to himself.

'Yes, Your Majesty. I understand,' she said, her voice dry and small. 'Your time has come. Let us complete your coronation. Let us prepare the Feast of Fools.'

'Good. Yes, let's.' A thrill rippled through the Holly King. Now the village would be his. About bloody time. He tossed the sack to the ground – resulting in curses from its occupants – clapped his gloved hands together and strode across the road to the nearest tree, one of the silver birch snow queens glowing in the moonlight. He went down on one knee before her and bowed his head. Removing the glove from his right hand, he rested his palm on the trunk, closed his eyes and bellowed a noise in a low register, somewhere between the boom that heralded the birth of the universe and the dread horns of the underworld.

The foraging fox bolted into the brambles. Birds scrambled for the skies in a flurry of beating wings. The birch lit up, blazing like a hearth right down to its roots. The other trees around it began to do the same, brightening with a strange energy. The raindrops on every branch shimmered and rose into the air, crystallising into icy flakes, each one a unique study in shining fractals.

The Holly King stood, still bellowing, and threw his arms wide. He paused for breath, then puffed his cheeks and blew.

Pearl covered her head and curled into a ball as the crossroads became the eye of a mighty winter storm. The Holly King's cloak billowed around him as he thrust his arms in the direction of the western road. The blizzard roared as it swept through the trees. It was heading for the village.

Interlude: The Trees Tremble

The trees brace in the sudden rush of the blizzard. Many bend. Their crowns touch the ground. Old oaks stand rigid and inflexible. A beech breaks. Any remaining leaves are scattered. All the trees wonder the same thing. Is this the end of the wood?

THE PRICE OF MERCY

'Kill the witches.' It was a simple request. Three words. Once it was done, Sid's father would be saved. Sid knew how to obey simple orders. It had been drilled into him throughout his training. Take that bunker, capture that flag, kill the enemy. The witches weren't his enemy. At least, they hadn't been until now. To be fair, until today he hadn't known the village even had any witches. Mrs Teach was just the village gossip, though now it was clear how she knew so much about everybody. Probably staring into a crystal ball. Miss Charlotte ... Yes, now that Sid thought about it, of course she was a witch. Living alone in a cottage in the middle of the wood. It wouldn't surprise him if the bloody thing was made of gingerbread. Faye was the one that shocked him. Just the thought of doing her any harm made him feel sick. To him she'd forever be that mouthy girl from school. Always an opinion on something or other. He'd heard more than one villager tell Faye that her gob would get her into trouble one day. But he'd never thought she was the kind of person who'd muck around with something like witchcraft. Still, Sid had a choice between a lippy girl he sort-of knew from school and his own father. If she had to go, then so be it. An order was an order. Identify the enemy, eradicate them with all speed. He took his mother's carving knife from a drawer in the kitchen. He checked its balance, weight, heft and sharpness, then he stepped out into the snow.

'They'll be at the crypt.' Alfie walked half a step behind Sid, boots slushing along as they marched in time. 'If you're quick, you can trap them in there, or get them on the way out. One-two-three!'

Sid caught a fleeting glimpse of Alfie miming a knife being thrust into three bodies. They'd become mates during bayonet practice when they were training. For some reason, they'd always ended up side by side, known to the training instructors as the 'Gruesome Twosome'. After the instructor's cries of, 'High port! On guard! Deliver the point!' they'd race each other to the heavy sack of sand dangling on a rope, roaring as they plunged their bayonet blades into the sack's belly. Sid would stick it with a powerful thrust, pushing in deep. Alfie would stab at it over and over, with quick and terrifying jabs, and always with a smile. He'd never had so much fun. He'd kept doing it until the instructor told him to pack it in.

A lot of the lads at the barracks had bragged about wanting to go to war. They'd all wanted to be seen as the most patriotic, the first to give the Narzees a bloody nose. But Alfie, he just wanted a fight. He loved nothing more. Sid had tried to give him a wide berth after their first meeting, but Alfie had stuck to him like a limpet, and after a while Sid resigned himself to the fact that they were a pair.

Then came that night in the Rising Sun in Salisbury, right before they were due to leave for France. A couple of lads from Birmingham took against Sid for some reason, shoving him around, trying to provoke him. Sid was about to offer to buy them a beer to keep the peace when Alfie went steaming in. He smashed a pint glass over the first one's head, then thumped the second one on the nose, knocking him flat on his arse. Turns out they weren't alone, and all hell broke loose. In seconds, everyone in the pub was exchanging blows. Alfie threw himself into it with a gleeful smile. Sid had managed to drag him out before the MPs arrived and he made himself Alfie's alibi. He owed him that much, he reckoned. No one could prove a thing and the next day they'd left for war.

After that, they were peas in a pod, always looking out for one another. Until it all went to pot. In training, everything made sense. One of the toffs in charge gave you an order, you did it, then you waited for the next one.

But in battle, the officers suddenly didn't have the first bloody clue. They weren't in charge anymore. The Nazis in the tanks, in the bombers, and with the machine guns – they were running the show now and they didn't play by the rules.

The worst was Lieutenant Fisher. A former grammar

school boy who all but bowed to his superior officers from Eton and Harrow and did whatever they commanded, even if it meant certain death for his men. Sid remembered Fishy Fisher's ridiculous walk – arms and legs moving in unison like a tin toy – as he'd cried, 'Follow me!' Few had. Most had dived for cover.

When they'd got split up from their regiment, Fisher had ordered a retreat, then to regroup while he checked the map and called for help on the radio. When no one answered, he sat on his hands, waiting for orders while the bombs dropped around them and the rattle of machine guns and the squeal of tank tracks came closer and closer.

It was every man for himself after that. They fell back to what remained of some bombed-out French town. Sid had been told what it was called, but he couldn't remember now. His job hadn't been to know things. It had been to do as he was ordered. But in the end, he hadn't even been able to do that.

Sid and Alfie had been told to check and clear the south side of a particular street. They'd moved from building to building, looking for the enemy. Fishy Fisher had given them orders to take prisoners, but Alfie wasn't having it.

'I'm going to kill every Nazi I meet, mate. Stick 'em with the bayonet, right in the guts.'

'What if they surrender?'

'Stick 'em anyway. They knew what they was lettin' themselves in for when they signed up. It's war, Sid. They won't do you the same courtesy, so don't do it for them.' Alfie had shown Sid a map of Europe he'd pinched from the officers' mess. 'See this? Every Nazi I kill, he's goin' on this here map. I'll draw a black dot for every one of 'em. By the time we reach Berlin, this thing's gonna look like it's got the bloody measles.'

That's when Alfie had scared Sid the most. The instructors back in Blighty had promised to make them into soldiers. With Alfie, they'd unleashed a blood-thirsty murderer.

It was in a smashed-up patisserie that Sid had come face to face with a young German private cowering behind the counter. He had dark hair matted with blood and sweat, and big blue eyes. Sid remembered how they'd glistened with tears as he'd raised his palms in surrender. He was gibbering. Sid didn't understand the words, but he knew the boy was begging for mercy as he trained his rifle on him. The German private had no weapons, no helmet, and his bootlaces were miss-ing. Sid had his orders, and this lad was his prisoner. He was about to call Alfie to help, but then he remem-bered his pal's bloodthirsty vow. This German would be the first dot on Alfie's grisly map.

Sid did what he thought was the right thing. He lowered his rifle and nodded to the street. '*Go!*' he whispered.

The boy blinked in disbelief, and Sid had to tell him again. 'Go on, get out of it!'

'*Danke.*' The boy ran, his legs shaking as he scurried away.

Sid felt a strange warmth as he watched him. In all

this madness, he'd shown mercy, and that gave him some hope that one day this war might be over. Him and that lad might one day share a pint and laugh about the time they—

'What'd you do that for, you soft sod?'

Sid spun to find Alfie emerging from the patisserie's back room, his face twisted with rage. He barged past Sid and ran out into the street, sliding the bolt of his rifle and taking aim at the fleeing soldier's back.

'Alfie!' Sid chased after his friend, shoving him aside as he fired. The bullet ricocheted harmlessly off the wall of the abandoned hotel opposite. 'You were gonna shoot him in the back?'

'It's war, Sid. Us or them.'

'He's just a kid.'

'So are you!'

'He was frightened.'

'Get out of my . . .'

Alfie trailed off. He'd seen something further down the street. Sid followed his gaze to find the escaped lad gesticulating at something around the corner.

'What's he doing?' Alfie plucked a roll-up from behind his ear, lit it and took a puff.

The lad was now pointing at them, and Sid felt a cold dread in the pit of his stomach. He was so fixated on the young soldier that he didn't see the barrel of the field howitzer until it was already taking aim from its hiding place in the old bank on the corner.

Alfie raised his rifle. 'Little bastard grassed us! Run!'

Sid had barely taken a step before the air around him

split into a billion thunderous shards. It was like being hit by a bus. He was blown through the window of the patisserie, crashing into an empty display cabinet that tumbled down on top of him. After that, everything went black.

He awoke at night. His ears still ringing. His arms and legs were dead weights, his head ached as if it were clamped in a vice. His legs almost buckled as he stood, and the world wavered around him. There was a cold, wet patch down one leg where he'd pissed himself. The streets were deserted, though the northern horizon flashed and boomed with the distant drumming of war.

He found Alfie – what was left of him – lying in pieces on the kerb. Sid was drawn to his eyes first. Yellow and bloodshot, they caught the light of the moon. Half of his face was completely untouched, a startled expression frozen there for ever, the roll-up cigarette still on his lip. His skin was grey and waxy, his lips and earlobes blue. His uniform carried a whiff of wet tweed, but the overwhelming aroma was a grisly mix of copper and shit.

Sid recalled how strangely calm he'd been at the time. As he'd crouched to retrieve one of Alfie's identity tags, he'd winced at his own cuts and bruises, but he was otherwise unhurt. If anything, being unconscious had left him refreshed, like after a long nap on a Sunday afternoon.

Sid knew he was looking at the remains of his friend, but he shoved all the horror and guilt he should have felt into a shadowy corner of his mind that he didn't visit very often. He just stood there, under the moon, staring at Alfie staring back at him.

'Blimey, will you look at the state of that.' It was Alfie's voice. It was the first time Sid saw Alfie out of the corner of his eye. In that moment, Sid knew he had gone mad and, to be honest, he was fine with it. In a funny way, it was the only sane solution to cope with what he had done. He'd surrendered to insanity, and it had been by his side ever since.

'Snap out of it, sunshine.' Alfie's voice brought Sid out of his daze. He felt the cold on the tip of his nose. He exhaled, sending puffy clouds into the air. 'We're here.'

Sid found himself standing outside the door to Saint Irene's crypt with a knife in his hand and murder on his mind.

The Devil's Door

After considerable hammering on the gibbet's hinges and lock, the only damage the witches had managed to do was to Bertie's hearing, his ears ringing from the clanging.

'Sorry about this, Bertie,' Faye apologised through the gibbet's bars. 'We'll get you out of this, I promise.'

'I should be the one apologising,' Bertie insisted. 'It's my fault I'm trapped in this ruddy thing. Maybe we just need a bigger hammer?'

Faye arched her back as she rose and turned to Mrs Teach. 'Didn't your Ernie have a shed full of tools?'

'Oh, he did.' Mrs Teach smiled wistfully at the thought of her dear, departed husband. 'But I gave them all away for the war effort.'

Faye had to wonder if Mrs Teach had given away all her Christmas decorations, too. It couldn't be easy for her to face her first Christmas alone, so perhaps she'd decided not to bother.

'We need something industrial,' Miss Charlotte mused. 'Larry Dell has a big table saw in Gustav.'

Mrs Teach blinked. 'I beg your pardon.'

'It's what he calls one of his barns,' Faye told her. 'It's a long story.'

'It's designed for cutting lumber,' Miss Charlotte said with a shrug, 'but it's bigger than a billiard table and has a blade like a Spitfire propellor. It should do the job.'

'Should?' Faye gestured at the gibbet. 'You're forgetting that poor Bertie will be stuck in there while that thing's whizzing inches from his head.'

'We've broken every blade we have, Faye. It's the table saw or Bertie lives the rest of his life behind bars.'

'We could use your goggles and flight helmet,' Bertie suggested. 'They should keep me safe.'

'It's too dangerous, Bertie,' Faye protested, but she could see he was starting to get desperate.

'I'll be fine,' he insisted.

'The table saw is bolted to the ground, if I recall.' Miss Charlotte narrowed her one good eye. 'I used it to cut some lumber for a bed last year. But it's on the other side of the village. How do we get Bertie all the way there? That thing weighs a ton.'

'Can't you make it fly?' Mrs Teach flapped her hands up and down as if that was all it took.

'I'll give it a go.' Faye, still a little light-headed from her last flight, closed her eyes, imagining herself flying alongside planet Earth, soaring through the universe. She rose a few inches from the ground, tingling with magical energy. Leaning forward, she gripped the tip of the gibbet. She focused on becoming one with it, and it rose with her.

'Mind the ancient stonework,' Mrs Teach warned, as behind her Faye manoeuvred the iron cage like a tiny Zeppelin towards the steps.

'Will you be quiet? I'm trying to concentrate!'

'There's no need to be quite so curt, young lady.'

'Just . . . shh.' Faye steered the gibbet to the first bend in the stairs.

Miss Charlotte brought up the rear, one hand on the gibbet and the other brushing against the stone wall to keep her balance on the steps. Losing sight in one eye had left her somewhat discombobulated, and she was prone to missing door handles and tripping on slabs. Mrs Teach had rustled up a black leather eyepatch from an old boot abandoned by one of the crypt's air raid occupants. Miss Charlotte had strung it around her head with a bootlace and carried it off with style.

'It's a bit tight, Bertie, but we're getting there,' Faye reassured him. 'Then once we're in the open air, you and I will whizz over the village to Larry's barn and—'

'What about us?' Miss Charlotte protested. 'You'll need someone who can operate a table saw, and I'm not walking. I'll hitch a ride, if it's all the same.'

'I'll walk,' Mrs Teach insisted. 'Flying is unnatural. Even for witches.'

'Let's get him outside first, shall we?' Faye said as they reached the top of the steps and the devil's door, as all north-facing doors in old churches were named. Through the draughty old oak beams was the graveyard. Mrs Teach jiggled the door's sticky handle and Faye rested her end of the gibbet on the top step.

213

The door creaked open, and she and Miss Charlotte shivered as they guided Bertie and his floating cage into the open.

'Gosh, it's turned very nippy.' Mrs Teach pulled her fur coat tighter. 'Looks like snow.'

Faye crouched down level with Bertie in the gibbet. His fingers threaded through hers. 'You all right in there, Bertie?' she asked. 'Not too—'

Faye became aware of a movement out of the corner of her eye, accompanied by heavy breathing and rushing footsteps.

'Move!' Miss Charlotte grabbed Faye and Mrs Teach by the scruffs of their necks, yanking them inside. Faye just about caught a glimpse of the shape of a man and the glint of a blade.

'No! Bertie's still—' Faye cried out as Bertie and the gibbet crashed to the ground, but before she could stop Miss Charlotte they were back inside the church. The devil's door slammed shut.

'Who the blazes was that?' Mrs Teach gasped.

'Sidney Birdwhistle.' Miss Charlotte leaned all her weight against the oak door. 'He has a knife.'

'Bertie!' Faye yanked at the door handle. 'We've left Bertie out there!'

Miss Charlotte put an arm between Faye and the door. 'He doesn't want Bertie.'

Faye was about to ask just who it was that Sid did want, when his voice came from the other side of the door.

'She's right. I don't want Bertie.'

'Hello, Sid.' Bertie's voice was chummy, if slightly fearful. 'How are you?'

'Shut up.'

'Wilco.'

Faye banged a fist on the door. 'If you harm so much as a hair on his head, Sidney Birdwhistle, I'll—'

Bertie cried out in pain.

'Bertie! Sid, what did you do?'

'I harmed a hair on his head, Faye Bright.' Sid's voice was close. The door creaked as he leaned against it. 'And I'll be doing more if you don't step outside right now.'

Faye did her best to keep her voice calm, fighting every urge to throw Miss Charlotte to one side and rush out there to rescue Bertie. She knew it would be a rash thing to do and that it wouldn't end well. She looked over to Mrs Teach and Miss Charlotte, desperately hoping they had some clever plan, or special magic, but they both slowly shook their heads.

'I'm all right, Faye,' Bertie called. 'Though I might have a bit of a bald patch. I've been a bit scalped.'

There was a clang as Sid kicked the cage. 'Be quiet!'

'Sorry.'

Charlotte leaned close to Faye and whispered in her ear. 'Keep him talking. I'll take the long way round and—'

'Let me hear the other two,' Sid said. 'Miss Charlotte and Mrs Teach. I don't want you pair trying anything sneaky.'

Miss Charlotte pursed her lips. 'Balls,' she said quietly, then raised her voice. 'I'm here, Sidney.'

'As am I,' Mrs Teach confirmed. 'Now, what's a nice boy like you doing with a big knife like that at this time of night?'

'Come outside and I'll show you,' Sid said. 'I'll explain everything.'

'I fear that would be a brief and somewhat stabby conversation.'

'That's the trouble, Mrs Teach. See, if you don't come out, then I will have to start stabbing people, and all I've got is Bertie here.'

'Sid, this isn't you.' Faye thought back to their last conversation at his front door. He'd been so reluctant to open it, and when he had, she'd seen something strange. Something lurking beside him. 'Is someone making you do this?'

'I'm going to count to three.' Sid's voice moved away from the door. 'After that, I'm going to cut one of Bertie's ears off.'

Metal creaked and clothing rustled as some kind of struggle ensued. Bertie gasped in fear.

'One.'

'Sid, please don't do this.'

'Two.'

'Sid, we can help you. I swear.'

'Three!'

'*Sid, do you still have two shadows?*' Faye blurted, then held her breath. She ignored the looks she was getting from her fellow witches. 'I saw it when I knocked at your door, Sid. A shadow over your shoulder. And it weren't yours.' She paused a second. 'I don't think the

Sid Birdwhistle I know would do these terrible things. I think someone's forcing you to do them. We can help you, Sid. I promise. We'll do everything we can.'

A chill wind buffeted the door and whistled through the keyhole.

'You can't help.' Sid's voice was smaller. All the fight had gone from him. 'No one can.'

Faye adjusted her specs as she came to a decision. 'I'm going out there.'

Four hands tried to stop her opening the door, but she slapped them away.

'Sid, I'm coming out.'

SECOND SHADOW

Faye swung the door open.

Sid was down on one knee by the gibbet, the point of his blade pressing into the soft flesh of Bertie's neck. Faye shuddered as she saw that a tuft of Bertie's hair was missing, blood matted around his scalp.

Her heart thudded in her ears, and she gave him what she hoped was a reassuring smile. He gave her one back, though the terror in his eyes was plain.

'Poor Bertie's had a hell of a night.' Faye slowly raised her hands. 'Why don't you let him go, Sid?'

Sid clenched his jaw and pressed the blade deeper into Bertie's skin. A tiny bead of blood glistened at Bertie's neck and he hissed through his teeth at the pain.

'I can see it.' Faye looked to Sid's left, where she could just make out a dark shape lurking over him, almost invisible in the gloom. It kept still, prey hiding from a hunter. 'It's there, Sid. I reckon I can get rid of it.'

Sid cocked his ear, as if listening to the shadow. A

sickly smile crept across his face. 'You don't even know what it is.'

'I know you didn't have it when you went marching off to war. So I reckon you got it when you were fighting. Am I right?'

Sid's smile faded. 'No. You're dead wrong, Faye. It's always been there. It's always been a part of me. I'd never let it out before, but over there … I had to. If I hadn't, I'd be dead, too.'

'If you were the one who let it out, Sid, can't you just put it away again?'

Sid's head twitched as he half glanced at the shadow beside him. 'It's out for good. It's who I am. I know that now. I'm a killer, Faye. A good one. They trained me so well, I actually enjoy it. I came home thinking I could leave it all behind, but it came with me. And now he says I have to kill you all.'

'Who says, Sid? Who is he?' Faye extended a hand and tried to keep the desperation from her voice. 'Please, Sid. Let me help you. Who's making you do this?'

'No one's making me do this.'

'Is it the shadow?'

Sid shook his head.

'The Holly King?' Faye asked, and Sid's eyes flashed. 'The Holly King. We know all about him, Sid.' That wasn't the complete truth, of course, but Faye felt a sinking feeling in her belly at the mention of the demigod's name. The beardy bugger had been busier than they'd thought. 'What did he promise you?'

Sid's face creased. 'If I kill you three, then my dad lives.'

Faye's heart twisted. If their situations were reversed, she'd do anything to save her own pa. 'Sid, it doesn't have to be like this. We'll help protect you and your dad from him, I promise.'

Faye heard doubtful murmurs from the witches behind her.

Sid heard them, too, and pressed his lips together tightly, his blade jabbing into Bertie's skin.

Faye bit her lip. 'Sid, don't. Please.'

Just then the chill in the air intensified. Faye felt her ears pop. Half a dozen jackdaws flapped away from the church's yew tree and a trio of rats skittered down the path past her feet. A sudden wind flattened her clothes against her.

She looked up, away from Sid. A billowing mass of snow and ice was thundering towards them, barging between the gravestones. Faye turned to find it coming from all directions, gaining speed and thickening into a blinding wall.

'What the blazes . . . ?' Miss Charlotte muttered.

Sid had followed their puzzled looks, the tip of his knife drifting away from Bertie's neck.

It was all the distraction Faye needed. She barged Sid to one side, then hurled herself at the gibbet and gripped its bars. Gritting her teeth and ignoring her aching body, she rose into the air, taking Bertie with her.

But Sid was fast. He sprinted, leapt onto a tomb

and jumped up after Faye, grabbing her ankle and yanking hard.

Faye kicked out at him, losing her hold on the gibbet, which landed loud as a church bell on the path. Bertie gave a yelp as he rolled through the lychgate and down the Wode Road, into the storm.

'Bertie!'

Faye leaned forward, ready to plunge into the blizzard after him, but an urgent cry from below tugged at her attention. She glanced down to find Mrs Teach and Miss Charlotte struggling with Sid in the slush of the graveyard. The women had him pinned down – Mrs Teach had his legs, Miss Charlotte his arms – but not for much longer. Sid thrashed about like a savage beast, kicking and screaming and cursing with spittle on his lips. His knife was still in his right hand. The blade trembled as he raised his arm. Even with Miss Charlotte's weight on him, he was able to point it towards her one remaining good eye. Both he and Miss Charlotte roared as they wrestled for dominance.

Faye didn't have a choice. Poor Bertie would have to wait.

She swooped down, kicking the knife from Sid's hand with her boot. It spiralled away, clanking against a gravestone somewhere in the blinding snow.

Faye's landing was ungainly. She slipped on the wet grass and landed hard on her backside. A yelp of pain came from somewhere in Mrs Teach's direction. Faye spun to see Sid kick her into a tomb.

'Oh, I say!' Mrs Teach's voice wobbled as she tried to compose herself.

Miss Charlotte had Sid's neck in the crook of her elbow, and for a moment Faye thought they had him, but he went berserk. Flailing his limbs about like a toddler having a tantrum, he managed to loosen Miss Charlotte's grip, then opened wide and bit down hard on her forearm.

The torrent of old Anglo-Saxon vernacular that came from Miss Charlotte was familiar to Faye from some of their more decadent nights at the pub, but even so, it was shocking to hear so much of it uttered with such rapidity and in a single breath.

Sid brought his own elbow up sharply into Miss Charlotte's nose, rolled away from her and looked around for his knife.

He saw Faye and froze.

Mrs Teach was on her feet again, Miss Charlotte two seconds from doing the same. And Faye stood her ground, fists at the ready, the moon at her command.

Sid did the sensible thing and legged it.

He ran into the mist, leaping over the stone wall and heading back towards the wood, without so much as a word.

'Sid!' Faye called after him. 'Sid, come back, please. We can help!'

'Faye.' Miss Charlotte hurried over to her, gripping her arm where Sid had tried to take a chunk out of her. 'We need to get above this snow.'

'It's just a bit of snow.' Faye shivered. 'What's the big deal?'

'This is no ordinary snow. Do you have a key to the bell tower?'

'There's one behind a loose brick by the drainpipe.'

'Fetch it. And hurry.'

'Is this what I think it is?' Mrs Teach covered her mouth and nose with a handkerchief as the snow whipped around them.

Miss Charlotte nodded. 'The Holly King is here.'

ɸ

The powdery snow billowed down every chimney, crept under every door. It woke every villager from their slumber. Despite the chill and the late hour, they were all compelled to dress in their finest. For each and every one of them had received an invitation in their dreams. The Feast of Fools was about to begin.

THE FEAST OF FOOLS

Go floppy. It was a piece of advice given to Bertie by a slightly sozzled Hurricane pilot in the pub a few months ago, and for some reason it had struck him then as something to file away for future use.

'If you're ever in a situation where you think you're going to crash, Bertie, fight every instinct you have to tense your muscles and brace for impact. You're more likely to break bones and tear ligaments if you're stiff as a board. What you need to do, Bertie old son, is go floppy.'

'Floppy?'

'As a rag doll. You'll be tossed about and get a few cuts and bruises, but you'll walk away in one piece.'

Bertie recalled the pilot's slurred voice as he'd doled out this wisdom, but he couldn't remember his name. He had to wonder if he'd taken his own advice, though, as the pilot had bailed out over the Channel in September and broken both his legs.

Nevertheless, going floppy was very much on Bertie's

mind as he barrelled down the Wode Road in his gibbet. *I wonder if this is what a bingo ball feels like?* he pondered as he whizzed past the pub, picking up speed as the storm gathered around him. The accelerating whirl of road-shops-sky-snow shifted suddenly as the cruciform silhouette of the Great War memorial emerged from the murk.

Bertie closed his eyes and made a conscious effort to go as floppy as possible, accepting that whatever happened, he had at least kissed Faye within the last twenty-four hours, and any day when that happened couldn't be all bad.

The gibbet came to an abrupt stop. There was no crash or clang of iron on stone, though Bertie's world flashed white as his forehead connected in a short, sharp fashion with one of the gibbet's bars. Typical. One of the few bits of Bertie he couldn't relax was his skull, and it hummed with the impact. He was able to wriggle a hand up within the rusty iron confines to touch his head to check it was still in one piece. There was a tender patch where Sid had sliced off a chunk of his hair, but it seemed to be otherwise intact.

Bertie opened his eyes, struggling to focus. For a moment he thought everything had gone dark, then he realised that he was in fact looking straight at the sole of a mighty boot. And not just anyone's boot.

The Holly King peered down at him. '*God Jól*, Bertie.'

'Hello again.' Bertie creaked a fearful smile into place, then frowned. 'What happened to your antlers?'

A flicker of irritation crossed the Holly King's face,

and he ignored Bertie's question. 'I'm so glad you could join us.'

'Us?' Bertie looked around, wondering if he meant Pearl, but she was nowhere to be seen.

The Holly King gestured back up the Wode Road. Bertie shuffled and rolled in his cage, watching as the mist receded over the roofs of the houses, then held position in undulating clouds like cavalry awaiting the order to charge.

The doors of every house started to open and the good folk of Woodville stepped outside, all fully dressed and looking rather dazed. They glanced at one another silently, exchanging polite smiles, all unsure why they were outside at this time of night, but certain that they had to be. Most were in their Sunday best, and a few were in uniform. Mr Loaf held his fiddle. Betty Marshall had her spoons. Finlay Motspur, the village's supreme plasterer, wore the full regalia of a one-man band, festooned with cymbals at his joints and a big bass drum on his back, and holding a flugel-horn in his hands. Every step he took was accompanied by a gentle *boom-tish*. Finlay only ever got his gear out for special occasions, and Bertie was about to ask just what the hell was going on when the Holly King decided to announce just what the hell was going on.

'Good people of Woodville.' The demigod's voice reverberated off every wall. All heads turned in his direction.

Bertie should have been surprised that the villagers showed no signs of being at all nonplussed by the sight of a ten-foot-tall Father Christmas in a Lincoln green cloak, a beard as white and voluminous as heavenly clouds, and eyes as red as berries. But, after all they'd been through this year, he supposed it was just another one of those peculiar things they all had to get along with. He'd grown accustomed to it, so why not everyone else? At least the Holly King had removed his antlers. Bertie suspected the pointy appendages might have caused some concern. The large writhing sack behind him was another matter, but Bertie decided that for the sake of his own sanity he would ignore it for the moment.

'*God Jól* to you all. Tonight is a very special night. One with many names. Shalako, Dongzhi, Yule, the bleak midwinter, the longest night. The Caesareans celebrated Saturnalia for thirty days and nights, but, alas, we have only one. Tonight, my friends, we banish darkness and celebrate the turning of the world, the slow return of the light. Between now and sunrise, we will revel in the Feast of Fools!'

The Holly King threw his arms to the sky, and, after a slightly bemused pause, those gathered gave a polite smattering of applause.

Bertie raised a finger. 'Mr Holly King, if I may?'

The Holly King, perturbed by the underwhelming reaction from the villagers, gave Bertie a nod without even looking at him.

'If this is a feast,' asked Bertie, who hadn't eaten since breakfast, 'then where's the grub?' Yesterday, he'd made himself leftover cabbage soup with a bit of shredded carrot and leek. Today, he was planning to make himself toast with scrambled eggs and diced rabbit leg, with enough rabbit leg left over to make a good lunch tomorrow. His tummy rumbled at the thought of it.

A smile made the Holly King's beard rustle. 'I'm glad you asked, Bertie.' The giant drew himself up to his full height and, with all due pomp, removed his crown and slowly raised it above his head. He chanted ancient words of summoning, his voice booming in the still air. The milky-white clouds, still roiling over the rooftops, rumbled ominously in reply.

The Holly King replaced his crown and gripped his sack, which was still wriggling and kicking. He carefully untied the knot in the rope, pinching the opening shut. Then, keeping a firm hold, he began to swing the sack back and forth, getting higher and higher with each swing. The crowd began to *ooh!* and *aah!*, rising in pitch until the Holly King was whirling the sack around like an out-of-control Ferris wheel. Teeth gritted, he gave a cry and tossed it upwards, sending it plunging into the mist.

For a moment there was only silence, and all held their breath.

The sack tumbled from the clouds. Empty and slack, it landed on the cobbles with a *flump*.

'Look!' Bertie pointed through the bars of the gibbet to the clouds.

They were pulsing with dots of colourful light. This drew some appreciative gasps from the crowd and a new round of applause. The lights intensified, shimmering, then burst forth in great plumes. Dozens of them arced overhead, twisting and turning like impossible fireworks. Bertie wondered what this evening's ARP Warden would make of all this, but then he saw Mr Paine standing in the middle of the road in his uniform and tin helmet, just as entranced as everyone else.

The balls of light spiralled down, whirling in between the villagers, who hopped around excitedly at the sight of such delights. Bertie watched from his cage as long shadows slid across the fronts of the shops and houses. The lights whirled faster and faster until the Holly King brought his hands together in an almighty clap. The lights froze in the air, burning until they were blindingly bright. Bertie squeezed his eyes shut. A gust of wind swept by, rolling the gibbet a little, and his ears popped.

'My friends!' the Holly King cried. 'Please welcome my little helpers.'

Bertie blinked his eyes open. The balls of light were gone. In their place were dozens of chubby fairies with translucent wings. But these were nothing like Pearl. They all had big, glassy eyes and fixed rictus smiles. Bertie shook his head, convinced this was some kind of hallucination, but they looked real enough. Almost.

A few days ago, Mr Gilbert had taught Bertie a new word. It had come up when they were looking at some Leonardo da Vinci prints, and Bertie had asked why they looked a bit fuzzy.

'*Sfumato*,' Mr Gilbert had explained. 'It's a

technique for blending tones and textures, creating a strange, smoky feel.' That's what these fairies had. They all looked a little too *sfumato* to be real.

Bertie was the only one who seemed to have noticed anything strange. The other villagers danced and laughed at the adorable little angels.

Finlay Motspur started a rhythm on his bass drum and cymbals, and Mr Loaf played a jolly jig on his fiddle. Captain Marshall gave an order and his Morris Men began to dance, handkerchiefs swirling about.

Bertie looked for Pearl among the angels, but she wasn't with them. The Holly King was running his own show now, and he looked absolutely delighted with himself.

The chubby cherubs soared back up towards the clouds, plunging into them and creating pulses of light. Moments later, they emerged carrying silver platters of food and drink, the likes of which the villagers hadn't seen since before the rationing. The fairies fluttered from person to person, offering little sausages wrapped in bacon, biscuits topped with exotic cheeses, tiny triangular sandwiches stuffed with glistening pink salmon. They circulated with goblets of wine and flagons of beer, which were gulped down, no questions asked.

Bertie shrank in his gibbet, hoping he wouldn't be offered any. His tummy grumbled in protest. This looked much nicer than leftover cabbage soup. But he didn't care how good the food and drink looked. There was something about the way the eyes of the fairies bobbed in their sockets that made him uneasy.

231

Bertie's Granny Joan used to warn him about accepting food from 'the little people', as she called them. They always wanted something in return. Bertie didn't want anything from them at all, and he was certain that any refusal would offend.

'Friends, before we continue with our revels, there is something I must do.' The Holly King's voice stopped everyone in their tracks, even the fairies. He held his crown high enough for all to see. 'For the period of the feast, I must relinquish my crown and my authority to another. To one of you.' He said this last in a teasing voice. The villagers whispered among themselves, each wondering if it might be them. 'Lo!' The Holly King dramatically cupped an ear and tilted his head. 'I hear him coming now. Pray silence, good people, as we welcome ... the Lord of Misrule.'

THE LORD OF MISRULE

From their vantage point at the top of Saint Irene's bell tower, the witches could see nothing but a blanket of sultry white mist draped over the village. A few chimney pots poked up, and there were strange pulses of light, but everything else was invisible. The Holly King's booming voice drifted up to them, muffled by the strange smog.

'Something about a Lord of Misrule.' Faye leaned on the stone crenellations, angling her ear in an effort to hear better. 'Who's he? Not another bloody giant, I hope.'

Mrs Teach and Miss Charlotte shared a look. Both were rather ragged after their recent scraps. Miss Charlotte's eyepatch covered the worst of her injuries, but her face was fixed in a grimace of pain. Mrs Teach's cheek was smeared with mud, and she had the beginnings of what promised to be a colourful bruise around her right eye. On top of that, the moisture from the mist was playing havoc with her hair, giving it an abandoned-nest quality.

233

'Not a giant, no,' Mrs Teach said.

'Quite the opposite.' Miss Charlotte moved her jaw as she thought. 'What poor sod do you think he's chosen?'

'I have a few ideas.' Mrs Teach saw Faye about to ask the same question again when she raised a silencing hand. 'The Lord of Misrule is a tradition that goes back to the Romans and their Saturnalia festivals.'

'Perhaps even further back than that,' Miss Charlotte added.

'A servant becomes king for the night.'

'All must obey his commands. Even the king.'

'A villager becomes king for the night?' Faye clapped her hands together. 'That's perfect. We whizz down there, find out who's king, have a word, and get them to command the Holly King to bugger off and leave us in peace.'

'If we go anywhere near *that* ...' Miss Charlotte peered over the edge of the tower to observe the white soup below. 'There's a good chance we'll lose our minds. Those clouds create a plane between our reality and that of the demigods, and everyone inside them exists under the Holly King's control, in a kind of waking nightmare. He'll force them to revel in a hedonistic orgy the likes of which hasn't been seen in centuries. It's known as the Feast of Fools.'

'Orgy?' Faye grimaced. She'd read the word in some of the racier books she'd enjoyed recently. The idea of her friends and neighbours getting all debauched made her shudder. 'I'm all for letting your hair down, but they can keep their drawers on for a start.'

Miss Charlotte's eyes flashed. 'They're going to have the time of their lives, and tomorrow morning they'll think it was all a dream.'

'That sounds like a lot of magic.' Faye stared into the hypnotic white mist.

'More than anything we can manage, that's for sure,' Mrs Teach agreed.

Faye began pacing. 'Right. So, we draw him out. We do something to get the Holly King's attention and distract him, and then we help the villagers escape.'

'It's not as simple as that, poppet.' Mrs Teach clasped her handbag a little tighter. 'The feast will last until sunrise, at which point the Holly King will take back his crown. Until then, he won't let it out of his sight.'

'He's not going anywhere,' Miss Charlotte said. 'Not least because once the feast is over and he has the crown back, he'll end the ceremony with a blood sacrifice that will make him more powerful than ever.'

'Blood sacrifice?' Faye's mouth went dry. 'I'm thinking that won't just be someone pricking their finger, then?'

Miss Charlotte spoke plainly. 'The Lord of Misrule, after being king for a night, has his throat cut.'

Faye went a little faint. 'But that could be Bertie. It could be my dad. It *will* be one of the villagers. We ... we can't allow it to happen.'

'You're right, Faye, we cannot.' Mrs Teach looked to Miss Charlotte. 'But I don't think your father or Bertie are in any immediate danger. I think I know who the Holly King has chosen to be the Lord of Misrule.'

Faye was about to ask who when it came to her in a flash. Of course. It had to be him. Poor sod.

ɤ

The Holly King watched as the villagers stood in silent anticipation of the Lord of Misrule's arrival. All apart from Herbert Butterworth, who asked if he could go to the toilet. He silenced the boy with a glare.

The fairies buzzed around the rapt villagers, ensuring that everyone's wine goblet was full. They all drank greedily, the red liquid spilling from their lips. Filled with good cheer, many raised their goblets to their host.

This was more like it. The Holly King had missed this.

He thought back to his original worshippers and the days of reverence and adulation. And how it had all gone wrong. The people in the little mud huts had continued to worship the Holly King and his brother for centuries, though he could sense their resentment building, especially when it came to the sacrifices. At the beginning they had been so willing, but newer generations had begun to ask impertinent questions, challenging the authority of their demigods. The Holly King and the Oak King smote the troublemakers, of course, but still the dissent continued to fester.

Then some of the humans began to travel, despite all his warnings about the dangers of the wood, with its bears and bandits. And when they returned – admittedly fewer in number, and many of them missing significant parts of their bodies – they brought with them stories.

The Holly King didn't like stories.

Well, he liked them when they were about him.

Well, he liked them when they were about him *and* were complimentary.

These stories were new and far from flattering. They were about lands whose inhabitants did not worship the Holly King or the Oak King – they hadn't even heard of them! – and yet the light returned after winter all the same. It was almost as if they didn't need to fawn and offer sacrifices to these gods. In fact, they could reject these gods entirely.

That was enough for the Holly King. He would not tolerate any blasphemy. And so he wiped them out. All of them. Which, in retrospect, might have been a bit of a mistake, for a demigod without followers is not much of a demigod. And when the Oak King found out, he was furious. The brothers fought one last time, and this time it was to the bitter end for both. They destroyed each other, condemning themselves to the aether where they drifted for millennia, forgotten and lost.

But now the Holly King had returned, and he would not make the same mistakes again. This was a new start. A new era. His new reign began now.

'Herald.' The Holly King beckoned Finlay Motspur, one-man band and newly appointed herald. He wore the herald's cloak of holly proudly, though it hung strangely over his bass drum and cymbals. 'A fanfare for our lord's arrival.'

Finlay nodded, thought for a moment, then licked his lips and raised his flugelhorn. A slightly flat flourish of notes ensued as a figure on horseback emerged from the mist.

Eric Birdwhistle, Lord of Misrule, wore a robe of purple velvet, trimmed with gold and silver tinsel. He was draped in ribbons of every colour, and bells and jewels jangled on his sleeves.

Finlay Motspur brought his fanfare to a suitably regal end, and there was a brief, eerie hush as folk tried to make sense of what they were seeing.

It was broken by a cry of, 'Eric!' from Shirley Birdwhistle. She ran through the crowd to him, arms outstretched. 'Eric, where have you been?'

'Patience, my good woman.' The Holly King's booming voice shook the glass panes in the windows, bringing Shirley staggering to a halt. 'Your time will come.'

'Hello, Shirley, my love.' Eric wiggled his fingers in a wave as he slid from the horse. 'Look at me now. It's been quite a day.'

The Holly King knelt before the village postman. 'Eric Marlowe Birdwhistle. Servant of the people of Woodville, honoured courier of messages, sacred keeper of secrets. I hereby bestow upon you the title of Lord of Misrule.' Even though he was kneeling, the Holly King still loomed over Eric as he lowered the wooden crown onto his head. The thing twisted and creaked as it shrank to a perfect fit. The Holly King felt exposed without it on his own head, but he knew to be patient. Soon, he would be all-powerful.

'Until the sun rises, all my authority shall rest with

you. I willingly relinquish my power and defer to you in all matters.' The Holly King rose suddenly and bellowed, 'All hail the Lord of Misrule! Hip-hip!'

The crowd hoorayed three times, as was traditional, and more wayward notes of celebration burst forth from Finlay's flugelhorn.

'Drink, my friends,' the Holly King bellowed. 'Drink!'

And they did. The fairies ensured that they did. If a villager displayed any reticence to imbibe, then a fairy would flutter up to them and tip their goblet back until they were forced to gulp down the wine.

It wasn't long until all were under the Holly King's spell.

'Before we resume the feast, we have two matters to attend to. First, the terms of power must be witnessed by all present.' The Holly King pulled a scroll from within his cloak and unrolled it. 'Hear ye, hear ye! Let it be known that on this Yule night in the year nineteen hundred and forty, a Lord of Misrule hath been appointed. His name is Eric Marlowe Birdwhistle. Until the sun rises, all shall yield to his wisdom and obey his word. All present shall be compelled to do his bidding, however repugnant it may be. His lordship has full power and authority to break all locks, bolts, bars, doors and latches. During his reign, there will be gluttonous revels for all you lusty guts.' That got a cheer from the crowd. Wonderful. They loved him. The Holly King's heart swelled, and he grinned as he read on. 'Swearing, drunkenness and fighting are allowed and encouraged.' More cheers. What joy to be so beloved again. 'But be warned: kissing any maid, widow or wife – except to bid welcome – is forbidden without his lordship's consent and will be punished!' The women cheered at this one. 'His lordship retains these rights and privileges until the rising of the sun, at which point he will be paid an honorarium of five pounds and be relieved of his command, and so on and so forth ...' The Holly King hurriedly trailed off as he rolled up the scroll. 'All hail the Lord of Misrule!'

He bowed to Eric and the crowd stomped and applauded. Shirley wiped a proud tear from her eye.

'Your lordship, the second matter before the revels commence.' The Holly King loomed over Bertie, now pale in his gibbet. 'You have before you a villager who has committed a grave transgression. O Lord of Misrule, will you hear the confession of Herbert Butterworth and pass sentence upon him?'

Eric looked down at Bertie in his cage, shaking his head in disappointment. 'I shall,' he declared, and the people cheered their Lord of Misrule once more.

In his cage, Bertie turned pale and crossed his legs.

Should Old
Acquaintance Be Forgot?

At the top of Saint Irene's bell tower the three witches had heard enough.

Faye was pacing again. 'We can't enter that mist cos we'll go doolally. So how do we stop the Holly King?'

'We find the person responsible for starting all of this.' Mrs Teach patted gently at her hair in a vain effort to restore its natural shape. 'There's one shrill voice absent from all the babble below.'

'Pearl.' Faye had been listening out for her cousin, too. Her voice could carry across oceans, but she hadn't heard a peep from her.

'Indeed. She has no interest in the Holly King's silly party. He's just a means to an end. What she really wants is revenge on you, young lady.'

'She's most likely the one who sent Sid to kill us,' Miss Charlotte said. 'If we find Sid, we might find her.' She nodded towards the wood. 'He headed off in that direction.'

'What about the villagers?' Faye asked. 'What about Bertie and my dad?'

Miss Charlotte considered their options. 'We can either stand here and pout and whine and do nothing, or we can find the little minx responsible and wring her neck. What's it to be?'

'Do we have to wring her neck?'

'You don't. But I will. She owes me for this.' Miss Charlotte pointed to her eyepatch. 'The villagers will be fine until sunrise. That's when it gets really messy.'

'Do you think we can track Sid down by then? He's a trained soldier, y'know.'

'I might have only one eye and be in constant agony, but no prey has ever escaped me yet.'

Faye shuddered. 'I'm glad you're on our side.'

'You should be.'

A raucous cheer came from the village.

Faye sagged against the crenellations, her heart heavy as she peered into the mist. 'I can't do it. I can't leave Bertie, Dad and our friends down there.' She turned back to Miss Charlotte and Mrs Teach, lifting her chin and doing her best to stiffen her resolve. 'You two go and find Sid. I'll take care of His Beardiness. If this Lord of Misrule has the crown, then maybe I could get my hands on it and destroy it?'

Mrs Teach tilted her head at an angle perfected specifically to deliver patronising advice. 'Faye, darling, I don't think that's a very good idea, do you?'

'Leaving them to suffer feels like a worse one.'

'You are familiar with the song "Auld Lang Syne", yes?'

Faye squinted one eye. 'What on earth's that got to do with old holly knickers?'

'The song asks if we should forget the past,' Mrs Teach said, 'and answers with a resounding no. The Holly King's métier is to dredge up the past and humiliate his victims with their forgotten wrongdoings. He has a long memory, and he never forgets.'

'*Should old acquaintance be forgot?*' Miss Charlotte mused. 'Nine times out of ten they most definitely should.'

'Legend has it that the Holly King would come upon a Yule night and beguile folk with his songs and gaiety, but after drinking his wine—'

'*Never* accept food from anyone from the other side,' Miss Charlotte interjected, ignoring a glare from Mrs Teach at the repeated interruptions. 'In fact, never accept any favour from any of that lot. There's always a catch. Apologies, Mrs Teach, continue.'

Mrs Teach made a little noise of disapproval at the back of her throat. 'After drinking his wine, people would find themselves compelled to make accusations and confess to sins. There's a description in the writings of Wilfred of Cirencester, a travelling scribe who came here in the Middle Ages, of a snowstorm that descended upon the village and drove everyone mad.'

'There's a reason it's called the Feast of Fools,' Miss Charlotte added. 'The new plane created by the mist and the Holly King's heady wine make people think they're in a dream. They do things they would never normally do in polite company.'

'Like what?' Faye grimaced.

'Best not to ask. Ouch. Oh, bloody hell.'

'Ouch?'

'I just winked with my bad eye. Look, the truth is, no one in living memory knows what it's actually like, but the Holly King is a degenerate muckraker who delights in sowing discord. I wouldn't want to endure whatever's going on down there.'

'But I ain't got nothing to be ashamed of,' Faye shrugged.

Mrs Teach arched an eyebrow. 'There's always something.'

'There's that business with me mum's book, I s'pose, but you lot already know about that. And I've done some quite passionate canoodling with Bertie, but I don't see anything wrong with that.'

Mrs Teach couldn't help but smile at such innocence. 'Faye, I'm warning you, he will dredge up *something* from your past. Something you will almost certainly have worked very hard to forget.'

Faye raised a hand. 'I've made up me mind. You two go and find Sid and stop Pearl. I'm going to crash the Holly King's little shindig and help our friends and neighbours.'

Mrs Teach was about to object again when Miss Charlotte intervened. 'You know, I think she's right. Faye is the only one of us who might be strong enough to make it through that fog with all her marbles intact.'

Mrs Teach tightened her lips. 'Very well. But before you do, Faye, see if you can get to the telephone box at the top of the Wode Road. Call Vera and the cavalry. We're going to need all the help we can get.'

Faye gave a thumbs-up. 'Wilco.'

Miss Charlotte turned her one-eyed glare on Mrs Teach. 'I thought *you* were going to report to Vera?'

Mrs Teach raised her chin. 'It may have escaped your notice, but things have been rather hectic today. When have I had a minute to make telephone calls?'

'I've been working under the impression they were already on their way.'

'I'm afraid they are not,' Mrs Teach said, with just enough defiance to almost convince Faye that she wasn't afraid at all.

Miss Charlotte set her jaw before muttering, 'We'll just have to do this on our own, then.'

'I'll make the call, Miss Charlotte,' Faye reassured her. 'Don't you worry.'

Charlotte rested her hands on Faye's shoulders and looked her in the eye. 'Faye, before you step into the mist, consider this: we think we know people, but we don't. Even our closest loved ones keep secrets from us, and that's a good thing. If we knew everything about everyone, we would never be able to like or trust anybody. Whatever you discover in there, just remember the good things about the ones you love. The good usually outweighs the bad.' She bobbed her head from side to side. 'Usually.'

Faye nodded, recalling the time she had pinched a

toffee from her dad a few Christmases ago, and wondering if that might come up.

'This may all be academic if we can't answer one simple question.' Mrs Teach gestured at the mist below, which now completely surrounded the tower and cut off the path to the woods. 'How *does* one get through a supernatural fog of considerable viscosity without losing one's marbles?'

'We go over it,' Faye grinned. 'You've not flown with me yet, have you, Mrs Teach?'

'Oh, good grief.'

Run Like Hell

Sid loved running. In training the others had complained about cross-country running – which they'd had almost every day, whatever the weather – but not Sid. He'd wanted more. When Sid was running, he found peace. The rest of the world could go hang. There were no voices in his head. No feelings of emptiness or guilt. Everything was drowned out by the rush of blood in his ears and his heart bashing at his ribcage.

He ran at Dunkirk. From the enemy and their tanks, planes and bullets. He ran from those begging for help, from people bleeding in the streets. He hadn't allowed himself to be distracted. Just him and the road as the war raged on all sides. Running kept Sid alive, and he wondered if that's why they did so much of it in training. Did the top brass know that their men would spend so much time on the run? Here's how to stick a Nazi with a bayonet, lads. And here's how you run like hell when the tanks start rolling. Sid had run until he'd reached the beach, and a little part of him had wanted to keep going into the Channel and all the way to Dover. He'd watched as a few soldiers tried to swim home. One was cut down by a diving Stuka bomber. Another quietly slipped beneath the waves. They returned with the tide the next morning. Bobbing about face down in the shallows, unsure if they were coming or going. Alfie told Sid that drowning was painful. How he knew this wasn't entirely clear, but Alfie rarely elaborated on his idle musings.

Alfie went away when Sid ran. He never had been much cop when it came to cross-country. All those fags had him coughing his lungs up half the time.

The silence in the wood was peaceful. Sid kept running. He had no idea where he was going, but it didn't matter. It was as if the trees had moved around to create a running track for him, and he gave thanks for it. His legs moved in a steady rhythm. Double time. He could do this for hours. No pain. No hurt. No guilt.

Only the path, the wood and the woodwose standing at the bend.

Sid's breath caught and his skin became suddenly clammy. He banked to dodge around the creature, but his knee gave way and he tumbled to the ground, rolling into a puddle of cracked ice. The chill water slid down his back, and he could only lie there, winded, his lungs burning, legs aching and skull thudding in time with his heart.

In the thin moonlight, the woodwose glowed like a spectre. Sid could see right through its muscle and sinew to the trees beyond. The woodwose silently offered Sid his oak club once more.

It was time. Sid wanted it. He knew that if he took it, he would be strong again. He could save his father and ...

Sid reached for the club, but it slipped through his fingers. He tried again, but it was ghostly, insubstantial. Sid lowered his head and slowly shook it from side to side.

His face still and inscrutable, the woodwose withdrew the club and raised it like a sword, tilting his head back and emitting a wordless cry. The short, startling noise reverberated around the wood, shaking snow from the bare branches. Chest heaving, he turned to face Sid again before melting into the darkness. The last things to disappear were those cold, black eyes.

'Hey, kid!' A new voice broke the silence. It was a woman's, American, like someone from a movie. Accompanying the voice was the sound of boots moving through slush. They stopped at Sid's side.

A young woman dressed in a mess of flowing lace peered down at him. Sid's mind reeled as it tried to make sense of who she was and how she had got here. She had hazel eyes and light brown skin and, despite her smile, looked royally pissed off.

'I'm Pearl. Merry Christmas.' She waggled her fingers in a jolly greeting, but Sid's eyes were drawn to the dagger on her belt. He tensed. 'Who was your friend?'

'It's called a woodwose.' Sid heard Alfie step out of the shadows behind him. 'He's this big hairy fella—'

249

'I know what a woodwose is.' Pearl cut Alfie off, turning to look into the gloom where the woodwose had faded away. 'I want to know what he is to Sidney here.' Pearl circled the puddle, and Sid saw something on her back that looked like wings. Broken wings.

'He's haunted Sid since Dunkirk,' Alfie told her. 'Sid thinks he can run away from him, but what he ain't figured out yet is that no matter how far he runs, the woodwose will never go away.'

It was like Alfie had plucked the thoughts straight from Sid's mind. Was this how to talk to fairies? Through a figment? Or were they both figments? Sid's head began to sway. His vision drifted in and out of focus.

'He's always been like this, Pearl.' Alfie scratched his chin. 'Running from his troubles. Never ready to face his mistakes.'

Pearl put a hand to her mouth in a mockery of shock. 'What're you sayin'? He's a coward?'

'Look at him.' Alfie gestured to Sid as he lay sprawled on the ground. 'His fear cost many a life over there, Pearl. Including mine.'

'But *he's* still alive and kickin'.'

Pearl and Alfie had been standing side by side. Sid watched, horrified, as Alfie began to dissolve into the darkness and Pearl stepped into the place where he had stood. For a brief moment their two images were overlaid, their lips moving in time as they both spoke the same words.

'You're ... you're him?' Sid gasped. 'No. You can't

be. Alfie's been with me since ... since Dunkirk. You're new, but ...' He dabbed his finger at her. 'You're real?'

Pearl smiled as she spoke the words he'd heard from Alfie so many times. 'Why you, Sid? Why are you still alive when so many others have died? Good, honest men, with loving families. Better men than you. What makes you so special?'

Sid lay in the dirt. He knew she was right. He was nothing. A failure. He didn't deserve to live. Barbed wire tightened around his heart and a sob burst from his lips. He curled into a ball. He wanted it all to end. If he just closed his eyes tight enough ...

'What if I could help you, Sidney?' Pearl crouched beside him and stroked his hair. 'Lord knows why I'd want to. You've let me down. But what if I could make it stop hurting? What if I could take all the things that don't make a lick o' sense and give them meaning? Would you like that?' Her voice was softer, almost kind, but he could still feel the poison underneath. 'But you gotta do something for me, Sid. You see, I gotta problem with this guy I know. We were working on a fun little Christmas party together, but he got all het up and angry and ...' She looked around, as if afraid to speak, leaning closer to him. 'I think he's gonna hurt me. He wants to pluck my pretty head from my shoulders and crush it into dust. His words, Sid. You wouldn't want that, would you, honey?'

Sid shivered. His eyes opened. He looked up into Pearl's face, blurred through his tears. She had Alfie's mild brown eyes. He could have sworn they were hazel earlier.

'And he don't just wanna hurt me, Sid. No. He's got your pop. That's right. As soon as the sun rises, he's gonna cut your daddy's throat.'

Sid tensed, wanting to run but not knowing where to go.

Pearl brushed his hair back from his brow. 'Hey, hey, take it easy, honey pie. There's still time. You can save me and your father, Sid. I can help you do it.'

Sid's voice cracked. 'How?'

'Here's the thing, sugar beet. You can't do it like this. I look at you and I see a boy who's scared and all messed up by guilt and shame.' She gently took his arm and drew him close to her. 'But there's something inside of you. And I can bring it out. It'll do what needs to be done. No hesitation. No remorse. Your daddy will live, your slate will be wiped clean, and you can run in these woods without a care in the world. That's what you want, isn't it, sweetie pie? To run and never stop?'

A calm settled in Sid's mind.

'What do I have to do?'

THE TRIAL

Someone had found Eric Birdwhistle a gavel. He sat in an ornate red leather wingback armchair that had been dragged from Mr Brewer and Mr Gilbert's antiques shop. Bertie noted that both men were absent from the revels. Mr Brewer was staying with Mr Gilbert at Hayward Lodge to oversee his recovery, putting them well outside the village boundary. He envied them.

'That's a bit off, isn't it?' Bertie objected. 'You can't just go rummaging through other people's property like that.'

'Silence, Bertie.' Eric banged his gavel on the little wooden paw at the end of the arm of the chair. Bertie winced to think what that might do to the resale value. 'I would remind you that I have the authority to break any locks and doors I please.'

'And it's only fitting that the Lord of Misrule should have a seat worthy of his status.' The Holly King gave Eric an obsequious smile, before snapping his fingers. 'The accused will now stand.'

Bertie shrugged from where he lay in the cramped confines of his gibbet.

'You two.' The Holly King picked out Mr Loaf and Mr Baxter in the crowd. 'Prop him up.'

Bertie had heard about kangaroo courts from his father, who claimed his cousin Percy had come a cropper with one during the Great War. He wasn't entirely sure where the kangaroos came into it, but he feared that proper law and order were about to be chucked out the window.

Eric's throne sat before the Great War memorial, which made this all the more twisted. He was flanked by Shirley, who had the decency to look frightfully embarrassed by the whole thing, and the Holly King, who was loving every minute. Fairies fluttered about, their dimple-cheeked smiles striking Bertie as unsettling and sinister as they served more drinks to the gathered villagers. They'd foisted a goblet on him, too, and he'd taken it through the bars of the gibbet with a hasty smile and an excited nod before tipping the contents away when no one was looking.

Mr Loaf and Mr Baxter hurried over to the gibbet and lifted Bertie from his prone position to face his accusers. Now that he was upright, he could get a good look at the villagers. They all shared the same vacant expression. Slightly happy and befuddled. It unnerved him, reminding him of the first time he had seen his father drunk. He recalled the disturbing feeling he'd got from seeing someone he'd always relied on suddenly lose all reason and good humour. It was doubly unnerving being a child

254

and having no idea if the next thing he said would get him a chuckle or a clip round the ear'ole.

'All shipshape in there, Bertie?' Mr Loaf asked, his words gently bumping into one another. The funeral director was the most sober man in the village. It simply wasn't the done thing for a gent tasked with ushering people's loved ones into the great beyond to be too jolly, and he never had anything stronger than a small sherry whenever he came into the Green Man. Yet here he was. Sloppy grin and eyes askew.

'I'm fine, thank you, Mr Loaf.' Bertie did his best to remain upbeat. 'Nice to be the right way up.'

Mr Loaf turned his head, his eyes following half a second later. He half laughed at Bertie's little joke.

Bertie leaned forward. 'Though I might need to go to the lavvy soon, so it would be nice to—'

'Bertie needs to go to the khazi!' Mr Loaf cried, and the villagers roared with laughter.

Mr Baxter rapped his knuckles on the iron of the gibbet and cackled. 'Number oneses or number twoses?'

'Order!' Eric banged his gavel, but the laughter still burbled away. 'Order!'

'Silence!' the Holly King bellowed, making everyone jump. They all shut up.

Eric might be wearing the crown, but Bertie could see who was really in charge here.

'If I may begin the proceedings?' The Holly King bowed low before Eric.

'Please do.' Eric gestured towards Bertie. 'Why has this young man been brought before me?'

'If it please you, my lord, it is known that I am a gatherer of truths. It behoves the Holly King in his role as guardian to know all about those who reside in his domain. No one can keep their secrets from me.' He slowly turned his head to the villagers, who now looked rather less enthusiastic at the prospect of having their dirty laundry exposed to all and sundry.

The fairies circled above them, as if searching for the next to be accused.

'I have made a list, which I have verified not once, but twice. And it is my sad duty to report that this young man, Herbert Hercules Butterworth, has revealed himself to be nothing more than a snivelling coward.'

The fairies started hissing, gesturing for the crowd to join in. Bertie was dismayed to see just how many did so.

He twisted his lips and frowned. 'I ain't no war hero, but I do my bit. I—'

The Holly King waved him into silence. 'Tell us, Bertie. Tell us all.' He swept his huge, gloved hand around him. 'Tell us the sad story of your mother.'

Whatever water was in Bertie's bowels suddenly froze. He didn't need the lavvy quite so badly now.

'W-what about her?'

'She died a few years ago, I believe.' The Holly King's voice turned solemn as he sat down, crossing his enormous legs. 'Cancer, wasn't it?'

Bertie's mouth was dry. He could only nod as he dreaded where this was going.

'Patricia Gabrielle Butterworth, née O'Farrell.' The

Holly King swirled her name in his mouth as though he were tasting a fine wine. 'She loved you, Bertie.'

Bertie felt numb. His feet were lead weights.

'And you loved her very much, didn't you?'

Bertie could only nod, turning his face away from the others.

'Then why did you not visit her in the hospital?'

'Dad . . .' The word came from Bertie's mouth with a croak. He thought of his father back at the farm, and what he might make of all this. Gulping, he tried again. 'Dad told me not to.'

'Are you lying to me, Bertie? You know what I think of lies. Tell me the truth.'

'I wanted to go.' Bertie felt a pain in his chest that he thought had gone for good. 'Then Dad came back from the hospital one night and said the mum I knew was gone. He said she was . . .' Bertie thought back to that night. The silhouette of his father in his bedroom door, bent and stooped like a man twice his age. 'He said she was barely there anymore. That she was empty, like a corn husk. That it were only a matter of time, and he didn't reckon I should see her like that. I wanted to go, I really did—'

'But you didn't, Bertie, you didn't. Why not?'

'Dad said I shouldn't.'

'You've defied your father before and since. Why not this time?'

Bertie felt his knees give way. If it wasn't for Mr Loaf and Mr Baxter holding up the gibbet, he would have toppled forward. He bowed his head, tears dripping to the slush. 'I was scared.'

257

'Imagine how scared your mother was.' The Holly King's voice remained soft. 'Lying alone in the dark, on the precipice of death, wanting nothing more than to see her little boy – her only son – one last time. But you, Herbert Butterworth, you expect us to believe that it was *you* who was frightened?'

Bertie looked up, his cheeks wet with tears. 'You bastard.' He sniffed and struggled to wipe his face dry. 'I was eleven.'

'Old enough to know it was wrong.'

'And I live with that every day. But even if I had gone, if I'd defied my dad, wouldn't you judge me for that, too?'

The Holly King's beard shifted as a slow smile crept across his face. 'Finally, Bertie ... finally, you understand.'

'Leave him alone!' a voice cried from the crowd.

Bertie could only turn his head so far, but out of the corner of his eye he saw Mr Paine and Mrs Yorke shoved aside as Terrence Bright limped forward on his dodgy knee to face the Holly King.

Terrence's eyes didn't have the same unfocused glaze as the other villagers'. Bertie wondered where he'd been while all this madness was unfolding. Then he remembered that Terrence regularly slept through air raids.

A fairy came fluttering to Terrence's side with a goblet of the Holly King's wine on a silver platter. He swiped it away and the platter flashed as it spun, clattering to the ground. He stood before Eric and the Holly King.

'Just who do you think you are, eh?'

'I am the Holly King.'

'Well, I ain't ever heard of yer.'

'Silence!' Eric banged his gavel.

'Oh, give it a rest, Eric. You of all people should show this lad some gratitude. Only yesterday, he was on patrol in the woods looking for whatever turned you into a gibbering wreck. Bertie's the first to volunteer for any dirty or dangerous work, so I won't have any of you accuse him of being a coward.'

Bertie could have hugged Mr Bright at that moment. If he wasn't in a cage. And if Mr Bright wouldn't have shoved him away because he hated hugs.

'He dishonoured his mother.' The Holly King's voice was loud as he spoke over Terrence's head to the attentive crowd. There were murmurs of agreement.

'And what if he did? Let's put aside the fact that he was only a child, confused and in bits because his dear old ma was about to die. So what if he was frightened and didn't know what to do? What business is that of yours? I'll answer that one for you, sunshine. None. None of your nosy rosy business.' Terrence turned to the crowd. 'We all do things we regret. That doesn't mean the whole world needs to know about it. There's a lot to be said for respecting people's privacy. For forgiving and forgetting. For leaving the past where it belongs.'

'Strong words for a man with such a ... colourful past.' The Holly King wore a knowing smile.

'I've got secrets, matey.' Terrence threw his arms

wide. 'Secrets and shame galore. You reckon you know my secrets? Good. If you like, we can start going through them right now. Do you want to go alphabetically or chronologically? I've got all night. You don't scare me, you big, hairy—'

Eric's gavel cut Terrence off.

'I have made my judgement and am ready to pass sentence.' Eric raised his chin and pursed his lips. He blinked rapidly, fighting the effects of the wine. His eyes darted about before finding a spot in the distance to focus on. Eric curled his lips in a smile. 'I find the defendant . . . not guilty!'

The crowd cheered.

'He is to be freed immediately.'

The Holly King made to protest. 'My lord—'

Eric waved him away. 'Bertie's a good lad, and Terrence is right. We all do things we regret. Release him now.'

The Holly King grimaced and gestured at the gibbet. The padlock clicked open and fell to the ground. Mr Loaf opened the squeaking door and Mr Baxter helped Bertie out. The lad flexed his uneven legs.

The villagers' cheers were silenced once more by Eric's gavel.

'I have one more judgement to make. Terrence Bright is found guilty of disrespecting the office of the Lord of Misrule. He will be excluded from tonight's feast and festivities.'

'Suits me,' Terrence muttered.

'What was that?' Eric squinted at him.

'Nothing.'

Eric pointed the gavel from Terrence to the gibbet. 'Put him in, gents.'

Terrence didn't protest as Mr Loaf and Mr Baxter ushered him into the iron cage.

But Bertie did. 'Eric, please—'

'Your lordship.'

'Your lordship, he was only sticking up for me.'

'I don't care, Bertie. I won't have rudeness.' Eric stood and addressed the crowd. 'Let the feast begin!'

The villagers roared as the fairies whooshed about, proffering teetering platters of food and drink. Mr Loaf and Mr Baxter locked Terrence into the gibbet, then dropped him to the ground as they hurried off to join the fun.

Bertie rushed to Terrence's side, cradling him in the gibbet as the older man winced from the fall. 'I'm so sorry, Mr Bright. I didn't mean for any of this to happen.'

'It's not your fault, son.'

'Thanks for sticking up for me.'

'Think nothing of it. Sorry I was late. I had a kip after closing, and when I woke up the whole village had gone stark raving mad.'

'Faye'll save us. I know she will.'

'Have you seen her, Bertie? Where is she?'

'She was with Miss Charlotte and Mrs Teach at Saint Irene's. They were having a bit of a kerfuffle with Sid.'

'Sid? I thought he was locked up in the chokey for the night?'

261

'I don't know nothing about that.'

'Are you all right, Bertie? You look like you're in pain.'

'Sorry, Mr Bright, but I really need the loo.'

'Then go! Use the one in the pub.'

'Ta very much. I'll be back in a jiffy.' Bertie limped off in the direction of the Green Man, glad to be free, but worried that Faye hadn't come to their rescue already. Where the blinking flip was she?

MISTY

Faye didn't have any change for the public telephone box at the top of the Wode Road, but there was a special number she could call that wouldn't cost her a penny.

She landed with Mrs Teach and Miss Charlotte by the bus stop, on the edge of the bank of mist. The telephone box was just a few yards away and Faye made it her first priority to call for help, as promised. Not the army or the Air Force, nor the police or the Secret Service. Fighting with rifles and bullets wasn't the answer. Only one particular emergency service would know what to do.

As Faye dialled the operator, she watched Mrs Teach and Miss Charlotte hurry off in the direction of the wood.

'Operator, how may I direct your call?'

'Westminster, six-one-six, please.' Faye bit her lip, hoping there wouldn't be any awkward follow-up questions.

'One moment, caller,' the operator replied, and the

line crackled. There was no ring tone. The receiver felt heavy in Faye's hand.

A loud electronic buzz startled her, hurting her ear. The buzzing cut off abruptly and a man spoke. 'Westminster, six-one-six. This is a secure line. You may speak freely.'

'I have an urgent message for Vera Fivetrees—'

'Is that the voice of Faye Bright I hear? I rather think it is!'

There was only one person Faye knew who asked and then answered his own questions. 'Bellamy Dumonde? Is that you?'

'As I live and breathe. How the devil are you, young lady?'

Faye brightened at hearing his voice. Only a few months ago, Bellamy had devised a ritual intended to thwart an impending Nazi invasion. It had got a bit hairy towards the end, but to everyone's astonishment it seemed to have worked.

'I'm tickety-boo, Bellamy,' Faye answered, in the manner of all British people when facing imminent disaster. 'Couldn't be better. How are you? They've got you on the late shift, then?'

'Indeed. I'm cooking up a few ideas to thwart the enemy. You know how it is. In fact, I've been meaning to run one or two of them by you. We might have a special mission for you, Faye Bright. Have you reconsidered Vera's offer?'

Faye tensed at the mention of special missions and Vera Fivetrees, but there was no time for that now.

'It's on the "to do" list, Bellamy, but this is a bit of an emergency.'

'Of course, of course. To what do I owe this surprising and delightful call? If you're after Vera, she's asleep in the cottage. Is it an emergency? Do I need to wake her?' He said this with a little too much eagerness. The pair had not entirely seen eye to eye, and Faye suspected there might still be some friction between them.

'Here's the truth of the matter, Mr Dumonde. When I said I was tickety-boo, well, that wasn't entirely true.' Faye took a breath and brought him up to speed on Eric's funny turn, the Holly King, Pearl, the sarcophagus in the crypt, Sid's attack, the Feast of Fools and the strange mist around the village. It all came out in one long babble. 'And once I'm done speaking to you, I'm planning to enter the mist to help the villagers, though none of us is entirely sure if that's a good idea or completely loopy, so there we are ...' Faye puffed out her cheeks, pleased that she had managed to summarise the palaver so succinctly.

The line crackled for a moment.

'Faye?' Bellamy's voice was small and distant. 'Are you still there? I heard "Here's the truth of the matter" and then it all went—'

The line clicked, and then died.

'Hullo?' Faye repeated this a few times and tried the operator again, but there was nothing. She looked up to find the telephone box shrouded in the icy mist.

'Oh, buggeration.'

It had sneaked up on her during the call and was now

creeping under the door of the phone box and pressing up against its windows.

Faye's heart began to race. She had envisioned taking her time before plunging into the mist. Having a little moment to prepare her mind before subjecting it to Miss Charlotte's promised 'living nightmare'. But now here it was, crawling up past her knees and filling the cramped booth.

'Sod it. In for a penny . . .'

Faye braced herself for the worst, swung the phone box door open and was immediately enveloped in white.

At once she felt a warmth wash over her. Muscles that had been tensed now relaxed. Her fingers tingled. She chuckled, and when she couldn't pinpoint a reason for the chuckle, laughed again. That laugh ended in a silly snort, and soon she was giggling uncontrollably. Giddy, she swaggered out through the mist in what she vaguely thought was the direction of the village, all her worries dissolving away into the haze. By the time she had taken a dozen steps, she had completely forgotten why she was there. And she couldn't care less.

A Soldier for the Wood

Sid followed Pearl through the wood. Those were definitely wings on her back. Broken wings. She hadn't said a word since they'd set off, and that suited Sid fine. As he tried to fathom who this overgrown fairy was, he wondered whether she could have been pretending to be Alfie all this time, or if she had somehow joined forces with him, or if Alfie had never been real at all. Ultimately, he wasn't sure how much he cared. That was another thing his training had hammered into him. Don't ask questions. Do as you're told. It didn't matter where Alfie was now, only that he'd shut his trap. It didn't matter who Pearl was, except she had promised to help his father and she seemed to have some kind of plan.

'Do you recognise this place?' Pearl came to a stop in a clearing and gestured to a large hollow oak tree. Sid rarely ventured into the woods, but he knew this tree. Everyone in the village did. As they approached, the wood fell silent, the waning moon their only witness.

The hollow oak wasn't as he remembered. It was scarred, a blackened wound running down its trunk. Slivers of charred bark lay scattered across the ground, mingled with broken branches.

'Struck by lightning?' Sid asked.

'Your pops was here when it happened.' Pearl stooped to pick up a branch. She turned it over in her hands, inspecting it closely. 'He was witness to the fight for supremacy between the Holly King and his brother, the Oak King.'

Sid looked about, as if he might find some evidence of his father having been here. His dad didn't like fights of any kind. He wondered if his old man had been scared.

Pearl carefully laid the branch in a specific place, shifting it back and forth in the snow until she was satisfied. 'Your father delivered the crown that rests on the Holly King's head. It's what gives him his power.' She gathered two more branches. 'No human has seen a demigod for generations. You should be very proud, toots.' She laid the branches in place and continued to search for more. 'This wood is very old, Sidney. One of the oldest in the land.' Sid watched as Pearl laid a final branch down. She had created a stick man among the roots of the hollow oak. Two arms, two legs, ribs, a spine. All that was missing was the head. 'It has a long memory. It remembers the old gods and the people who worshipped them. The blood of their sacrifices runs deep in its soil. The wood carries their voices within it if you know how to listen.' Pearl cocked an ear and

Sid did the same, but there was nothing other than the barest rustle of leaves and a faint ringing sound that had plagued him since that day in France with Alfie. 'What your daddy saw was the manifestation of a woodland memory. Ancient and forgotten demigods made flesh. The Holly King don't belong here no more, but if we don't stop him, he won't ever leave. He's trapped the villagers, playin' 'em all for saps. He's made your daddy king for a day, letting him wear the crown. While he does, the Holly King is vulnerable, but when the sun rises, he'll cut your daddy's throat and reclaim his crown and after that, there ain't gonna be any stopping him.'

Sid tensed. His first instinct was to run to the village and fight, but he wasn't dealing with soldiers in a pub, or even Nazis. Old gods and Holly Kings were beyond his understanding.

'I know, I know, it's a lot to take in.' Pearl raised her palms. 'But we can help each other, Sidney. We can save your father, and the village.'

'How?'

'The woodwose.' Pearl glanced down at the body she had constructed from the branches. 'There was a time when this wood was vast, covering every inch of the land like a blanket. And it had a guardian. Someone who protected it from the ravages of men and the whims of gods.'

Something in Sid perked up. 'Like a soldier?'

'I guess so. Yes. A soldier for the wood.' Pearl smiled as she sauntered closer to him. 'And we can bring him back.'

'Like you did with the Holly King?' Sid curled his lip. 'I'm not stupid, Pearl. If you know all about this manifesting of old gods, then I reckon you're the one who brought the Holly King back. And now he's threatened you, so you want rid of him.'

Pearl grinned. She gently pressed a hand on Sid's chest. 'What if I could gift you the powers and strength of a woodwose, Sid?'

'I can't.' Sid lowered his head. 'I tried.'

'What?'

'He offered me his club. I tried to take it, but it ...' Sid frowned, wondering how to explain what had happened.

'Let me guess. It slipped straight through your fingers, like it wasn't even there?' Pearl arched an eyebrow.

Sid nodded. 'How did you know?'

'You can't just *take* the club, Sid. You have to earn it. The woodwose has had many names – Enkidu, pilosi, salván, leshy, orke – but the ritual is always the same. He's the wild man and guardian of the wood, and the only one with the ferocity to defeat the old gods. To gain that kind of power requires a sacrifice.'

Sid took a good look at the branches arranged on the ground. The long arms and hunched shoulders, like a child's drawing of a stick monster. He reeled, as if standing on the edge of a cliff, as a thought struck him. 'Are you ... going to turn me into a woodwose?'

'It ain't permanent. If I take a *teensy-weensy* bit of your human blood now, I can use it to turn you back. By sunrise, you'll be your old self again and your father – not to mention everyone else in the village – will be saved. You'll be a hero, Sidney.'

'How much blood?'

Pearl squinted and held her thumb and index finger half an inch apart with a grin. 'About a pint.'

'You're a witch, aren't you?' Sid got only a wry smile in response to that. 'Why don't you do your own dirty work?'

'Magic won't save your father, kid. Sure, it makes for a good distraction, but only brute force can stop a demigod like the Holly King. I can give you that strength.'

'Temporarily, you say?'

Pearl nodded.

Sid scratched his chin. 'I've been lied to so many times. *This won't hurt. It'll all be over by Christmas.* I'm not a fool. I know when someone's telling me only what they want me to hear rather than the truth. And I know that when a man fights, something changes in him that'll never be the same. I'll never be my mother's little boy chasing birds and butterflies again. I'm not even the lad who volunteered anymore. He's long gone. I'm just the mess you see standing here now. So don't lie to me.'

Pearl folded her arms and raised her chin. 'All right. There's a good chance it'll change you. Your mind might never be the same, but I'm thinking you're in need of a change of mind. I promise you this, kid. I will make you whole again.' She looked up at the moon. 'The transformation takes a while, sugar. If we delay any longer, you're gonna be late. Your pops will die, and the only choice you'll have left will be how to explain to your mother that you had the chance to save him but didn't.'

'You ain't got nothin' else planned, have yer?' Once again Alfie stood on the periphery of Sid's vision, hazy through cigarette smoke. 'Here's the deal, sunshine. Do this, and you and me are quits. The slate'll be wiped clean, and you'll never hear from me again.'

'And what's in it for you?' Sid asked out of the side of his mouth, one eye on Pearl as she waited for him to make a decision.

'She's told me if I can get you onside, then she'll show me the way to paradise. Can't say fairer than that.'

'You're her, aren't you? You've been mucking me about all this time.'

'Maybe I'm you, Sid? Ever thought of that? I'm a part of you that let her in. A part of you that wants to hear what she has to say. Don't matter either way. We all know you've come too far to turn back now. Like she said, think of your dear old ma. You've had more than your fair share of luck. It's time to pay the piper, Sidney, my lad.'

Sid looked back into the dark of the wood. The path to the village was lost in the gloom. He turned to Pearl. 'How do we do it?'

THE GREAT
PYRAMID OF BOOZER

Faye had never been happier, though she couldn't explain it. Meandering through the mist, hands stuffed into the pockets of her flight jacket, she was simply content to be alive. Any cares and worries could wait, not that she could recall a single one of them. And you know what? It didn't matter. She whistled 'Jingle Bells' as she went, bobbing her head from side to side. The mist began to clear, revealing the Green Man pub at the top of the Wode Road. 'Oh,' she said, surprising herself. 'I'm in the village. Okey-dokey.'

The sound of music mingled with cheers and laughter from somewhere down the road.

'Ooh, a party.' Faye smiled, clapping her hands together. 'I wonder if I'm invited?' She chuckled and resumed her whistling, slipping slightly on the icy road as she moseyed on down the street.

☙

Bertie washed his hands with red carbolic soap in the Green Man's outside lavvy. He pondered his next move. Going back to the feast would mean he could keep an eye on Terrence and step in if there was any further danger. Though Bertie had to admit that he wouldn't be much use when it came to a showdown with a demigod. And the gibbet was most likely the safest place for Terrence to be. Bertie had got a few bumps and bruises during his time in the cage, but it had also saved him from broken bones and worse more than once. No, Bertie needed help. Magical help. He didn't know where Faye and the others had gone after their showdown with Sid at the church, but he had to find them.

Bertie dried his hands on an old tea towel that Terrence had hung on a hook on the lavvy door. As he put it back, the door opened a crack and he saw it.

A fairy was searching the backyard. Small and cherubic, it was dressed in ragged lace, grey and dirty where it had dragged along the pavement. It sported a tightly tied festive red ribbon in its blonde hair. Its blank, doll-like face wore a fixed grin, but its eyes lolled about in their sockets. The *sfumato* fuzz around it made it look like something from his nightmares. The thing floated between the stacked crates, wings thrumming, its pudgy little hands extended like a predator's claws.

Patience, Bertie, he told himself, trying to stay calm as the fairy drifted about. It stopped for a moment and lowered its hands, gazing slack-jawed at the vast white mass of icy cloud on the other side of the wall.

Constantly undulating, the cloud looked like a wave on the verge of crashing down. Bertie wondered how dense the mist was and longed to jump through it to freedom. *Patience, Bertie.*

The fairy's shoulders jerked as it chuckled to itself. Its wings flapped harder, and it started for the gate. Just a few more seconds and it would be gone.

Bertie took a step back into the shadows of the indoor loo, but as he did so his heel kicked against an empty tin of whitewash. Bertie couldn't be sure if it was in fact the loudest noise ever recorded, but in that moment it blimming well felt like it. The lavatory walls acted as a kind of echo chamber, boosting the volume of the impact.

The fairy snapped its head around, leaning forward as it flew to investigate.

Bertie pressed his back against the brick wall, wishing he could conjure up one of those glamours that Faye had told him about and disappear from sight. Instead, he tucked himself behind the door as far as he could and held his breath. The patch on his head where Sid had cut off a handful of hair started to throb.

The fairy's wings flapped intensely, making the air vibrate. It hovered half-in, half-out of the doorway as it peered inside and inspected the lavvy, its eyes drifting down to the toilet bowl.

Where Bertie's terrified expression could be seen reflected in the water.

'Bugger,' he said as the fairy lunged at him, hissing and baring its teeth. He pushed the door hard, squashing the creature against the frame. It cried out, grasping at him with little sausage fingers. The sound coming from its mouth became an inhuman, gasping rattle, and Bertie knew it was only a matter of time before its fellow fairies heard it and came to its aid.

He grabbed the fairy by the ribbon on its head and threw it against the cistern. As the thing continued to thrash about, he shuffled out of the door and pressed it shut quick smart.

There was no lock on the outside of the lavvy, and the fairy's wailing intensified as it barged against the door. Bertie looked around desperately, his eyes landing on a nearby stack of crates. He could use them to blockade the door and trap the fairy inside. He reached out for the crates, his fingers brushing against them. They were tantalisingly close, but not close enough.

The fairy was throwing itself against the door with a rhythmic regularity now, each crash accompanied by a furious cry. Bertie found the rhythm and waited for the right moment. *Smash-cry-beat*, *smash-cry-beat*, *smash-cry*-now! He lunged for the crates, yanked hard and leapt away as they came crashing down. They blocked the door. Almost. It juddered as the fairy barged it open an inch, its fingers wriggling out and grasping the door's edge. Bertie got onto his knees and gave the crates a shove, slamming them against the door. The fairy let out a strange whinny as it withdrew its fingers.

Bertie got to his feet, hobbled over to the side gate and opened it a crack. The feast was in full swing.

Fairies buzzed around with their silver platters of food and drink. Tables had been dragged from the surrounding houses out into the street, and Mrs Pritchett was dancing to Finlay Motspur's best rendition of 'Knees Up Mother Brown', a cacophony of fiddle, bass drum, hi-hat, clapping and whooping. They had been making their own racket. No one had heard Bertie struggling with the fairy.

But if Bertie could see them, then they might see him. He had to find another way.

He turned to face Terrence's Great Pyramid of Boozer. An unstable triangular stack of empty crates awaiting collection by the brewery. They were pushed against the backyard's wall, beyond which was the rippling cloud.

Bertie flexed his fingers. Fortune favours the bold and all that.

He clambered up onto the first crate, which wobbled beneath his uneven legs. He waited until it steadied before moving on to the next, but that one slipped and caused the whole edifice to shimmy. Bertie splayed his arms out like a tightrope walker. On the other side of the wall was a lamp post. Once he got within reach of that, he could slide down it and be on his way, but he still had half a dozen crate steps to go.

The outdoor lavvy door was banging again, gradually inching open as the fairy smashed into it over and over.

Biting his lip, Bertie threw caution to the wind and hopped up the next two crates. This was when he realised that he might have been better off taking the risk of slipping out of the side gate, and the thought annoyed him because now he would make just as much noise getting down as he would going up.

'Onwards and upwards, Bertie,' he muttered as he tentatively placed a foot on top of the next crate. It felt firm. Didn't budge. He put his weight on it. The pyramid swayed like a ship at sea. The top of the wall was within reach and Bertie hurled himself onto it, swinging his legs over. He leapt from the wall to the lamp post and slid down into the alley behind the pub.

'Job done.' Bertie dusted his hands. Just then a noise like a Luftwaffe bombing raid came from over the wall as the crates crashed down. 'Oh, bugger.'

He scurried along the alley into the mist, realising as soon as he did so that he'd made a terrible mistake. A crushing despair bore down on him out of nowhere. Voices in his head berated him to turn back immediately. Visions of Terrence, bleeding and battered in his gibbet, flashed before his eyes.

Bertie kept moving. He knew magic when he saw it. The Holly King's mist closed in on him, thickening until he was completely blinded.

'Turn back!' the voices whispered, swirling around him. 'There is nothing you can do. You are nothing. There is only pain ahead of you.'

'No!' Bertie cried, his words deadened by the fog. 'You can't stop me. I'm not listening!'

'Pain, only pain ...'

'Shut up!' Bertie balled his fists and kept running.

The alley would end soon, and he could find a path that led to the church.

He stumbled into a dustbin, sending it clattering like the London Philharmonic's percussion section tumbling down a stairwell.

'Sod it.' He righted himself and picked up the pace, running blindly onwards.

'Pain! Pain!' the voices around him cried, but he ignored them.

There was something up ahead. A shape floating in the air. It was coming directly for him.

Before Bertie could stop, there was a blinding white flash as he was punched in the face by the fairy with the red ribbon. It had escaped and hunted him down.

He fell back, clutching his nose, warm blood seeping through his fingers.

The fairy cackled with glee. Wings beating hard, it grabbed Bertie by the hair and dragged him back to the village.

℘

The Wode Road was on an incline, which did little to help Faye's overwhelming sense of discombobulation as she approached the revels. The first thing that made her mind wobble was the sight of little fairies flying about, dispensing food and drink to all. Faye put them to one side for the moment, as she couldn't quite cope with that just yet.

Eric Birdwhistle sat on a throne, bedecked in purple robes, his wife Shirley by his side. Both wolfed down chicken legs like they were Tudor royalty. Eric wore a crown of oak and holly, which suddenly felt important, though Faye couldn't quite recall why. The Holly King sat beside them, keeping a watchful eye on the feast. And what a feast it was.

Tables were set out for a street party, though they sat askew with little thought given to presentation. They creaked under the weight of food and drink. Dishes heaped with roasted chickens and geese, sausages, onion stuffing, mountains of spuds, Christmas puddings with rum sauce galore, bananas and apples, and biscuits and cheese. It was a free-for-all and everyone's plates were piled high.

Faye couldn't help but giggle to herself to see her neighbours letting themselves go. This was hardly the bacchanalian orgy she had worried it would be, though from the vacant looks on everyone's faces it was clear they were all under the Holly King's spell.

Mrs Pritchett played an upright piano that Faye thought she recognised from the saloon bar of the Hand and Heart, Woodville's less salubrious pub, albeit home to an excellent darts team. Finlay Motspur kept time with the *boom-tish* of his one-man-band bass drum and cymbals. Mr Loaf played his fiddle as if in competition with the devil himself. Mrs Nesbitt – one of the oldest women in the village, who wouldn't normally say boo to a goose – was dancing around the piano in what looked like an attempt at the Lindy Hop. She whooped and cackled raucously, occasionally flashing her bloomers.

Miss Burgess was arm-wrestling Mr Hodgson and winning. She was cheered on by Mrs Yorke from the bakery who, from the look of her rolled-up sleeves, was next in line.

Doctor Hamm was stuffing his face with Christmas pudding, as were Constable Muldoon and family in between tearing open their Christmas gifts of rag dolls, slippers, tin soldiers and a pink blouse.

Betty Marshall and Milly Baxter – or, as Faye thought of them, the terrible twosome – were giggling as they showed Milly's younger sister, Dotty, how to light a cigarette like Greta Garbo. Faye looked for Mrs Baxter to give them a telling off, but she was laid out on a table, snoring like a steam train, an empty wine bottle in her hand.

Reverend Jacobs sat alone, wild-eyed and presumably having some crisis of faith as he nursed a sherry. This wasn't helped when Edith Palmer, volunteer ambulance driver and his lodger at the vicarage, flung herself down next to him and squeezed his knee. He froze like a rabbit caught in headlights.

Miss Gordon had her archery kit out and was taking aim at an apple placed on the top of Mr Baxter's head. He was giggling like a loon. She was wavering like a willow in the wind.

Close by, Miss Moon and Miss Leach, long-time companions, sat together swaying gently to the music. They looked into one another's eyes and kissed tenderly.

Mr Paine – the tall and broad ARP man and news-agent for whom Faye had the utmost admiration, and not just because he gave her sherbet lemons when they were on duty together – teetered down the road with a vacant stare, gripping a bottle of stout and muttering, 'Put that light out,' over and over.

Captain Marshall and the Morris Men danced in a frenzy, circling and whirling like dervishes as the fairies hovered above them, clapping faster and faster, urging them on with wicked grins. Sweat dripped down the faces of the Morris Men, their bells jangling louder and their sticks clacking harder as they built to an almighty crescendo.

The world around Faye tilted, and she thought she might pass out. The happy delirium she had experienced in the mist had become a kind of insanity, and she was on the verge of letting it sweep her away when she heard a voice call out to her.

'Faye!'

It was Bertie.

Faye spun to see a grim-faced fairy with a red bow in its hair pulling the lad along by his ear.

Faye sobered up like someone had thrown a bucket of cold water in her face. That's why she was here. To save Bertie. To save the villagers from the Holly King.

'Bertie, you're out of that bloody gibbet!' Faye ran to him, but the fairy buzzed between them, its little fists raised.

Faye was about to give it what for when she noticed Bertie stiffen, his eyes sliding to something over her shoulder. She realised the sounds of the revelry had faded away, leaving an eerie quiet.

She slowly turned to find the party had ground to a halt. Everyone was staring at her, including her father, who gave her a meek wave from inside the gibbet.

'Oh, blinkin' flip, Dad. How'd you end up in there?'

He shrugged, at least as much as a man could when encased in iron. 'Long story.'

'I'm all ears. I want a word with you, by the way.' Her mind might still have been a bit fuzzy, but she had questions for him about her mother and Pearl. Terrence looked suitably worried and shrank into his cage.

The Holly King stepped down from the war memorial, a sly grin rustling his beard. 'Faye Bright. I hadn't expected to see you again.'

Any certainty Faye had felt about destroying the crown and saving the villagers crumbled as the demigod loomed over her. Had he grown again? She raised her chin and forced a measure of defiance into her voice. 'I'm like a bad penny, sunshine. Better people than you have tried to kill me and failed.'

'Indeed. Nevertheless, I'm so glad you're here. Now the real jollity can begin.'

BECOMING WOODWOSE

Sid lay among the roots of the hollow oak, the wooden bones of the Oak King arranged around him. It was cold and wet in the snow, and he was beginning to think he had made a terrible mistake. Pearl had taken an awful lot of blood, cutting his arm and squeezing it into a tartan Thermos flask, of all things. The wound throbbed and his mind drifted, threatening to float away entirely.

Pearl circled around him, swinging a black candle on a string. The flame was green and left strange streaks on his eyes in a colour that he had never seen before. She spoke words that Sid did not understand in an urgent whisper, as if she was in a hurry, though Sid felt like he had been lying there for ages.

Enough was enough. It was time to get up and go home.

Only he couldn't.

His limbs were heavy and numb. He made to raise an arm, but it wouldn't budge. He tried wriggling his

285

fingers and toes. They tingled with cramp and stiffened. His heart began to race and his chest tightened. He struggled to breathe.

'Stop, please stop, I've changed my mind, please, I'm begging you, stop,' was what he meant to say, but all that came out was a series of incoherent moans.

Pearl continued reciting her strange words while raising a finger to her lips – *shh* – and giving him a sickening smile.

Something just out of sight made a snapping noise, followed by a groan. Sid tried to move his head to see, but by now he could barely blink.

He looked on, helpless, as above him the roots of the hollow oak shuddered into life, growing and wrapping around him in a terrifying embrace. Sid wanted to break free, but all he could do was spasm as they tightened their grip and dragged him under the earth.

※

There is no going back. He understands this somehow as the soil fills his lungs. He hears the song of the trees, mournful and poetic, old as time. He understands and promises to keep them safe. An ancient part of Sid is awakened. Something that lingers in all of us, from before we became human and scorned the living things around us. It steps forward, out of the darkness. The woodwose stands before Sidney Birdwhistle, offering his club. There is an unspoken promise. Sid takes the club, finally gripping it in his fingers. It is dry and heavy. Hard as granite and cool to the touch. His

*fingers entwine with the handle and the club completes
his arm. The woodwose draws Sid into his embrace.
Sid's hands sink between the woodwose's ribs. Their
hearts beat in time. He rests his head on the creature's
chest, but when he looks up, it is through those black
eyes. All his pain and rage are unleashed. His blood
boils, his muscles rip and tear and heal over and over.
His bones creak like the pine of a galleon's mast as they
grow and strengthen. His mind shrinks. Words elude
him. His mouth no longer forms speech. But he can
hear the footsteps of two women approaching. He can
smell their blood. He is hungry.*

℘

Mrs Teach struggled to keep up with Miss Charlotte,
even in her best winter walking boots. 'Do slow down,'
she called as she watched her fellow witch bound up
the woodland path with that ridiculous Samurai sword
strapped to her waist.

Charlotte took a breather, leaning against a tree
and drumming her fingers as Mrs Teach tottered
to catch up.

'I know you're in a hurry for vengeance, but I simply
wasn't built for running.' Mrs Teach skipped daintily
over an icy puddle.

'I'm not only after vengeance.' Miss Charlotte
sounded almost reasonable. 'We have to stop Sid from
doing something stupid. Again.'

The two witches resumed walking side by side.

'I don't blame you for wanting to get your own back.'

Mrs Teach glanced at her companion. 'Though you must admit, the eyepatch is rather fetching. You pull it off with élan.'

'I'd rather have two working eyes.'

'Of course. How badly does it hurt now?'

'Like a bugger.'

'More ointment?'

'Later. The pain sort of helps, if that makes sense?'

'None whatsoever. Still, no point dwelling on the past, as you said.'

'What's that supposed to mean?'

Mrs Teach did her best to look innocent. 'Are you suggesting there was an ulterior subtext?'

'I know that tone of voice, Philomena.'

'I merely think your advice to Faye was somewhat wayward. How does one learn from one's mistakes if one doesn't acknowledge them?'

'What if those mistakes *include* an inability to let go of the past?' Miss Charlotte's voice took on a spiky quality familiar to Mrs Teach. 'And what if that led to summoning a demon to resurrect a loved one, which in turn resulted in an attack on a village by a small army of scarecrows? Just hypothetically, of course.'

'Touché.' Mrs Teach cleared her throat. 'Nevertheless, I learned some important lessons from that episode, and I shan't forget them in a hurry.'

'I'm not saying we shouldn't learn from the past,' Miss Charlotte said, her voice softening. 'I'm simply saying that some of us – especially those of us who have been around the sun a few more times than most – might have changed over the years.' She pressed a hand to her chest. 'I know at least one hypothetical woman who won't be the same person she was when she made many of her hypothetical terrible lapses in judgement.'

'I think the hypothetical lady doth protest too much.'

'Maybe she does, but she's also happy to have outlived all of her accusers and since tried to be a better person.'

'One armed with a Samurai sword?'

'She's not completely stupid.'

'I suspect the Holly King is older even than you, dear.'

'That's why he has to go.'

Mrs Teach realised she must have pulled a face of disapproval, as Miss Charlotte snapped at her.

'What? You don't have anything to hide?'

'It's the bloodlust I find disturbing. Of course I have things I would prefer to keep to myself. We all do.'

'All except Faye, it seems.'

'She's young,' Mrs Teach said wistfully. 'She still has plenty of time to make her blunders. It's up to us to ensure she doesn't hurt anyone in the process.'

'I refuse to be anybody's nursemaid. She can look after herself.'

Mrs Teach shook her head. 'There you go again.'

'Where do I go again?'

'You have a distinct habit, Miss Charlotte, of putting distance between yourself and those who care for you.'

'Care for me? Why should *I* care—' Miss Charlotte crouched abruptly, drawing her sword.

Mrs Teach remained standing. 'What the devil are you—'

'Get down!' Miss Charlotte hissed. 'She's in the clearing.'

Mrs Teach hadn't paid much attention to their surroundings as they chattered and was quite surprised to find they were so close to the hollow oak.

'It's too late,' she said. 'She's seen me. Hello, Pearl. Out for a walk? Can't fly with broken wings, I suppose.'

The fairy stood her ground in the clearing, and as Mrs Teach approached, she noticed the branches arranged on the ground. 'Our friend the Oak King?'

Pearl's eyes flashed briefly with wickedness, and she shrugged. 'Had a little bust-up with his brother.'

Miss Charlotte, back on her feet, started to move clockwise around the clearing. 'And I suppose you had nothing to do with it?'

Mrs Teach took this as her cue to move anticlockwise – better to offer two slightly more difficult to hit targets than one – but something about the Oak King's remains puzzled her, and she kept her eyes on them as she went.

'It's not my fault they didn't get along.' Pearl's attention was fixed on Miss Charlotte, no doubt wondering what she was intending to do with that sword.

'Hasn't exactly gone to plan, though, has it?' Charlotte wore an I-told-you-so grin that Mrs Teach knew all too well. 'Must be quite galling.'

As she drew nearer, Mrs Teach crouched to take a closer look at the soil around the branches. It had been disturbed. All the snow and slush had melted away.

'Looks like your little lapdog has abandoned you to do his own thing. Must be humiliating to be left out in the cold. Again.'

Mrs Teach reached into the soil and took a handful. It was warm and soft and crumbled through her fingers.

'C'mon, Missy.' Pearl had her back to Mrs Teach as she followed Miss Charlotte circling the clearing. 'It's been a long night. Things were said, deeds were done, the Holly King wants me dead, and by now we all want the same thing.'

'I want revenge.'

'Revenge? The whole eye for an eye, tooth for a tooth thing? Where does that get us?'

'It gets me a little pouch full of your eyes and teeth.'

The ground beneath Mrs Teach began to tremble. The Oak King's wooden bones shook in an eerie dance. She rose and stepped back. 'Pearl, what have you done?' she demanded. 'Where's Sidney?'

Miss Charlotte looked towards Mrs Teach's feet and instantly understood. She readied her sword.

At that moment the ground burst open, throwing up clods of earth in all directions. A towering figure sprang from the chaos, muscle and sinew flexing as he gripped his club of ancient oak. His nostrils flared as he fixed on Mrs Teach's scent and went straight for her.

Mrs Teach made to run but stumbled on a root. She fell on her back, completely helpless.

'Woodwose!' The creature stiffened at once. Pearl's voice echoed again in the clearing. 'To me.'

It bowed its head and scurried to her side.

Mrs Teach, gasping for breath, propped herself up to get a better look at the thing.

It might once have been human. Covered from head to toe in coarse hair, its arms and legs were long and muscular, ending in fists the size of boxing gloves that looked like they could smash rocks into powder. Its jaw jutted outwards, revealing yellow incisors, and its brow was low and thick, like a Neanderthal's. Its dark eyes lay within deep sockets. Its nose was more of a snout, and wet as a dog's.

'Sidney?' Mrs Teach found her voice. 'What have you done to him?'

He stood two feet taller than Pearl, though with a gesture she brought him to his knees before her. 'I have given him purpose.' Pearl stroked the hair on the back of his head. 'As I was saying, honeys, we all want the same thing. The Holly King out on his ass. With the guardian of the wood on our side, we can make that a reality. I propose a truce. What do you say?'

THE TRUTH

Faye stood before the Holly King, hands on hips. 'Jollity? No, sunshine. It's time for you to sling yer hook.'

The Holly King frowned. 'Sling my ... ?'

'Scarper,' Faye clarified. 'Skedaddle, vamoose, bugger off. Leave!'

'Leave?' The Holly King swept a gloved hand towards the villagers. 'But our revels have just begun. You would deny these fine folks the feast they deserve?'

'The feast they deserve is a nice Christmas dinner with their loved ones. Not some half-arsed orgy.'

'And who are you to decide what's right for them, hmm?' The Holly King's eyes flashed and he raised a finger. 'I know. Let's ask them.' He drew himself up to his full height and clapped once.

The fairies took this as a signal to swoop low over the villagers, sprinkling some kind of glittering dust over their heads. They dodged Faye, but scattered handfuls over Bertie and her father in the gibbet, then

293

finally Eric and Shirley Birdwhistle. The villagers blinked and rubbed their eyes. Their vacant looks were gone, replaced by the kind of bloodshot bleariness that usually came with a thundering hangover.

'Good people of Woodville. There is one among you – Faye Bright here – who would bring the feast to an end. What say you?'

Unhappy grumbles rolled like thunder.

'It seems the villagers disagree, so—'

'They don't know you like I do.'

'Oh, I think we've come to know each other quite well.' The Holly King raised a goblet to the villagers, spilling red wine onto the snow. 'Haven't we?' The grumbles turned into cheers. The Holly King made to drink from the goblet, then paused. 'But how well do *you* know them, Faye?'

Faye peered over her specs, making sure to draw attention to her unimpressed half-mast eyelids. It's something she'd seen Bette Davis do in the flicks, and she'd been practising in the mirror. 'I've lived here me whole life, you great loon. These are my friends and neighbours.'

'Indeed.' The Holly King smiled like a card sharp. 'Then let's ask them how well they know you, shall we? Starting with the man of the moment, the Lord of Misrule.' The Holly King bowed before Eric as he sat in his throne. 'My lord, if you would be so kind as to share your unvarnished thoughts on Faye Bright.'

Eric looked doubtful for a moment, the glitter from the fairies still twinkling on his cheeks. He glanced at Shirley by his side. She nodded.

Eric took a deep breath. 'She's childish and needy,' he blurted out.

Shirley leaned over his shoulder, chin pointed at Faye. 'She talks too much and her voice makes me want to smash things.'

Faye puffed out her cheeks. *Okey-dokey. It's going to be like that, is it?*

'She's a witch and we hate her!' This screech came from Milly Baxter, which was no surprise.

'And she dresses like a boy,' added Betty Marshall, the other half of the terrible twosome.

'She's a brazen hussy,' Dotty Baxter chipped in, though Faye was sure that if she were pressed to explain what that meant exactly, young Dotty would struggle.

'She's too loud by half,' boomed Mr Baxter, with no sense of irony.

'And she's a bell-ringer,' one of the Morris Men said, getting jingles of agreement from his bell-bedecked colleagues in their ridiculous outfits.

'And an average ringer at that.' Mr Hodgson's eyes went wide, as if he couldn't quite believe what he had just said.

Neither could Faye. This was the first one that really hurt. Mr Hodgson had always sounded so encouraging when he was teaching her to ring.

'She's not half as good as she thinks she is and has much to learn.'

Faye's heart sank a little, but they were only getting started.

'She's too flighty by half,' Mrs Pritchett said. 'She needs to grow up, and quick.'

'Oh yes, she's very immature,' Miss Gordon added, her voice quivering.

Miss Burgess was more forthright. 'She thinks she's being cheeky, but she's just insolent.'

'She's reckless and lippy,' Captain Marshall said with a sneer.

'She's frightfully impertinent,' Reverend Jacobs said, getting a nod from Edith next to him. 'And she's a heathen.'

'Not to say disrespectful.' Constable Muldoon stood and wagged a finger. 'She needs to get a grip on herself and mind her p's and q's.'

'Her voice grates.' Mr Loaf's own voice cracked. 'And every time I hear her, I want to scream.'

'She's overfamiliar.'

Faye's cheeks reddened as she saw Mr Paine about to speak. *Not you, too, Freddie?*

'Every night we do ARP duty, she tells me all sorts of personal things that I have no interest in hearing, thank you very much. And she constantly scrounges sherbet lemons off me.'

This got an *Ooh* of disapproval from the crowd.

Faye wanted to scream that *he* offered them to her, but she held her tongue.

Mrs Brew, possibly the most good-natured and soft-spoken woman in the village, stepped forward, a sweet smile on her face. Perhaps now Faye would hear some words of kindness?

'She's a proper little bossyboots and a know-it-all cow,' Mrs Brew declared. She turned to the other villagers. 'And when she gets all hoity-toity, like she is right now, she's got a face like a slapped arse!'

Perhaps not.

Faye was familiar with the term *stiff upper lip*, but she'd never really appreciated its meaning until hers collapsed. Her bottom lip failed her, too. Together they formed a pout that wobbled like jelly in an air raid. Tears streaked down her cheeks, but she wasn't about to give anyone the satisfaction of wiping them away. She sniffed and raised her chin.

'Bertie?' The Holly King's voice cut through her. 'Is there anything you would like to say?'

Faye's eyes darted towards the lad. He shook his head, tight-lipped.

The Holly King snapped his fingers. Before Bertie could move, two fairies rushed at him. One pinched his nose until he gulped for air, then the other poured wine from a goblet into his throat. He choked and coughed up some of the red liquid, but more went in than came out.

'Faye!' Terrence cried, just as another pair of fairies raised a barrel over his gibbet, sending a torrent of wine cascading into his open mouth. He spluttered and spat the excess away, gasping for breath.

'Bertie?' The Holly King put an expectant hand to his ear.

The lad was trembling, the tendons in his neck straining as he tried to keep the words in. He gritted his teeth and held his breath, but it was no good.

'I love her,' Bertie said, his chest heaving.

Faye's heart warmed and she wanted to rush over to him and—

'But she don't half go on a bit, and sometimes I wish she'd dress more like a girl.' Bertie gasped at his own words before slapping a hand over his mouth.

Oh, Bertie. Faye had wondered why he kept pointing out dresses in magazines. She mustered all her dignity. 'Thank you for that, Bertie, and you're not wrong. I know I can waffle on at times. But I'll dress how I want if that's all the same to you?'

Bertie, hand still firmly clamped over his mouth, nodded.

Faye chuckled. Biting her lip and blinking away her tears, she flashed a smile at the Holly King. 'Is that it?'

'Terrence?' the Holly King asked.

Faye turned to her father, trapped in the gibbet, which was being propped up by Mr Loaf and Mr Baxter. Soaked in the Holly King's wine, his eyes were twisted shut and he writhed inside the cage in agony.

'Speak,' the Holly King urged him.

Terrence shook his head, tears leaking from his eyes.

'Leave him alone.' Faye put herself between the gibbet and the Holly King. 'You're hurting him!'

'The pain will not cease until he speaks.' The Holly King turned over his palms in an *I-don't-make-the-rules* gesture.

'Dad, it's all right.' Faye gripped the bars of the gibbet. 'There's nothing you can say that will upset me. Please.'

298

Terrence stopped shaking and opened his eyes.

'It's tickety-boo, Dad. Honest.'

Terrence blinked, glitter bright on his eyelids. His voice was barely a whisper. 'I love you, Faye. You know that,' he said, and Faye smiled back at him. 'I look at you and I see your mother. And sometimes it makes me happy. Other times it breaks my heart.'

Faye reached through the bars and took her father's hand. 'I understand, Dad, of course I do.'

'That's not all, is it, Terrence?' The Holly King beckoned as if to tease the very words from Terrence's mouth. 'Dig deeper, my good man. Tell her the whole truth.'

Terrence convulsed, his face contorted in agony.

'Terrence, my friend,' the Holly King spoke gently, 'the truth will end your suffering.'

'There are days ...' Terrence stopped himself, wincing in pain.

'Go on, Dad.'

'There are days ... if someone offered me a choice. If they said I could bring her back, or I could keep you ...' His eyes were red and brimming with tears. 'I'd choose her.'

The words sliced into Faye's heart. She knew it was true. She tried to say something, but to speak was an invitation to sobs and she didn't need that now. Not in front of these people and that overgrown Father Christmas. She glanced around. Bertie had his head in his hands. The other villagers looked on with an odd mix of defiance and shame, as if they knew they were doing a rotten thing, but were going to continue doing it because it was their bloody demigod-given right. Eric and Shirley led the way, puckering their lips in right-eous indignation. Only the Holly King and his fairies were smiling.

'Righto. I see.' Faye tried to ignore the swelling behind her eyes. She took a few breaths, her chest hitching. 'I came here to save you lot. To stand up to the Holly King and put a stop to all this madness. But it looks like you're all happy with things the way they are. So, if it's all the same to you, I'm going to be the immature child you all think I am, and I'm off to find a quiet place to have a good old-fashioned sulk.'

'Faye ...' Terrence's anguished voice pricked at Faye's ears.

'Dad.' Faye couldn't bring herself to look at him. 'Not now. I need a minute.' She wrapped her arms around herself and marched with uneven steps back up the road.

'Faye, we're sorry!' Bertie called after her. 'We really are, aren't we?'

No one replied.

Faye kept her head down, putting one foot in front of the other, unsure where she was going next.

Finlay Motspur's flugelhorn broke the silence, and the villagers cheered as their revels resumed.

AN EASY UNEASY TRUCE

Sid's mind was drowsy in the body of the woodwose. Or was it Sid's body still? Ransacked and transformed by magic into a vessel worthy of this savage woodland spirit. His bones ached to their marrow, his muscles burned with every move, but he fizzed with energy to spare and had to resist the urge to leap into the trees. Pearl would not like that. A scrap of Sid's mind knew he needed her to get back to his old self. He loped alongside the witches through the wood like a circus performer on stilts. At first, he had wobbled like a newborn deer, but before long he was moving surefootedly, weaving between the trees and using the club as a counterweight. The wood was alive to him in a way he had never dreamed possible. The tangy whiff of rabbit pellets at the foot of an ash. The lone, urgent chirp of a rudely awakened robin laying claim to a beech and its rusty remaining leaves. The hard scent of frost in shaded places where the sun never dared reach. A distant vixen calling for her mate, her cry as soulful as any song he had ever heard. Sid saw the world anew and he surrendered to the spirit of the woodwose, trusting it to cosset him until the job was done.

∅

Miss Charlotte made a habit of not trusting anyone. It was an attitude that had kept her alive for centuries and – until today – in one piece. Curiously, she found that it also made it easier for her to form tactical alliances. If you came to the negotiating table with the base assumption that the other person would do everything in their power to betray you, you knew exactly where you stood.

There was great comfort in the cast-iron guarantee that your enemy would let you down exactly as you expected them to. Charlotte simply assumed that the very second Pearl got what she wanted she would turn on them, and she was more than happy to proceed on that basis.

Mrs Teach, by no means gullible but perhaps a more trusting soul, was less enamoured with the arrange-ment. She looked on edge as they trudged through the snowy wood behind Pearl and the woodwose formerly known as Sid. Her eyes darted about as if another of the creatures might leap on her out of the shadows.

'You look worried, Mrs Teach.' Charlotte drew up beside her.

'One is embarking on a mission to destroy a demigod armed only with a handbag.' She glanced at the sword strapped to Miss Charlotte's waist. 'At least you have a proper weapon.'

'A fat lot of good it did me earlier.' Doubt bubbled in Miss Charlotte's gut and she tamped it down firmly. 'I just hope the damn thing lives up to its name.'

'Yes, remind me.' Mrs Teach waved a hand in the air as she tried to recall. 'Something in Japanese, meaning ... ?'

'God Slayer. I know. It sounds ridiculous when I say it out loud. They told me the blade was designed to kill all manner of gods and demigods. I can't help thinking that I'd be better off with a reliable machine gun.'

'Did you pack one?'

'Sadly not.'

'A shame. I'm not sure our current armoury is quite up to the task.' Mrs Teach nodded ahead to Pearl and the woodwose. 'What do we have? Myself and my handbag, a bitter fairy with broken wings, a hairy wild man in his first day on the job, and a half-blind witch with a sword that she's beginning to suspect came from the Yamabushi equivalent of a tourist gift shop. This plan is doomed, I tell you.'

'What choice did we have? I didn't much fancy being torn to shreds by a woodwose.'

'Neither did I.' Mrs Teach raised her voice to get Pearl's attention. 'Young lady! Just how are you expecting us to defeat a demigod at the peak of his powers? You were somewhat vague on the specific details.' They came to a stop at the old Roman bridge. On the other side was the Holly King's wall of cloud.

The witches, the fairy and the woodwose stood before its dense and rippling mass. Miss Charlotte picked up a stick and tossed it into the mist. It vanished without a sound.

The woodwose growled, but Pearl gripped his arm. 'Easy, kiddo.' She stroked his hair, calming him.

Mrs Teach pulled her fur coat tighter. 'Is one correct in assuming that to step into that means to lose one's mind?'

'You lose your cares.' Pearl nodded slowly in appreciation of such a diabolical creation. 'The mist allows the Holly King to manipulate those who enter it, and that's the easiest way to draw people to him, make them malleable before the real fun begins. You feel great. Happier than you've ever felt before, and you don't know why, and frankly you don't give a hoot. This time of year it's dark, cold and there's precious little hope doing the rounds.'

'Especially this year,' Charlotte muttered.

'All them poor saps in there'll be flocking to him like moths to a flame.'

'Those *saps* are our friends and neighbours,' Mrs Teach snapped.

'Those *saps* are giving the Holly King his strength.'

'The Feast of Fools,' Miss Charlotte said. 'He throws them an old-fashioned knees-up and as they worship him—'

'He grows in power,' Mrs Teach finished.

'Yeah, don't drink the wine,' Pearl warned them.

'We know.' The witches were united in their disdain.

Pearl looked up for the moon, but it was obscured by clouds. 'While Eric wears the crown, the Holly King is vulnerable. That's where the woodwose comes in. We distract the fairies. Sidney attacks and kills the Holly King. But we gotta get this done by the time the sun comes up. After that, Eric will be sacrificed, and His Majesty will be unstoppable. And that's when he'll destroy your cute little village.'

Mrs Teach blanched. 'I beg your pardon?'

'Oh, yeah. This all used to be his domain, sweetheart.' Pearl gave an insincere shrug of apology. 'You're all trespassing on his turf. When he's got the power, he'll sing to the trees. Their roots will rise up and start breaking your homes apart.'

Mrs Teach thought of the damage done to the crypt by the roots of the old yew tree.

'He won't stop till there ain't nothin' left. He's got a real bee in his bonnet about it. He wants you all living in mud huts, worshipping him like the good ol' days.'

Mrs Teach turned back to the wall of watery whiteness. 'But he's not that powerful yet. He's getting his strength from everyone worshipping him at the feast. So we have to crash the party, so to speak.'

'Precisely. Make some noise, break the spell, then we break his neck, right, honey?' Pearl scruffed behind the woodwose's ears.

'Pearl, the woodwose is an ancient guardian of the wood,' Miss Charlotte said tersely, 'not a bloody Labrador. Give him some dignity. Look, how are we

supposed to get through that with our minds intact?'
She gestured at the sultry mist.

'Simple. Resist the bliss.'

Mrs Teach blinked. 'What?'

'You're gonna get an overwhelming feeling of happiness. Festive cheer. Forget that. Think about the worst Christmases you ever had.' Pearl gave a dark chuckle, suggesting she had plenty of material to work with. 'Every argument, every break-up, every fight. The misery, the disappointment, the despair.'

'Got plenty of those.' Miss Charlotte clapped her hands together. 'Let's have at it.'

'Attagirl.' Pearl looked into the woodwose's eyes. 'Somehow, I don't think this all applies to you, sugar, but just in case, you think bad thoughts. You got that? 'Course you do.'

As the others took a step towards the wall of cloud, Mrs Teach hesitated.

'Mrs Teach?' Charlotte frowned, then realisation dawned. 'Oh, Philomena. I forgot. I'm so sorry.'

'What?' Pearl gestured impatiently to the waiting wall.

Miss Charlotte rested a hand on Mrs Teach's shoulder. 'This is her first Christmas without her husband.'

Pearl smirked. 'He run off with a waitress?'

'He died, you heartless wench,' Mrs Teach snapped.

'Then he came back as a scarecrow,' Miss Charlotte added.

'That was not him!'

'Of course not.' Charlotte squeezed Mrs Teach's shoulder a little tighter.

'That means your worst is yet to come,' Pearl smiled.

'Try not to be so gleeful,' Mrs Teach said, her voice wavering.

'Use it.' Pearl pointed at the wall. 'Do whatever you gotta do to get through the storm. We lose you, we're down to me, the dogman and the cyclops.'

'Charming.' Mrs Teach raised her chin, pushed Pearl aside with the tips of her fingers, and marched towards the cloud. 'I shall see you on the other side.'

In the Thick of It

Faye marched onwards through the mist. Head down, fists in her pockets. It had been a while since she'd wallowed in a good old-fashioned sulk. It simply wasn't the done thing in a time of war, hardship and rationing. Posters on the walls and voices on the radio constantly reminded people to keep their chin up. A stiff upper lip was required at all times, and selflessness was the order of the day.

But Faye had done her bit. Lord knows, she had. Volunteering to collect scrap metal when war was first declared, trying to join the Home Guard (it wasn't her fault there were no girls allowed!), signing up with the ARP, not complaining too much when her beloved bell-ringing was banned, and being the first to step up when any of her family, friends or neighbours needed help. And this was how the ungrateful buggers thanked her. With laughter and humiliation.

Sod 'em. Sod 'em all. If any of those ungrateful scrotes ever needed anything from her ever again, they could take a running jump.

Getting angry felt good. She thought back to what Pearl had told her. *Wynter women don't forgive.* Faye liked the sound of that. The clatter of rage in her head almost stopped her thinking about what Bertie and her father had said. *Oh, Dad, why did you have to open your big gob?* Because the Holly King forced him to, that's why. *Doesn't matter. How could he say those things?* It's the truth. Isn't it better to know the truth? *Is it? Wouldn't you be better off not knowing?*

'No!' Faye's voice was deadened by the thick fog around her. She didn't know if it was the first word she had spoken since entering it, or merely the loudest.

The white mist clung to her like silk. Bright as day, it left tiny droplets of moisture on her specs. She took them off to wipe them dry on her blouse, only then realising that she was just as blind with them on as off. She held the specs at arm's length. Her hand faded into a blurry shadow.

Where the bloody hell was she? She vaguely recalled marching up the Wode Road, so by rights she should have reached the church by now, but all around her was a great white nothing.

No. Not quite. Something was out there. Its movement sent ripples through the air. It didn't surprise Faye that the Holly King might have sent someone to follow her. Her heart beat faster as she put her specs back on. She wasn't alone.

ℬ

Charlotte could have sworn she was two steps behind Mrs Teach as she strode into the fog, but she was nowhere to be seen.

'Mrs Teach?' Charlotte's words struggled to find any purchase in the dense air. 'Philomena?'

Either the silly woman had hurtled off to the village, or there was something strange going on here.

'*Resist the bliss*,' Pearl had warned them. That wouldn't be difficult. Charlotte tried to think of the last time she had been truly happy. Pudding Lane, London. Spring, 1593. In bed with Lizzie as the sun rose. Everything since had been woe and misery. Resisting bliss was Miss Charlotte's default. This would be a doddle.

Martine's smile came to her mind's eye.

The French resistance fighter also had little to smile about, but when she did, it was in Charlotte's arms. They didn't waste any energy on silly chit-chat. All they needed was one another, and they were happy.

Oh, bugger it.

Charlotte shook her head as a warm and fuzzy feeling threatened to overwhelm her. She thought of friends long gone. All the souls she had known who had died so needlessly. Lovers she would never see again. *Should auld acquaintance be forgot—*

Charlotte and Martine had made a promise to speak on New Year's Day as dawn broke. Martine would scry for her and they would enjoy the birth of a new year together. Charlotte's heart bloomed at the very thought of it. *Gah! Stop it. This is not the time.*

Martine's laughter echoed around Charlotte. She was somehow close by and yet out of reach.

'Martine?'

How could she be here? It was impossible. She was sabotaging the Nazi occupiers in France with her cell of partisans. Could she have been given leave? A special break over Yule to surprise her lover? Of course. That was typically French.

Martine's laugh came again. It was further away than before. Charlotte was losing her.

'Martine, I'm coming! Wait for me. I'm here,' Charlotte cried as she ran blindly into the depths of the mist.

✄

The Christmases of Mrs Teach's youth had often been miserable affairs. Her father Wallace was a dressmaker of some considerable talent, but modest ambition. He was happy to provide the women of Woodville with dresses made to measure at a reasonable price. Her mother, Norma, was a midwife whose intense disapproval of the loose morals of the same women who bought her husband's dresses radiated from her like a summer heat haze. Wallace had died when Philomena was only sixteen. A heart attack during Christmas dinner. He had been laughing uproariously at a joke that his daughter had told, about a snowman going to work on an icicle, when he'd suddenly looked confused, then fallen face-first into the trifle.

Nana came to stay with them a few days later. She

and her daughter Norma agreed on little and could not be more different. Nana was a warm soul who hugged Philomena at every opportunity. She soon realised that her granddaughter shared her magical abilities, and over the next year she showed her how to harness the gifts of plants and trees to heal others. Philomena's mother disapproved of Nana filling her daughter's head with such nonsense and sent the old woman back to London two days before Christmas.

The following autumn, Norma fell in love with a travelling cigarette salesman who spoke of settling down and opening a tobacco shop in the village. She welcomed him into her home with uncharacteristic glee, and Philomena delighted in seeing her mother smile again. He vanished one morning, taking the contents of Norma's purse with him, but leaving her carrying his child. Unable to face the shame, the widowed Mrs Norma Cranberry sat down by the fire that Christmas Eve and wrote her daughter a letter before consuming an entire bottle of sleeping pills. The eighteen-year-old Philomena found her mother slumped in an armchair, her dead eyes staring into the embers of the fire.

Pearl's comment that Mrs Teach's worst Christmas was yet to come was laughable. But she wasn't wrong that this time of year would be unspeakably hard without Ernie by her side.

Philomena and Ernie had made a show of going to church and singing carols and all the usual festivities, but they had both hated Christmas. Ernie's father had spent every Christmas drunk, beating his wife and children. It took Philomena and Ernie two Christmases together to realise they shared an apathy for all the paper hats and decorations nonsense. Their one concession to the festivities was to burn a yule log for twelve days. They would pour wine over it and feed it into the hearth, then light it with the remnants of the previous year's log. Its warm glow would reflect in their eyes as they held hands, looking forward to the return of the light, the turning of the year, and the hope that lay ahead beyond the darkness. That's what she would miss the most. Sharing the long nights with him. She missed him now, with this bright mist pressing on her from all sides. What she wouldn't give to take his hand in hers now. Just for a moment. She knew the mist was trying to entice her. Tickling the palm of her hand until she could almost feel the roughness of his fingers. It opened a door in her mind, beckoning her to step through with promises of unbridled happiness. But Philomena Teach welcomed the darkness and sadness. It reminded her how lucky she had been to know such joy with her Ernie, even for a short time. And nothing could ever match it. Mrs Teach realised with a tug of sorrow that she hadn't yet lit this year's yule log. If nothing else, she had to survive the night in order to do that.

The mist began to thin, as if realising she was a lost cause. Mrs Teach could see the cobbles of the Wode Road beneath her feet. Somewhere in the distance, a trumpet blared and a bass drum pounded an irregular beat.

∅

It didn't matter how thick the mist was, it meant nothing to the woodwose. He could not be lulled by festive cheer. He was a creature of instinct and action. The path ahead was clear to him, and he followed the fairy with sure feet. He could hear the high-register hiss of light, taste the bitterness of sound, and see the intensity of fear in the woodland creatures that scurried from his path. Sid was one of them now. Sharing a body and mind with something unknowable and ancient. A thing created long ago to watch over the wood, gifted with a perception of his environment that went beyond any mere animal. The only thing he could not do was speak, and that suited him fine. Words can be twisted. He had seen it happen with the witches on the bridge. Words had left the mouth of the fairy in one shape and arrived at the ears of the witch with the handbag in another. He understood all of it, though. Better than ever. He could see truth and lies. He knew the fairy would turn on them all in time. But the woodwose had no choice. Her magic meant that he was bound to her. She spoke. He obeyed.

He ached all over. All he wanted was to run free in the wood. But until the fairy released him, he would be in pain, weighed down by obligation. A shadow of what he could be.

Sid knew this all too well. Orders. Duty. These were not just words. They meant something to a soldier. They meant even more to a woodwose.

315

The mist was clearing. They were close now. The Holly King's aura shone like a beacon. Soon Sid would smash the demigod's skull with his club, rip out his throat, and then he would be free. He tensed, ready to run at him, teeth bared, raving and drooling.

The fairy stopped just ahead of him, wary and alert.

He sensed it, too. Someone else was in the mist with them. Someone they knew. The fairy strode towards the newcomer, away from the Holly King. Sid ached with yearning. He was so close. So close to sating the bloodlust that would ensure his freedom. But he was compelled to follow the fairy, and his fur thickened in anticipation of a fight.

❧

Pearl's reserves of Christmas misery were endless, and she had little problem fending off the mist's festive allure. She strode through it with confidence, despite not being able to see beyond the end of her nose. Flying would have been easier, of course, but her wings were broken and numb. Still, a good walk never hurt nobody. Especially when at the end of her little hike she would get to see the Holly King's throat ripped out by her very own woodwose. Soon the old bastard would be choking on his own blood, and—

'Pearl!'

She stopped, unsure if the voice was one of the others calling for her, or if it was in her head. That had happened quite a bit since, y'know, dying. Death can really

316

mess with a girl's constitution and she didn't much fancy going through it again.

'Pearl, don't die, please.'

Pearl's heart had stopped working some time ago, but that didn't prevent the damn thing from tightening in her chest.

'I didn't mean it.'

Pearl knew that voice and those words all too well. She'd never thought she would hear them again. Why would she? They were some of the last words she'd heard before she died.

ø

Faye couldn't help where she was going. Wherever she placed her boots, the ground rose up to meet them and tilted and veered until she was headed where she was required, the mysterious figure always there but always out of reach. She'd stopped fighting it. The mist was disorientating, and for a moment she didn't know up from down. Beneath her feet the cobbles seemed to have gone, replaced by twisting roots and crisp snow. How had she ended up in the wood?

Gradually the mist retreated, and Faye found herself on the path to the hollow oak. It was still the middle of the night, but the snow made everything bright.

She stopped. This was all very familiar.

She wasn't floating. She wasn't in her jim-jams and slippers, but otherwise this was very much like her dream.

She turned in a circle, looking for someone she hoped she wouldn't find.

But there they were. A figure in a hooded winter coat dragging a body on a stretcher through the snow. Faye's mother and Pearl. A vision from decades past.

What else could she do but follow?

Mrs Teach, Party Crasher

Mrs Teach emerged from the mist, surprised to find herself by the Green Man pub at the top of the Wode Road. How had it taken her so long to cover such a short distance? She glanced around. And where the bloody hell were the others? Miss Charlotte should have been two steps behind her.

Mrs Teach was not alone, however. The Roberts twins were here. Big lads and hard to miss in their bright yellow sou'wester oilskins. These two respected members of the village – bell-ringers and volunteers for the Royal National Lifeboat Institution who had helped with the evacuation from Dunkirk – were dancing around a lamp post, singing an obscene rugby song about the Mayor of Bayswater's Daughter. They were so blotto that they hadn't noticed Mrs Teach's arrival. They weren't the only ones. The whole village was gathered around the Great War memorial at the bottom of the road for a raucous knees-up.

Music played. Well, if you could call Finlay Motspur

emptying his lungs into that cursed flugelhorn of his *music*. Several villagers were staggering about singing songs in competition with one another. If the assault on Mrs Teach's ears was anything to go by, this was a contest in which everyone lost.

Mrs Teach was no prude, but the sight of her neighbours in such a state was really quite scandalous.

Mrs Pritchett lay unconscious on top of an upright piano, flecks of vomit caked on her twinset. Finlay Motspur's lips were failing him as his flugelhorn emitted a series of bum notes, and his bass drum had a hole in it courtesy of Mrs Nesbitt's head. She had somehow lost all of her outer garments and looked lost and chilly as she extracted herself and continued to wander around in her corset and bloomers. Mr Loaf's fiddle sported a broken string that bounced around in time with his playing, though his instrument was so out of tune that it would hardly have made a difference.

Mrs Teach had to look away from Miss Burgess, who was spending a penny in one of the Wode Road's drains. Mr Hodgson and his wife were asleep in the gutter, arms wrapped around one another with what Mrs Teach recognised as the afterglow of recently joined lovers. Mrs Yorke stared at a row of Champagne bottles as if calculating with advanced algebra how they had come to be suddenly empty. Doctor Hamm was vomiting repeatedly onto his own welcome mat. Constable Muldoon's children were screaming and fighting over broken tin soldiers and decapitated rag dolls as their parents shouted at them to be quiet. Betty,

Milly and Dotty were pulling each other's hair as they squabbled over their last misshapen cigarette. Edith Palmer slapped Reverend Jacobs across the face. Miss Gordon tended to an arrow sticking out of Captain Marshall's shoulder. Miss Moon and Miss Leach had joined the Morris Men in their whirling dance. They circled Mr Paine and whacked their sticks on his tin ARP helmet as he laughed like a madman.

'Absolutely disgraceful,' Mrs Teach muttered.

The drunken villagers were attended to by flying fairies. They looked vaguely similar to Pearl, but without her sense of fun. They each wore the plastered-on grin of acolytes determined to ensure you had a great time, even if it killed you.

One of the Roberts twins collapsed. The other retched into the gutter. The twins were no lightweights when it came to alcohol consumption. If they were suffering, how much longer would the other villagers last?

Mrs Teach felt conspicuous against the vast white wall of mist. She ducked into the porch of the pub.

Pearl's plan had been to break up the party before the Holly King became too strong. The plan had also relied on Pearl and the others actually bloody being here to execute it. Where in the name of buggeration were they?

Mrs Teach surveyed the scene at the war memorial. Eric sat on his throne, wooden crown on his head, clapping along with at least two of the competing songs at once. The Holly King sat directly behind him, cross-legged and eyes closed. Several little fairies floated around him, like planets orbiting a star. Each had their arms folded, eyes surveilling the crowd for troublemakers. Mrs Teach was confident that any attempt to wrestle the crown from Eric and destroy it would surely end in her grisly demise. She noticed that something odd was happening to the Holly King's antlers. The last time she had seen him at the crossroads, at least one had been broken off. Now both were longer than ever and glowing as bright as the sun. Just as Pearl had predicted, he was gaining strength from the revelry.

Mrs Teach looked around for anyone who could help. There was no sign of Faye. She had last seen the girl by the telephone box about to enter the mist herself. Had she somehow become lost in its fog? She spotted Terrence and Bertie close to the war memorial. For some reason, Bertie was now out of the gibbet and Terrence was the one locked inside. Bertie had his arms draped over the iron bars and seemed to be sobbing. Terrence covered his eyes with his hands. All the fight was gone from them. What on earth had happened here? Was there no one who could help?

Shirley. Yes. Eric's wife Shirley stood behind his arm-chair throne. Her shoulders were tense and rounded, and the sober and disapproving grimace on her face told Mrs Teach all she needed to know. Mrs Teach would get to Shirley and tell her she wasn't alone. Shirley would order Eric to pack it in, and the Holly King's hold on the villagers would be broken. With any luck, Miss Charlotte, Pearl and the woodwose would be here by then, and they could send the demigod on his way.

Mrs Teach took a long look at the wall of mist, willing Miss Charlotte to come marching through with that ridiculous sword in her hands, but the white mass remained undisturbed.

'Well, Philomena, it's been some years since you crashed a party,' she told herself. 'Let's hope you haven't lost your touch.'

She strode over to the closest of the Roberts twins, plucking a silver goblet from his slack grip. Inside were the dregs of red wine. Fairy wine. The fools. She tipped the rest of it away and gripped the goblet. She skipped over one twin and stooped over his brother, whipping the bright yellow sou'wester hat from where it rested on his face. She popped it on her head at a suitably rakish angle and staggered towards the party, a filthy old song on her lips. *'I've seen it, I've seen it, I've been in between it ...'*

❦

Bertie's heart weighed heavy in his chest. If only he could claw his words back from the air. He hadn't meant to say anything to Faye. It had all just fallen out of his mouth. And now that he'd said it out loud, it didn't make any sense. Of course Faye should wear whatever she liked. Bertie did. So why not her? All he wanted to do now was run after her, into the mist, and beg her forgiveness. But that would mean leaving Terrence.

The poor man hadn't said a word since she'd left.

Mr Bright was always full of get-up-and-go, so it unnerved Bertie to see him staring blankly at the grey slush congealed around a dark puddle of melted snow. There were few signs of life. The occasional blink, and a shudder as his breath caught. Staying here and making sure Faye's dad didn't come to any harm was all Bertie could do.

A pint glass smashed nearby, scattering tiny shards across the cobbles. Bertie winced. Glass had been in short supply since the start of the war, and if he dropped one in the pub, he would get a well-rehearsed lecture from Mr Bright on how much it had just cost them.

Now, Faye's dad didn't even look up.

'*And the hairs on her dicky-di-do hung down to her knees.*'

That was new. A tuneful voice mingled with the chaos. Bertie knew the song, of course, but who was the singer?

'*One black one, one white one, and one with a bit of shite on ...*'

There. A yellow sou'wester hat weaved its way through the orgy, circling the Morris Men's half-hearted pissing contest and heading for the war memorial. Its owner dared to look up from under the brim. Mrs Teach! Bertie was so surprised he nearly blurted her name out loud. She caught his eye, some-how managing to convey, *Don't you say a bloody word, Bertie Butterworth, or I'll wring your neck*, with just a raised eyebrow.

No one else noticed her, not even the fairies circling the Holly King. They were focused on the revellers. She had their *sfumato* fuzziness about her, too, and Bertie wondered if that was her witch's glamour. Had he been hanging around Faye for so long that they had less of an effect on him? Perhaps it was just because he was desperate for someone like Mrs Teach to save the day. But where were the others?

Eric, the Lord of Misrule, puffed his cheeks out as a fairy offered him another chicken drumstick. His wife Shirley yawned and sipped at a glass of red wine she had managed to make last all evening. And the Holly King was too busy glowing like a Christmas tree as his antlers continued to grow to notice Mrs Teach getting closer.

ჽ

The Holly King tingled all over. Embers of the forgotten fire within him burst into flames, searing away his shame. He was so close now. Soon, the sun would rise and meet the light within him. With a simple offering of blood, he would be all-powerful once more.

ჽ

The wine tasted sweet in Shirley Birdwhistle's mouth. Finally, she and Eric were getting the respect they deserved. Without them, the village would grind to a halt. Without their deliveries of letters and bills, there would be chaos. Why had they been so looked down upon for so long? Well, not anymore. Shirley gazed at her husband. Lord of Misrule. She had made the crown that rested on his head. It had come to her in a dream. A voice that whispered to her constantly between sleep and waking. Shirley had worked every spare minute she'd had – and there were precious few of those – to create the most beautiful thing she had ever seen.

That wasn't quite true. Her son was the most beautiful thing she had ever made. Her heart ached to think of how he had changed since coming back from Dunkirk, but it wouldn't last. He would get better soon. He had to. He'd be her Sidney once more. The laughing lad without a care in the world, chasing birds and butterflies all day. That's what the voice had told her. Make the crown and your boy will return. And it had been right. Shirley had only finished the crown the other night, and Sidney had come walking through her door the very next day. That had also been the morning of Eric's funny turn. It hadn't made sense at the time, but when in the presence of someone like the Holly King, one can go a bit doolally. She could feel it now. Her thoughts of tomorrow, the past and the now all mingling like clouds before a storm. It had been painful to see the man she had married raving like a loon, but in the end he had been proven right. The Holly King had come, and now they were all happy. There had never been such a party as this in the village before. She wished Sidney were there to enjoy the fun, but he needed his rest. He had been saying such strange and silly things. How could her boy have died on a beach in Dunkirk, when she could see him clear as day? He was talking in daft riddles. Ah, but that was her Sidney. Such an imagination. Her boy was full of life. Nothing could stop him, not even the Nazi armies. There was a reason he'd come home when others hadn't. He was brave, strong and clever. Everything a mother could want. She was so proud of him. 'Our little soldier,' she and Eric had called him. She'd left him at home in bed tonight. He was exhausted, poor lad. That's why he was talking such nonsense. The last thing he needed was a late-night party for grown-ups. Yes, leave him to rest. She would take a few of these fairies' sausages and do her boy a proper fry-up in the morning. Eric, too. They both deserved it. Eric had been made lord for the night and her son would be back to normal in the morning. Right as rain once more.

'Shirley!'

The voice was a hissed whisper.

'Shirley, down here!'

Shirley looked down to the foot of the war memorial and saw someone lurking there, but her mind couldn't quite put together what she was seeing. It was a figure in a bright yellow hat, clutching a bottle of cider. Their features were obscured, as if behind a veil, but Shirley knew that voice from somewhere.

'Shirley, we have to stop this. Tell Eric to command the Holly King to end the party. If you don't—'

'Mrs Teach!' Shirley blurted. Yes, she could see her now. The witch's face blinked into sharp focus.

'Please, Shirley, if we don't end this now, then Eric will be—'

'My lord, Your Majesty!' Shirley grabbed Mrs Teach's sou'wester hat and whipped it off her head. 'A witch!' The fairies orbiting the Holly King instantly fixed on the two women, ready to pounce if either threatened the demigod. 'Mrs Teach is here to ruin everything. The party, Eric, my boy. She wants to spoil it all. You have to stop her.'

Eric leapt off his throne and placed himself between Shirley and the witch. 'Back, you old hag!' he cried.

Shirley flushed with pride. What a brave man her husband was. She could see where Sidney got it from.

'It matters not,' the Holly King boomed. His eyes remained closed, and his antlers were as tall and sprawling as the apple tree at the bottom of Shirley's garden. 'The time is upon us. I shall reclaim what is rightfully mine.' The Holly King's eyes opened. They were as golden as the sun's first rays. He took a deep breath, chest heaving. Opening his mouth wide, he began to sing. A low bass note. It was soft at first, almost childlike, but it grew louder and louder, filling the air and pressing against Shirley's ears. She clapped her hands to the sides of her head. Eric, Mrs Teach and the others did the same, even the floating fairies. The light in the Holly King's eyes glowed as bright as his antlers. His voice buffeted the roiling clouds that surrounded the village. The endless white now beat a retreat, breaking into tiny globes before dissolving completely. The stars above shook like sequins, as if excited to be seen again, and the first hint of dawn's red light washed the edges of the sky.

'Dawn is coming,' Mrs Teach cried over the Holly King's droning song. She hurried to Shirley and grabbed her by the shoulders. 'Dawn is coming, and at first light Eric will be sacrificed. He's going to die!'

MISTLETOE AND WINE

Faye called after her mother, 'Mum, it's me!'

But the young Kathryn showed no sign of hearing Faye. She continued to drag the body on the stretcher into the clearing where the hollow oak stood.

Faye knew it was a vision, but she had to try. There was her mother, in three dimensions, flesh and blood. The imperfect wise angel that her father loved so much.

Faye only had one photograph of her mother. And, while she treasured it, she realised now that the glossy little scrap of paper couldn't capture the light in her mother's eyes. A kindness mingled with the sort of determination that didn't stand for any nonsense.

'Mum, please!'

'She can't hear you, honey.' Pearl emerged from the mist, standing by Faye's side.

Faye tensed and bunched her fists. The last time she had seen Pearl, the fairy had been intent on killing her. But there was something different about her now. Less of a swagger in her step. Murderous rage was replaced by cool curiosity as she stared at the vision of her younger self and Faye's mother.

'Stay back,' Faye warned her.

Pearl glanced down at Faye's fists. 'Relax, will ya? I'm not here for a fight.'

Faye's fists remained clenched. 'You sent Sid to kill us.'

Pearl tilted her head to her shoulder in a half-shrug. 'That mighta been a mistake. A lot's happened in the last few hours. The Holly King wants me dead and, hey, I even made a truce with your buddies.'

Faye longed to see Miss Charlotte and Mrs Teach step out of the mist, but they didn't come. 'Why should I believe you?'

'Believe what you want.'

'Where are they? Where's Sid? Have you seen Bertie?'

'Slow down. We all got split up.' Pearl squinted one eye. 'All except you and me.' She returned her attention to the vision of herself and Kathryn Wynter. 'I think we're the only ones who're meant to see this, kiddo.'

Faye looked back at the clearing. Kathryn rested the stretcher between two familiar wooden sarcophagi. Faye had never got this far in her dream before, and her need to know more extinguished the aggression she felt towards Pearl.

'What is this?'

'It's the night I died,' Pearl replied matter-of-factly. 'Hold onto your hat, this is going to get a little nuts.'

Kathryn undid the straps on the stretcher with trembling hands. 'Pearl, can you hear me?' She cradled the girl's head. 'Say something!'

Young Pearl's eyes bulged open. She lurched to the side on her hands and knees and vomited a bloody mess.

Faye grimaced as she looked from young Pearl to fairy Pearl. 'Poison?'

'Not exactly. I was trying a potion and a ritual your momma showed me. I wanted to communicate with my old family.'

Young Pearl retched again. Kathryn held her hair and gently patted her on the back.

Faye covered her mouth. 'What the bloody hell was in it?'

Fairy Pearl narrowed her eyes and counted off her fingers. 'Vinegar, red wine, a half-pint of Kentish ale, a dozen berries—'

'What kind of berries?'

Pearl winced as her younger self threw up again. 'Mistletoe.'

'Mistletoe's poisonous!'

'I was young. I thought I was invincible. Ooh, look, here comes the frog.'

'The ... what?' Faye spun to see young Pearl retch again. What came out was dark, throbbing and frog-shaped. It steamed in the snow, one of its legs twitching.

'I was desperate.' Pearl wagged a finger in Kathryn's direction. 'But what your momma did next was a lot dumber.'

Faye turned to find Kathryn emptying white ash

from a sack. She was making a circle around Pearl and the wooden boxes.

The younger Pearl rolled on to her back and moaned. 'Kathy, I ... I can't feel my legs, sugar.'

'I'm nearly there, Pearl, just keep breathing.'

'We were cousins,' the fairy Pearl said, her voice softening, 'but we shared secrets like sisters.'

Faye felt a tight twist of jealousy in her belly to think that this interloper from across the pond had known her mother better than she did. 'Make it stop, Pearl.'

'I'm not doing this.'

'Then who is? Why are we seeing this?'

'This is the work of the Holly King. You ever wonder why at Christmas people get drunk and tell the people they love what they really think of them?' Pearl smirked. 'That's the Holly King's speciality. The ugly truth. If you've been good, you'll be happy. If you've had any misfortune, he'll make you remember and relive it over and over. Most of us only remember when we get drunk, or when we're tryin' to sleep at 3 a.m., but this mist ...' Pearl glanced around at the thick whiteness that now hovered at the edge of the clearing. 'When he's got you right where he wants you, he uses it to wring out every single damned detail and make you remember it all. It might look like heaven, but it's the pits. Worse than Detroit.'

Young Pearl convulsed in pain. Kathryn rushed to her side and took her hand.

'I'm dyin', Kathy. I can feel it. Gimme somethin' to knock me out.'

'Don't be daft. We can stop this. All I need—'

'Kathy!' a new voice cried. 'Oh God, what have you done?'

'Dad!' Faye said with a gasp, as her father, young and sprightly, dashed into the clearing with a cardboard box tucked under his arm. 'Oh, my good grief, look at his barnet.' Faye knew there were more important things to be focusing on than young Terrence's impressive mound of curly chestnut hair, but she couldn't take her eyes off it. 'It's like he's got a giant pine cone on his head.'

Kathryn beckoned Terrence closer. 'Quickly, Terry, she's not got long.'

He scurried over with the box.

'Now, go,' Kathryn told him firmly. 'Forget you saw any of this. Don't tell a soul. Promise me, Terry.'

'I . . . I promise.'

Faye's heart melted. Her father's unquestioning devotion felt very familiar.

Pearl leaned closer. 'Aww, he's just like your Herbie.'

'Bertie,' Faye corrected her. 'And he's nothing like him.'

'Tickety-boo,' young Terrence said, and Faye flinched.

'Y'know, they say some girls just want to marry their poppas,' Pearl teased.

'If you don't shut your gob right now, I'll—'

Young Pearl screamed in pain, clutching her belly. Her leg jerked out, kicking Terrence in his left knee.

'Ow, bugger that!' he wailed, falling on his backside.

'Terry?' Kathryn turned to him, worried that she

335

now had an extra patient to care for, but he waved her concerns away.

'It's nothing. I'll be all right.'

'Go, Terry, now!'

Terrence decided he'd better do as he was told and limped back the way he came, taking one last look behind him as he disappeared into the mist.

'War wound, my arse.' Faye's voice was tinged with hurt as she watched him hobble away. 'He lied about that, and never said a dicky bird to me about this. And then he tells me ...' Faye faltered, her heart twisting as she thought back to the terrible things he and Bertie had said. 'Why did he keep this a secret? How many more bloody secrets has he kept?'

'Oh, plenty.' Pearl raised a knowing eyebrow.

'Like what?' Faye demanded, but Pearl had turned her gaze back to the action.

Kathryn took something from the box Terrence had left behind. For a moment Faye thought it looked like a wreath, but as Kathryn laid it before the sarcophagi, she realised she'd seen one like it before.

'A wooden crown,' she whispered. 'Oh, Mum, what are you doing with that?'

Pearl grinned at Faye as she waited for the penny to drop.

'No.' Faye shook her head as the dread realisation sunk in. 'She can't have been that daft? Why the bloody hell was Mum summoning demigods?'

'We didn't know the rules.' Pearl shrugged. 'The two boxes used to be here all the time. Did you know that?

People would let their dogs pee on them. No one ever questioned it. You know what the villagers are like.'

Faye couldn't argue with that.

'But your mom wasn't like the others. She always wanted to know more. We became obsessed with these boxes. We wanted to know everything, but we didn't have a Mrs Teach or a Miss Charlotte. So, how do you find out about this stuff?'

'There's a mural in the church crypt,' Faye said. 'Mind you, you have to know to look there in the first place.'

'You got your mom's smarts, kid. That's where we started. The Reverend back then was a fella called Skipwith, who knew more than he let on about the old ways. He showed us the mural, told us the tale of the Holly King and the Oak King, how they fought for control of the year, how they brought sunshine, rain and snow, and how – if you asked them nicely—'

'They can heal people.' Faye snapped her fingers. 'When Eric came into the village with his holly cloak, he said the Holly King healed him. That he could heal us all.'

'That's why she brought me here. That's why she did—' A thud silenced Pearl.

They both looked up to see the lid of one of the sarcophagi rocking on the ground. Kathryn gritted her teeth as she heaved the second one off. The tendons in her neck went taut and her slim arms shook as it toppled, landing on its corner before pivoting into the snow.

Kathryn gasped and pushed her hair back, before reaching into her coat and producing two hand mirrors. Faye recognised one with an ivory handle. She had the very same mirror in her bedside drawer. One of the few belongings of her mother that she still possessed. She watched as Kathryn held the mirrors high, angling them to catch the light of the moon.

'What's she doing?'

When Pearl spoke, it was accompanied by the gentle ripple of a shudder. 'Opening doors.'

The light from the mirrors dazzled them momentarily as the earth began to shake beneath their feet.

'That felt real.' Faye crouched, resting her palm on the ground. Echoes of tremors vibrated against her hand, accompanied by a low and thunderous moan.

A giant with skin of oak clambered out of one of the sarcophagi. The Holly King heaved himself out of the other. Kathryn and young Pearl embraced as they cowered beneath them.

'These fellas start beatin' the snot outta each other any second now,' Pearl told Faye. 'You might wanna rest your tush. It takes a while.'

LOVERS, OLD AND NEW

Miss Charlotte was lost. Martine's voice had fallen
silent some time ago and it was all she could do to
keep moving. She had a feeling that if she stopped,
she would be lost here for ever. She only had herself
to blame, of course. A life of solitude is what she had
wanted and that's what she had got. Only, this year,
that had started to change. First, there was Faye and
her annoying curiosity and meddling, which had
somehow brought the village witches together in a
bizarre solidarity. Then Martine and her ability to
listen. Good gods, it was like being in a confessional.
Charlotte would find herself waffling on about all the
terrible mistakes she had made over the centuries, and
every time, Martine would remain patiently by her side,
taking in every word, asking infrequent but perceptive
questions, and holding Charlotte when she was done.

'I like your eyepatch.'

Charlotte froze. She hadn't heard that breathy
London voice in a very long time. Except in her dreams.

It was accompanied by the distinct aroma of camomile, sage and rose petals.

Lizzy stood by her side. Charlotte's first love. The wonderful barmaid at the Cheshire Cheese in Fleet Street. They'd had a brief and wonderful spring together, making silly plans to open an alehouse of their own, or jump on a boat to the New World. Until the plague had come for Lizzy. Charlotte Southill's life had never been the same.

'You're lost, Charlotte.'

'You're not real.' Charlotte looked straight ahead.

'This place makes the unreal real. It's all about the truth in here, Charlotte.' Lizzy's smile gave her dimples, and Charlotte's heart flipped despite herself. 'And there's nothing more real than the truth.'

Charlotte's chest felt heavy. She didn't like where this was going one little bit. 'You sound like her, but you don't speak like her. This is the Holly King's stupid mist playing tricks with my mind.'

'You keep telling yourself that, Charlotte, but it won't change the fact that you ain't got the foggiest.' Lizzy snickered at her pun. 'Turn left, right, go back the way you came, or carry straight on. Don't make no difference. You're not leaving until you face the truth.'

Charlotte rounded her shoulders and tucked her hands into her armpits. 'Which is?'

'You've pushed folk away all your livelong life. You don't give yourself to no one, and sooner or later you destroy the lives of those you love.'

'Exactly. The people I grow close to usually end up

getting hurt. Better to spare them the pain.' Charlotte hoped the words would come out cold and hard, but her voice wavered and she cursed herself.

'Spare *them* the pain? Most of us do end up dead before our time, but yes, I suppose we don't feel anything once we're gone.'

'*C'est vrai.*'

Charlotte spun to find Martine strolling out of the mist, wearing a long coat and a woollen hat. She had a sub-machine gun strapped over her shoulder. 'She made me leave.'

'Don't lie, Martine.' Charlotte's mind whirled. Could Martine possibly, actually be here? 'You wanted to fight.'

'*Oui.* And I wanted you to come with me, but you twisted my words and pushed me away. Why? To spare *yourself* the pain.'

'That's not fair.' Charlotte pointed an accusing finger at them both. It was trembling. 'I wept for you. I wept for both of you.'

'You let us go,' Lizzy and Martine said in unison.

'No. The things I did for you, Lizzy. You'll never know—'

'I know exactly what you did.' Lizzy turned to Martine. 'She removed me from her mind. Plucked me out like a weed. All so it wouldn't hurt *her*. She'll do the same to you, you'll see.'

Charlotte fell to her knees. 'I won't, Martine, I promise. I'll come for you. We'll fight side by side, we'll—'

'It's too late.' Martine opened her long coat, revealing

a claret stain across her belly. Blood seeped through the white of her blouse. 'I was shot two days ago in a raid on the farmhouse where we were hiding. I took an hour to die. You allowed this to happen.'

Charlotte's bad eye burned. The white nothingness tilted around her and she thought she might pass out. 'No. We'll speak on New Year's Day, and we'll laugh about it, and we'll curse this mist and the Holly King's ridiculous games.'

Lizzy crouched and took Charlotte's hand. Her fingers were rough and cold. 'You won't be doing any of that, my love,' she told Charlotte. 'Until you twig who you are and what you've done, you're stuck here.'

Would that be so bad? Miss Charlotte wondered. To stay in this void for all time? Not like this, though. Not with the two women she loved taunting her for all eternity.

She blinked a tear away from her one good eye, glancing up just in time to catch Martine and Lizzy sharing a conspiratorial grin.

And that's when Charlotte had a moment of clarity. What a fool she had been. There was a very simple solution to this dilemma. Lizzy was right, in a way. Charlotte *did* have to face a terrible truth. That she had let her guard down and been soft enough to fall for such a cheap trick.

In a flash, she jumped to her feet, drawing her sword and swinging it around. Lizzy's head retained its dimpled smile as it parted company with her neck. It landed nose-first on the ground with a crack. A rush of air burst from her headless body, and in the blink of an eye it had transformed into that of a winged fairy. It dropped out of the air, tumbling next to its head, the features of which no longer belonged to Lizzy. A cherubic face stared back at Charlotte with a surprised scowl. As it rolled on the ground, it burst into countless glittery fragments that were whisked away into the mist.

Martine was so stunned that she didn't have a chance to even think about running before Miss Charlotte's blade was at her throat.

'Show me who you really are.' Miss Charlotte prodded the soft flesh.

Martine twisted her lips and closed her eyes. A rush of air mussed Charlotte's white hair as the fairy transformed into her true self. Her wings buzzed as she prepared to fly away, but Miss Charlotte pierced one of them through the translucent membrane, bringing her down. She pinned the fairy to the ground.

'Don't ... don't kill me,' the fairy pleaded.

'Kill you?' Charlotte shook her head. 'Not yet, darling. First, you're going to get me out of this fog. Take me to the Holly King.'

The Woodwose of Woodville

Sid the woodwose followed Pearl until her silhouette faded to nothing. Her scent, a unique mix of frost and fuchsia and vengeance, evaporated, and she made no sound. He called after her. He meant to cry her name, but all that came out was a guttural grunt. The ground beneath his feet hardened. The snow was deeper here, and more compacted. A breeze carried with it a new smell of sweat, violence and greed. Sid ran towards it and the mist parted to reveal three men on horseback. They wore tricorn hats and scarves over their noses and mouths. Sid's nostrils tingled with the tang of caramel and smoke. Burned powder from the flintlock pistols in their hands. One of the three spotted him, raising the alarm as the horses reared up and whinnied in fright. Another fumbled to reload his flintlock, while the third reached for his sword. They moved as if in deep water. Sid would have been little more than a shadow to their eyes as he leapt through the air, swinging the club in his hand and smashing their brains in. The highwaymen's bodies fell like puppets with their strings cut. The woodwose ripped out their throats and feasted on their guts. The horses fled their masters, galloping into the mist which once again gathered around him, whipping itself into a violent storm.

A new aroma came to him. A funk of passion, pink flesh and sin. He bounded through the snow to find a couple in powdered wigs and untied bloomers making hurried love by a bare willow tree. The man's face twisted in fear. He pushed the woman away, told her to run. Sid let her go. The man with the white-painted face held up his undergarments with one hand and a drew a dagger with the other. Sid bit into his wrist, relishing the taste of marrow and flesh as both hand and dagger broke away. The man fell, his wig tilting at a peculiar angle, billowing cheap flour and pomatum. Sid gripped his dagger and slashed at his thigh, blood hissing as it spilled onto the snow. The man thrashed for a while before the life drained out of him.

Sid could smell another hunter in the fog. He found him stalking a deer through knee-high snow. The man wore a leather jerkin and stank of filth and mead and turnips. He was so focused on the deer that he didn't see the woodwose until it was leaping at him. To his credit, he was fast. He managed to loose an arrow while Sid was still airborne, but it went wide of its mark. Sid made no such mistake, bringing his club down on the man's bow arm, cracking it like dry bread. The woodwose's jaws closed around the hunter's face. It came off like a rubber mask, chewy in Sid's mouth.

346

The hunter's screams hurt his ears, so he silenced him quickly by snapping his neck.

Sid hunted more prey through the mist and the ever-deepening snow. A clutch of warriors with iron swords and shields decorated with bronze. A Roman centurion, wounded from battle and dying in a ditch. A farmer in furs with an axe. A creature that looked human, but was half the height and moved like an ape. Sid slaughtered them all until there was no one left to fear him.

To keep going would lead to oblivion. Somehow, he knew that. A sweet, everlasting peace that would end his pain. It called to him, and he wanted to answer. He could end the terrible history of the Woodwose of Woodville here and now.

He felt the song before he heard it. Rumbling through the earth, carried on the roots of the trees. An old song. Perhaps the oldest. One celebrating the turn of the year. From here on in the light would creep back, bringing with it hope. The storm's death came in a sudden cascade. The wind dropped; the snowflakes spun off into droplets. The mist backed away like an emperor's courtiers, and the woodwose's bloodlust faded with it. Sid recognised himself again. Trapped inside this beast, he shivered to think how close he had come to annihilation. He heard the song and knew the singer. He flexed his legs and ran, following the vibrations in the air back to the village, where he would slay the Holly King and save his father.

A GLASS OF WARM,
SALTY WATER

Faye had seen her fair share of fisticuffs in her time –
she was a pub landlord's daughter, after all – but the
brutality of the fight between the Oak King and the
Holly King was truly something to behold.

'They really don't like each other, do they?' she
observed as the Oak King grabbed his brother by the
antlers, bringing his knee into short, sharp contact with
the Holly King's nose.

'They're fighting for their lives.' Pearl sat with Faye
on a bough of the hollow oak. From there they had the
best possible view of the punch-up. Pearl sorted through
a handful of powdery-blue juniper berries in her palm
and popped one into her mouth every few seconds.

Faye shook her head in dismay. 'And they did this
every year?'

'*Twice* a year,' Pearl corrected as the Holly King
retorted by kicking his brother in the nethers. The Oak
King doubled up. The Holly King's hand was a blur as

it punched into his brother's back with a crunch that made Faye wince. His biceps tensed and, with a cry that shook the branches, he ripped out the Oak King's wooden spine.

'Oh, my good gawd!' Faye slapped a hand to her mouth.

Her mother, still hiding with young Pearl between the sarcophagi, did the same.

The Holly King stood over his brother's body, shoulders rising and falling with each breath. This was not the same lucid Holly King that Faye had encountered earlier today. This one looked as though he had been abruptly woken from a deep Sunday-afternoon nap. His heavy-lidded eyes and slack mouth suggested he was still in that strange netherworld between sleep and waking. As they watched, he tossed the Oak King's spine away.

'Please.' Kathryn stood slowly, the wooden crown in her hands.

'Oh, Mum, what are you doing?' Faye pressed her hands to the sides of her head. 'Sit down, this is not the time.'

'Told ya, she can't hear you.' Pearl offered the berries in her hand to Faye. 'Juniper berry?'

Faye shook her head, her attention fixed on her mother.

Kathryn presented the wooden crown to the Holly King.

'That's what really gives him his power,' Pearl said between chews. 'Once it's on his head, it's all but impossible to stop the big galoot.'

'Please help my friend.' Kathryn lowered her eyes.

The Holly King reached for the crown tentatively, as if not quite recognising it.

'Please,' Kathryn repeated, taking a step towards him.

The Holly King growled and swiped at her with a backhand that sent her flying across the clearing, landing in a heap in a holly bush.

'Mum!' Faye cried.

'No!' young Pearl croaked at the same time, lunging feebly at the Holly King. He bent and wrapped his fingers around her neck, hoisting her off the ground. She kicked out to no avail as her face began to turn blue. He drew her closer, a deathly snarl on his face.

Fairy Pearl nudged Faye in the ribs. 'Watch this.'

Kathryn hauled herself out of the holly bush, rushing into the clearing. Drawing a dagger from within her coat, she reached up as high as she could and plunged the blade between the Holly King's ribs, pushing it up towards his heart. The demigod convulsed. The crown slipped from his fingers. His back arched and his arms tensed.

Young Pearl's neck snapped in his grip.

They both fell, lifeless, limp and heavy.

'No! No, no, no!' Kathryn cried, kneeling by young Pearl and gripping her hand. 'Pearl!'

'And that's how I died.' Pearl popped the last juniper berry into her mouth and clapped her hands clean. Still chewing, she turned to Faye as one might do after a movie. 'Whaddya think? Nuts, huh?'

Faye's eyes were closed, hidden behind her fingers,

a hand pressed to her face. She wanted to yell at her mother and ask her what the bloody hell she was thinking, but another part of her knew that in her shoes she might have done exactly the same thing. She opened her eyes to find that Kathryn had hers closed, hidden behind her fingers, a hand pressed to her face.

'What happened next?' Faye asked, self-consciously lowering her hand. She got an immediate answer. Kathryn spotted the crown of oak and holly, which had fallen from the wounded Holly King's grip, and scrabbled towards it, sliding across the ice and snow. She snatched it up, gritting her teeth. As Faye watched, she wrenched it apart with her bare hands.

'Merry Christmas, you murdering bastard!' Kathryn cried, tossing the crown's remnants aside.

The Holly King moaned as he desperately reached for the broken pieces.

Around them the air darkened and a thunderous crack shook the clearing. A gaping fissure split the ground and Kathryn just about managed to scrabble clear as the hole shook itself wider, swallowing the Holly King, his sarcophagus and Pearl. A blizzard howled through the trees. Kathryn curled into a ball, pulling her hood over her head as the Oak King's sarcophagus toppled to the ground. An intense flurry blinded Faye, though it ended as quickly as it came, leaving only a few pirouetting flakes.

The Oak King's body was gone, though his sarcophagus remained. Kathryn got to her feet, alone in the clearing with the ancient wooden coffin. 'Pearl?'

she said, her voice trembling. The world turned bright white as the vision dissolved.

Faye and the fairy were still sitting in the bough of the hollow oak. The mist had cleared. Through the parting clouds, Faye noted the moon hanging low in the sky. The first light of dawn diluted the night.

Pearl hopped off the bough. 'I don't know exactly what happened next, Faye. I was kinda busy falling through an infinite void of despair in a plane between realities. At least, that's how the Holly King explained it to me when I eventually found him again. We became close. You do when you're lost in the aether. And we weren't like the other mindless blobs there.'

Faye recalled the Holly King's little helpers and their vacant faces. 'Those fairies. They were once people, too?'

'A long time ago.' Pearl's ever-present smirk faded. 'The Holly King brought them with him and turned them into fairies for his own amusement. His own little army of disposable, mindless serfs. That's what happens if you spend too long in the aether. You become kind of a lost soul. A faint memory of yourself. Well, I didn't want that to happen to me, and neither would you. So I did what I had to do. Me and the Holly King, we discovered we had similar ambitions. See, your mom had woken him up from a sleep that had lasted thousands of years. He'd forgotten who he was. But then he'd got a taste of his old demigod life and he wanted it like never before. Me, I wanted to live again. And I wanted my revenge.'

Faye hopped off the bough, tightened her lips and shook her head. 'A glass of warm, salty water.'

'Huh?'

'That's all she needed to avoid this mess. If she'd given you a glass of warm, salty water then you might have thrown up the poison and none of this would've happened. She was daft, there's no getting away from that. But you were dafter.'

'I died because of her! She was the one who woke the demigod.'

'She was trying to help. You died because of both of you. Two silly girls who thought they knew it all. And don't think I haven't noticed that you're still here and she's not. You didn't do so badly out of this after all.' Faye found her hands had bunched into fists again. She flexed her fingers. 'But what's the point in gettin' angry now, eh?' The snowy clearing, once the scene of so much bloodshed and terror, was empty and quiet. 'I reckon ... I reckon we need to put this behind us, Pearl. Mistakes were made. Bloody big ones. But the past is the past and we don't live there. We're in the here and now. So, here. Now. Still want revenge? Still want to kill me?' Faye tensed, ready to leg it if the fairy jumped her.

For the first time since Faye had met her, Pearl looked uncertain. The fairy puffed her cheeks and wiped a hand over her face. She stood for a moment, hands on hips, tapping her toes, before her eyes landed back on Faye. 'When I look at you, I see her. I hated her for so long that I didn't know how to think any other way.

But ... watching what happened, it's different from how I remembered.' Pearl stepped back and folded her arms. 'I don't wanna kill you no more. But I don't like ya, either.'

'Feeling's mutual.' Faye found herself folding her arms, then realised she was mirroring Pearl. She wanted to stop, but reckoned that if she did then Pearl would count it as some sort of small victory. 'Oh, sod it.' She dropped her arms to her side, wincing slightly at Pearl's grin. 'I don't like you, you don't like me. My mum might be a little bit responsible for you poppin' your clogs, but you might be a little bit responsible, too. That's where we are, right?'

'Agreed.'

'Then the important thing now is that we need to stop the Holly King. Let's put all that old nonsense where it belongs in the past, and work together.'

'Suits me.'

'Good.' Faye looked into the depths of the wood. 'We need to find the others.'

'Oh, I found them.' Pearl beamed, but her smile vanished abruptly. 'Then I lost them. They were right behind me, but I guess the mist got them, too.'

Faye felt a familiar dread building in her gut. Were Miss Charlotte and Mrs Teach out there having visions like the one she'd just had?

She shoved her hands into the warm pockets of her flight jacket and started marching back along the path. 'C'mon, move your arse. I came from the village and they weren't there, so who knows where they are now?'

Pearl cackled and hurried after Faye. 'You came from the village? Let me guess. The Holly King got to you, didn't he? What'd he do?' Pearl twisted a knuckle by her eye and pouted. 'Did he make you cwy, widdle one?'

'I didn't cry.' Faye kept marching, trying not to blush. 'You don't know what it's like in this village. Almost everyone here knew my mother better than I did. And they all tell me she was this wise angel with healing hands, and I know they all want me to be just like her.'

Pearl's brow twitched. 'And now how do you feel?'

Faye quickly glanced back the way they'd come. 'I should be disappointed with her. That she was so daft. But the truth is . . .' A smile crept across her face. 'It's like a weight's come off, if you know what I mean? She was just as reckless as I am. Mind you, I would never have done something as dangerous as that.'

'The night is young,' Pearl muttered. 'So how did the Holly King make you cry?'

'I told you, he didn't. I was pissed off.'

'With him?'

'With everyone.' Faye didn't know why she so readily confessed to Pearl, but she had a feeling that the fairy could be the only one who might understand.

'Did he do the secrets thing?'

Faye said nothing, but a sideways glance gave her away.

Pearl smirked in recognition. 'Yeah, he used to do that when we encountered new souls in the aether. As if the poor bums hadn't suffered enough already. Now they get to drift in empty space for all time, knowing

their mothers were disappointed in them. It's a pill.'
Pearl slapped Faye on the shoulder. 'Who cares what
they say, huh? You save their sorry asses and they'll
love you for ever.'

Faye wondered how much she wanted their love now.
'I s'pose.'

'You *suppose*?' Pearl hurried to block Faye's way, but
Faye dodged around her. 'Hey, that's not how to win
wars, kiddo. You *suppose* you wanna save your friends
and neighbours? No. You gotta believe it. Otherwise,
His Highness will see your doubt and he'll exploit
it, and then we all end up drifting through infinity
knowing that our mommas hated us. Or worse.' Pearl
playfully punched Faye in the arm. 'So c'mon, Faye.
You really wanna save these people?'

Faye wanted to rub her sore arm, but as with the
folding-arms dilemma, she didn't want to hand Pearl
another little victory. Being around the fairy was
exhausting. She continued to trudge through the snow
in silence.

'You don't hafta answer now, that's dandy,' Pearl
reassured her, before hurriedly grabbing the crook of
her elbow. 'But what's the plan, toots?'

Faye didn't reply. She didn't have a plan. No plan,
and no idea if she even wanted to save the villagers after
all they'd said to her. All she wanted to do was to keep
walking. Drifting in emptiness for infinity was actually
starting to sound like a nice change.

Her boots slid beneath her and for a moment she
thought she was slipping on ice. That's all she needed.

To fall flat on her arse in front of Pearl. But the ground surged, sending them both tumbling to the ground.

'Earthquake?' Pearl looked puzzled as she got to her knees.

'Maybe . . . No, wait. Listen.' Faye raised a finger and cocked an ear. 'The trees. They're singing.'

'ALL HUMANS ARE BASTARDS' AND OTHER SONGS OF THE TREES

Mrs Teach had a fair few remedies in her cellar for hangovers, but nothing had quite the immediate sobering effect as sheer terror. As the Holly King's voice rattled the village windows, the fairies dived for cover and the drunken villagers ceased their revels. They blinked in confusion. What on earth were they doing? Avoiding eye contact, they hurriedly gathered up whatever belongings were nearby and dashed back to their homes, eyes wide with fear and faces red with mortification.

Bertie remained beside Terrence, who was still locked in the gibbet. Mrs Teach was getting an earful from Shirley, who refused to believe her Eric was in any danger.

'You just can't bear to see Eric get the respect he deserves.' Shirley jabbed a finger at Mrs Teach's chest.

'You're so used to hogging all the attention that you're just jealous. You're nothing but a green-eyed—'

'I am trying to save his life, you ridiculous woman.' Mrs Teach ducked around Shirley and crouched next to the postman, who was curled up on his armchair throne with his hands over his ears as the Holly King's one-note opera continued.

'Eric, you're still the Lord of Misrule.' Mrs Teach shook him by the arms. 'He has to obey your commands. Get the Holly King to tell you the truth.'

Shirley shoved Mrs Teach aside, sending her tumbling down the memorial steps. 'Don't listen to her, my darling, it's a trick!'

'Mrs Teach!' Bertie's voice barely carried over the Holly King's deafening melody. He was pointing at something. 'Mrs Teach, is that supposed to be happening?'

She followed his pointing finger to the bottom of the Wode Road, where a silver birch tree by the ARP shelter was shaking like a belly dancer.

'Oh no.' Mrs Teach's voice was swallowed up by the noise. 'No, Bertie, it is not.'

⁊

The Holly King's song brought him joy like no other. Not only could he torment the infestation of humans on his land, but with his deepest notes he could commune with his oldest allies. The Holly King sang to the trees.

360

ɸ

Few people realise this, but trees are terrible gossips.

The first trees, the earliest ferns of the Carboniferous Period, had learned how to swap tips on dealing with pesky insects and coexisting with fungi. Over millennia, they developed a complex language using scent, electricity and sound vibrations carried via their roots. The trees understood that their accumulated knowledge – essential to their ongoing existence – needed to be passed on from generation to generation, across all species. It needed to be easy to remember, and they found a solution that came naturally to them. Song. To this day, the ground resonates with trees sharing their memories through subsonic melodies. As is the way of things, new generations of trees became bored of the same old songs and decided to expand the repertoire. They didn't abandon the classics entirely – a jolly ditty on coping with nibbling caterpillars is always useful – but they invented the concept of music for pleasure thousands of years before humanoids first clacked rocks together in a groovy rhythm.

What even fewer people realise is that these newer songs are incredibly catty. The trees sing about dim-witted mountains who deserve all the erosion they get. They recite lyrics mocking squirrels and their addiction to nuts. They pour scorn on moronic rivers who gleefully slide into oceans only to become air-headed clouds, before tumbling back onto the same hills they started from. There is a choral piece devoted to the tediousness of the rain cycle that takes the trees over twenty thousand years to perform in its entirety (trees might be bitchy, but they're also very slow).

But trees reserve their most venomous verse for the new kid on the evolutionary block. Humanity. These bipedal pests have proven to be the trees' deadliest enemy. They could tolerate dinosaurs tramping over them, birds setting up their nests all over the place, bears defecating in their collective, even fungi and beetles collaborating to wipe out poor old elm. But these fast-breeding humans adopted arboreal genocide with unbridled glee, felling trees in unprecedented numbers and using their lumber for anything and everything they could think of. Firewood, log cabins, coffee tables, pencils. This last proved to be a cruel irony, as a handful of humans actually used these pencils to write their own poems and songs about their alleged love of trees.

The trees joined forces with plants and grasses to develop chemical weapons, but ultimately hay fever turned out to be little more than an irritant to a select few humans.

And so they had to fall back on composing and sharing songs with titles like 'All Humans Are Bastards', and swapping scandalous stories of the awful things humans were doing to the world and to one another. The trees could recognise when a species was headed for extinction and they decided to bide their time. Once humanity was gone, they would take back their land and churn all of its creations into dust.

But every now and then, the trees were given an opportunity to cause a little havoc in a way that humans would understand. And one of these moments had just presented itself.

The arboreal demigod, the Holly King – a spirit born from the seeds of a tree – was singing to them, urging them to rise up. The song spread through the root network, and soon the whole wood had joined in a harmony that even the humans could hear. This lost chord vibrated through the ground and the air, carrying a simple command.

Grow.

It started with a birch tree at the bottom of the Wode Road, on the corner by the ARP post. Isolated from the other trees, it stood closest to the Holly King. The silver birch flexed. Sections of its white bark – hanging like flaky wallpaper – snapped like flags in the wind as the layers closest to the trunk tightened, cracked and popped. Its roots shook off loose soil and icy slush. They rose from the ground like creeping, gnarled, pale fingers, paving slabs buckling as they spread. The birch's branches trembled, twigs blowing like wisps of hair as the song found another voice.

The other trees in the Wode Road began to join the chorus. All were surrounded by concrete and cobbles at street level, but their roots went deep. Further down the road, close to the woodland path by the stream, a wych elm took up the melody. Over ninety feet tall, its voice reverberated up and down the streets. Those villagers still outside staggered about in panic. At the

roundabout by the railway bridge, the solitary dog-
wood planted in the centre of the raised bed spread
itself out, sending bricks and soil tumbling onto the
road. By the telephone box a bare hazel tree caused
such sudden subsidence that the panes of glass in the
red booth all smashed at once.

At Saint Irene's Church, the big sycamore joined
forces with a nearby cherry tree to send tiles slipping
off the lychgate roof and smashing onto the path.

But the foremost blasphemy was reserved for the
great yew. Primeval and deathly, it had overseen the
church graveyard for centuries. Its branches bent and
twisted, mirroring the contortions of the countless
grief-stricken mourners it had witnessed over that
time. Its roots cradled the dead in their coffins before
reaching under the church and its tower, holding them
in balance.

When the song came to the yew, it was accompanied
by the thoughts and commands of the Holly King.

He had a different instruction for the old giant.

Retreat.

If I do that, said the yew, *I will surely die.*

*Your time has come, old friend. You have earned
your rest. Retreat.*

The yew was reluctant, but it was tired and no longer
had the energy to argue with the Holly King, as it had
done so many times in the distant past. It acquiesced,
and hastened its demise. Its roots shrank and shrivelled, leaving gaps in the foundations of the church.
The crypt walls cracked and crumbled. The bell tower

began to sink. The entire edifice tilted until the clappers surrendered to gravity and the bells pealed of their own accord. The tower was heading for collapse, and nothing and no one could stop it.

SAINT IRENE'S LAST PEAL

Faye and Pearl staggered through the quaking wood as branches tumbled around them. Owls and robins took to the air, darting to safety. They had the right idea, Faye thought.

'Sod this for a laugh.' Her eyes raked Pearl from head to toe, sizing her up. 'How much do you weigh?'

The twisted branch of a hazel tree came crashing down next to them.

'Doesn't matter. Hold on tight.' Faye grabbed the fairy around the waist, drawing on the power of the moon as they rose silently, sliding up through the trembling branches of the singing trees. The eastern horizon was a violent red. Somewhere, church bells rang.

'What the hell?' Faye spun in the air, nearly dropping Pearl.

'Hey!' the fairy complained. 'Watch it. If you hadn't broken my wings, maybe I could fly myself.'

'Shut up,' Faye snapped, her heart kicking at her ribs. The bell tower didn't look quite right. It seemed to be tilting like the Leaning Tower of Pisa. The bells clanged mournfully again, but this was no peal. Faye knew no one could be ringing the bells.

Something unthinkable was happening. The bell tower was collapsing. She gripped Pearl tighter, imagined them both as a tiny moon orbiting the world, and flew as fast as she could.

It wasn't fast enough.

Faye knew the tower was designed to wobble. When the bells were being rung, she could feel it swaying beneath her feet, but she always felt safe, secure in the knowledge that it had been built with that elasticity in mind. A few cracks had appeared in the outer walls over the centuries, but those had been reinforced with iron bars decades ago. It was the most solid building for miles around.

For the tower to fall, something truly catastrophic would need to happen, like a bomb, or a—

Faye thought of the yew tree's roots in the crypt, intertwined with the stone foundations. She looked at the trees below, their roots writhing, and a sudden cold dread filled her belly as she understood what was happening.

The first cracks appeared in the tower's window reveals. The lead frames buckled and the glass shattered, sending shards tumbling to earth. Faye was thankful that at least the stained-glass windows were in storage somewhere, but her gratitude was short-lived. The iron bars securing the old cracks bent and surrendered to the weight of cascading stone. The flint walls popped as long fissures slashed like knife wounds through their sides. Faye heard the timber bell frames snap like bones as the bells gave one final round of chimes.

The bell tower of Saint Irene's came crashing down onto the graveyard, crushing the yew tree that had betrayed it.

'No!' Faye cried, her stomach tightening as she and Pearl landed heavily by the lychgate, which had also tumbled over in the embrace of the sycamore tree.

'He's taking it back,' Pearl said, though her voice was muffled in Faye's ears.

Her beloved bells were cracked. Broken hearts lying in the rubble of the dead tower. She would never feel their old, familiar weight again, never feel that connection with her mother, who had rung the same bells. Nothing would ever be the same again.

All because of one big, bearded, antlered bastard.

Pearl's words finally reached Faye, and she sifted them in her head. 'What's he taking back?'

'The village.' The fairy gripped her arm. 'He kept talking about it, but I didn't think he was crazy enough to do it. He's singing to the trees, Faye. He's telling them to take back the land, to become his wood again. They're going to destroy the whole village.'

Faye had felt anger before, of course. She was known to lose her rag on occasion, though she was always quick to recover and apologise.

But she had never felt such rage as she did now. It filled her up inside with a quivering white heat. No one, but no one, messed with her bells.

'Pearl.' Faye was surprised at the calm tone of her voice. 'How do I kill a demigod?'

'Wouldn't you know it, toots, you've been able to do it all along.' Pearl curled her lips into a wicked smile and leaned closer to Faye. 'You kill him with kindness.'

※

The collapse of the bell tower was like something from a nightmare. Bertie couldn't believe what he had seen, and yet there had also been something strangely inevitable about it, like his own eventual demise. It had even shaken Terrence out of his stupor. That, and the ongoing destruction wrought by the trees. Paving slabs were rising all around them as roots stretched up from the ground. A lamp post by the butcher's came crashing down.

'What the bloody hell was that?' the landlord asked, his voice making some recovery to its usual strident self.

'My bells ...' Bertie, like most bell-ringers, felt a kind of proprietorial kinship with the bells in his tower. They were his to ring, protect and care for, and now he had failed them, too. 'They're gone.'

As the dust began to clear, he peered up the Wode Road towards the church and the pile of rubble that had once been the bell tower. He thought he could see people dashing for cover, and his heart trilled at the thought that Faye might be coming to the rescue, but when he blinked they had vanished. He was silly to think she would come back. Why would she, after all they had said to her? Bertie wondered if he would ever see her again.

'Get me out of this bloody thing, Bertie!' Terrence rattled the door of the gibbet. 'Someone here needs to be taught a lesson.'

Bertie glanced over to the glowing Holly King and his floating guard of watchful fairies. 'I don't know if that's such a good idea, Mr Bright.'

'I will not rot in this poxy cage, Bertie Butterworth.' Terrence reached through the bars and gripped Bertie's wrist. 'You and me, we've done wrong by our Faye. I know I never meant to say what I did, and I reckon you were the same.'

Bertie nodded frantically, his words tumbling over themselves as he replied. 'It's true, it's true, it just came out. I didn't want to say it, any of it. Honest, I didn't.'

'What's done is done, but we can try and make amends for it.' Terrence nodded up the Wode Road, where Bertie saw a wych elm keel over onto the roof of Mr Loaf's funeral parlour. The crash of glass and tile was almost as loud as the bell tower's collapse.

'There's tools in the pub, Bertie. No time to lose.'

THE WILD MAN OF WOODVILLE

Mrs Teach shut out the racket around her and focused on Shirley Birdwhistle, only momentarily distracted by the sound of iron scraping on cobbles as Bertie dragged Terrence and his cage up the road.

'You're nothing but a ratty gossip and a liar.' Shirley scowled at Mrs Teach. 'Eric won't listen to a word you say.'

'You think me a liar, Shirley? A *ratty gossip*?' Mrs Teach bristled but kept her calm. 'Take it from me, Shirley Birdwhistle, I haven't even begun. You think he's the only one who keeps secrets?' Her eyes flitted to the Holly King, still singing and glowing like a lantern, surrounded by his floating fairies. 'I know about every last one of your husband's deliveries. I know that he wears lifts in his boots. I know that he's taken the Civil Service exam three times and failed, and I know that you resent him for it, and want to take it yourself just to show him what for. I know that he uses Dr Scholl's Solvex for the itching in his toes. I know that on his first day on the job he went from door to door looking for a house named "Fragile". I know that he ran over Miss Moon's cat with his bike and tossed the half-dead moggy in the river to make it look like it had drowned. I could ruin him with whispers, and it would be oh so easy. But you, Shirley, I'll save the best for you.' Mrs Teach took some satisfaction from the sight of the other woman's face turning the colour of a china teapot left in the sun for too long, but as another tree crashed into a house, she realised she was running out of time. 'I know what has become of your son, Shirley Birdwhistle.'

'My son is at home in bed.'

'Is he? Then fetch him.'

'I do not fetch and carry for the likes of you, Philomena Teach.'

'Your son has become something quite extraordinary, Shirley.' Mrs Teach allowed herself a smile. 'He'll be here soon. You won't recognise him at first, but I'll be happy to point him out to you ... if you make this stop now.'

Shirley clenched her fists. 'My son is a hero. You should get on your rotten, grubby knees and thank him for what he's done, rather than—'

'What was that about Sidney?' Eric shuffled forward, eager to hear.

'Eric, be quiet,' Shirley snapped.

'He looked ever so troubled when he came home. I wasn't myself and I'm afraid I said some terrible things to him.'

'Eric, keep your trap shut!'

Mrs Teach held Eric's pleading gaze. 'Take the crown off, Eric. Help me destroy it.'

Eric winced. 'I . . . I don't think I should.'

Mrs Teach grabbed the crown and tugged on it.

'Ow!' Eric cried, stumbling into her embrace. Mrs Teach pulled with all her might, but the crown was as much a part of Eric as his own hair. It wouldn't budge or break.

She huffed as she released him, nodding towards to the Holly King. 'Then make him stop. Make him stop, and I'll tell you everything you need to know about Sid.'

'Eric, don't you dare.'

Eric shrivelled under his wife's radioactive glare, but on balance he found that Mrs Teach frightened him more.

'O Holly King,' he cried, and the Holly King opened one eye. 'Cease this thing you are doing with the trees, I command you.'

The Holly King continued to sing, his eyes bearing down upon the crowned postman.

'I command you, as Lord of Misrule!' Eric hollered, his voice breaking a little.

The Holly King stopped. He set his jaw, breathing heavily through his nostrils.

Mrs Teach's ears rang in the silence that followed. Somewhere a dog barked, and in the distance came the metal clang of hammering. She wondered what Bertie and Terrence were up to.

Eric's lip half-curled at this little demonstration of his power. 'Thank you,' he said.

'I suggest you relish what little remains of your reign, my lord.' The Holly King raised a hand to the lightening sky. 'Come sunrise, I will rule once more.'

Eric chuckled nervously. 'About that. She was just joking, yes?' He looked from the Holly King to Mrs Teach. 'About you killing me at sunrise?'

The Holly King said nothing.

Shirley took Eric by the arm and tried to pull him away. 'Don't be so daft.'

But Eric shook her off. He shuffled back and forth in the armchair, wringing his hands. 'Tell me, Holly King. I command you to tell me. Is it true? Will I be executed at sunrise?'

The Holly King leaned forwards, hands on his knees. 'It will be quick, Eric Birdwhistle. And painless. You have my guarantee.'

'You'll have to get through me first.' Mrs Teach placed herself between the demigod and the Birdwhistles. She held her handbag tightly, like a little leather shield.

'Very well.' The Holly King drew back his fist.

Mrs Teach tensed, bracing for what might be her incredibly painful last moments. She wished her Ernie was with her. As she did so, two fairies dropped down behind her, seizing Eric and Shirley by the arms. The couple kicked and cried for help as they were dragged away.

Mrs Teach winced at having fallen for such a cheap distraction.

'Begone, witch.' The Holly King lowered his fist and held his belly as he chortled.

Mrs Teach glanced up to see the other fairies scrutinising her as though she was a dessert. She could probably thump a couple of them into unconsciousness with her handbag, but not the lot. Still, never let it be said that she didn't go down fighting.

'Don't just float there, gawping,' she told them, raising her chin and sneering in the face of death. 'Get on with it.'

At that moment a shadow leapt from the roof of the butcher's. It was no more than a blur as it flew through the air, swinging a club made of ancient oak. The Holly King was fast, catching the club in his mighty grip before it could crack open his skull. The woodwose tumbled into him, sending the pair of them sprawling onto the cobbles. The club rattled out of reach as the woodwose pummelled the Holly King with a flurry of savage kicks and punches.

The circling fairies lost all interest in Mrs Teach and pounced on the hairy man, but he batted them away like flies.

The Birdwhistles gawped in horrified astonishment as they wriggled in the grip of their captors.

'What is that disgusting creature?' Shirley asked, her face contorted by fear and repulsion.

'Some kind of monster.' Eric looked like he was about to vomit at the mere sight of the thing.

Mrs Teach's heart sank. What could she tell them? Despite her promise to identify Sidney to his mother, she didn't have the heart to do it now. Not yet. And not while he was doing what she could not. If not actually saving them from a demigod and his minions, then definitely buying them some time.

The rhythmic clang of a bell came from the ruins of Saint Irene's bell tower. Somehow, Mrs Teach knew the bell tolled for her. She was being summoned. It was time for a strategic retreat.

℘

Sid's blood rushed as he battered the Holly King. The old demigod had been caught on the hop when Sid had crashed into him, raining down blows without mercy. The fairies had piled on, but they were little more than an annoyance. He sent them spinning like tiddlywinks.

Sid became aware of a familiar sound. His parents' voices as they kicked and wailed, thinking they were surely next. Sid chuckled out loud. He couldn't wait to see their faces when Pearl changed him back. Mum never liked to admit she was wrong and would try and make out that she knew all along, and that her screaming was just an act. Dad would lecture Sid for telling lies before going off in a huff.

A bell was ringing. Mrs Teach was running away. Sid made his first mistake, allowing himself to be distracted. That was all the Holly King needed to break free from his hold. The demigod took the woodwose by the scruff of the neck and hurled him through the air. Sid's head slammed against the cobbles, and for a moment everything went white and his ears whistled.

He realised that he would never defeat the Holly King like this. His human compassion and concern for others were drawing his eye from the task at hand. To win this fight, he would need to become a ruthless creature of instinct. He would need to give himself entirely to the woodwose.

It made so much sense now, and Sid was surprised by how easy it was. The woodwose's rage and thirst for blood washed over him like waves on the shore, and he welcomed it. The woodwose was in control now. He shook his head clear, hopped to his feet and charged at the Holly King.

DENOUEMENT WITH A DEMIGOD

Faye stood amid the rubble of the bell tower, a chunk of flint in her gloved hand. She brought it down again and again on the cracked tenor bell, which she had discovered lying on its side in the ruins. It chimed with each strike, though not the joyous ring she was used to, but a flat clang of dead iron. It would have to do.

Pearl was close by, hands covering her ears. She was yelling something and looking over Faye's shoulder. Faye turned to see Miss Charlotte clambering across the rubble to join them.

'Oh, Faye, I'm so sorry,' the witch said with surprising sincerity as she surveyed the wreckage.

Faye shrugged as she continued to hit the bell. 'It's been one of those nights.'

'Faye! Miss Charlotte!'

They turned to see Mrs Teach not exactly running – that wasn't really her bag – but *hastening* in their direction up the Wode Road. In the distance, Faye could see the Birdwhistles being held captive as the woodwose fought against the Holly King and the fairies. He was strong but wildly outnumbered, and no matter how many times he whacked the fairies away, they always came back for more.

'Faye, I tried destroying the crown, but it's stuck on Eric's head like a limpet,' Mrs Teach said, gasping for air as she arrived at the foot of the rubble mountain. 'Our only hope is to help young Sidney.'

'We will.' Faye stopped ringing and tossed the flint away. 'And here's how.'

⌀

With a final tap from Terrence's mallet, Bertie knocked out the last pin holding the gibbet door in place. Its clatter echoed around the backyard of the Green Man pub as Bertie helped the landlord clamber out.

'About bloody time.' Terrence stretched his limbs and tilted his head from side to side until something went *pop*. 'That's better.'

'What do we do now, Mr Bright?' Bertie cracked open the gate and peered out into the alley. 'You said something about making amends?'

'I did, didn't I.' Terrence marched past the lad and swung the gate wide open. 'We can start by rousing the Home Guard, loading our rifles and unleashing several rounds of *amends* on the big beardy bastard.'

'You weren't there when we first met the Holly King, Mr Bright,' Bertie said as he hurried to keep up with the grim-faced man. 'Bullets just whizz round him.'

Terrence stopped where the alley met the Wode Road.

'We've got a new problem, Bertie.' He nodded towards the war memorial, where a tall, hairy man was fighting the Holly King while several fairies tied Eric and Shirley Birdwhistle to the stone cross. 'Whose side do you think the hairy fella's on?'

'Doesn't matter,' Bertie said with a tinge of optimism in his voice. 'Cos *they're* on ours.' He nudged Terrence and pointed up the Wode Road.

Striding down the cobbles like a sheriff and deputies on their way to a gunfight were Faye, Miss Charlotte, Mrs Teach and Pearl. Bertie was slightly bemused by the presence of Pearl.

'The last time I saw that one,' Bertie said, 'she had me locked in the gibbet and was trying to kill Faye.'

'The last time I saw that one ...' Terrence took a deep breath. 'She buggered my knee.'

Bertie frowned at him. 'I thought you got your dodgy knee playing football?'

'It's been a long and peculiar night, Bertie.' Terrence rested a hand on the lad's shoulder. 'And it's a long and peculiar story. For another time. Anyhow, I reckon Faye might've won her over. It's the sort of thing she does,' he added with a little wobble of pride in his voice.

'Don't suppose we can put this off any longer, can we?' Bertie looked to Terrence.

'No, lad. Time to take it on the chin.'

Bertie called Faye's name and hurried across the cobbled street as fast as his uneven legs would allow. She and Mrs Teach came to a stop. Miss Charlotte and Pearl kept marching.

'Have fun, kids.' Pearl wiggled her fingers in a wave as Miss Charlotte drew her sword. 'Remember what I said. Kill him with kindness.'

Bertie wondered what that could possibly mean, but he had other priorities. 'Faye, I'm so sorry. I don't know where to start. I didn't mean what I said. Well, yes, I suppose that perhaps I did mean it, and I sometimes get thoughts that I don't want to say out loud, because they're not the best part of me, but ... I don't want to hurt you, and of course you should wear whatever you want. I do, so why shouldn't—'

Faye raised a hand.

Bertie shut up just as Terrence arrived at his side. He said nothing to his daughter. The pained expression of regret on his face said it all.

Mrs Teach stood some distance away, and Bertie wondered if she did so to get out of range of the torrent of rage that Faye was perfectly entitled to unleash on them.

'I've got something for you.' Faye reached into the fur-lined pocket of her flight jacket. Bertie wouldn't have been surprised if it was a cosh, but what she whipped out was quite unexpected.

A sprig of mistletoe.

As he boggled at it, Faye kissed him on the cheek. Then did the same to her gobsmacked father.

Bertie dabbed the wet patch on his face. 'What ... what was that for?'

Faye's specs were smudged. She popped them off and breathed on them before giving them a quick clean with the end of her blouse. 'Pearl told me the Holly King used to come here every year at Yule to test people. He'd reveal everyone's secrets and have a jolly old time watching folk turn on each other.' Faye slid her glasses back on and leaned closer. 'But she told me the secret to defeating him.'

Bertie crinkled his nose. 'It's not guns, is it? I was just telling your dad that bullets go right round him.'

'Is it anything to do with the hairy fella?' Terrence asked. 'He's certainly giving him what for.'

Faye shook her head. 'No, it's not guns. And the woodwose is part of the plan to keep the Holly King occupied. Miss Charlotte says she's bumped off a couple of the fairies with her sword already and wants to do more, and Cousin Pearl is going to lend a hand while we do our bit.'

'And what's that?'

'Yuletide is a time to forgive and make peace with the past,' Faye said. 'The Holly King has divided us and we need to come together again. I'm planning to do that by forgiving anyone that's done me a wrong'un, and by apologising to anyone that I've annoyed.'

'We could be here all night,' Terrence smiled, his face getting its familiar cheerful crinkle back.

'What are you apologising for?' Such was the intensity of Bertie's frown that his eyebrows almost met in the middle.

'If we're going to stop the Holly King, I need the villagers on my side, but they all think I'm a know-it-all bossyboots.'

Bertie squinted. 'But you're *not* a know-it-all bossyboots.'

Terrence made a noise at the back of his throat. 'She has her moments, Bertie.'

'Don't we all? Why does *she* have to be sorry for it?' Bertie turned his hands over, showing his palms. 'You don't have to apologise for anything, Faye.'

'Normally I'd agree with you, Bertie. And there are times to put your foot down, but this don't feel like one of them. If I'm going to save this lot, then I have to show them I understand and there's no hard feelings. And they'll have to see that I mean it.' Faye thought for a moment, then grimaced at her father. 'Do you remember when that politician came here a few years ago, going door to door?'

Terrence sighed. 'Silly sod was chased out of town.'

'I feel a bit like him. Like I'm spinning a line to get what I want.'

Terrence shook his head. 'He was lying through his teeth to get votes. You're putting aside your pride and eating a bit of humble pie to save the village. We all have to do stuff we don't like, Faye. All part of growing up. And I'm proud of you for it.'

'I s'pose so,' Faye grumbled, twisting her lips to hide how misty her eyes were getting. She began to march down the road, and Terrence and Bertie both limped after her.

'Oh, and by the way, dear Father, I discovered how you really got that war wound.' She glanced down at Terrence's knee.

Bertie leaned forward and whispered, 'He didn't get it playing football.'

'Oh, I know.' Faye gave her father a wry smile. 'But we'll have plenty of time to discuss it later. Before that, I need you two to do a little digging for me. Here's what you have to find.'

℘

Sid was losing himself. The harder he fought, the less Sid-like he felt. The thing called Sid came and went like the sun behind summer clouds. With each punch, it drifted further and further away. But he didn't care. Sid was his weakness. All that mattered was to destroy the demigod and protect ... these people. A man and a woman. Feeble, frightened. Dead soon. Humans lived and died in the blink of an eye. So why bother? Why save them? The fight was all that mattered. The woodwose bared his yellow teeth and bit down on the Holly King's nose.

℘

Miss Charlotte weighed the sword in her hand as she and Pearl approached the melee at the war memorial. Eric and Shirley wailed in fright, tormented by the hovering fairies, as the Holly King and the woodwose punched and kicked and slashed at each other with increasing savagery. The woodwose's eyes were bright, his teeth bared in a primal grin. As he chewed on the Holly King's nose, blood gushing across both their faces, he looked like he was having the time of his life.

'What did you do to that boy?' Charlotte muttered to Pearl.

'I set him free.' Pearl smiled and batted her eyelids, quite proud of herself. 'We've all got this inside us. We just never invite it to parties.'

'With good reason,' Charlotte said as the woodwose headbutted the Holly King and elbowed a fairy in the face. 'And you're sure you can bring him back?'

Pearl produced a tartan flask from within the billowing expanse of her gossamer dress.

Miss Charlotte frowned. 'With a strong cup of tea?'

'Blood.' Pearl shook the flask like a cocktail mixer. 'Sid's blood before he became that thing.'

'You bled him?'

'It's been blessed by me. There's just enough of this to restore the kid to his jolly old self. Of course, he's gotta drink it before sun-up.'

'What happens if he doesn't?'

'Oh, he stays that way. Permanent, like.'

Charlotte winced as the Holly King grabbed the woodwose by the neck and slammed him into the memorial's stone steps. She took a breath. The nerves behind her damaged eye throbbed and pain sliced through her. Time for a little revenge.

'Let's give him a hand, then,' she said, raising her sword and charging.

LET'S GET THIS OVER WITH

Even as Faye delivered her apology to Mr and Mrs Baxter, she began to question the wisdom of her chosen course of action. It was eight in the morning, an hour before sunrise, and the couple stood in their doorway, overcoats hastily thrown on over their night things. Mr Baxter had one hand propping him up against the door frame. Mrs Baxter had a confused and hungover expression weighing down her jowls.

Faye continued, regardless. 'I realised that you were absolutely right and that I do speak at a volume that some might find annoying.' She kept her voice low, careful not to antagonise the Baxters any further. 'And so I should like to apologise for any discomfort that I might have caused.'

'What?' Mr Baxter cupped his ear. 'Speak up, girl. What do you want?'

'I *want to apologise for being too loud!*' Faye blurted. She didn't have to turn to sense Mrs Teach wincing behind her. 'I should also like to thank you,

Mr Baxter, for everything you do with the firefighting volunteers, and thank you, Mrs Baxter, for the splendid work you do running the Saucepans for Spitfires collection.'

Something happened to the Baxters. His shoulders dropped. Her eyes softened. Mrs Baxter clasped her hands before her, pursing her lips thoughtfully before speaking. 'Faye, it's been a long and confusing night. I know we all got a little raucous earlier, and ... Well, I'm sorry, too, young lady.'

'So we're all tickety-boo?' Faye grinned.

Mr Baxter nodded. 'Oh, that was never in doubt.'

'Lovely stuff. Merry Christmas to you both.'

'Is it?' Mrs Baxter looked puzzled as she made to close the door. 'Yes, I suppose it is, near enough. Merry Christmas, Faye.'

Faye dusted her hands and skipped down the path to where Mrs Teach waited for her by the Baxters' garden gate.

'Do you hear that?' Mrs Teach cupped a hand to her ear. She didn't wait for Faye to answer. 'That's the sound of the ghosts of suffragettes past crying at your betrayal, Faye Bright. Never apologise to anyone for speaking your mind. Especially a mutton-chopped ironmonger like him.'

'I don't like it any more than you do, Mrs Teach, but I have to do what's necessary to make peace with everyone. Who's next?'

Mrs Teach consulted her list. 'If we take a shortcut through Perry Lane, we could get to Mr Hodgson's—'

'Hold up.' Faye raised a hand and sniffed the air.

Mr Baxter's house was on the corner of Unthank Road. An alley ran along its rear and was a popular spot for young people who wanted to do certain things away from the prying eyes of parents and police officers. But they hadn't reckoned on Faye's keen sense of smell. The pungent tang of phosphorous and cheap tobacco tickled her nostrils. She put a finger to her lips and beckoned Mrs Teach to follow her.

They turned into the alley to find Betty Marshall, Milly Baxter and her younger sister Dotty sharing a roll-up cigarette. Milly and Dotty froze as if keeping still might make them invisible.

Betty, as always, was as defiant as one would expect from the daughter of the captain of the local Home Guard. 'What do you two want?'

'I'm here to make peace,' Faye said.

'Then get lost.' Betty laughed and took a drag on the cigarette.

Faye stuffed her hands into her flight jacket pockets and rocked back and forth on her heels. 'You were right, Betty. I am a witch, and I do dress like a boy. But ...' She raised a finger. 'I do draw the line at being called a brazen hussy.'

Dotty, a perky combination of big teeth, freckles and curls, sniffed. 'Sorry, Faye.'

She was rewarded with a glare from Betty. Milly drew her closer.

'I'm sure you didn't mean it.' Faye gave Dotty a friendly wink, then turned to Betty and Milly. 'And as for you pair, I know you think I'm peculiar, but I ain't gonna change. The sooner we all accept each other for who we are, the better we might get along.' Faye's heart thumped a little harder. It had been months since her last proper conversation with these girls, and they'd never really seen eye to eye. They kept their distance, warding her off with scowls and sneers. All this reconciliation lark was a bit terrifying, but speaking to them now made Faye kick herself for not doing it a lot sooner. 'And for my part, I reckon what you girls do in the WAAFs is nothing short of marvellous. I know it ain't easy, and I admire you for keeping going. I don't know if anyone's told you that recently, but there it is.'

Milly and Dotty smiled. Betty kept her curled lip of disdain in place as she sucked on the roll-up, but Faye could see it was just for show now.

'Anyway, Merry Christmas, girls.'

'Merry Christmas, Faye,' Dotty said, sincerely.

As Faye made her way back down the alley, she could hear Mrs Teach speak as she leaned closer to the girls.

'Smoking stunts your growth, you know,' she told them. 'And it shrinks your bosom.'

Faye glanced back to see Betty, horrified, dropping the roll-up and grinding it out with the tip of her shoe.

'Who's next?' Faye asked as they passed under the railway bridge.

Mrs Teach checked her list. 'Mr Hodgson.'

Faye's feet felt heavy. The things Mr Hodgson had said about Faye and her ringing hadn't been delivered with any malice, but in a cold, matter-of-fact way that had hurt all the more.

She nodded. 'Let's get this over with.'

⚕

Terrence and Bertie hurried as they circled the rubble of Saint Irene's bell tower, clambering over boulders of flint and ragstone.

'Here it is!' Bertie cried, beckoning Terrence over.

Some of the north wall was still standing, jutting up at a perilous angle like a broken tooth. The devil's door was remarkably undamaged.

Terrence gestured at the door. 'And it's in there, is it?'

Bertie plastered on a brave smile. 'In, then down some steps.'

'Oh, triffic.' Terrence rolled up his sleeves. 'Let's get this over with.'

⚕

Miss Charlotte had been to war on occasion. She'd fought in duels, and once hastened the demise of Matthew Hopkins, the Witchfinder General. But she had never been in a scrap as strange as this one.

Eric and Shirley Birdwhistle were tied to the stone cross of the war memorial, caterwauling in fear, as their son Sidney, inhabiting the form of a woodwose, attempted to knock seven bells out of the demigod known as the Holly King.

Around that central punch-up was a melee of an altogether different kind, as flying fairies dive-bombed

Charlotte and Pearl Wynter – a fairy herself, albeit one with broken wings.

Between bombing runs, the fairies buzzed around the Holly King's empty sack where it lay on the cobbles. Three of them held it open while their winged comrades darted in and out, somehow emerging with a curious selection of festive weapons.

One fairy rummaged eagerly in the sack, tongue poking out from between her lips, and cackled as she brought out a bright, shining seven-pointed star, the kind you might put at the top of a Christmas tree. Hefting it in her pudgy hands and squinting one eye, she took aim and hurled it at Miss Charlotte, who ducked just in time.

The star juddered as its deadly points stabbed into the roundel of a lollipop bus stop.

Charlotte was quick to grab it and hurl it back towards the fairy. Her aim was true. It sliced through the air before lodging deep in her target's forehead. The fairy's eyes crossed as she looked up at the star. Her legs kicked uselessly in the air, and she gave a pathetic squeak of panic before bursting into a billion golden glittering shards.

'Nice shot!' Pearl said, ducking a blow from a red-and-white-striped candy cane. The fairy wielding it darted just out of her reach before diving to deliver another blow. This time the candy cane struck Pearl's back with the heavy thud of an iron bar. She gasped a curse as it knocked the wind out of her. A second blow cracked against one of her already broken wings and the useless appendage snapped clean off. Pearl scrabbled for it, but the fairy pulled a length of tinsel from her waist, twirling it about her head like a bull-whip. With a crack of her wrist, it snapped around Pearl's neck. The fairy rose into the air and Pearl went with her, feet kicking and eyes bulging as the noose tightened.

Charlotte ran and leapt onto a nearby bench, boosting herself just high enough to cut through the tinsel whip with her sword.

Pearl hit the ground and rolled over, grabbing her useless wing. She snapped away the scapula, wielding it like a javelin. As the candy cane fairy swooped down for another attack, Pearl hurled the pointed missile. It pierced the membrane of the fairy's wing and sent her spinning onto the cobbles, where Pearl snatched up the candy cane and brought it smashing down onto her head. This fairy, too, burst into countless tiny splinters of light.

Pearl gasped air into her lungs and beamed. 'Isn't this fun?'

'If you say so,' Charlotte said. She swung her sword into another flying fairy, which gave a tiny *eep!* before exploding into stardust. She allowed herself a smile. This might just bloody work. She gripped the sword tighter and muttered to herself, 'Let's get this over with.'

༄

The Holly King had initially relished the fight with the woodwose. His old foe had been gone far too long.

He'd toyed with him at first, and looked forward to breaking his bones, plucking off his limbs and devouring his essence. But the hairy beast wouldn't submit. And when the savage had gnawed on the Holly King's arm, the novelty had worn off. Now it was just plain tiresome. He had communed with the trees, staked his claim for what was rightfully his. The Holly King wanted nothing more than to wear his crown again and to finally rule. But first, he needed to dispose of this irksome woodwose. The crown would help, of course, but he didn't need it to defeat this hairy pup. He knew exactly who could help him. It was time for Pearl to pay her dues. He growled to himself. 'Let's get this over with.'

§

The woodwose felt something he had not encountered before. A kind of boredom. No matter how much he punched the Holly King, his opponent kept coming back for more. The woodwose liked a worthy foe, but what was a fight for if not victory? He wanted to snap the Holly King's neck and be done with it, but no matter what he tried, he couldn't get close.

Something pricked at the woodwose's biceps. It was followed by another stabbing sensation in his neck, then another in the lobe of his ear. Holly leaves whistled through the air, jabbing into the soft skin of his cheeks and throat. These tiny stars of pain grouped themselves into clusters, infesting his entire body. The woodwose caught a glimpse of the Holly King's face.

The demigod's eyes were glassy, his jaw slack, as he guided the holly leaves towards the woodwose. More came, covering the hairy man from head to toe.

Lesser creatures might have cowered, wasting time trying to brush off the spiky leaves. Not the woodwose. Pain was his friend. It gave him strength. He would use it now to kill the Holly King.

He cried out as he leapt up to wrap his arms around the demigod's head and—

He never got that far. The Holly King's fist was fast, cracking into the woodwose's ribs. The wild man cackled as his back was brought down onto the Holly King's knee. He bent but didn't break. This was more like it. One way or another this would be over soon, as one of them would surely be dead. A thought came to the woodwose, from the soldier inside him. *Let's get this over with.*

THE BATTLE FOR WOODVILLE

Faye knocked on Mr Hodgson's front door, but there was no answer. She felt an odd mix of relief and guilt.

'Knock harder,' Mrs Teach suggested. 'He'll be as hungover as the others.'

Faye took a step back and looked at the house, its blackout curtains drawn. She could hear Mrs Hodgson snoring, but she was solo tonight without Mr Hodgson's usual harmonies.

'He's not here.'

'Are you sure?' Mrs Teach asked. 'Then where is he?'

'He's where I would be.'

It was a short walk to the rubble of the bell tower. Mr Hodgson was indeed there, as Faye expected, but he wasn't alone. The other ringers were gathered around in silent mourning. Mr Hodgson sat cradling the cracked tenor bell like a poorly child. He wore a dressing gown over his shorts and vest.

The Roberts twins sat together, one with a bright yellow sou'wester and one without. Miss Burgess and

Miss Gordon held one another tight in their grief. Mrs Pritchett exhaled blue cigarette smoke as she saw Faye and Mrs Teach clambering over the ruins.

'Faye, darlin'. Have you seen this? What happened?'

Faye floundered, wondering how on earth she could explain this without giving them conniptions.

Before she could make something up, there was a creak and a thud, followed by Bertie coughing as he emerged from the devil's door in a cloud of yellow dust. He waved the air clear as Terrence joined him.

'Dad! Bertie! Are you all right?' She noted they were empty-handed and felt a flutter of panic. 'Couldn't you find it?'

Terrence pointed back towards the dusty darkness beyond the door. 'Nah, nah, we got it. Just give us a mo',' he wheezed. 'Just ... just needed some air.'

The two men shuffled back into the darkness, where sounds of cursing mingled with something heavy being dragged.

'What on earth are they doing?' Mr Hodgson demanded to know.

The answer came as Bertie backed out of the devil's door carrying one end of a large wooden sarcophagus. 'Whoa, whoa, whoa, down!' he cried, all but dropping it on the door's threshold. He gave Faye a grin. 'It's quite heavy.'

She dashed over to help him.

'What happened here, Faye?' Mrs Pritchett asked.

Bertie caught Faye's eye. He must have seen a glimmer of panic there and came to her rescue. 'Stray bomb,' he said, with a certainty no one could challenge. 'Saw it meself. Junkers Ju 88. Probably shedding its payload before heading home.'

Faye tried to stop herself from smiling. It was the way Bertie casually used the word 'payload' to underline his expertise in the matter. She cherished that wonderful boy.

'Bastards,' Miss Gordon muttered, with a venom she normally reserved for people who were cruel to cats.

Bertie continued with his story. 'And we're helping, er, rescue whatever artefacts we can find.' He patted the sarcophagus on the lid.

'Good lads,' Mrs Pritchett said before tossing her cigarette away. 'Faye.' She folded her arms and cast her eyes down. 'Those things we said earlier . . .' She looked to the others, almost pleadingly. Was she going to have to do this on her own?

Miss Burgess stepped forward. 'We weren't ourselves.'

Miss Gordon nodded eagerly. 'We didn't mean it.'

Faye raised her palms. 'Ladies, it's all right. I know you did mean it, and it's all tickety-boo, because . . . you were right. I need to grow up. And I'm going to start right now. And Mr Aitch . . .' Faye crouched beside the venerable ringer and rested a hand on his shoulder. 'You were right, too. I'm not as good a ringer as I think I am. I have lots to learn, and I hope you'll teach me.'

'Teach?' He turned to Faye, his eyes and cheeks wet with tears. He gestured at the remains of the tower around them. 'How?'

Faye picked up a fragment of flint from beside her boots. She turned it over, its surface smooth and shining. She handed it to Mr Hodgson. 'We'll rebuild.' She patted him on the back and stood. 'I reckon by the time this war's over, we'll have our tower back again. Then we'll celebrate with a peal or two. What do you say?'

The Roberts twins nodded enthusiastically. Misses Burgess and Gordon applauded.

Mrs Pritchett gave a lopsided grin. 'Sounds good to me,' she said.

The smiles vanished as screams echoed from the end of the Wode Road.

'What the bloody hell was that?' Mrs Pritchett applied a fresh cigarette to her bottom lip.

'Everyone, go home,' Faye commanded. 'It's not safe.'

'What's happening down there?' Miss Gordon asked.

Mrs Teach cleared her throat. 'There is something of a kerfuffle by the war memorial. Miss Charlotte has it all under control. But Faye is right. You should all go home, close your doors, have a hearty breakfast, and, uhm, keep away from the windows.'

Faye leaned closer to Bertie. 'How long till sunrise?'

He checked his wristwatch. 'About thirty minutes.'

'We need to get a move on. Mrs Teach, who's next on the list?'

⚨

The problem with the fairies was that the little buggers just kept coming. For every one that Miss Charlotte slashed with her sword, two more would clamber out of the Holly King's sack, armed to the teeth. They were dumb creatures, but fast, vicious and relentless. Miss Charlotte had been taught by her sensei to fight with grace and poise, much like a dancer. That was all well and good when sparring with others who had studied the same form, but these little demons were manic agents of chaos. It was all Charlotte could do to strike at each one as they flung themselves at her.

'Pearl Wynter!' The Holly King's voice strained as he wrestled with the woodwose, who was still covered in holly leaves, and as such had become a somewhat prickly opponent. 'I thought we were friends? I thought we had an understanding?'

'So did I,' Pearl said, socking a fairy on the jaw. 'But then you went and said you were gonna pluck my pretty head off my shoulders. Somethin' about that made me figure you weren't on my team no more.'

'Oh, no, no, no.' The Holly King shook his head as he clamped his hands around the woodwose's jaw, keeping it from biting his face off. 'I still want to help you, Pearl. It's the least I can do after you helped me. But the rising of the sun dictates that I must prepare the feast and the sacrifice, and so on and so forth. You of all people know how important ritual is.'

Miss Charlotte twinged with angst as she saw Pearl nodding in agreement. 'Don't listen to him, Pearl!'

'You could rule by my side, Pearl,' the Holly King managed between gasps as he attempted to throttle the woodwose. 'Queen of the Fairies. How does that sound?'

Pearl beamed. 'Oh, I think I like that very much. Would I get a crown?'

'Of course!'

'And no more threats of decapitation?'

'None at all, I give you my word.'

'Pearl, he's lying!' Charlotte cried, slashing another fairy to dust.

'And the fairies.' Pearl waggled her fingers at the various winged cherubs whizzing around them. 'They'd do whatever I say, right?'

'They would be at your command,' the Holly King said, bringing his fist up into the woodwose's snout.

'An army?' Pearl blushed and pressed her fingers to her cheeks. 'For little ol' me?'

'I can think of no finer gift.' The Holly King tossed the woodwose against the stone cross. It fell limp at the feet of Eric and Shirley, who recoiled from the hairy man, still unaware that they were looking at their own son.

'Pearl, for the sake of all that is good and sane …' Miss Charlotte backed away, her sword held low as the fairies surrounded her. 'Do not do this.'

Pearl looked from the Holly King to Miss Charlotte and back again. Shadows darkened the fairy's face, and a sick grin hoisted itself into place. 'I accept.' She reached out a hand to the Holly King.

Miss Charlotte suddenly felt very alone.

Faye, Mrs Teach and Bertie hurried away from Reverend Jacobs' cottage in search of the next name on their list. They had found the Reverend breakfasting with Edith Palmer.

'At least they had the decency to look ashamed,' Mrs Teach observed.

'Oh, I think they make a lovely couple,' Faye replied. 'Nothing to be ashamed of.'

'I meant after what they did to you. The Reverend should have known better.'

Faye couldn't disagree. For a man who preached about the everlasting love and forgiveness of Jesus Christ, he could be quick to judge. She had taken a little wicked pleasure in advising him to have a strong cup of tea before checking on the state of the church bell tower this morning.

So far, the reconciliations had gone well. The Reverend and Edith had apologised unreservedly. And Bertie had been press-ganged into delivering Faye's message to Mr Loaf, who found her voice so annoying, so as not to antagonise him any further. By the time they had left, he had been begging Faye to speak to him.

'Well, he should've thought of that before, shouldn't he?' Bertie grumbled and nudged Faye. 'Still, I didn't like doing that. Please don't make me do it again.'

'Thank you, Bertie.' Faye gently squeezed his hand. 'I know it don't feel like it, but you have to think of these as victories for us, too. If we can bring everyone together then we've all won. They just don't know it yet.'

Their encounter with Mrs Brew had admittedly gone less well. She still insisted that Faye was a 'bossyboots little cow', but you can't please everyone, and allowing Mrs Brew to vent had actually seemed to calm her down.

Bertie raised a finger as they rejoined the Wode Road.

'Bertie, you don't have to ask for permission to speak.' Mrs Teach gently lowered his finger. 'You're not in school.'

'I've noticed something peculiar,' he said.

Faye raised her eyebrows. 'On tonight of all nights? That's impressive, Bertie.'

'When you speak to the villagers, and they realise how rotten they've been, something happens to their eyes. Have you seen it?'

Faye pursed her lower lip. 'Can't say I have, Bertie. What happens to them?'

'Their eyes brighten. It's like they're waking up. For all my doubts about your plan, Faye, I think it's actually working. You're breaking the Holly King's hold on them.'

'Let's see, eh?'

They crossed the Wode Road to Mr Paine's newsagent's and Faye steeled herself for another awkward reunion.

Just then there came a crash and a scream from down the street. The fight at the war memorial was still rumbling on and the distinct howl of Miss Charlotte's war cry reverberated up towards them as she despatched another fairy.

Bertie couldn't help but glance in Charlotte's direction. Mrs Teach placed her hand on the top of his blond mop and swivelled it until it was facing the shop. He

winced. There was a sore patch on his head where Sid
had chopped off that clump of hair.

'Sorry, Bertie, but we cannot be distracted. They
have their job, and we have ours.'

Faye was about to knock on the door, but Mr Paine
was already up and had spotted her. The big man came
towards them, lumbering from side to side. He opened
the door with a tinkle of the bell and stood before
them. Silent. Impassive.

Faye thought of all the nights they had spent together
on Air Raid Precaution duties, watching the skies,
ever vigilant.

She cleared her throat. 'Mr Paine, I am sorry for
burdening you with all my idle gossip and woe on our
ARP shifts. I was overfamiliar and I made them a trial
for you, and they're hard enough as it is, and I had no
right to be such a bletherer. I also apologise for taking
advantage of your generosity with the sherbet lemons.
I hereby offer to replace them at the earliest instance,
but in the meantime, I hope you will accept these as
temporary compensation.' Faye reached into the pocket
of her flight jacket and pulled out a small brown paper
bag, twisted shut at the top. 'Liquorice Allsorts. I know
you're partial to them.'

Faye gave Bertie a quick, apologetic smile. 'Sorry,
Bertie, I know they were a gift from you, but as we're
all sharing the truth and apologising and such, you
should know that they give me terrible wind.'

Bertie blinked, smiled and nodded, noting it for
future reference.

Mr Paine slowly lowered his eyes to the bag in Faye's palm. He reached for it, gripping it so tightly that Faye feared he had squeezed them all into one giant Liquorice Allsort, which might actually be a bonus if you liked the blessed things.

When he looked up again, Faye saw it.

The light had returned to Mr Paine's eyes. He was his old self again. Bertie was right.

Mr Paine drew Faye towards him and wrapped his arms around her. No words were needed as he held her tighter than he had the liquorice.

'Er, Faye.' Bertie's voice was muffled by Mr Paine's arms blocking her ears.

Mrs Teach bristled. 'Bertie, what did I tell you? We have our job, and they— Oh ...'

Mr Paine eased his hold on Faye, and she was able to see the war memorial and its terrible tableaux. The woodwose lay unconscious, his hairy body riddled with holly leaves. Miss Charlotte was surrounded, malevolent fairies closing in on her from all sides.

'This ends now.' Faye set her jaw.

Mrs Teach brandished the list. 'We haven't reconciled with the Morris Men.'

'Sod 'em,' Faye said. 'We have to draw the line somewhere. And Miss Charlotte needs our help.'

SLING YER HOOK

Sid could feel the edges of his mind fraying like an old rug. He might have lingered here a little too long. The ancient instincts of the woodwose were part of him now. As much as Ardennes, Escaut and Dunkirk. War had ravaged Sid's mind, leaving it fractured. All the certainties he had taken for granted were now in tatters, leaving him silent and afraid. He found that his thoughts were no longer his own. The voices of others – be they Alfie, or Pearl or the Holly King – crept in and plagued his waking moments. But the magic had changed him, too. His mind and his body. Now he shared both with an ancient being as sharp and deadly as flint. It was unsettling to be confronted with something so certain of its place in the world. Most folk go their whole lives trying to discover who they are and what their purpose might be. Not the woodwose. It was simple. He was the guardian of the wood. It was his to protect. And no demigod was going to take it from him. A fire as pure as the stars in the sky burned within Sid. His muscles ached and a few of his bones were fractured, but he would stand soon. He would rise and he would bend the Holly King's back and break it.

In a moment.

First ... first, he needed a rest.

Darkness clouded his mind like ink in water. Sounds fell away. Infinity beckoned.

'Oi! I wanna word with you!'

The voice cut through the murk.

'You, sunshine, are no longer welcome in this village.'

Some might call the voice grating, or annoying, or too loud for a girl, but it was certainly effective at commanding attention.

'So sling yer hook.'

Sid clung onto the words. Time expanded and contracted around him, and he fought against the pull of oblivion. Then something came to him on a tiny wisp of light. Bait on a hook. And he grabbed it with both hands.

ᛈ

Faye helped Bertie and Mrs Teach carry the Oak King's sarcophagus down the Wode Road, using her magic to lighten the load. As they approached the Holly King, they gently lowered the wooden box to the cobbles. Terrence hurried over to join them. She had asked him to fetch something from her room. He handed Faye her mother's hand mirror with the ivory handle. He hadn't asked her why she needed it. He knew better than to ask these days. Faye tucked it into her inside

410

pocket, then stood before the Holly King in her flight jacket, hands on hips and, no doubt, with a face like a slapped arse.

'It's over, Your Majesty.' Faye's words bounced off the walls of the village's houses and shops, returning to her as if uncertain and wondering if she had really meant to say them.

'Over, is it?' The Holly King gestured at the broken body of the woodwose. 'Your champion is fallen, and I still have my sacrificial lamb.'

Faye glanced to where Eric and Shirley were tied to the stone cross. Pearl drew her dagger as she approached Eric, a gleeful, bloodthirsty grin on her face. Faye's chest tingled and her breathing quickened as she questioned her easy trust in her wayward cousin.

'You are surrounded and outnumbered.' The Holly King raised his hands to the fairies as they encircled Faye, Mrs Teach and Bertie. 'And our fairies now have a queen.' He genuflected to Pearl, who giggled and snapped her fingers. A winged fairy buzzed over to her, ostentatiously nestling a diamond tiara into her hair. Queen Pearl bobbed her head from side to side, getting used to the new adornment. Then she pressed the blade of her dagger to Eric's throat, ready to slice on command.

The Holly King nodded approvingly. 'I suppose, in a way, you are correct, Faye Bright. It *is* over. The sun will rise within moments. Eric here will be sacrificed in honour of the return of the light—'

Shirley gave an involuntary sob.

'And my rule will be restored.' The Holly King clenched his gloved fists. 'The wood will consume your feeble homes of bricks and mortar. You will become my servants or perish, and I shall reign over this domain for all eternity.'

Faye puffed out her cheeks and looked at her fellow witches. 'Blimey. He might have a point there. What do you reckon, ladies?'

Mrs Teach, an accomplished actress in her youth, adopted her finest stage voice and spoke from her diaphragm. 'One does not like to shrink in the face of overwhelming odds, Faye, but it does seem as if they are stacked against us somewhat.' She pressed a dramatic hand to her chest. 'After all, we are merely witches, and he is a demigod.'

'Oh dear.' Faye flexed her lips. 'That doesn't sound good. Miss Charlotte?'

The white-haired witch made a show of sheathing her sword. 'We've tried blades, fangs and claws, but they've had little effect. I think he's got us, Faye.'

Faye tutted, briefly shaking her head. 'And, of course, he set the whole village against us, so we can't rely on our friends and neighbours to come together.' Faye clapped her hands, and her face brightened. 'Or can we? Bertie, would you do the honours, please.'

Bertie took a handbell he had found in the rubble of Saint Irene's bell tower from his pocket and started ringing.

The Holly King's beard bristled. 'What are you doing, foolish girl?'

Faye heard footsteps on the cobbled street behind her. She resisted the urge to look back. Instead, she took a moment to enjoy the bafflement on the Holly King's face as Mr Hodgson arrived, flanked by an army of villagers. Bertie stopped his ringing.

'Hello again, Mister Aitch,' Faye said cheerily. 'We all present and correct?'

'We are indeed,' Mr Hodgson replied.

'Ta very much.' Faye had to wave to get the Holly King's attention, so fixated was he on the silent mob before him. 'Your Maj? Down here. Hello. First of all, I applaud you for doing what the Nazis couldn't. You divided us. You took our secrets and turned us against one another and we all fell for it, hook, line and sinker.'

Faye decided it was time to face the villagers. And what an indomitable lot they were. The Baxters and the Marshalls. Mr Paine and family. Constable Muldoon with his truncheon at the ready. Even the ringers stood in solidarity with the Morris Men. Faye flushed with pride as she turned back to the Holly King.

'And it almost worked. But tonight I learned that no one's perfect and that it's time to grow up, and so I apologised to everyone I'd narked off and we made amends. We're all friends again.' Faye raised a defiant finger. 'Our village is as one!'

'Not me!' came Mrs Brew's voice from the back. 'I still think you're a know-it-all little mare.'

Faye winced. 'Except Mrs Brew,' she conceded. 'Can't please everyone, I s'pose.'

'But,' Mrs Brew continued, 'I hate that big, bearded lump even more, so I'll stand with you.'

In a strange way, Mrs Brew's words of bile, infused as they were with reluctant solidarity, warmed Faye's heart more than any others she'd heard this morning. She couldn't help but smile.

'Your hold over the village is broken, O king of the holly bush. And do you know why?' Faye gently wagged a finger at the demigod. 'I think you do. I think you know this already, but you don't want to admit it. And I don't blame you. Believe me, I know. It's a hard thing to face the truth.'

'What are you chattering about, you impudent little shrew? What truth?'

'Your time has passed. We don't need you anymore. We're living through tough days, that's for sure, but we're not the peasants of old. We don't have to doff our caps to no one if we don't want to, and we certainly don't need to bow and scrape like fools to an old demigod like you. We have each other. And you ... your time is up, sunshine.' Faye jabbed a thumb towards the sarcophagus behind her. 'So, I suggest you clear off before things get really ugly.'

The Holly King's cheeks reddened and his eyes shrank to tiny beads of hate. 'It matters not, you ridiculous child. All you have done is hasten the deaths of these pathetic people. They will curse your name as I smite them with a stroke of my hand.'

Faye heard some murmurs of doubt behind her. Time for the big reveal.

'Ah, yes. Violence.' She scrunched her nose. 'We tried that, didn't we, Miss Charlotte?'

'Didn't work.' Miss Charlotte looked over at the still form of the woodwose where it lay at the feet of the writhing Birdwhistles. 'But that was when we were outnumbered.'

Mrs Teach put a finger to her chin as she thought aloud. 'What if we had an ally? One who had an army at their command?'

Miss Charlotte drew her sword again. 'That would certainly even the odds.'

'Queen Pearl of the fairies.' Faye curtseyed. 'What do you say?' She looked up from her bent position, pushing her glasses up her nose to better see the fairy's face.

Pearl remained motionless, her blade pressed against Eric's throat. For a moment, the whole world held its breath.

The sun's first beams rose between the rooftops, the light returned, and somewhere a robin sang.

'Fairies,' Pearl said, and every fairy head snapped towards their newly crowned queen. She removed the dagger from Eric's throat and pointed it at the Holly King. 'Get 'im!'

THE FATE OF SIDNEY
BIRDWHISTLE

The fairies piled onto the Holly King without a moment's hesitation. He was fast and he was strong, managing to slap many of them into sparkling dust in the first frenzied seconds of the attack. But their numbers were overwhelming. More and more armed fairies came spewing from his enormous sack, toppling him over and pinning him down.

'Mrs Teach. Bertie. Now!' Faye commanded, and the pair hurried to remove the lid from the Oak King's sarcophagus. It was dark inside. Just an ordinary wooden box to the untrained eye.

Faye took her mother's hand mirror from the inside pocket of the flight jacket, closed her eyes and slowly rose into the chill air above the sarcophagus.

The Holly King writhed under the countless fairies holding him down. He uttered oaths and curses that were very unbecoming for the time of year. His rage did not diminish.

Faye raised the mirror and her free hand. She felt the power of the waning moon in her palm. Not as powerful as a full moon, but it was all she needed. She hoped.

She angled the mirror so that it caught the moon's energy and directed it into the open sarcophagus. The bottom of the coffin lit up like clouds in a lightning storm. Darkness and light swirled together to create a vortex that howled as it spilled over, gaining momentum and power.

Faye glanced over her shoulder to see her dad herding the villagers to a safe distance. A squeal made her look back. The Holly King batted a chubby fairy from his face, and she cried out in fright as she was sucked into the sarcophagus, vanishing into the roiling, flashing clouds. Banished to the aether. Faye planned the same fate for the Holly King, but unsurprisingly he was reluctant to go quietly. He kicked and screamed like a toddler, thrashing about and hurling more and more fairies into the roaring maelstrom. He reached out with his big, gloved hand, gripping the stone cross of the war memorial as the remaining fairies continued to pummel him.

Miss Charlotte dashed towards the Holly King, sword raised. Her white hair whipped around her face as she brought the blade down on his wrist. It bit hard and true, breaking his radius bone. He howled in agony as she wriggled the blade out and hacked again, slicing through his ulna and detaching his hand completely.

Miss Charlotte bared her red lips, showing her teeth. 'That's for my eye, you bast—'

He swiped at her with his forearm and stump, sending her sliding across the street.

The Holly King's injury only fed his rage. His remaining hand was a blur as it grabbed fairies, slapped them on the cobbles like rag dolls, then tossed them into the sarcophagus. He chortled as he did so, a booming, 'Ho, ho, ho!' that rattled the surrounding windows.

Faye spotted Pearl scurrying around the back of the war memorial, cradling the tartan flask with Sid's blood. She crouched by the woodwose's still body, then looked to Faye.

Now was the time. If Sid was ever to be himself again, this was it. The woodwose would drink Sid's blood, his body would remember itself, and he would transform back into Sidney Birdwhistle, giving his parents – still tied to the stone cross and screaming their heads off – the shock of their lives.

The Holly King hurled more fairies into the storm. Faye watched helplessly as they vanished. She desperately wanted to join the fight, but if she lost the moon's light in the mirror, then the doorway to the aether would be gone. She had to stay in position while the fairies attacked. There were only a handful left. The Holly King's sack was empty.

He got to his feet with a hateful holler. He might have lost a hand, but he was as strong as ever.

Pearl unscrewed the lid of the flask.

'No!' Faye cried, her throat tightening. Could she really do this? 'We need him. We need the woodwose.'

'Faye, this is his last chance.' Pearl pointed to the

glow of dawn beyond the rooftops. 'He can't change back once the sun is up.'

Faye's eyes darted to Sid's parents. They held hands as they cried in terror, with no clue that the fate of their son was being decided before their very eyes.

The Holly King tossed away the final fairies, their bodies spinning into the whirlwind.

'Wake him!' Faye cried. 'Wake the woodwose.'

Pearl nodded gravely. She put the flask down, crouched by the hairy man and whispered into his ear.

Immediately, his eyes snapped open. Alert, primed.

He looked up to see the Holly King, blood dripping from the stump of his left arm, raising his right fist to strike Faye and smash her mirror.

Still covered in holly leaves, the woodwose leapt to his feet, gripped his club and clambered up the stone cross like a demented squirrel. He launched himself at the demigod.

The woodwose's club smashed into the Holly King's skull. Something crunched, and the Holly King roared in shock and pain. His knees buckled and he fell forward.

The vortex had him.

The woodwose sprang clear as the Holly King was gobbled up by his brother's sarcophagus. It wasn't a pretty sight. Stuffing an oversized semi-deity into such a relatively small box meant breaking bones, unnatural contortions and blood-curdling cries of pain.

'Lid on! Now!' Faye cried.

Bertie was the first to hobble over to the lid. He was

joined by Miss Charlotte, still dazed from her attack, and Mrs Teach, who swiftly took command.

'Lift, quickly, quickly!' she said as they grabbed the lid of the sarcophagus.

'This isn't over, Faye Bright!' the Holly King cried as the swirling storm tore him apart.

Faye held the mirror in place, training the light of the moon on his face.

He winced. 'This isn't over by far. You've been a very, very naughty g—'

The lid was dropped into place with a satisfying *thud*. It silenced whatever lay beyond.

The Holly King was gone.

℘

As the light faded to nothing, the Holly King returned to the aether. He thought of his brother, and he hoped to find him here and beg forgiveness. All he found was stardust and loneliness. No one would worship him, but no one would know his shame.

℘

Faye tucked the mirror into her inside pocket and dropped to Pearl's side, her fingers grasping for the flask.

'Faye, it's too late,' the Queen of the Fairies muttered, even as she handed the flask over.

Faye wasn't listening. She gripped the flask as she approached the woodwose.

The hairy man's chest heaved and the sound coming

through his nostrils made her think of a stream train in a station after a long journey. He began to pluck holly leaves from his body. Countless tiny cuts started to bleed, matting his coarse hair and turning it black.

She looked into his pitiless eyes, hoping to see some glimmer of Sid.

There was none.

'Drink this.' She slowly raised the flask. 'And you'll be yourself again, I promise.' Her eyes flickered to the Birdwhistles, who were no longer screaming, but were still tied up and very confused. Faye knew she couldn't use Sid's name. Not now. They'd hear it and there would be too many questions. 'Please.' She was close enough to reach out. She took his hand. His palm was as rough as glass paper. His breath was as fetid as the pub's bins in the summer. She raised the flask to his mouth. 'That's it. Drink up.'

He was clumsy. Lapping with his tongue through the flask's narrow opening. Faye gently tipped it forward, slowly pouring the rest of the blood into his mouth.

The woodwose closed his lips, swirled the liquid about, and spat it all over Faye.

'No!' she cried. Her first instinct was to shake the flask to see if there was any left, but it was empty.

The woodwose shoved her aside and bounded over to where the Birdwhistles were tied to the cross. He leaned close to both of them, sniffing their faces. Faye feared that he might bite them, but instead he got down on his haunches, gripped the rope that bound them and gnawed through it. It fell away and they were free.

The woodwose nodded as if satisfied. He raised his club in salute, then turned and ran towards the wood, leaving only eddies of gently falling snow in his wake.

The whiff of burning wood reached Faye's nostrils. She turned to find the sarcophagus smouldering, Miss Charlotte stoking the nascent flames.

'Better safe than sorry,' she said, and Faye agreed.

Mrs Teach and Bertie hurried to help the bewildered Birdwhistles. Eric and Shirley fell to their knees, holding one another tight. The crown of oak and holly slipped from Eric's head, rolling onto the cobbles.

'Our boy.' Shirley's voice trembled as she looked around in vain. 'Has anyone seen our Sidney? Where is he?'

Interlude: The Trees' Regret

The trees do not retreat. That is not their way. Their roots remain in peculiar places across the village. A reminder to the humans of what lies beneath. That doesn't mean the trees aren't a little ashamed. Allowing the Holly King to manipulate them so easily had ended in chaos. They vow never to fall for such cheap temptations again.

Unless they absolutely need to.

CHRISTMAS MORNING

Faye had a delivery to make.

She got up early, slinging a knapsack onto her back. There was no post on Christmas Day, no milk deliveries, and she was the first one up, well before the sun peeked over the horizon. The snow had gone, leaving in its wake a few burst pipes and mounds of grey slush on the kerbs.

Things seemed normal enough, but the village had been wounded and Faye knew it would never be quite the same again. Most who lived there had feared some kind of irreversible change was on the horizon since Mr Chamberlain had spoken to them on the wireless in September 1939, but they had expected it to arrive under the banner of a swastika. Instead, it had come in the form of a jolly man with antlers and a huge beard who had turned them all against one another. They hadn't seen that coming, and who could blame them?

Vera Fivetrees had arrived the day after the battle

with her potions, intending to wipe the memories of the villagers, but by then a curious thing had happened.

No one appeared to remember that night. Or at least no one spoke of it.

Oh, in passing, perhaps, someone might mention a raucous night of revelling that had given them an almighty hangover, a feast that had got out of hand, but they were soon silenced by the glares of others, daring them to say more on pain of a thick ear.

As for the bell tower, Bertie's story of a stray bomber had gained its own curious momentum, with other eyewitnesses stepping forward and swearing blind that they, too, had seen the bombs fall on Saint Irene's. Promises were made to rebuild. Mrs Teach started a fundraiser, bringing the villagers together as only she could.

They had sung carols under the stars at the fallen tower that night. Many of the wounded servicemen had come from Hayward Lodge, including Mr Gilbert, who was making a fine recovery.

Miss Charlotte had been absent. She had received a telegram informing her that Martine had been wounded in action and was recovering in a hospital in Portsmouth. She'd left without a word, and Faye and Mrs Teach had no idea when she would return, if at all. Her home in the wood had been destroyed, after all. Mrs Teach suspected that Miss Charlotte might join Martine in France with the Resistance.

'This has changed everything,' she'd told Faye on the way home that night. 'Don't expect things to be the way they were. This war will pull and shove us in every direction, you mark my words.'

Pearl had also left for New York the day after the Holly King's defeat. She'd taken his sack with her. Already, Faye could see signs of fairy life returning within it. And Pearl's wings were growing back, too, though she kept them tucked away underneath a long coat extracted by Miss Charlotte from the rubble of her cottage and donated for the purpose.

'I got some old scores to settle,' Pearl had told Faye when she'd seen her off at the train station. 'Most of the putzes who done me wrong think I'm long dead. Boy, are they gonna get the shock of their lives when they see me comin'.'

℘

Faye marched along the path into the wood, pulling up her hood to warm her ears. Ahead of her, a robin made a defiant violin-string squeak before darting between the trees. Faye thought of last night. Christmas Eve. After last orders and closing up, she and her father had found time to talk. There had been tears and apologies.

Then her dad had said something unexpected. 'That night in the woods changed your mother. I hardly saw her for the next ten years.' He'd sat by the fire, hypnotised by the reflection of the flames in his glass of sherry. 'We'd been close friends. Not stepping out or anything like that. Not yet. But we trusted each other. She blamed herself for Pearl dying, though, and said she wouldn't let another death be her fault. She took it upon herself to study magic and locked herself away with her books. She had her poorly mother to look after, too, but that's another story.' Terrence swirled his sherry. 'Then the Great War came along. She drove an ambulance. She would heal people, or comfort them as they died. She became this ...' Terrence's brow crinkled. He glanced up at the top of their little Christmas tree. 'Angel. A wise angel. And I loved her for it. And she loved me back. We started stepping out in the summer of 1922. What a year that was. We were married soon after. We weren't getting any younger, and we realised that if we wanted a family we should get a move on. And so you came along the next year. Happiest days of our lives.' Terrence finally downed his sherry. 'I'm sorry I've kept things from you, Faye. There's more to tell, and I could spend the rest of my days doing so.'

'What books?' Faye had asked, her heart quickening. 'You said she locked herself away with her books. Witches aren't allowed books. It's all handed down from witch to witch. Who did she study with?'

Terrence shook his head. 'Like I said, she all but disappeared. There were some things she kept secret, even from me.'

Faye realised the more she learned about her mother, the less she really knew about her. But that was tickety-boo. Everyone was entitled to their secrets. Even the dead.

§

Faye arrived at the clearing with the hollow oak. It held the icy morning moon in its branches. Scars of snow lay about its roots. The ground was hard as iron and all the fissures had healed, leaving only dead leaves. A solitary redwing looked her up and down like a nightclub doorman, then fluttered away. But she wasn't alone.

Something was watching her. He had been since she'd entered the wood. This place was his to guard now, and if he didn't want Faye here, she was sure he'd let her know.

She shrugged off the knapsack and opened it, carefully removing the crown of oak and holly. It had slipped from the Holly King's head after the final, crushing blow of the club, and now she placed it in the tree's hollow, took a reverential step back and cleared her throat.

'I reckon this is yours,' she said in a voice loud enough to carry to the highest branches. 'We talked about destroying it, but then Vera Fivetrees said that as long as this one exists, then no other like it can be made. And I think it's safer with you than with any witch. Don't want anyone getting any daft ideas.'

The oak's few remaining leaves rattled as a chill wind passed through in a hurry to get somewhere.

'Everyone . . . everyone thinks you're dead. Pearl told them a story. That you'd volunteered for ARP duty and were up on the roof of the bell tower when it was bombed.' Faye listened for any kind of reaction. There was none. 'Your parents . . . They're heartbroken, of course, but you're their hero, too. You're getting medals and all sorts. Funeral's next Wednesday if you're interested. Full military honours, I'm told.' Faye lowered her head, studying the crown. 'I wanted to tell them the truth. But what could I say that wouldn't just upset them all the more? I've let you down, Sid. I've failed you. I'm sorry.'

Faye thought back to Pearl's train leaving the station. She had leaned out of the carriage window as it started to pull away. 'And now you have a secret, Faye,' she'd hollered over the chuffing of the engine. 'One that, if it gets out, will ruin you. You've become your momma. Congratulations. You finally grew up.' She'd cackled as the train gathered speed, her laughter blending into the thunder of its wheels.

Faye could hear it even now.

'She's wrong, though. I've still got a lot of growing up to do. Would you like to know a secret?' Faye looked up into the bare trees. Nothing moved. Nothing made a sound. There was such an abundance of nothing that it had to be hiding something. She continued anyway. 'Bellamy's offered me a job. A mission, he called it. It's dangerous, but he keeps insisting that only I can do it. I don't know about that ... but it's something I really want to do. It feels like the right time. Mrs Teach can look after the village, you can look after the wood, and Dad and Bertie can look after each other. I want to go off and ... have an adventure.' Faye nodded to herself. 'I'm sure you couldn't give a tinker's cuss, but I really wanted to tell someone. And I'm fairly sure you can keep a secret. Thanks for listening.' She thrust her hands into the pockets of her flight jacket. 'If you're even there.'

Faye gave the clearing one last look, then turned to walk back to the village. In the distance, a vixen cried like a witch burning at the stake. The wind danced around Faye again. She sensed something coming from the nothing. She spun on her heels.

The crown was gone.

⚲

Sid leapt from tree to tree, the crown snug atop his head, meshing with his hair. It didn't matter how acrobatic or sudden his jumps were, the crown always stayed on.

He saw that Faye was taking the old path to the village. She radiated the contentment that came from knowing what she was going to do next. He saw it with the birds. Free to fly, they were never happier.

Sid saw and heard lots of things now that he was a woodwose. The colours of time, the songs of the trees, streaks of matter left by the stars.

He could smell spring coming. The wood was moving through its cycle and it was the task of a woodwose to ensure that nothing stopped it. Not even his own grief.

Sid's heart ached for his parents, but they were safe now. And their son was a hero, apparently. No longer the frightened boy who'd cowered on the beach at Dunkirk. There would be medals and memories and pride, and no one could take that away from them. As much as he was tempted to go to his own funeral, he had a job to do. His reward would be spring, then summer. And then he could chase birds and butter-flies again.

ℰ

There had been talk of a church service with carols in the rubble of Saint Irene's this morning. Faye had been invited, but she had other plans for Christmas, and they started with putting the kettle on. As soon as she got home, she would tell Dad about the mission, put up with all his arguments against her going, and then go anyway. Of course, she would have to tell . . .

Bertie was waiting for her at the old Roman bridge. Faye's blood ran cold. She wasn't ready for this. Not yet. She needed some tea before she could tell him. At least two cups. She couldn't let Bertie down on an empty stomach.

'Mornin', Faye.' Bertie bit his lip and shuffled on his uneven legs.

Faye opened her mouth to speak, but he beat her to it. His words tumbled out, most of them in the right order.

'I've been thinking about what you said – growing up, and all that. You're right, we ain't children no more. And that got me thinking about me and you, and this, and bein' frightened all the time. And when I was stuck in that gibbet, I got to thinking then, too. Life is short and there's bombs falling from the sky, and none of us knows how long we've got and, well—'

'Bertie, my love, skip to the end.'

Bertie nodded and brushed back his hair.

'Faye Bright ...' His voice cracked. He cleared his throat and tried again. 'Faye Bright, will you marry me?'

THE WITCHES OF WOODVILLE
WILL RETURN ...

ACKNOWLEDGEMENTS

The author has been reminded by members of the Woodville Village Council (in a motion proposed by one Miss Araminta Cranberry) that no book is written in isolation, and he should like to thank the following:

Georgie Leighton for her editing skill and enthusiasm, and to all at Simon & Schuster for banging the Woodville drum.

Lisa Rogers for her forensic expertise on words and choke holds.

Ed Wilson and the gang at Johnson & Alcock for their good cheer and those lovely emails with 'remittance advice' in the subject heading.

Ian W Sainsbury and Julian Barr and Topaz Postma for their feedback on the early, messy drafts.

The staff at the archives of the Postal Museum for their wisdom and patience.

Fadzi Kasambira for his feedback on Pearl.

Mike Shackle for his wise words on swords.

To Georgie Lou Godfrey, Kenichiro Shimada, Fadzi Kasambira, Robyn Sarty, Wendy Coath, Richie Janukowicz and my friends on the BXP Team who helped me get the name right for Miss Charlotte's sword.

And finally, my sincere thanks to Richard Cave and Duncan Moyse for sharing their experiences of PTSD. Gents, you made all the difference. Thank you.

Organisations like the Royal British Legion offer support to people like Richard and Duncan who have served and returned home as changed men. Find out more here: https://www.britishlegion.org.uk